LEGEND OF THE FIVE RINGS

The realm of Rokugan is a land of samurai, courtiers, and mystics, dragons, magic, and divine beings – a world where honor is stronger than steel.

The Seven Great Clans have defended and served the Emperor of the Emerald Empire for a thousand years, in battle and at the imperial court. While conflict and political intrigue divide the clans, the true threat awaits in the darkness of the Shadowlands, behind the vast Kaiu Wall. There, in the twisted wastelands, an evil corruption endlessly seeks the downfall of the empire.

The rules of Rokugani society are strict. Uphold your honor, lest you lose everything in pursuit of glory.

ALSO AVAILABLE

The
FLOWER
PATH

A Daidoji Shin Mystery

JOSH REYNOLDS

ACONYTE

First published by Aconyte Books in 2022

ISBN 978 1 83908 150 7

Ebook ISBN 978 1 83908 151 4

Cover art by Grant Griffin

Rokugan map by Francesca Baerald

Distributed in North America by Simon & Schuster Inc, New York, USA

Printed in the United States of America

9 8 7 6 5 4 3 2 1

ACONYTE BOOKS

An imprint of Asmodee Entertainment Ltd

Mercury House, Shipstones Business Centre

North Gate, Nottingham NG7 7FN, UK

aconytebooks.com // twitter.com/aconytebooks

For Anjuli, who keeps things going.

CHAPTER ONE
Daidoji Shin

Daidoji Shin emptied his cup of tea with a grateful sigh. "Nothing more fortifying after a long night than a good cup of tea," he said, adjusting the intricately embroidered sleeves of his robes so he could refill his cup unhindered.

"Expensive tea at that," his guest murmured, her gaze on the ledger open before her. "Silver Needle, unless I miss my guess." Iuchi Konomi was a handsome woman. A courtier of his acquaintance had once described her as someone to ride the plains with, and Shin could not help but agree. There was a vivacity to her that was startling, and she possessed a keen mind as well. It was why he enjoyed spending time with her.

Konomi was tall and muscular beneath her violet robes; taller than he was, even, and he was not short by the standards of the Crane. She was built for a life in the saddle, riding to battle beneath the horsetail banners of the Unicorn. Shin, in contrast, was slim, handsome, and white-haired, the epitome of a Crane courtier in his finest azure robes. Or such was the impression he sought to give. There were standards to be maintained, after all.

They sat together in Shin's private box in the newly refurbished

Foxfire Theater. In less than two hours, the drum would sound, and the doors would open to the public for the first time in more than a year.

For weeks, an army of theater pages had papered the City of the Rich Frog with advertisements for the first performance under the theater's new management – Chamizo's *Love Suicides in the City of Green Walls* – and a full house was expected.

"You guess correctly," Shin said, watching her leaf through the ledger. "The expense is due to the time-consuming method employed in its harvest as well as the limited nature of the harvest itself…" He paused. She wasn't listening, her eyes on the sums before her. "Is that one of my ledgers?"

Konomi didn't look up. "Yes."

"Are you going through my accounts?"

"Yes."

"Why?"

"My own amusement," Konomi said. She closed the book and looked up, smiling. "You spend quite a bit of money. How have you not run out yet?"

"Sound investments. Where did you even get that?" He felt a flicker of annoyance but was careful not to let it show on his face. It wouldn't do to let Konomi know she'd succeeded in irritating him. Besides, it wasn't the first time she'd gotten into his records – at least the ones he left for people to find. It was hard to hold it against her; she might be an inveterate snoop, but so was he.

"Lord Kenzō kindly let me borrow it," Konomi said. As an auditor for the Daidoji Trading Council, Kenzō was one of the few who possessed the authority to look into Shin's finances. He was also a spy, come to report on any shameful activity on Shin's part.

Shin had managed to distract Kenzō for a time by unleashing him on the theater's account books, which had been in a less than optimal state when he'd purchased the business. But the accounts hadn't occupied him for long. He'd started sniffing around once more as the repairs neared completion. Shin had begun to fear the auditor was planning to stay until he found something damning. "Well, that doesn't sound like him," he said, an eyebrow raised.

Konomi shrugged. "He did take some convincing, I admit." She paused. "He might be under the mistaken impression we are to be engaged."

Shin froze, startled. "What?"

Konomi laughed gaily and arranged herself beside him – not too close but closer than propriety strictly allowed. She, like Shin, found that boundaries were for testing rather than respecting. He found he didn't mind. There was something about Konomi that put him at ease. "Oh, relax, Shin. It was a ploy, nothing more. I was curious."

"I can only imagine what he'll tell my grandfather," Shin said, rubbing his brow. He suddenly wished for a scrap of willow bark to chew. "The letters, Konomi. Did you even think of the letters I will have to write?"

"Yes. That was part of the fun." She tapped the ledger with a finger. "You really have spared no expense on this place."

"I wanted to get it right," Shin agreed, rather pleased with himself. It wasn't often he saw things through, and when he did, he felt somewhat entitled to bask in the afterglow of accomplishment.

Konomi snapped open her fan and gave it a lazy flap. "You should be proud."

"I am." Shin glanced around. Like the other boxes that

encircled the upper level of the theater, his had been tastefully decorated with cushions and curtains of deepest blue as well as wall hangings chosen especially for their innocuous beauty. The wooden slats that acted as the ceiling had been carved with scenes from the great plays of the previous century.

Each box was divided into two parts by a paper wall. The outer part was a small foyer with stools for servants and bodyguards. The inner was for the box owner and their guests. Five people could sit comfortably in each box. There were thin privacy curtains that could be pulled to hide those seated in the box from the auditorium. When not in use, the curtains were held out of the way by silken cords.

"You do not seem proud."

"No?"

"No."

Shin looked at her. "And how do I seem?"

Wordlessly, she indicated her cup with her fan. Shin refilled it, and she said, "Frustrated. Tired. At the end of your cord."

"I can be all of those things," Shin protested, somewhat unnerved by how easily she'd seen through his façade of pleasantries. Looking for something to occupy his hands, he snapped open his metal-tined fan and gave it a languid flutter, stirring the air.

He'd come to discover that running a theater was like waging a war against an implacable foe. There were a hundred niggling details that afflicted him like stinging insects; the moment he brushed one aside, two more took its place. Too many problems and not enough time to solve any of them.

But despite the difficulties, the theater had risen from the ashes like the proverbial phoenix, thanks to him – not to mention an altogether exorbitant amount of money. He'd hired the best architects and tradesmen money could buy, and as the Crane clan trade representative to the City of the Rich Frog, he'd had the necessary contacts to procure all the necessary materials for them to go about their work.

The new theater barely resembled the old at all, which he considered a blessing. At the time of the fire, it had been little more than a rickety backstreet venue. Age and neglect had worn its glamor thin, but the new building had charm to spare.

Konomi gave him a level look. "You look tired, Shin."

"It has been a stressful night."

"Several nights, I would say."

Shin made to protest again but instead sighed and said, "You would not believe the week I've had, Konomi. One disaster after another."

"I did warn you," Konomi murmured. "Still, all worth it, though, wouldn't you say?"

"That remains to be seen."

"I think you are nervous." She was teasing him now.

"I am a Daidoji. We do not get nervous."

"Nor should you be." She smiled wickedly. "It's not as if everyone who is anyone is attending or sending someone to attend in their place. The Lion, the Unicorn, the Dragonfly, even the Scorpion, strange as it sounds. Everywhere is a-twitter with talk of this performance." She gestured with her fan as if to indicate the city.

"Probably hoping it will go spectacularly badly," Shin remarked sourly. He had invited representatives from all the major clans with interests in the city as well as the imperial governor. He did not expect all of them to attend – renting a box was a polite way of expressing interest or wishing someone good luck in their venture. But some would, and would be seen to attend by the masses who made up the bulk of the audience. It was the latter he was hoping to impress. They were the ones who would attend, week after week, and determine the success or failure of the new Foxfire Theater.

Konomi snorted – an unladylike sound. "Don't be morose. You have more friends in this city than enemies these days."

"Then where are they?"

"Well, I'm here," she said pointedly.

Shin paused and relaxed if only slightly. "Yes, and for that I thank you." He looked at her. "I do not know what I would have done without you, Konomi. Your support has been invaluable these last few weeks."

"Think nothing of it, Shin." Konomi paused. "Truthfully, I wouldn't have missed this for the world." She paused and gave another evil grin. "It's going to be an utter disaster."

Shin glared at her, and she gave a throaty laugh. "I'm teasing," she said, touching his wrist. "It will be fine. Among the Unicorn, it is well known that the Fortunes favor the bold, Daidoji Shin, and you are nothing if not that."

"I hope you are right," Shin murmured, awkwardly patting her hand. "I've forgotten what it's like to gamble with actual stakes, I think. But this… this might be the biggest gamble I've ever attempted."

"Bigger than unraveling political intrigues and criminal conspiracies?"

Shin hesitated but nodded. "Yes. This time it's my head on the block." He sighed. "But sometimes you just have to charge the enemy and hope for the best. Not a very Daidoji view of things, but there it is," he said.

"As a daughter of the Unicorn, I fully agree." Konomi laughed. She paused and tapped the ledger. "But I will say this. Your

Lord Kenzō is not someone to be taken lightly, whatever you imagine."

"I give him as much consideration as he is due, I assure you."

"I do not think you do. He's cunning, that one. More than he lets on."

Shin smiled. "He's a Daidoji auditor, of course he's cunning. He wouldn't be much use otherwise."

"I mean it, Shin. Kenzō has been studying your accounts the way a samurai studies an opponent's defenses. He's looking for a weakness. That's why I borrowed this. I wanted to see for myself if there was anything here that might draw his eye."

Shin looked at her. "Why the sudden concern?"

"I do not wish to see you taken advantage of by such a petty little man." Konomi tapped the ledger again. "Money is power, Shin. It buys everything one could need."

"Not everything."

"Everything worth having. Money is freedom. Even for such as us. Enough money and even the emperor himself would listen."

Shin peered at her. "And what would you say to him, Lady Konomi? What words of wisdom do you have for our beloved potentate?"

"Are you making fun of me, Shin?"

"Only a little bit."

A sudden commotion from outside interrupted her reply. She frowned and turned. "That doesn't sound good."

"Well, it's certainly bad for someone. I gave express instructions that we weren't to be disturbed." Shin rose smoothly to his feet and hurried to the screen door that separated the box from its foyer. Konomi rose and followed, still sipping her tea.

His manservant, Kitano, was waiting in the foyer. "My lord, it appears we have a guest," he said doubtfully. Kitano was a seedy looking middle-aged man, despite the quality of his robes. Shin ensured his servants wore only the best. He scratched his cheek with a prosthetic finger as he spoke. "Master Odoma."

"Ah. I was wondering when that particular snake would strike." Shin pulled out his fan and smacked it into his palm. "Of course he would choose today."

"And who is this person?" Konomi asked, taking a swallow of tea.

"A persistent annoyance," Shin said as Kitano slid open the door to the corridor for them. Shin stepped out into the hall to find a confrontation taking place. As Kitano had warned, Odoma was there, accompanied as always by his two bodyguards. The latter were a pair of ragged looking men with frayed hems to their sleeves and scruff on their cheeks and chins. They were both armed, but their hands were nowhere near their weapons.

This was largely due to the fact that facing them was his own bodyguard, Hiramori Kasami, who watched them warily but without any apparent anxiety. For once, she was not clad in armor but in a simple kimono dyed in clan colors, though like Odoma's men, she was armed with a sword. Despite being a head shorter than the tallest of the two, Shin knew who he'd have put money on to win a fight.

A daughter of the Uebe marshes, Kasami had been born into a vassal family but now served the Daidoji directly, her skills refined to lethal deadliness. Odoma's men clearly recognized this, for they watched her the way a bird might watch a snake and seemed almost absurdly relieved when Odoma waved them back. "Finally," the merchant said. He was short and heavy with a round head that gleamed in the light of the paper lanterns strung throughout the theater.

"Playing nicely, I hope," Shin said, ignoring Odoma.

Kasami grunted wordlessly, not taking her eyes off Odoma's men. Konomi's own bodyguard, a lanky samurai named Hachi, stood ramrod straight against the wall, his hands folded before him and the Iuchi insignia displayed proudly on the breast of his kimono. "She hasn't killed them yet," he said as he nodded amiably to Shin.

"Small favors, Hachi," Shin said. The samurai flushed slightly, pleased Shin had recalled his name. Shin snapped open his fan and turned his attentions to Odoma. "Well then, Master Odoma. What can I do for you on this fine day?"

Odoma bared his teeth in an ugly smile.

"Well, you can give me my damn theater back for one."

CHAPTER TWO
Merchant Odoma

"I thought you were a fool, you know," Odoma said with a degree of cheerfulness Shin found obnoxious. Then again, he found most things about the other man obnoxious. "Buying this place. Barely worth what it would cost to tear it down. That's what I told Ito." The merchant smelled strongly of rice wine despite the relative early hour of the day, and his robes, though richly brocaded, were stained in places.

Shin had thought it best to discuss matters in the privacy of the box. He'd had the curtain pulled, and Odoma had left his bodyguards outside. Konomi, of course, had not taken the hint, and instead sat watching from the corner. Odoma either didn't recognize her or was simply happy to have a witness.

Shin nodded and forced a smile. "Yes. He told me."

"I bet he did!" Odoma slapped his knee and laughed. "Not one to soften a blow is Ito. He drove a hard bargain nonetheless. Told me you wanted it for the wood." He shook a finger in mock accusation. "Told me you were going to sell it."

Shin gave his fan a languid flutter and was rewarded by a glint of annoyance in the other man's eyes. "I did, as it happens. At least all that could not be repurposed."

Odoma laughed again, but this time, Shin could hear an undercurrent of bitterness. The merchant had thought himself clever, unloading the property so soon after the fire that had all but destroyed the original theater. He'd thought the land worthless, though he'd wanted a good deal of money for it nonetheless; more than it was worth in fact.

Shin had been happy enough to pay the merchant's asking price but had allowed Ito – a Crane merchant of his acquaintance – to act as go-between and haggle on his behalf. A good haggle, while thoroughly entertaining, was not considered a worthy activity for a man of Shin's standing. While Shin didn't often concern himself with what others thought, there were times when even he had to bow to societal pressure.

"Yes, well, you've certainly made something of the old place, I admit," Odoma continued. "I don't recall it looking this fancy when I owned it."

"I have made a few improvements," Shin admitted, not without some satisfaction. He caught Konomi's eye, and she gave a slight shake of her head. A warning but an unnecessary one. He was well aware Odoma was up to something.

"Yes, you certainly cleaned it up nicely, my lord." Odoma smiled. "My compliments to you. Though I cannot help but feel somewhat… cheated."

Shin snapped his fan shut with a flick of his wrist. "How unfortunate. And yet, a fair price was paid. More than a fair price, some might say." Ito had warned him this might happen. Odoma thought they'd played him false, all evidence to the contrary.

"A fair price for lumber, yes, but not for a venue such as this, my lord."

Shin paused. "You could have restored the theater yourself.

You certainly have the funds. You are one of the wealthiest men in the city."

Odoma chortled. "If I have wealth, my lord, it is only because I do not cast it frivolously upon the waters of chance. I am but a humble soy merchant and must reinvest the greater portion of my earnings in my business." He clasped his hands over his stomach and looked about. "But then the Crane have wealth to burn, it is said."

Shin dipped his chin, acknowledging the point but neither agreeing with nor disputing it. At times, a reputation for bottomless coffers was helpful. Other times, as now, it was a hindrance. Odoma, like many merchants, thought a fair price was one slightly above what a customer could pay.

The door to the box slid open to admit Kitano. He set a tray of tea down on the bench provided. The tea was a common variety; Shin saw no reason to waste his quality stock on a man like Odoma. Shin smiled apologetically. "I would offer something stronger as I recall your tastes do not run to tea, but unfortunately, we do not have it to hand."

Odoma brushed his words aside. "Tea is fine, my lord." His gaze lingered on Kitano as he bowed and retreated. "I see you still have that disreputable peasant in your employ."

"I will grant you that he's disreputable, but he's no peasant." Shin poured steaming tea into the two cups provided. "I've come to learn that his father was a ronin of some small infamy. He turned his skills to banditry, and then piracy, before finally winding up on the wrong end of a Lion spear."

Odoma's eyes widened in surprise. "How did you learn this?"

Shin handed him a cup. "I asked him, obviously." He glanced at Konomi and tapped the pot. She shook her head, and he settled back on his mat. "You know Kitano, then?"

"I employed him. Once."

"I trust he gave satisfactory service."

Odoma grunted and set his cup aside, untouched. "I'm not here to talk about him."

"No, I did not think so." Shin sighed. "It might interest you to know that the Daidoji Trading Council recently dispatched an auditor to check over my records – Junichi Kenzō. Have you heard of him?"

Odoma's expression went through several interesting contortions before settling on a look of mild interest. "I believe I might have, yes. He has a forceful reputation."

Shin suspected Odoma already knew Kenzō since it had likely been his complaints that had given the Trading Council the excuse needed to dispatch an auditor to his doorstep. "Indeed. He has been most helpful in my efforts to restore this venue."

Odoma frowned. "I'm sure," the merchant said, his previous boisterousness gone.

"If you truly believe yourself taken advantage of, I would happily introduce you to him. I'm sure between you, you could come to some accommodation." Shin reached for the bell resting beside the mat he knelt on. "I could have Kitano fetch him if you like."

"That won't be necessary, my lord," Odoma said hurriedly. "I can see now that I was mistaken. I must apologize for wasting your time in such a manner." Odoma bowed as low as a man of his girth was able to while sitting.

"No need to abase yourself. We are men of the world, and such misunderstandings often occur in our business." Shin smiled. "I trust you will be staying for the performance. I have set aside a box for your use if you wish. You would do me a great courtesy by attending."

"Yes, I would, wouldn't I?" Odoma straightened. "Some might consider it an endorsement."

"Some might." Shin did not, but he saw no reason to say so.

"I expect you have invited everyone of importance in the city, eh? Not just myself."

"I have sent out several invitations, yes." He caught a flicker of a smile from Konomi but pretended not to notice. She was enjoying this.

Odoma grunted. "Unlike others, my endorsements do not come cheaply. As I said, I am but a humble merchant. I cannot afford to give away goodwill for free."

Shin set his cup down. "I have provided the box. You may use it or not as you wish."

Odoma smiled. "I have insulted you."

"If you had insulted me, you would know," Shin countered in a mild tone. He'd fought this particular duel a dozen times since he'd purchased the theater, and it was becoming tiresome. Odoma was trying to wear him down, to eke out some token payment in order to assuage his own ego.

Odoma hesitated and then tried a new tack. "You Crane do much business in this city. Paper, mostly, isn't it?"

"Yes, I believe so." Ostensibly, Shin was the Crane Clan's trade envoy to the City of the Rich Frog. But he was a firm believer in a hands-off approach to overseeing the merchants under his authority. They knew their business – Ito especially – and did not need him prying into their affairs. So long as the money continued to come in, Shin saw no reason to unduly involve himself.

Odoma paused. "I'd heard you weren't interested in playing the merchant prince, though. That you had, ah, other hobbies, one might say." He peered at Shin, and there was a sly gleam in his eyes.

Shin paused. This was a new tactic. He wondered where it was leading. His hobby, as the merchant called it, was rather more than that. He had begun to make a name for himself in the city and beyond as a solver of puzzles, often delicate ones. The sort of puzzles that arose in a place such as this. Thefts, disappearances, even the occasional murder. All told, a more interesting way to spend one's time than shuffling trading licenses and import tariffs.

"One tries to keep busy," he said after a moment. "I have my puzzles and you, your interest in dice." Odoma flushed. Like many rich men, including Shin himself, he had his share of vices. Gambling was one of the more pedestrian examples of Odoma's bad habits. The merchant won more than he lost but only because he rarely went anywhere without armed guards to enforce his views on the outcomes of certain dice rolls. Or so Kitano had told him. From the look on Odoma's face, it was most likely true.

"Now I am the one who's insulted," the merchant said, cheeks flushed with embarrassment. Shin paused, studying Odoma. Was the other man clever enough to bait him into a trap? No. Not unless someone had coached him.

"My apologies. I did not intend for you to take my comment in that way. As I said before, I would be most grateful if you chose to attend the day's performance. As you might have heard, I have secured the services of the actress, Noma Etsuko. Today will be her first appearance on the stage in our fine city."

Odoma grunted. "So I've heard. She's a great beauty. How did you manage such a feat? I was told she refused any offer to leave the Imperial City."

Shin snapped open his fan and gave it a wave. "I can be quite persuasive, or so I'm told. I take it you will stay, then?"

"Perhaps." Odoma looked at him and gave another sly smile.

"It might go some way to soothing my ruffled feathers as you Crane say."

"Do we say that?" Shin asked innocently. "I've never heard such a thing."

Odoma cleared his throat and rose awkwardly. "Yes, well. I suppose I should go."

"If you must." Shin did not rise but rang the bell, alerting Kitano so he could slide open the doors for Odoma. "Until next time, Master Odoma."

Odoma departed wordlessly. Konomi waited until he was gone and said, "What a vile little man. Is he trying to blackmail you?"

"In his own clumsy way, possibly." Shin sighed and looked at Odoma's untouched cup. "What a waste of tea."

"I take it this has happened before?"

"Several times. It always follows the same script. He implies that I cheated him, demands compensation in some oblique manner, and I soothe him with a token show of largesse. It was amusing at first, but it's becoming tiresome."

"What is he a merchant of?"

"Soy. Why?"

"No reason. I assumed rice wine, given the smell." Konomi waved her fan as if to clear the air. "Why do you allow it?"

"Odoma is the head of the local merchants' association. I cannot be seen to bully him. He knows this and is using it to his advantage."

Konomi nodded. "He's hoping you'll pay him off."

"It's that or kill him."

"I know which I would advise."

Shin laughed. "Kasami said much the same. Sadly, I fear I will just have to endure it, at least until Lord Kenzō has returned home." He frowned. "Then again, I could have them both killed. A tad expensive, though." He paused as if truly considering the matter. "No, no, best to leave it."

She stared at him a moment as if wondering whether he was joking before uttering a sharp laugh. "I'm pleased you followed my suggestion to hire Noma Etsuko," she said, changing the subject.

"A good idea is a good idea, whoever it comes from," Shin said primly.

Konomi gave a throaty chuckle. "I was worried you might have been put off by her reputation." She fixed him with a calculating gaze. "Still, she brings a bit of welcome notoriety to your new venue."

"Do you really think me capable of such calculation?"

"If I didn't, we wouldn't be friends," Konomi said. "She is quite popular and not just with the audience."

Shin smiled. "This sounds like gossip."

"Does that mean you don't want to hear it?"

"Oh, to the contrary. You know I can't resist a good scandal."

Konomi chuckled throatily. "It's one of the things I find most agreeable about you."

Shin made to reply but was interrupted by the thud of a drum from somewhere above, signaling that the doors were about to open. Konomi looked up. "I forgot you managed to inveigle Tetsua into granting you permission to construct a drum tower," she said, referring to the city's imperial governor, Miya Tetsua.

"The least he could do, considering," Shin said. The drum and the flat tower it occupied had been something of a coup; only theaters with the favor of the imperial court could possess a drum tower on their roof. It told the patrons the Foxfire was a cut above – a place to be and to be seen at. Tetsua had given him permission as a reward for services rendered earlier in the year, during the affair of the poisoned rice.

"There was a rumor an imperial representative would be attending today's performance," Konomi said. "Not Tetsua himself, I assume."

"No, sadly." He sighed and stretched, trying to loosen up the tension in his muscles. Too much sitting of late, not enough sword practice. That was what Kasami said. He wasn't certain he agreed, but he had to admit he was feeling stiffer than he liked. "No time for gossip now, I'm afraid. I must greet my guests as is a good host's responsibility."

They rose at the same time. She smiled and patted his arm. She paused at the door. "Oh, by the way, there's someone I want you to meet. A cousin of mine."

"Where do all these cousins come from?" Shin asked. "It seems as if you have a new one every time we speak."

"The Iuchi are a large family, and we enjoy meeting new people," Konomi said with a slight frown. "Stop trying to change the subject. Shinjo Yasamura."

Shin blinked. "Wait. The son of the Unicorn clan champion? *That* Shinjo Yasamura?"

"Do you know of another?"

"He's your cousin?"

Konomi made a fluttering gesture. "Technically, he is the half brother of one of my cousins, but it all amounts to the same thing really."

"Does it?"

"Stop asking silly questions, Shin. He wants to meet you."

"Why?"

Konomi smiled. "Why wouldn't he? You're very interesting. You tell me so yourself incessantly." She rapped his knuckles –

gently – with her fan. "You'll like Yasamura. He's a vain peacock who fancies himself a wit." She paused. "You have much in common."

Shin ignored that. "When?"

"He's attending the performance today as my guest. He's told me he's rather looking forward to it. And to meeting you." She looked him up and down with a critical eye. "Do try to be on your best behavior, Shin. I wouldn't want you to embarrass me."

CHAPTER THREE
Noma Etsuko

After showing Konomi out, Shin dispatched Kitano to find out which of his guests had arrived early and who wasn't planning to arrive at all. While his servant did so, he took a moment to finish his tea, hating to let it go to waste.

Kasami entered as he was emptying the last of the pot into his cup. "You look stiff," she said, apropos of nothing.

Shin glanced at her. Younger than Shin, she often treated him as if the reverse were true. Her tone often bordered on disrespectful, and he prided himself on being able to provoke her out of her dutiful shell. He gave his fan a flutter, knowing it annoyed her. "It will pass," he said, knowing that would annoy her as well.

"You look nervous," she said as if he hadn't spoken.

"I'm not nervous," Shin said, more sharply than he intended. First Konomi, and now Kasami. It was irritating to find out he'd let his mask slip and all the worse because she was right. He was nervous. He'd never attempted anything like this before. Until now, his whole life had been about not doing things, pointedly so in fact.

Kasami continued, unperturbed by his tone. "You did not sleep last night. I heard you pacing till all hours."

"I slept," he said in protest. Not well, admittedly. But some.

"Not long enough from the look of you."

Shin ran a hand over his head, careful not to muss his white hair. "Are you my bodyguard or my nursemaid?"

"At times, I think you need both," she shot back. "Look at the state of you."

Shin self-consciously smoothed the fold of his robes. "You're one to talk."

Kasami snorted. "Childish."

"I don't see you sleeping."

"No. If you see a bodyguard sleeping, they are a bad bodyguard." Kasami sniffed and tapped the hilt of the sword sheathed at her side. Normally, she would not have worn it indoors, but it was a public venue, and she'd ignored his request to leave her blade out of sight. "Though I have no doubt this performance will do its best to put me to sleep."

"You are a savage." He slapped his fan into his palm. The metal spokes rattled slightly as he did so.

She shrugged. "Kabuki is boring."

"*Love Suicides in the City of Green Walls* is a classic of the genre and Chamizo's masterpiece," Shin said. "It is a story of shame and obligation, of love and loss but also triumph over tragedy. It has everything an audience could want."

"Swordplay?" Kasami asked.

"Quite a bit. Were you even listening to me when I explained the plot earlier?"

"No."

Shin sighed and shook his head. "Sometimes I despair of you."

"Why choose a play everyone has already seen?" Kasami asked.

"Because they have already seen it, my lady."

Shin and Kasami turned. Wada Sanemon, master of the Three Flower Troupe, the theater's resident kabuki troupe, stood in the open doorway. "The, ah, the door was open, my lord. I hope I am not… interrupting?" he asked as he ran a hand nervously across his bald pate. He was a large man, broad and bulky like many former soldiers. His face and hands bore the scars of his previous profession, and he wore his ill-fitting robes like armor. Despite his appearance, he was pathologically nervous around those he regarded as his betters. His pate was, as always, dappled with a light sheen of sweat.

"Master Sanemon," Shin greeted, gesturing for him to enter. "I trust everything is on track for today's performance?"

Sanemon swallowed. "That is what I came to speak with you about, my lord…"

Shin felt a sudden spike of panic but forced a smile. "Oh? Then by all means, Master Sanemon, say on!"

"It's Lady Etsuko, my lord."

"What about her?"

"She wants to see you."

Shin traded glances with Kasami. "Well, I will be most happy to speak with her after I have greeted my guests."

Sanemon swallowed again. "You don't understand, my lord. She wants to talk to you, well, now." He glanced over his shoulder and gestured. Shin rose and went to the door. He peered into the corridor and saw a sight that would take the breath from any sane man.

Noma Etsuko swept down the corridor toward his box, trailed as ever by the diffident form of her protégé, Ashina. At first glance, Etsuko was a small, curvaceous woman of an age with Shin. There was a rumor she had her costumes tailored slightly too small to better emphasize her natural gifts, but Shin wasn't sure she needed such aid. She fairly bristled with charisma, her hair untidily pinned, eyes wide, mouth set in a firm line as she stalked toward them, chin thrust out.

Ashina, in contrast, was tall and demure. She was younger than Etsuko but only by a few years. Shin had heard she was considered a promising actress, but since coming into Etsuko's service, she'd only rarely gotten the chance to be onstage. She had an apologetic look on her face as she followed her mistress.

Sanemon tried to intercept the actress but was brushed aside as if he were of no more importance than a fly. "My lord, this is intolerable, simply intolerable," Etsuko cried, her voice carrying all the way along the corridor. "Unendurable!"

Shin sighed and plastered a sympathetic expression on his face as he stepped into the corridor. "I'm sure, Lady Etsuko. Though, if I might inquire, what is it, exactly, that you find intolerable?" *This time* he wanted to add but didn't. Etsuko had been complaining about one thing or another since her arrival. He was beginning to wonder if Konomi had suggested he hire her as a prank.

It was true Etsuko was accredited as the greatest actress of her generation, but she was also the most temperamental woman he'd ever had the misfortune to meet. It wasn't simply her incessant complaints but also her ever-increasing demands on his time and his attention. Etsuko thought highly of herself, and she was determined that others do so as well.

She came to a halt before him, back as straight as an iron bar and a look of utter desolation on her face. Shin recognized the look, for he'd seen her employ it more than once onstage. It was a good expression, very potent, but empty of true feeling. She wrung her hands. "The nameboards, my lord. Oh, it is too embarrassing for words." She covered her eyes and turned away as if overcome by emotion. "Think of my reputation!"

"What about the nameboards, my lady?" Shin asked more firmly than before. The nameboards stood out in front of the theater and listed the cast, usually in order of appearance, as well as sketches of the actors in costume. He glanced at Sanemon, who unhelpfully shook his head in evident dismay.

"My name, my lord – my picture – they are in the wrong place," Etsuko breathed, not quite leaning toward him. "Someone is trying to sabotage me, my lord... and yourself, of course. That is the only explanation."

"Or perhaps it is merely a mistake," Shin said soothingly. He raised his hands but was careful not to touch her. While the gesture would have been an innocent one, Etsuko might well see more meaning in it than was intended. Every time their eyes met, Shin saw something in her gaze he found unsettling. A hunger, but for what, he could not say.

Etsuko closed the distance between them to an almost improper margin. "They placed me below him," she said, eyes wide. "As if I were no more than a junior member of the cast."

Kasami appeared as if from nowhere and thrust her arm out, separating them. "Step back," she said flatly.

Etsuko shot her a glare, but it vanished quickly, and she retreated to a proper distance, head bowed. "Below whom?" Shin asked, but he already knew.

"Nao," she growled, and for an instant, she seemed like another person. "He is trying to sabotage me, my lord. Ever since I arrived here, he's been waging a war against me." It was a familiar accusation, and one he'd heard often since Etsuko's arrival.

Shin made a placatory gesture. "I know Nao can be difficult, but he is lead actor. You are only newly arrived, and it will take time for the troupe to get used to you."

Etsuko pulled herself erect. "I have been here for nearly six months, my lord. If they are not used to me by now, I suggest you hire a new troupe." She glanced at Sanemon as she said it, and he frowned but made no protest.

"I will take it under advisement," Shin said.

Etsuko smiled. "I know you will, my lord. You are a man of rare insight and distinction. That is why I agreed to act for you." She touched his arm before Kasami could intervene. "I know you will do what is best for this theater. For all of us."

With that, she spun and strode away, Ashina trailing in her wake. Shin watched her go in some bemusement. Then, with a sigh, he turned to Sanemon. "I suppose I don't have to ask if our new lead actress is fitting in."

Sanemon sighed and shook his head. "We are doing our best, my lord. Lady Etsuko is a woman of... forceful personality."

"That's a polite way of putting it. Tell me the truth."

"She is rude, demanding, and lacking in decorum. She regularly insults her fellow actors, the crew, and, well, myself."

Shin smiled weakly. "At least she is a good actress."

Sanemon grunted. "Yes. Sadly."

Shin was quiet for a moment. "As good as Okuni?" he asked softly.

Sanemon was silent. "Better, in some ways. Okuni slid too easily into her roles. She lacked the sheer presence a good lead player requires. She did not command the stage. She simply insinuated herself."

"Like a cat, you mean."

Sanemon smiled weakly. "If you like, my lord." He cleared his throat again, clearly hoping to change the subject. Nekoma

Okuni was something of a sore spot for both of them. She had been Sanemon's lead actress before the fire. She'd also been a shinobi, and it was due in no small part to Shin that she'd been forced to flee the city. They'd both hoped she might return, albeit for different reasons. That hope had thus far proven unfounded.

Shin had reluctantly made the decision to hire a new lead actress. He'd learned that Noma Etsuko's contract had been under review by her previous troupe and had swooped in to steal her away. Despite her popularity with audiences, her old employers had not put up much of a struggle. Shin had begun to understand why.

"Actors are temperamental by nature, my lord," Sanemon went on. "Even the most placid of them can turn on you in a moment. But Lady Etsuko is…" He trailed off.

"Not placid," Shin finished for him.

"No, my lord. Definitely not that." He managed a weak smile. "But I'm sure she will find her place given time."

"Let us hope so, Master Sanemon. The future of your troupe, and this theater, might well depend on it." Shin regretted the words as soon as he said them. It wasn't Sanemon's fault. He sighed and waved the matter aside. "Never mind. It will be as it will be. Thank you for attempting to warn me." Shin paused. "Would it help if I visited the cast and crew before the performance begins? A show of support, you might say."

Sanemon gave him a weak smile. "It might just, my lord. I know the actors, at least, would appreciate it."

Shin nodded. "Good. I will do so immediately." He clapped Sanemon on the shoulder. "There's a Daidoji saying – start as you mean to go on."

Sanemon frowned. "I've never heard that saying, my lord."

"Well, no. I just came up with it. Good, though, wouldn't you say?" Shin gestured. "Now, shall we? There's not much time and quite a few people I need to see."

CHAPTER FOUR
Backstage

Kasami sidestepped a panicked embroiderer as the man hurried into the costume room, picking at a loose seam in a set of vermillion robes. The room was the largest backstage out of necessity. Every wall was studded with shelves upon which costumes were carefully folded and stored. Dressmakers, embroiderers, and dyers sat on scattered stools and saw to last-minute alterations and repairs for waiting actors.

Rin, the master of costumes for the Three Flower Troupe, stood at the center of the room, a long bamboo pole in one chubby hand. He was a short, narrow man with perpetually red cheeks and a wide smile. He used the pole to indicate shelves and costumes for his youthful assistants to select and make ready for the actors. "Hats, headdresses, and footwear, my children. Do not forget a single one, else I'll take this pole to your rears!"

His assistants laughed at his words. Rin was far too genial to ever carry out such a threat, and they knew it. He chuckled and looked at Shin. "As you can see, my lord, I have made good use of your largesse – a costume for every occasion!"

Shin nodded, clearly pleased by the comment. Kasami stifled a grunt of disapproval. It was not for her to say how Shin spent his money, at least not in public.

A trio of actresses swanned into the room. Kasami recognized one of them – Chika. One of the few members of the troupe Kasami could stand. They weren't friends; it wouldn't be proper. But they were friendly. The young woman often played grandmothers or matron aunts, not because she looked particularly old but because she had a raspy voice and an excellent sense of comedic timing. The right wig and a bit of bending and she might have been any grandmother in the market.

Chika sauntered toward her, casting a glance at Shin as she did so. He'd wandered farther into the room, away from her. "He looks excited," she murmured.

Kasami grunted. "He cannot help himself."

"None of us can." Chika glanced down at Kasami's sword. "Worried someone's planning to drop a sandbag on him?"

"He has enemies."

"Everyone does," Chika said.

Kasami glanced at her. "Even you?"

Chika laughed and touched Kasami's arm in a friendly gesture. "Oh, you are an innocent, my lady. Actors have enemies the way gamblers have debts. And that's just backstage. Why, Lady Etsuko herself once threatened me with a knife." She leaned close and added conspiratorially, "And I'm not the first."

Kasami snorted. "I am not surprised." Etsuko was a troublesome woman. She was loud and arrogant and utterly without a proper awareness of her own place in the scheme of things. Over the months since her arrival, Kasami had often daydreamed about teaching the other woman a lesson in good manners.

Chika laughed again. "You should come out with us. After the

show, I mean. Let Lord Shin see to his own safety for a night."
She gave a sly grin. "Or better yet, bring him along…"

Kasami's reply was interrupted by a sharp thwack of bamboo
against the floor. Rin snapped his fingers at Chika. "You. Here.
Now. We need to do a proper fitting."

Chika rolled her eyes and sighed. "Yes, Master Rin." She
winked at Kasami. "Think about what I said, my lady. A bit of fun
might do you good."

Kasami grunted again, unimpressed by Chika's argument. A
part of her, a small part admittedly, thought a life without such
small indulgences to be a sad thing, rather like a ceramic fruit –
pretty to look at but otherwise lacking. Yet indulgence could lead
to mistakes. She had been taught all her life to put duty before
everything. Anything less was a failure, and failure was anathema
to her.

She sought out Shin and saw he was still in the midst of his
unnecessary inspection. He'd already visited the small properties
room and the storerooms, checking over everything. She knew
he'd linger backstage until the performance began – or even
after – if he had his way. It was all so unnecessary. Thankfully, he
had other commitments.

She retreated into the corridor, satisfied Shin was safe for
the moment. Rin was no threat, and the craftsmen were too
preoccupied with their labors to even notice his presence. Once
outside, she took up a position next to the door, arms folded.

The backstage area was a semi-octagon, parceled up by
dividing paper walls into a nest of interconnecting corridors and
a dozen rooms. The largest rooms, such as the one she'd just left,
had been set aside for the storage of props, costumes, and the
like. The remainder had been allocated to the actors as changing
rooms.

Below them, she knew, was a maze of paper and wood stretching all the way to the front of the theater. And beneath that was the city's water course – a warren of stone tunnels and running water. Kasami had made it a point to know the location of every point of ingress and egress as well as every trapdoor, sliding panel, and hatchway in the building.

Backstage was heaving this close to the curtain call. Actors made their way to the communal dressing room, accompanied by fitters and assistants. A trio of craftsmen hurried past, carrying armfuls of severed heads made from wood and stuffed full of red-dyed shavings. They bowed awkwardly to her, even as they gave her a wide berth.

Many of those who worked backstage had tasted Kasami's wrath at one point or another since Shin had purchased the theater. If Shin was the benevolent lord, doling out rewards and compliments generously, then Kasami was his iron fist, dispensing reprimands where necessary.

Kasami pretended not to notice their wary respect, but it pleased her. She was a traditionalist at heart and never more pleased than when others knew their place. If only Shin could do the same. She brushed the thought aside even as it passed across her mind. The truth was, Shin did know his place. He always had. It was the source of much of their difficulty.

Of late, however, he'd shown a certain contentment with his lot. A desire to better himself. Many of his previous vices had ceased to be of any interest. Instead, he preoccupied himself with murders and thefts. Hardly suitable work for a man of his station but better than gambling away his stipend on a weekly basis.

But this latest indulgence – it might well be the death of him. She'd never seen him in such an agitated state. He was as nervous as a boy on the eve of his gempuku. His talk with Lady Konomi hadn't settled him as she'd hoped. As far as Shin's companions went, Iuchi Konomi was the only one she truly approved of. She was of noble blood and, even better, seemed remarkably able to tolerate Shin's… well, Shin-ness.

Her ruminations were interrupted by the arrival of a familiar, grubby figure. "Kitano," she said, packing as much disappointment into his name as she could. "Looking for something to steal?"

"Not this time," Kitano Daichi said with a louche grin. He was all rough edges and shifty looks, and he had tried to kill Shin once. Shin had shown mercy, disappointing Kasami to no end. She'd settled for taking one of Kitano's fingers. Despite her misgivings, Kitano had proven himself useful as a servant – if somewhat incorrigible.

Kitano scratched at his unshaven cheek with his prosthetic finger. "Is he going to be much longer?" he asked, peering into the fitting room.

"Why? What do you want, gambler?"

"He has someone waiting for him in his box," Kitano said. "One of his guests."

Kasami grunted in surprise. "Which one?"

"The Scorpion." Kitano paused. "Unpleasant bunch."

"They always are," Kasami murmured. It wasn't unknown for guests to visit their host prior to a performance. But Shin had never met his opposite number from the Scorpion delegation. The Scorpion did little in the way of trade in these waters. That they had a delegation was a formality more than anything.

She wondered what they wanted, even as she dismissed Kitano with a gesture. "Go make yourself useful and get some tea ready. I'll collect his lordship."

But Kitano lingered. "Is Chika in there?"

Kasami frowned. "Yes. Why?"

"No reason. Just curious."

She gave him a smack on the side of the head. Not a hard one; just enough to remind him of his place. "Curiosity is a privilege. One you do not have. Go. I will bring him." Kitano went, his smile still in place.

Kasami sighed. The problem with men like Kitano was that they pushed their luck too often. And eventually, they'd push it too far. She peered around the edge of the door and gave a sharp whistle. Shin turned and frowned. She motioned for him to follow her. A few moments later, he stepped out of the costume room. "All is well, I trust?"

"Yes. We should get you to your box. You have a guest."

"Who?"

"Bayushi Isamu, the Scorpion envoy."

Shin scratched his chin. "That's odd." He shrugged. "Oh well. Saves us having to visit his box, I suppose. But first, I'd like to wish the rest of our actors good luck." He turned and froze. "Oh dear," he murmured.

Kasami followed his gaze and laughed softly as a familiar, frowning face appeared at the other end of the corridor, just visible over the bowed heads of a crowd of workmen. Junichi Kenzō was a narrow man, needle sharp and blade straight. He wore a permanently pinched expression as if he'd recently smelled something not to his liking.

Despite his status as a courtier, Kenzō dressed modestly in robes of pale blue. He held an accounts ledger close to his chest, cradling it as if it were his own child. He looked around, eyes narrowed, as if searching for someone. Luckily for them, the corridor was packed with crew and craftsmen, and Kenzō hadn't spotted them yet.

Kasami allowed herself a smile. "He looks unhappy."

"He always looks like that. Even so, let us absent ourselves before he spots us." Shin turned and started quickly down the corridor. Kasami followed at a trot. "Does the man not sleep?" he asked somewhat plaintively as they walked. "Everywhere I turn of late, he's there, haunting me!"

"He's an auditor," Kasami said. "That's what he does."

"I thought he would have gone home by now, honestly," Shin said, glancing over his shoulder. "I can't imagine why he's still here."

"Because he likes it," Kasami said.

Shin looked askance at her. "Likes what? Going over my finances?"

She shrugged. "You knew what he was like when you suggested it. Did you think he'd get bored? Because his sort don't."

"I thought he'd have figured it out by now is all."

"Maybe he has."

"Obviously he hasn't," Shin retorted.

"Have you asked him?"

"Don't be ridiculous."

"Then how do you know?"

"I intuited," Shin said, tapping the side of his head. "If he had figured it out, he would have confronted me by now. Instead, all he wants to do is drone on at me about fiscal matters. It's as if he's decided to appoint himself my secretary, my own thoughts on the matter be damned."

"Would that be so bad? You hate looking at ledgers."

"You must admit they're not the most compelling reading," Shin said.

Kasami snorted. "I wouldn't know. A samurai does not concern themselves with such matters. That is why men like Kenzō exist. Why not let him do it?"

Shin didn't reply. She knew he had no good reason for distrusting Kenzō's motives – save for his enduring suspicion that the courtier had been dispatched not by the Daidoji Trading Council as he claimed but by Shin's grandfather. He'd never spoken of it to her, but she could read him well enough after all this time.

She sighed inwardly. To say their relationship was strained was an understatement. The old man had never made any secret of his disappointment. He had long regarded Shin as a problem to be managed rather than a grandson. Shin, for his part, saw the old man as an obstacle to be overcome… or an enemy to be outsmarted. Their duel had preoccupied Shin for most of his life and likely would continue to do so until the old man passed.

She'd never met the old man herself, not even when she'd been formally entrusted with Shin's life. From what she'd heard of him, he was a hardened pragmatist – a samurai of the old school and a man with little patience for foolishness. The antithesis of Shin.

Kasami glanced back. No sign of the auditor. They'd lost him for the moment, but the theater wasn't that large. Eventually he'd run Shin to ground. She smiled at the thought.

"What are you smiling about?" Shin demanded.

"Nothing," Kasami said. "What do you think the Scorpion wants?"

Shin sighed. "I suppose we might as well find out."

CHAPTER FIVE
Sanemon

Wada Sanemon gnawed discreetly on a thumbnail as he watched the backstage crew prepare the stage for the first performance the Foxfire Theater had hosted in over a year. The first performance since it had been all but gutted in a fire and left little more than a heap of smoldering ashes. Not to mention the first performance of the Three Flower Troupe since the loss of their lead actress.

It was always the same every opening day – nerves, the anticipation – it was all so overwhelming. Like a drug. He took a deep breath, trying to slow the rapid pace of his heart. It wouldn't do to suffer a fainting spell – or worse – today of all days. Not when so much was depending on him.

Most companies had their own stage manager in addition to the troupe leader, but the Three Flower Troupe had long done without. Sanemon had taken on the responsibilities himself, overseeing the performance as it happened, keeping the actors on schedule, and ensuring the stage was made ready for each scene in the proper order. He was also responsible for ensuring any last-minute changes to the cast or the scene went off as smoothly as possible. It kept him busy when he would be otherwise worrying.

Hopefully none of it would be necessary today. It was always tricky, trying to slip things past an audience, especially an attentive one. A group of musicians hurried past, momentarily distracting him. They were heading for the stage and the black-slatted façade that would hide them from the audience. He gestured in greeting, and they bobbed quick, awkward bows as they continued on their way.

Many of them were new; the troupe's previous musicians had erred on the side of enthusiasm over skill. Another example of Lord Shin's largesse – and another example of their new patron fixing something that hadn't necessarily been broken.

Not that he wasn't grateful, of course. Lord Shin had rescued them from penury. But with money came obligation. Sanemon had been so eager to secure a patron, not realizing what it meant. At the end of the day, the one who held the purse strings made the decisions.

He glanced toward the opposite wing of the stage where a handful of workmen were diligently working on one of the windlasses that controlled the revolving dais at the center of the stage. They'd been at it for an hour already and seemed in no great rush to effect their repairs. He wondered if he ought to go over and say something to the crew leader, Ishi, but he decided against it. Ishi knew his business, and Sanemon saw no reason to distract him.

Even so, it nagged at him. It was just the latest in a string of accidents that had afflicted the theater and the troupe over the last few months. Missing tools and damaged scenery, stolen costumes, falls and fires. Little stones that added up to an avalanche. It hadn't crashed down yet, but it was only a matter of time.

That it was just a part of theater life only made it worse. There was nothing to be done about it, except to buy new tools and fix what was broken. Even so, some of the more superstitious troupe members were claiming it was all the work of a ghost. Specifically, that of Okuni, who was somehow haunting them, even though everyone knew she was alive, just… not present. Others whispered of a different sort of spirit, that of the old theater, angry at what it must see as a desecration of its sacred place.

Nonsense, of course. But nonsense could take on a life of its own under the right conditions. Thus far, he'd managed to keep a lid on it. He'd even managed to keep Lord Shin from finding out, though he suspected it was only a matter of time. No telling what would happen then. He'd probably want to investigate or some such nonsense.

"Master Sanemon!"

Sanemon flinched and turned. He saw the auditor, Lord Kenzō, striding toward him, an accounts ledger clutched to his chest. Stage crew scattered before the courtier like startled birds, though he paid them little mind. "The very man I wished to see," Kenzō continued. "We have things to discuss, you and I."

Sanemon bowed his head. "Lord Kenzō. A pleasure as always."

"An obvious lie, but I'll accept it as it was intended," Kenzō said, grinning. Unlike Lord Shin's easy smile, Kenzō's grin reminded Sanemon of nothing save a tiger preparing to leap. He peered past Sanemon toward the stage. "How goes it?"

"It has not gone anywhere yet, my lord," Sanemon said. Despite the difference in their status, he felt strangely at ease with the auditor. Kenzō was not friendly by any stretch of the imagination – he was still a courtier, after all – but he was a pragmatic sort, especially when it came to money. Sanemon liked to think of himself as much the same. Over the past weeks,

Kenzō had proven to be a good source of advice on cost-cutting measures.

Kenzō laughed politely. "It will, Master Sanemon. Of that I have no doubt." He paused. "Sales of tickets have been exceptional, I understand."

"Better than expected."

"You do not sound pleased."

Sanemon hesitated. "A full house brings its share of difficulties, my lord."

"It also brings in money," Kenzō said, patting his ledgers. "Lord Shin has spent quite a hefty sum getting this place in working order. It would be a shame if he could not recoup his losses."

"A shame for all of us, my lord."

"Yes, yes." Kenzō peered past him at the stage. "What are they working on?"

"The windlass, my lord."

"Is it broken?"

"Apparently so. We discovered it last night."

Kenzō frowned. "I believe there have been a number of such difficulties of late."

Before Sanemon could reply, there was a sudden and all too familiar eruption of shouting from the direction of the dressing rooms. He recognized the voices instantly – Lady Etsuko and Nao. No one else argued quite so… theatrically.

"What is that racket?" Kenzō demanded, a startled look on his face.

"Another difficulty," Sanemon growled. Lord Shin had waxed poetic about the actress before she'd arrived. Upon meeting her, Sanemon had realized that it was just that – poetry. The reality of Noma Etsuko was anything but poetic.

She was as arrogant and demanding as any lady of the court

with a fishwife's temper and a voice that could shake the pillars of heaven. Not a day went by that she didn't cause some trouble. Sanemon did his best to ignore her outbursts when they weren't aimed at him. But, eventually, Lord Shin was going to have to do something about her, whether he admitted it or not. The troupe wouldn't survive otherwise.

"My apologies, my lord, but I must attend to this," Sanemon began.

Kenzō nodded. "Of course. I will come with you."

Sanemon would have preferred otherwise but wasn't quite sure how to dissuade the auditor without insulting him. So instead, he simply nodded and headed in the direction of the argument, Kenzō following behind. They weren't the only ones either. He caught sight of Chika and a few of the other actresses hurrying that way. The confrontations between Etsuko and Nao had become legendary backstage. People even wagered on them at times. Sanemon didn't approve of it but neither did he move to stop it. The troupe needed its outlets, however disreputable.

The battleground for the latest engagement appeared to be the wig room. A crowd had already gathered, and Sanemon saw money changing hands. As the name suggested, the wig room was a room filled with wigs, manned by a single elderly wig dresser named Uni. While most troupes had several wig dressers on staff, the Three Flower Troupe relied solely upon Uni. Though she was bent and shrunken by age, she moved with startling speed when she wished. Everyone backstage knew to stay out of her way.

At the moment, she was all but dancing about in panic, hands fluttering like the wings of a startled bird. Several wigs lay scattered on the floor, and another rested in the grip of the troupe's newest member, who was brandishing it like a weapon at her rival.

"Give it back," Etsuko shouted, jabbing at Nao with the wig she held. In contrast to his rival, Nao was tall, slim, and effete. In the right light with the right costuming, he could pass for either a man or a woman. He had used this talent to great effect in his career, playing a diverse array of roles that had won him much acclaim if not accompanying success.

Nao looked down his nose at Etsuko, a supercilious expression on his face. Sanemon realized he had a wig as well, though his was cradled protectively against his chest. "It's mine, and you know it," he said flatly. "You were trying to steal it."

"I stole nothing," Etsuko said with no give in her tone. "That wig is mine. You can tell it is mine because it is made from real Ujik hair and not horsehair... like these ratty things you wear." She brandished the wig she held more forcefully, provoking a cry of distress from Uni. Sanemon reached out to physically restrain the old woman.

"Both of you, cease this childish display," he barked. Neither actor paid him any attention. He hadn't expected otherwise, but he'd had to try.

"Horsehair," Nao breathed. He touched his chest as if she'd struck him a physical blow. "Horsehair! How dare you insinuate such a thing, you – you... *amateur*!"

Etsuko paled. "What did you call me?"

"You heard me."

Etsuko drew herself up, eyes sparking. "If anyone is the amateur here, it is you. I have trod the boards with legends. What have you done that anyone has ever heard of?"

Nao flushed and made to reply. Sanemon took a deep breath and roared, "Quiet!"

A hush fell over the corridor. Even Etsuko looked stunned. Sanemon stepped away from Uni and glared at the participants.

"Fools, the pair of you. Quiet, I said," he snapped when Etsuko made to protest. He snatched the wig out of her hand and passed it to the sobbing Uni. "Do we not have enough to worry about today without you two making things worse? I don't care which of you started it. I am ending it here and now."

He looked around. "Today is the most important day of our lives. If today's performance goes well, our troupe's future is secured. If it goes poorly, we'll all be looking for new employment come tomorrow." He fixed Etsuko and Nao with a hard eye. "That includes both of you. Stop it."

Etsuko sniffed and gathered her dignity about her. "I do not have to stand here and listen to this. I am no child to be chastised. I must get ready." She turned and then rounded on Sanemon. "And I expect that sign board to be changed before I go onstage!" With that, she stalked away, and the crowd started to disperse.

Sanemon caught Nao's eye and gestured for him to remain where he was. He wanted to talk to the actor after he'd gotten rid of Kenzō. He turned back to the auditor and bowed. "My apologies, my lord. You should not have had to witness that."

"No, no, it was quite edifying, Master Sanemon," Kenzō said. "I had wondered how you kept things running. Now I see. This is your fiefdom, and you are its lord."

Sanemon flushed. "I am not sure I would put it that way, but thank you."

"Though I must say, this is not the first time I have witnessed such an altercation. I hesitate to say it, but taken along with all the accidents, it does not seem to bode well for today's performance."

Sanemon paused. "It is considered good luck to have a few problems on opening day, my lord."

Kenzō looked askance at him. "Is it?"

Sanemon nodded. "Oh, absolutely, my lord. Can't have a good

show without something going wrong, that's what they say." He wasn't lying. It was an old saying, just not one anyone with any sense ascribed to.

The auditor hesitated, then leaned close as if to share a confidence. "Between us, it would make my task easier if this effort failed."

"Failed, my lord?"

"I speak in hypotheticals, of course. Lord Shin's triumph is that of the Crane. That is why I have lent him my aid. But one cannot predict how such things will turn out. The performing arts are notoriously resistant to accurate prediction. For instance, if something were to happen, the audience might ask for refunds – the bane of any creative endeavor."

"Why would the audience ask for such a thing, my lord?"

"Oh, any number of reasons," Kenzō said slyly. Sanemon stiffened.

"We are not in the habit of giving refunds."

"Exceptions must sometimes be made." Kenzō was speaking softly now. "And then, well, a new venue would need to be found. A new patron as well. Though that would not be difficult for you, I think. It is not empty flattery to say that I think your troupe is among the finest of the mid-tier repertory companies. You could easily find a more suitable place to ply your trade if you wished." He smiled. "Why, I would even lend my services to the cause, should it be necessary. It would be the least I could do."

"I am humbled by your words, my lord," Sanemon said, bowing his head. He chose his next words with care, uncertain as to what the auditor was trying to accomplish with such a suggestion. "But we have just started the season. To leave now for any reason would surely harm our reputation."

Kenzō gestured dismissively. "Easily fixed if there is need."

He paused. "Not that I am saying there is. I am sure everything will proceed as planned. Have you seen him, by the way? I must speak to him."

"Lord Shin?"

"Who else would I mean, man?"

"My apologies." Sanemon hesitated. "No, my lord. I believe he's greeting his guests."

Kenzō frowned. "Very well. I shall speak to him later." He sucked in a breath and turned but paused. "Think on what I said, Master Sanemon."

"I will, my lord," Sanemon called to the courtier's retreating back. He felt slightly sick as he considered the auditor's words. Something was going on. Something that spelled trouble for him and his people. When lords clashed, it was often the peasants who suffered. But the question was, should he get involved or leave them to it and hope for the best?

"Fortunes protect me from scheming Cranes," he muttered. On the other side of the stage, Ishi began to curse as something went wrong with the windlass. Sanemon hurried across the stage to deal with this new difficulty with something approaching relief.

This, at least, he knew he could handle.

CHAPTER SIX
Nao

"What did the Crane want, then?" Nao asked as Sanemon entered the wig room, a hangdog look on his face. "The other Crane, I mean. Not ours." He heard the echo of the drums, thudding down from above. It set his heart to racing as always.

"Nothing," Sanemon said curtly. He sounded tired. They were all tired. Today was a new beginning for all of them, but if it went poorly, they would not get a second chance. Nao knew it. Even the stagehands knew it. The Three Flower Troupe had been given a reprieve, but it was only temporary.

Nao frowned. "I didn't start the fight this time."

"It doesn't matter who started it. It matters that someone like Kenzō saw it."

Nao sighed and gestured irritably, dismissing the troupe's elderly wig dresser as she tried to clean up in the wake of whirlwind Etsuko. "I'll reorganize them myself, Uni, thank you," he said sharply. Then, softening, he added, "Why not go make yourself a cup of tea to settle your nerves, eh? It will all be tidy by the time you get back, I promise."

The old woman bobbed low and scuttled out, murmuring disapprovingly to herself. Nao and Sanemon watched her go. Uni was an indispensable member of the troupe and had been since it had had a different name and different master. She was, perhaps, the oldest member of their little found family, and they all had much affection for her.

"Our new leading lady made no friends there," Nao opined. Not that Etsuko would particularly care, he thought. She viewed the stage crew as little more than furniture.

"She needs time."

"What she needs is a–"

"Nao, please," Sanemon said. He sat down heavily on a stool. "You have to stop this."

Nao inspected his fingernails. "It was hardly a fight. A spat at best."

"Keep pushing and she may well quit. Then where would we be?"

"Weak-kneed with relief?"

"Nao, please," Sanemon said somewhat plaintively. "We need her."

"That is debatable."

"No. It is not. Lord Shin is counting on us. He has given us everything we could want, and in return, all he asks is that we fill seats. Etsuko is the best way to do that."

"Again, debatable. And Lord Shin is a Crane. He has more money than he knows what to do with." Nao picked up a fallen wig and carefully dusted it off. He found a certain comfort in the wig room. It was a room of possibilities. It was as if each wig was another spirit, waiting to be invoked, be it master or maiden, courtier or peasant. They were like old friends. He'd worn most of them during one performance or another.

Sanemon gave an annoyed grunt. "Perhaps, but no coffer is bottomless, and there may well come a day when he decides to cut his losses. I intend to put that day off for as long as possible. It would be nice if you helped me in that."

"I am helping." Nao set the wig back on its mannequin with a reverence he was certain Etsuko did not share. She was not alone in this. There were few actors these days who understood such things. The magic of story, of transformation and tradition. The magic of hearts and minds. With command of such, one could bring an audience to tears or fill them with laughter. There was no greater power, Nao thought, and no greater responsibility.

"And how exactly? By fighting with Etsuko in full view of the crew?"

"Yes, actually." Nao looked at the other man. "If it weren't for me, she'd be terrorizing the costumers or the embroiderers or some poor curtain puller. She prefers easy prey, that woman. But luckily, she also can't resist a fight. So, I give her one. Really, you should be thanking me. They're already nervous enough about this place. They don't need the added stress of her regard."

"I keep telling them it's not haunted," Sanemon said in exasperation. He fell silent. "Did you really steal her wig?" he asked after a moment.

Nao smiled. "What do you think?"

Sanemon shook his head and heaved himself to his feet. "I think you will be the death of me." He paused at the door. "And if you are not careful, she will be the death of you."

"And what is that supposed to mean?"

"Lady Etsuko has friends, Nao. Important ones from what I hear. If you irritate her overmuch, they might just decide to intervene on her behalf."

Nao sniffed. "It wouldn't be the first time I had to deal with an overambitious suitor."

Sanemon snorted. "Yes, but this time they wouldn't be yours."

"If that's the way you feel, perhaps I should leave."

Sanemon looked at him. "What?"

"You heard me. Perhaps a clean break would be best." It was meant as a joke, but there was an edge to it. Nao had seen too many troupes caught between rivalrous actors. He did not intend to let the Three Flower Troupe suffer that fate.

"Don't be ridiculous." Sanemon hesitated. "Just… think about what I said. Please. For Okuni's sake if nothing else." He was gone a moment later.

Nao sighed. Okuni. The troupe's former lead actress had not been as skilled as Etsuko, but she'd been more agreeable. She'd also been a shinobi, and she'd contributed to the troupe in other ways than acting. She was gone now, having fled. Nao didn't blame her. She'd gotten involved – gotten them all involved – in something far too dangerous for the likes of them. But thanks to their new patron, she'd escaped.

Nao sometimes wondered where she'd gone after leaving the city. But it was better he didn't know. In the wrong hands, knowledge was a deadly weapon. He knew that better than most. Idly, he stroked one of the wigs, enjoying the feel of it beneath his fingers. Not horsehair, this, but human and well cared for by Uni.

Of late, he'd begun to wonder if perhaps Okuni had had the right idea. Maybe it was time to move on. To go elsewhere and be someone else.

"Are you all right, master?"

Nao sighed and turned. "Yes, Choki." His understudy was young, and pretty rather than handsome. He had aspirations of being a leading actor but was as yet only a journeyman. "What do you want?"

The youth bowed. "Master Sanemon thought you might need some help. With the wigs, I mean." He looked around. "Though Uni usually doesn't let me in here."

"With good reason. There is an order to this place, and most of you have never bothered to learn it."

"Why would we, master? That is what wig dressers are for."

Nao clucked his tongue. "Yes, but what if there is no wig dresser or the one you have is incompetent? Because I have experienced both, and neither is an experience I'd care to repeat." He tapped a wig with long sides and a raised bun. "Here. What is this one?"

"A formal style, worn mainly by unmarried young women," Choki said with no hesitation. Nao smiled thinly.

"And?"

Choki paused. "And, master?"

"Look at the style of the bun – loose, deceptively untidy. Not the hairstyle of a chaste maiden or the sensual fashion of a geisha but the flared comb of a courtesan, say of Journey's End City." Nao traced the messy curve of the bun. "Wigs tells stories, the same as every part of a costume. What you wear is almost as important as how you wear it. You must learn these things if you wish to have a career on the stage."

Choki nodded. "I will learn, master." He hesitated. "But I think I have learned much already. And I could learn more onstage than back here."

"Is that what you think?" Nao asked lazily.

"I wish to be an actor, master," Choki said. "But I cannot learn hanging about in the background or speaking a single line in a single scene. I am ready for more!"

Nao sighed. He'd heard those words before from other young men in Choki's position. Their voices alight with fire and ambition. Every single one of them had seen themselves as masters-to-be of the stage. "Do you know what it means to be an actor?" he asked as gently as he could manage. "For once you step onto that stage for the first time – truly step on it, I mean – your path is set, and there can be no deviation. No retreat. Like a soldier you must advance or perish."

Choki swallowed. "I am not afraid."

"I did not ask whether you were afraid. I asked whether you understood."

"I do."

"I do not think you do. To be an actor is to give of yourself, to surrender your life to the stage." Nao took Choki's chin in his hand and forced the youth to look at him. "The stage is your kingdom, your master, your god. It is your bride, your lover. It is all things. And it is nothing. For in the end, the stage cares nothing for those who walk the flower path. We are but grist for the mill."

Choki looked away, two spots of color on his cheeks. He was embarrassed. Nao smiled sadly. "Choki, you have been an excellent understudy. You have observed me for weeks, months even. Ever since we came to this city and you joined our troupe. But you still have much to learn." Nao smiled. "Now, I must go get ready for today's performance." He started for the door but paused. "Finish cleaning up in here for me if you would. Then come help me with my costume."

Choki could not hide his disappointment, but he nodded. "Yes, master." Nao studied the disconsolate slump of the young man's shoulders for a moment and then left him to it. While he sympathized with Choki's impatience, he knew no good would come of letting the boy go onstage in a lead role too soon.

Many young actors abandoned the theater when their dreams proved too arduous to make real. Others went on to great success with their chosen troupe. Only time would tell which path Choki would find himself on. But until then, Nao would do his best to teach the young man what he could. As he himself had been taught in his callow youth.

But the sad truth was, Choki would likely never become the actor he imagined himself to be. His talents were mediocre – adequate, perhaps, for an unsophisticated audience – but nothing more. Nao had never said this to him, of course. There was no reason to crush the lad's spirit, not when mediocrity had its uses.

Every troupe needed those actors who were neither exceptional enough to lead nor poor enough to be noticed. Adequacy was sufficient for some roles; the bit parts and boring roles that filled out the ranks of any cast of characters. The messenger, the rowdy, the tittering maiden. Choki was eminently suited for these roles, and Nao had said as much to Sanemon. The latter was no stranger to such roles himself, for he'd excelled in them during his brief time as an actor, or so he claimed.

Nao had never seen Sanemon act. They had not met until well after the troupe leader had traded the stage for backstage. Sometimes he regretted that but not often. Nao himself had been acting in a provincial theater in a small marsh town, one of only a handful of actors in the Red Turtle Troupe, when Okuni had hired him to star opposite her in the Three Flower Troupe. He'd acted in better, but Sanemon's troupe was a step up from the Red Turtle. And a permanent berth in the City of the Rich Frog had its perks.

It wasn't the City of Lies, for one thing. Nao grimaced as

he reached his dressing room and pushed the thought aside. Memories of the city he'd grown up in were like a bad smell – unpleasant but fleeting. He paused in the doorway, thinking of Choki staring at wigs. He shook his head and slid the door shut behind him.

The profession of the kabuki actor was largely a hereditary one. With few exceptions, the players of most troupes were connected by blood, however thin those ties might be. Many were descended from the great acting families of previous generations. Even their names were handed down. Nao was not the first to call himself so nor would he be the last.

Names such as his were at once a blessing and a curse. For though one could call on the weight of tradition to guide oneself, one was also beholden to those who had come before. Audiences knew the history of every name worth remembering and comparison was inevitable. Nao had done his best, but sometimes he wondered what his predecessor would make of him. Then Shosuro Nao had been hard to read, even at the best of times, her every expression and word calculated for best effect. She had been a good teacher, though. Better, he thought, than himself.

"Finished playing with your wigs?" Etsuko asked as he entered the dressing room they shared. It was the largest as befitted the lead actors. Once, he'd shared it with Okuni. On the whole, she'd been a far more agreeable roommate.

Etsuko was getting dressed with some help from her understudy, Ashina. Nao smiled kindly at the young woman, but she avoided his gaze. She had been with Etsuko for several years and likely knew better than to acknowledge anyone her mistress disliked.

"Finished cleaning up after you, you mean? Yes. You really

should apologize to Uni, by the way. Not wise to annoy the wig maker."

"I have my own wigs," Etsuko said dismissively. "I have a sensitive scalp. You think you are so clever, Nao. But you're really just a child."

"Better a child than a crone."

Etsuko's gaze snapped toward him. "What did you call me?"

"You heard me." In actuality, Etsuko was no older than himself. She was still young enough to believably play the part of a lovestruck teenager – if one overlooked certain endowments.

"How dare you speak to me so!"

"I shall speak to you any damn way I like," Nao snapped. He squared off with her, knowing even as he did so that it was a mistake. It was too soon after their last fight. She gestured sharply, and Ashina scurried away, her eyes wide and face pale. Etsuko reached into her robes and pulled out a short-bladed knife. Nao was so surprised he was momentarily at a loss for words.

Etsuko brandished the blade. Her previously polished tones had become rough. "I ought to cut your tongue out." She took a step toward him, and he stumbled back, bumping against his makeup table. She leaned close. "I know you took more than my wig, Nao. Where are the letters?"

"What letters?"

"Don't play the fool. My private letters."

Nao paused, recalling the uproar she'd made a few weeks earlier about some papers of hers being stolen. He hadn't given it much thought at the time. She'd blamed Chika, but nothing had come of it. "Are you still going on about those?"

Her eyes flashed. "As I will continue to do until I get them back."

"I took no letters. Now, put that knife away before someone gets hurt," he said softly.

"The only one who's going to get hurt is you, you preening fop." Etsuko held up the knife, then paused. She gave him a sneer that would have set the first three rows alight had they been onstage, and made the knife vanish. "But I don't want to get blood on my clothes. You will return the letters to me by the end of the performance. Or else."

"Or else what?"

"Or else I shall tell my new fiancé that you have insulted me." She turned away so Ashina could finish helping her get ready.

Nao stared at her in surprise. "Fiancé?"

"Yes. It seems I am to be wed at last."

"And who is the unlucky suitor?"

"Bayushi Isamu," she said, watching him in the mirror. "A familiar name, I think."

Nao paused, startled despite himself. Bayushi Isamu? Here? The thought of it sent a chill through him. "Not to me."

"That's not what he says."

"Scorpions lie," Nao said with a shrug. He tried to ignore the sudden spurt of panic that gripped him. "They are much like us in that way."

"I do not think he is lying. In fact, he told me quite a bit about you, Nao. Would you like to know what he said?"

"No."

Her smile chilled him to the bone. "Are you certain?"

Nao said nothing. He didn't intend to give her the satisfaction of seeing how much that name had rattled him. Her smile faded to be replaced by a sneer. "Very well. My letters, Nao. Otherwise, you can speak to my sweet Isamu in person."

Nao glanced at her in his mirror, studying the satisfied smile on her face. She thought she'd won. His anger turned cold. She wanted to upset him? Fine.

Two could play that game.

CHAPTER SEVEN
Bayushi Isamu

When Shin and Kasami arrived, there was a single Scorpion standing before the door. She was willowy beneath her robes of black and red, and her face was completely hidden beneath a mask that resembled a demon's grinning countenance, including an impressive pair of horns. She was armed and kept her hands close to the hilt of her sword as she faced them sidelong. "You are the Crane," she said.

"Am I? That's a relief. I thought I might have put on the wrong robes this morning." Shin smoothed the fold of his robe and gave her his most winning smile. Despite this, she did not relax. Shin paused. "I am. Yes. And this is my box."

"My master is within," she said, her gaze sliding toward Kasami. The two women stared at one another for several moments. Shin could almost hear the clangor of battle as they sized one another up. A truce was reached, and the Scorpion stepped back, opening the path to the door. "Your bodyguard may stay here."

"How considerate of you," Shin said before Kasami could protest. "And in my own theater, no less. So kind. I can't imagine why the Scorpion have the reputation they do." He glanced at Kasami. "Keep her company. Be hospitable." He took her wordless growl for assent and stepped to the door. A servant – not one of his – opened it.

"This way, my lord," the masked servant murmured. Shin raised an eyebrow but didn't comment. The Scorpion were as infamous in their own way as the Crane were in theirs when it came to matters of courtesy. As a general rule, Scorpion courtiers were obnoxious. Everything they did was designed to take the advantage in any given situation and hold tight to it. Where the Crane used courtesy to accomplish the same end, the Scorpion used discourtesy. An interesting tactic and one Shin himself had used to great effect more than once.

There were four courtiers waiting for him in the box. Each wore a mask crafted in a different fashion – subtle differences, signifying rank, taste, and other variables. Three of them sat on the available cushions – two men and a woman. The fourth member of their quartet stood at the front of the box, overlooking the stage.

They'd opened the privacy curtain – likely so people would notice their presence. "I do hope you are all looking forward to the performance," Shin said, bowing slightly to them. The courtiers watched him silently from behind their masks.

The fourth turned as Shin spoke. "*Love Suicides in the City of Green Walls*. An uninspired choice but a safe one."

"And you must be Bayushi Isamu," Shin said, ignoring the insult.

Bayushi Isamu was thin and graceful, the lower half of his face hidden behind a tasteful veil. He wore robes of black and gold with outspoken embroidery on the edges. His black hair was worn loose much like Shin's own, save for a golden, scorpion-shaped band that kept it out of his face. He glanced at his fellow courtiers. Without a word, they rose and filed out of the box, leaving only Isamu and Shin.

Shin watched them go. "Are they not staying?" he asked. Inwardly, he felt a flicker of amusement. It was a signal that Isamu wished to speak privately. An old tactic, though somewhat ostentatious.

"Not for this," Isamu said.

"Shame. I'm always at my best before an audience."

"So I have heard." Isamu's tone implied that what he'd heard had not been particularly impressive.

They studied one another in the way of courtiers everywhere, searching for exploitable weaknesses even as they waited to see who would make the first move. Shin, no stranger to these games, ceded the opening round to Isamu. "You are new to the city, then," he said, making the first move.

Isamu gave a brief nod. "You are not."

"No. It suits me."

"Something else I have heard."

"My fame precedes me."

"It is said that 'infamy stretches like a shadow.'"

"Kazushi," Shin said, acknowledging the quote. He straightened the hem of his sleeve. "'The sun of our deeds casts the long shadow of infamy'. I take the comparison as a compliment."

"This too I have heard."

"You hear much."

"I listen where others speak."

"I find I can listen even while speaking," Shin said. "A talent of mine." He tilted his head. "How are you finding it so far?"

"The city? Adequate."

"You must not be getting out much."

"I do not share your predilection for peasant vices."

Shin raised an eyebrow. "Another thing you heard?"

"I did not have to listen very hard. Most of the city is awash in gossip relating to your exploits. You are the subject of much discussion."

"How thrilling," Shin murmured. He decided to go on the offensive. "You seem to know quite a bit about me. Am I so interesting, then?"

"Not to me," Isamu said but hesitated. A mistake or a feint? Shin circled the statement carefully before deciding not to take offense.

"I should hope not. I am but a humble courtier, after all."

Isamu gestured. "Two intrinsically opposed concepts – humility and the courtier."

Shin smiled. "Yet it is said that 'humility is the keenest blade and mercy, the sharpest edge.'"

"'Cut a man's spirit, and he bleeds just the same,'" Isamu said. "Hiroki. *Ode to the Gentle Blade.*" He sounded as if he disapproved of Shin's choice. A flaw in his defense or another feint? Shin decided to find out which.

"A foundational work, in my opinion," he said.

"'Opinion, o'pinion, thus flies the Crane,'" Isamu replied so quickly that Shin thought he must have been waiting for the opportunity.

He raised an eyebrow. "I've never heard that one."

Isamu straightened all but imperceptibly. "Something of my own."

There – an opening. Shin struck. "Ah. Well, we all have our little hobbies."

Isamu's gaze sharpened. "Yes. I am told you solve mysteries."

Shin fanned himself and made a feint of his own. "You flatter me."

"It was not intended thus."

Shin covered his mouth with his fan to hide his smile. "I am chastened."

"I doubt that." Isamu looked around the box as if noting its many imperfections. "I was surprised to receive your invitation."

"Were you?" Shin asked. Now that they had tested their edges on one another, it was time to get down to business. "I don't see why. You are a personage of some importance in the city. It would be more surprising by far if I did not invite you."

Isamu turned to look at a point just over Shin's shoulder. "I am told that today is to set the tone. If it is a success, you will be much lauded. And if it fails…"

"I will be back where I began, no great harm done."

"An optimistic outlook."

"'One does not have to stare into darkness to understand shadow'," Shin said.

"Harada. A third-rate philosopher."

Shin shrugged. "Even so, she makes some good points. Is this why you came to see me? To cast aspersions on my choice of philosopher?"

"I came to inform you that today will be Lady Etsuko's last performance."

Shin paused. "Oh?"

"Indeed. She and I are to be wed."

"Oh." Shin paused again, digesting this new information. Whatever he'd expected to come of this meeting, it hadn't been this. "I see."

"You seem displeased."

"Merely surprised. I spent a considerable sum buying out her previous contract. Had I known…" He paused. "Might I ask how this came to be?"

Isamu flinched – not obviously, but there was a slight tightening of the skin around his eyes. "And what business is that of yours?" More rudeness, intended to deflect this time rather than draw in.

Shin pressed his momentary advantage. "As she is currently under contract to me, I consider it a matter of some importance. For instance, it would not do to let one of my actresses be pressured into an engagement. Imagine what people might think."

"I assure you, there was no pressure applied by me," Isamu said. A curious way of wording a denial. Very particular. Shin filed it away for future analysis. There was something there, just beneath the surface. He wondered if he could tease it into the light.

"I will take your word for it," Shin said. A bit crude, but the point connected. He gave Isamu no chance to recover. "Though, given the variety of suitors who have asked for her hand, one is naturally curious as to how you won it."

"Were you one of them?" Isamu asked. A blunt question – almost an accusation.

"No."

"Ah. Forgive me. I'd heard your tastes ran to actresses."

"My tastes are varied and egalitarian," Shin said, fluttering his fan. "Why, I have even dallied with a Scorpion or two."

Isamu grunted softly. "Yes. My cousin warned me."

"Your cousin?"

"Bayushi Chiasa."

Shin paused, momentarily wrong-footed, as memories of a young woman, laughing behind her veil, surged to the fore. But he recovered swiftly. "I believe I know that name."

"You should. You kidnapped her, after all."

Shin snapped his fan shut. "Hardly that. A bit of youthful

mischief in which she was a willing participant. Enthusiastic even, one might say."

"It was the eve of her betrothal."

"And did she wed the fellow in the end?"

"No," Isamu said flatly.

"Well, then I expect that was the reason for her enthusiasm." Shin paused. "You did not answer my question."

"Poetry," Isamu said.

"Yours?"

"Some." Isamu took a breath. "'How desolate the past, those sad years ere I chanced to see thee; better to forget those days before we met.'"

Shin smiled politely. "How lovely. Tetsua Atsu, I believe. Though I must admit I have always preferred Kana." He cleared his throat. "'The blossom color washes away in the rain, even as my charms do wane – both bloomed, sweet sadness, in vain.'"

"I assure you, Lady Etsuko's charms are not on the wane," Isamu said.

"Such was not my intent," Shin said apologetically. He gestured somewhat dramatically and quoted, "'Lying on the silent sands, this day I remember distantly the agony of my first love.'" He prodded the air with his fan as if to push the words toward Isamu. "Ishihara. Such a way with words, that man."

"A trifle maudlin for my taste," Isamu said. "Shika says it better, I think. 'The water is gone, poured out and lost; dew slides like pearls from the blossom.'"

"And that's not maudlin?" Shin asked.

"It's more subtle at least."

"Subtlety is overrated. A weapon for cowards."

Isamu peered at him. "Are you sure you're a Crane? That sounds like something I'd expect a Lion to say."

Shin chuckled. "Given whom I heard it from, that is not a surprise. You are acquainted with Akodo Minami, the Lion garrison commander?"

Isamu hesitated. "Not intimately."

"I am surprised."

"Why? I have only just arrived as you said."

"She was – is – enamored of Lady Etsuko." Shin smiled. "Or so I have heard."

"Trust a Crane to offer gossip without being asked."

Shin clutched his chest. "A palpable hit. Gossip is among my vices, I admit. Still, you will forgive me. I am somewhat shaken by the news that I am losing my new star."

Isamu gestured dismissively. "Of course. That is why I wished to tell you myself. I did not wish for there to be any awkwardness between us should we meet again."

"I am sure we will," Shin said, peering at him. Yes, there was definitely an undercurrent of – what? Unease? Frustration? Hard to say. Isamu was unhappy about something and endeavoring not to show it. This, too, Shin filed away to analyze at his own convenience. "Still, though it is unfortunate for me, I will congratulate you and wish all the happiness the Fortunes might provide."

Isamu sniffed. "Yes. Thank you. I will leave you now. I am certain you have others to speak to." He paused. "I am told that Tonbo Yua is attending. Is that true?"

"Yes," Shin said, betraying none of the curiosity this question engendered. He'd invited Tonbo Kuma, the current spokesperson for the Dragonfly delegation to the city, but they pleaded prior commitments and sent one of their cousins, Yua, in their place. Whether Kuma did, in fact, have prior business or there was some lingering bad feeling over their previous encounter with

Shin during the affair of the poison rice, Shin could not say. He had not pegged Kuma as one to hold a grudge, but still waters ran deep, it was said.

"Excellent. I have matters to discuss with her."

"Trade matters?"

"Something like that," Isamu said. He bowed stiffly. "I will take my leave now." With that, he ushered himself out, accompanied by his servant. Shin followed them to the door and watched the whole bunch of them – courtiers, servant, and bodyguard – depart in the direction of their own box.

"I do not trust them," Kasami said bluntly. Shin glanced at her. She stood stiffly near the door, arms crossed. "The Scorpion do nothing without reason."

"He came to tell me he was getting married," Shin said idly. "To Lady Etsuko."

Kasami grunted in surprise. "Poor fool," she said before she could stop herself.

Shin sighed. "I feel a bit foolish myself. Still, it's a problem for tomorrow." He looked around. "Where's Kitano? I thought you sent him to prepare the tea?"

"Here, my lord," Kitano said from behind them. He looked somewhat more downtrodden than usual. "They, ah, sent me away. Said it wasn't necessary." He rubbed the back of his neck in embarrassment. "I thought it best not to argue."

Shin waved the excuse aside. "No matter. Have the other invitees arrived?"

Kitano nodded quickly. "Yes, my lord. All accounted for."

"Excellent." Shin looked at Kasami. "Shall we make the rounds?"

Kasami pushed away from the wall and nodded. "If we must."

"We must. Kitano, have some tea ready for me if you would. Oh, and close the privacy curtain. I wish to be undisturbed when I return." Shin started down the corridor, his hands clasped behind his back, still ruminating on Isamu's visit despite his intentions to leave it for later. Without turning, he added, "If all goes well, I'll be back before the performance gets underway."

CHAPTER EIGHT
A Good Host

Shin stifled a yawn as he made his way down the corridor. Kasami grunted disapprovingly. "Straighten up," she chided. "What will they think if they see you lurching about like a drunkard?"

"Presumably they would assume I was inebriated. Which I might well be before the day is out. Especially if things do not go well." He shook himself and straightened up. They were approaching the private box Shin had gifted to the Dragonfly for their exclusive use. "Still, I take your comment in the spirit it was intended."

A single guard was on duty outside the box, perched on a stool. She was dressed much like Kasami, though she lacked the latter's air of competence. She was new to her duties, Shin thought. But she had obviously been expecting them, for she rose as they approached. "Lady Yua has just arrived, my lord," she said nervously, bowing her head. "She awaits you in the box."

"Wonderful," Shin said. "I will speak to her now." The guard slid open the door and glanced warily at Kasami as she took up a position opposite. Shin paused in the doorway. "Play nice," he said, pointing a warning finger at Kasami. Kasami grunted but did not reply. Inside the small foyer, two servants in the colors of the Dragonfly bumped their foreheads against the floor as he stepped past them and into the box proper.

Greeting the Dragonfly first was as much a matter of courtesy as convenience. Officially, the city was controlled jointly by three clans – the Lion, the Unicorn, and the Dragon. Unofficially, the Dragon had ceded their portion to their vassals, the Dragonfly. Of the three powers, the Dragonfly were the weakest both militarily and economically. Thus, they were the safest to greet first.

"Lady Yua," Shin said as he entered and bowed politely. Tonbo Yua was an older woman, frumpy and practical. She dressed in an understated fashion and had a severe expression on her face. Shin knew little of her, save that she was one of several trade envoys who oversaw the clan's holdings in the City of the Rich Frog.

"Lord Kuma sends their greetings and their apologies, Lord Shin," she said, stiffly. "As they said in their letter, they are unable to attend the performance and have sent me in their place. It is hoped you will not be insulted," she added.

Shin inclined his head. "Never. I do hope you will enjoy the performance. Are you a devotee of the performing arts, by chance?" He glanced around and saw she had a writing desk set up and several ledgers stacked beside it. A box filled with dried tea leaves and more ledgers sat nearby. The smell of the leaves was strong – a potent tang that clung to the paper. It might as well have been a signature.

"I consider myself well educated," she said simply. She looked about the box, her face betraying no sign of what she might be thinking. She paused, then added, "I am told you procured the services of Noma Etsuko. Quite a coup, my lord."

Shin forced himself to smile. "So I am told. Are you a fan of her work?"

"As I said, I consider myself well educated." Something in her tone implied that it would be wiser not to pursue the current line of questioning. Shin heeded the unspoken warning and turned to the stage.

"Well, you should have a good view of the flower path from here," he said, indicating the narrow gantry that extended from the stage to the rear of the audience. It allowed actors to enter from amid the audience, which always provided some enjoyment for those seated in the benches.

"How considerate of you," she said flatly.

Shin ignored her tone and went on, a trifle desperately. "I've also ensured a supply of Iron Benten is on hand with our local tea sellers. I understand it is the favored beverage among the Tonbo…"

"I prefer Spring's Smile."

"Of course," Shin said, still smiling. That was the smell, then. The dried tea in the boxes. She must truly prefer it if she used it for packing material as well as refreshment. "I shall ensure some is on hand should you wish to partake. As far as food, I can recommend a delightful noodle seller–"

"I have brought my own repast."

"How wise of you. One cannot entirely trust food prepared by another." Shin felt himself flailing. It was another unfamiliar feeling, and he found it unpleasant. Yua seemed determined to be rude, and he could not imagine why. Maybe she just wanted to be alone. Either way, it was his duty as host to make her stay pleasant. He tried to erect one last bridge. "I spoke to Bayushi Isamu earlier."

"And of what interest is that to me?"

Shin frowned. There was something sharp in her tone, almost an accusation. "He mentioned he wished to speak to you."

Her gaze narrowed. "Why?"

"He did not say."

She straightened and turned away. "Forgive me. I am overtired."

Sensing he had outstayed his welcome, Shin made his apologies, bowed, and made his exit, feeling a slight sag in his burgeoning enthusiasm. In the corridor, Kasami was talking quietly to the Dragonfly bodyguard. They fell silent as he slid the door shut behind him. "Come," he said.

Kasami pushed away from the wall and nodded her goodbyes. "New friend?" he asked when they were out of earshot.

"Her name is Hira. She's a Koshei. Trained with the Shiba. This is her first duty."

"You found all that out in a few moments?"

"She's very nervous."

"I would be too with a mistress like that," Shin said.

"Didn't go well, then?"

"If I didn't know better, I'd say Kuma was trying to insult me. Lady Yua does not appear to be pleased with my hospitality."

Kasami snorted. "How terrible for you."

"It is like a knife in my heart, I tell you," Shin protested. Despite his best efforts, Kasami didn't understand how much effort went into being a good host. Any flaw in his pattern could lead to talk among his peers. Shin knew he was thought of as a layabout and an eccentric, but if people began to think he was a bad host as well – he shivered; it did not bear thinking about.

Kasami shook her head. "Where next?"

"The Lion, I think. Konomi will understand."

"I bet she will," Kasami murmured. Shin stopped and gave her a sharp look.

"What was that?"

"You heard me."

"I did. What are you implying?"

Kasami grunted wordlessly, and Shin waited, hands folded. Finally, she said, "You've been spending a lot of time with her since we got back from the lands of the Unicorn."

"Is that a problem?"

"No. But people talk."

Shin gestured dismissively and turned away. "Let them. A bit of gossip is healthy."

"Word may get back to your family."

"By way of our visiting auditor, you mean? Yes, it might. But I can't imagine even my grandfather objecting to Iuchi Konomi." He laughed softly. "Though I'd like to watch him try."

"So, you are courting her?"

"What?" he said, startled by the bluntness of the question. "No. We're friends. Nothing more. Whatever gave you such a ridiculous idea?"

"She would be a good match for you."

Shin shook his head, hands in the air. "No. Stop. We're not having this conversation. You're my bodyguard, not my matchmaker."

"Ensuring you are safely wed is a form of protection," Kasami said mildly. Shin peered at her in suspicion. The truth was, his only real objection to marriage was that it was expected of him. He had made it a point to never do what was expected of him. Kasami knew that. No doubt that was why she was suggesting it.

"You've been thinking about this, haven't you?"

Kasami pointed. "Lion."

Shin turned and nearly collided with a scowling Lion samurai. The warrior glared at him. He was broad and well built; vaguely familiar, though Shin could not recall from where. "Lady Minami awaits you," he growled. From his tone, Shin could tell he'd been sent to look for them. Minami was the impatient sort.

"Does she? How delightful." Shin beamed at the samurai. "Lead on, then. It has been too long since her ladyship and I have spoken." The samurai grimaced but turned away.

The Lion and the Crane had never gotten along in the history of the empire. Too much blood had gone under the bridge for that, but in Shin's opinion, a certain modicum of civility was nonetheless expected. Besides which, he knew his exaggerated notions of courtesy annoyed them. Being simultaneously polite and annoying was a skill he'd spent much of his life honing to obnoxious lethality.

The Lion box was slightly larger than the one reserved for the Dragonfly as was only proper given their status as a great clan. A second samurai stood on guard in front of the door, and she looked them up and down warily before stepping aside. Shin gestured, and Kasami came to a halt, waiting patiently. He was confident she would not unduly provoke the Lion samurai, but nonetheless, he thought it best to make this visit a quick one.

A single servant waited inside – a brusque older woman – who bowed and showed him into the box proper where a single occupant waited for him. As the door slid shut behind him, he said, "Lady Minami. A pleasure as always."

Akodo Minami was a short woman and sturdily built. A warrior rather than a courtier. She looked uneasy and perched on her knees as if preparing to spring to her feet at the first hint of trouble. Nevertheless, she didn't rise as Shin entered but gestured for him to sit. "I was surprised to be invited," she said after a moment.

"Right to it, then," Shin replied.

"Unpleasant duties are best done quickly," she shot back. "Why did you invite me?"

"To do otherwise would be to risk insulting the Lion." Shin smiled and looked around. "I trust everything is to your satisfaction?" He gestured to the Akodo family sigil – a reserved lion face divided into two distinct halves – carved into the paneling above their heads. Draperies in the colors of the Lion decorated the interior of the box – even the cushions had been sewn with that heraldry in mind. Scrolls honoring the great battles in the history of the Akodo hung from the framework of the box, and the privacy screens had been decorated in similar fashion.

Minami followed his gesture and grimaced. "I do not like the theater."

"And yet, you have chosen to attend. I am flattered."

"I did not do it for you, Crane," she said. Her body language was as easy to read as ever. She was uncomfortable. Nervous.

Shin smiled and nodded, pleased to have the upper hand. "My condolences, by the way." He pitched his voice low and snapped open his fan. "They say Lady Etsuko has left a trail of broken hearts in her wake."

"I don't know what you mean."

"I've just learned that Lady Etsuko is engaged to Bayushi Isamu."

Minami stiffened. "That is of no import to me."

"Then why did you come? Hoping for one last look, perhaps?" Shin fluttered his fan, studying her from behind its tines. He'd been surprised to learn Minami was one of Etsuko's suitors, not because he doubted the actress's charms but because he could not fathom how they'd met in the first place. "How did you come to meet her, by the way? Given that you do not like the theater, I mean."

"That is my business."

"No offense intended, I assure you. I was merely curious."

"I have no intention of satisfying that curiosity." Minami gave him a warning look, and he sat back, symbolically withdrawing. Even so, he was determined to make it a fighting withdrawal. He cleared his throat.

"Have you ever seen her perform? Lady Etsuko, I mean."

"I have not," Minami growled.

"Then you are in for a delightful experience, my lady."

"I am certain."

"I look forward to talking to you about it at length."

Minami gave a wordless grunt, and he judged the audience at an end. Shin rose, bowed politely, and left. As with Yua, he found himself somewhat dissatisfied with how it had gone. Though he enjoyed tweaking Minami's nose, her heart had not been in it today. Usually, she gave as good as she got. Perhaps she was distracted by the thought of Etsuko marrying another. He shook his head, annoyed on her behalf.

He plastered on a thin smile as he stepped into the corridor. He indulged himself with a polite nod to Minami's bodyguards and then started away. Kasami ambled in his wake. "That was quick," she said.

"She was in no mood for our usual banter."

"Well, you are very tiresome."

Shin glanced at her. "Careful. That bordered on disrespectful," he teased. Before she could reply, he added, "Kaeru Azuma should have arrived by now. Come. I want to make sure he's comfortable."

"I'm sure he's fine."

Shin gave her a pointed glance. "Given that he is here in his capacity as a representative of the governor as well as an enthusiast of the performing arts, you'll forgive me for wanting to make certain of it."

"Meeting with him before you meet the Unicorn might be seen as favoritism," Kasami said. If it had been anyone else, he might have thought she was teasing him. As it was, he decided to use the jibe as a teaching opportunity.

"Only to the uneducated." Shin flung back the edges of his sleeves to free his hands for the emphatic gestures to come. "In reality, by visiting the Unicorn last, I show that I bear no undue bias on their behalf but simultaneously reaffirm the bond between our clans. They are last, and therefore the least important, but by visiting them last, I might spend more time with them, thus showing that they are, in fact, more important to me."

Kasami stared at him. "Do you actually listen to the words that come out of your mouth, or are you simply speaking to hear your own voice?"

"I am trying to teach you something important."

"I do not need to know this."

"I feel the same way about swordplay, and yet you insist on a daily training regimen."

"That reminds me, you have not practiced in some time."

Shin dismissed her comment with a wave of his hand. "I have been busy. Besides, as I always say, different battlefields require different tactics."

Kasami peered at him suspiciously. "That's from Kakita's *The Sword*," she said.

"Is it?"

"Yes."

"How odd. Well, great minds think alike," Shin said cheerfully. The box reserved for use by the imperial representatives was almost at the dead center of the walkway, directly over the flower path. It was also the largest of the lot as was only appropriate.

Three Kaeru bodyguards stood outside, glowering at anyone who came near. They were a hardy looking bunch, even out of uniform. He could easily imagine them fighting pirates on the deck of a burning ship or breaking up a smuggler's hideout.

The Kaeru technically owed allegiance to no one save the Miya, and that was only because they were being paid. Yet they were inextricably tied to the city. Even their name spoke to their ultimate loyalty – Kaeru meant frog – and in some ways, they had as much claim to the city as the great clans who openly vied for its ownership.

Like the Lion, they had clearly been expecting him. As he was shown inside by one of the servants, he heard a familiar laugh and paused, nonplussed. "Oh, do stop lurking, Shin. Come in," Konomi called from inside the box. Shin put on a smile as he stepped in.

"Lady Konomi, what a surprise!"

"A pleasant one, I hope," Konomi said. "I thought you might save us for last, so we decided to save you some effort." She tapped Azuma on the forearm with her fan. "Besides, it has been too long since I last took tea with Lord Azuma."

Azuma raised an eyebrow at this familiarity but did not seem unduly troubled. Even seated, Azuma was tall and whip thin with hard features and hair that was going silver. He was dressed well but modestly. He nodded in greeting to Shin. "Lord Shin. My thanks for inviting me to this performance."

"You have my thanks for choosing to attend," Shin replied smoothly. He made to sit and then paused and looked at Konomi. "You said we…"

Konomi smiled and indicated the third occupant of the room, whom Shin had not noticed thanks to his surprise at Konomi's presence. Shin turned to see a slim, handsome man, clad in a richly decorated kimono, seated opposite Konomi and Azuma, his back to the stage. He smiled widely as he studied Shin.

"This is him, then?" he said in a mellifluous tone.

Konomi snapped her fan shut. "Lord Shin, might I introduce you to Lord Yasamura. Shinjo Yasamura … meet Daidoji Shin."

CHAPTER NINE
Flower Path

Sanemon stood in the wings, watching as the benches filled and the boxes were opened up. The drum was like thunder overhead. He found himself clutching the edge of the auxiliary curtain as the musicians began to play a soothing melody, reminiscent of a summer rain. It would keep the crowd from becoming overly raucous as they found their seats. Only once the last seat was taken would the large, barrel shaped drum set behind the musician's screen sound, signaling the rise of the curtain.

He glanced toward Lord Shin's box and saw that the curtains were still closed. That boded well. It meant he was satisfied, wonder of wonders. While he had nothing but respect for Lord Shin, the nobleman had proven himself an incessant busybody. There'd been a number of complaints from the crew concerning Shin's… enthusiasm and need to oversee every single detail – even those which did not require his participation.

One of the secondary actors, an older man named Botan, who specialized in comedic parts, hurried up to Sanemon. "How's it looking?"

Sanemon frowned. "Crowded. Why aren't you in costume?"

Botan looked down at his disheveled robes. "I am. I'm playing the monk, remember?"

"Yes, but that's not the costume Rin picked out for you."

"I know. It's better."

Sanemon shook his head. "Don't let him hear you say that." He gestured toward the gantry that extended from the stage through the seating area. It could be reached from backstage by way of a concealed passage that curved around the inner wall. "The flower path calls, Botan. Try not to trip like last time."

Botan laughed and straightened his frayed robes and started for the concealed passage where he would take his place with the others entering from the back. "They loved it. Every performance needs a good pratfall or three."

"You nearly broke your neck."

"But did you hear the applause?" Botan said over his shoulder. "It was worth it!"

Sighing, Sanemon turned away from the stage and nearly collided with Nao's understudy, Choki. He steadied the youth with a firm hand. "Easy now, lad. You're out of breath. What's wrong?"

Choki was practically hopping from one foot to the other. "It's Lady Etsuko, master!"

Sanemon sighed. He felt the beginnings of a headache somewhere behind his eyes. "What's she done now?"

"Nothing, master. It's not really her, it's–"

Choki's explanation was interrupted by the arrival of Etsuko and Ashina, walking determinedly toward Sanemon. A heavyset form trailed in their wake, hands outstretched in a gesture of pleading. Sanemon bit back a curse and hurried to meet them. This same scene had played out more than once since Etsuko had joined them, often enough that he'd become all too familiar with her pursuer.

Ichiro Gota was a short, burly man with a build similar to Sanemon's own. There the similarities ended. Gota was a son of the Badger Clan and a well-known merchant besides. Word was, he'd followed Etsuko upriver from Otosan Uchi, uprooting his life and business just to be near her. Etsuko, as far as Sanemon could tell, did not return such devotion. "You must listen to me, Etsuko," Gota said. "I beg you for but a moment of your time. Surely you can spare me that much…"

Etsuko ignored him. She caught sight of Sanemon and jerked her head, indicating that his intervention was once again required. He sighed and stretched out a thick arm, forcing Gota to stop. Sanemon bowed low as Etsuko and her understudy hurried on. "Apologies, my lord, but Lady Etsuko must take her place on the flower path. Might I be of service?"

When he straightened, he saw that Gota's bodyguard was staring at him. He felt a chill run along his spine. The Ujik – Sanemon didn't know his name – was dressed in dark robes of foreign cut but bearing the Badger insignia prominently. His hair was bound up in an informal topknot and his face was unshaven. He looked as if he were only playing at civilization. His hand rested on the hilt of the curved sword sheathed at his side.

The Ujik accompanied Gota everywhere. He never spoke, to Sanemon's knowledge, and only rarely acknowledged others. Even so, he disturbed Sanemon. He was no stranger to violence, and the Ujik radiated it. The man was a murder looking for a place to happen.

Gota waved the Ujik back. "No," the merchant said curtly. "No, you cannot. What I have to say is for her ears alone." He drew himself up in a gesture that reminded Sanemon of an avalanche in reverse. "Not for the likes of you."

Sanemon accepted the chiding with an amiable expression.

Gota was not like Shin or even Kenzō. He was a traditionalist in many ways, especially when it came to dealing with those he perceived as his social inferiors. Two weeks ago, Gota had ordered his Ujik to beat a stagehand who made the mistake of moving out of the way too slowly. Sanemon had considered mentioning the matter to Lord Shin but had eventually decided against it – mostly because the Ujik had taken a rather lackadaisical approach to the beating – a few gentle taps with the back of his hand. Also because involving Lord Shin meant involving his bodyguard, Kasami, and that would inevitably lead to bloodshed.

"The performance is soon to begin, my lord. You should take your seat." Sanemon hesitated, then added, "You would not wish to miss Lady Etsuko's grand entrance."

Gota peered at him, face twisted into an expression of frustration. His big hands clenched, relaxed, and at last fell by his sides. He blew out a breath and turned away. His Ujik paused, gave Sanemon a respectful nod, and then followed his master.

Sanemon did not allow himself to relax until they'd gone. He turned back to the stage and started as he realized Nao was standing behind him. He was wearing a fine kimono, costumed for his part as one of the secret lovers. Etsuko played the other half of the classical duumvirate, of course. "Which one was that?" Nao asked. He gestured, and Choki, who'd been watching it all, wide-eyed, darted off on some errand.

"Gota."

"Ah. She's engaged, you know."

Sanemon paused. "What?"

"She told me. Someone actually proposed to that pit viper. Can you imagine?" Nao smirked as he said it, but his sneer didn't reach his eyes. He was worried, and that, in turn, made Sanemon worried.

"She hasn't said anything to me," he said, gnawing on a thumbnail. His eyes darted in the direction Etsuko had gone. "Who is it?"

"Bayushi Isamu."

"The Scorpion envoy?" Sanemon blinked in surprise. That was fast work. From what little he knew, the man had only recently arrived in the city. "Did she say when?"

Nao shook his head. "Soon, I imagine. Else she wouldn't have mentioned it. You know what this means, don't you?"

Sanemon rubbed his head. "Yes."

Nao glared at him. "The season has only just begun, and that woman has already sabotaged us. I warned you."

"Maybe it won't change anything," Sanemon said helplessly. But he knew better. If you were a prominent actor like Nao or Etsuko, marriage to someone wealthy or noble or both was often your end goal if you had no desire to teach. And while the well-to-do were happy to patronize the theater, they did not want their significant other parading about onstage in wigs and makeup. That was just how it was.

"Someone will have to tell Lord Shin," Nao said.

"Perhaps you could do it?" Sanemon asked hopefully.

"I'm not in charge."

"Since when has that ever stopped you?"

Nao shook his head. "You wanted to be our leader, Sanemon. So lead. Go tell our patron he wasted his money on a flighty leading actress who is planning to abandon us for a life of ease and contentment." He turned toward the stage. The music was changing tempo. The last of the audience would be arriving soon and the doors closing.

Sanemon bowed his head. He felt as if the world had fallen in on him. "I'll tell Lord Shin." But even as he said it, he wondered what Lord Kenzō might make of the news. And whether it was worth letting him know first. Nao was right, after all. Sanemon was the leader. He had a duty to ensure the Three Flower Troupe prospered. Even at the possible expense of their current patron. Still, whatever he decided, it would have to wait. Maybe by intermission he would have some idea of what to do.

He was still debating the matter when one of the troupe pages ran up to him. The pages were the lifeblood backstage. They carried messages back and forth, helped move props, and alerted the crew to problems, all for the price of a meal and a warm place to sleep. "Message, master," the boy panted, out of breath. He haphazardly flapped a piece of paper in Sanemon's general direction, forcing Sanemon to snatch it from him.

"A message? For me?" Sanemon frowned and unfolded the paper. He paused. "What is this?" There were no words, merely a symbol – and a curious one at that. It reminded him of a clan sigil, but he couldn't say which one. He heard Nao hiss and glanced at the actor. "What? Do you know what this means?"

"No," Nao said.

Sanemon stared at him. "You're lying."

"I am not," Nao protested.

"I've endured you long enough to know when you're lying, Nao. What is this? Some prank of yours? If so, I am not in the mood."

"You're never in the mood, but no, it's no prank of mine." Nao gingerly took the message from him and peered at it. "It's a family crest but mixed up. Like a child's puzzle."

"Which family?"

"The Bayushi," Nao said too quickly.

"How do you know that?"

"Lucky guess." Nao looked at the boy. "Who gave this to you? Where are they now?"

Startled, the boy half turned and made to gesture. Nao caught his shoulder quickly. "No, don't point. Just tell me."

"B- back there," the page stuttered. Nao released him, his eyes sweeping the opposite end of the wing where it gave way to the backstage area properly. Sanemon stared at him.

"What is this, Nao?" Sanemon demanded. "You know something. Tell me."

Nao shoved the note into Sanemon's hand. "I don't know anything. Neither do you."

"I know this is a message from Etsuko's fiancé," Sanemon bit out. "Isn't it?"

"Who knows? Ask her." Nao turned away, gathering his robes about him. He paused. "This might be a blessing in disguise, Sanemon. The sooner she's gone, the better. We can't afford to get tangled up with the Scorpion. Take it from me, they make poor patrons." A moment later, he was gone, losing himself in the crowd of actors taking their places.

Sanemon shook his head, bewildered by the sudden turn of events. He'd never known Nao to be frightened of anything, but he was clearly scared now. Sanemon wondered if he ought to be as well. He carefully folded the missive and slid it into his robes when he caught sight of the Scorpion.

The warrior stood serene and untouched by the chaos around him. The crew and the actors both gave him a wide berth. Sanemon couldn't blame them. The Scorpion wore a filigreed eye mask of gold with a veil of red silk covering his mouth and nose. His gaze flitted across the crowd as if searching for someone.

Sanemon hesitated, then made his way over. "Is there something I can help you with, my lord?" he asked nervously. "I am Wada Sanemon, the troupe leader." The Scorpion paused and then looked at him.

"Where is Lady Etsuko's dressing room? I wish to bring her the compliments of my master, Bayushi Isamu."

"Ah, her fiancé, yes," Sanemon said.

"Yes." The Scorpion paused again. "You received my message?"

It was Sanemon's turn to hesitate. "I- I did, yes. Though, I confess I did not understand it." He made to retrieve it, but the Scorpion gestured languidly.

"That is to be expected. The one it was intended for will have no difficulty, however."

Sanemon frowned. "Lady Etsuko, you mean?" he asked, though he suspected the man meant someone else. The Scorpion gave a slight twitch of his head but did not elaborate. Sanemon wanted to ask why he'd been sent a message for someone else but, given Nao's reaction, decided it was safer perhaps to hold his tongue.

"The dressing room," the Scorpion said again.

Sanemon gestured in the direction of the dressing rooms. They were easy enough to find if you knew your way backstage. However, something told him the Scorpion already knew where they were. "She is already on the flower path, however. If you wish to speak with her, you're a bit late."

The Scorpion inclined his head. "Of course. I will speak with her later." He turned on his heel and departed, moving without hurry or hesitation. Sanemon watched him go and wondered why he felt a sudden chill of worry.

From above came the final crash of the drums.

The performance was about to begin.

CHAPTER TEN
Shinjo Yasamura

Shinjo Yasamura smiled amiably at Shin as the latter sat down on the available cushion. "Konomi has told me much about you, Lord Shin. I understand you are a student of the Kitsuki Method."

"I am, yes. You know of it?" Shin glanced at Konomi, who pretended not to notice. Azuma seemed quietly amused, which Shin took as a good sign. Shin turned his attentions to Yasamura, studying him with open curiosity. Yasamura was handsome in an angular sort of way with an air of roguish good humor about him. His hair was close-cropped, and his facial hair was artfully trimmed to cover a square jaw. He was clearly a man who took some pride in his appearance.

"Enough to find it ridiculous," Yasamura said. Shin frowned.

"Hardly that," he said.

"Oh, but surely you must agree that it sets a disturbing precedent." Yasamura fanned himself and arranged his face into an expression of dismissal. "It makes a mockery of our legal system and creates a false equivalence between the classes. The word of a peasant cannot carry the same weight as that of his betters. To even consider it is preposterous."

"Why?" Shin asked, careful to keep his tone even. Was he being teased? It was hard to tell. Yasamura was difficult to read, like any experienced courtier.

"What?"

"Why is it preposterous?"

Yasamura laughed, as if he'd been expecting the question. Konomi cleared her throat and patted her cousin's knee. "I should have warned you, Shin. My cousin enjoys teasing others. Do not take such comments seriously."

Yasamura smiled broadly. "Nonsense. Ignore her, Lord Shin." He leaned forward. "I am always ready to engage in polite debate," he said, studying Shin with a newly speculative eye. "Especially when my opponent is passionate about the subject. Tell me, have you read Yomei's treatise on the nature of man?"

Shin relaxed. This was a game, then. "I have, yes." He took a breath and quoted, "'Every soul a gem, with its own facets and flaws. Its own worth.'"

Yasamura nodded, pleased. He leaned forward. "And you will agree that some gems are worth more than others, of course?"

"But worth is not intrinsic nor is it objective," Shin said. "It is based upon subjective reasoning. The worth of gems is derived from the value placed upon them by those who trade in them. If I place worth upon the word of a peasant, does that not then grant it comparable value to the word of their social better?"

Yasamura laughed and clapped his hands. "Oh, well reasoned. Nonsense of course, given that worth is determined by the stewards of heaven, but well said."

"The idea that worth is determined by heaven is a flawed one," Shin said, smiling in pleasure. Debate was always more fun with a willing partner. "It is we who must translate the decrees of heaven, even as the servants of the court interpret the whims of the emperor. As Shogo said, 'The truth invariably depends on where one is standing.'"

Yasamura glanced at Konomi. "And now he drags Shogo into the debate. You said he was a philosopher, not a theologian."

"I have studied both," Shin said, a trifle more defensively than he'd intended. He'd had similar arguments before with others. These debates were largely good-natured but occasionally acrimonious. It was hard to tell which way the wind would blow sometimes.

"As have I," Yasamura countered in obvious amusement. He snapped his fan shut. "You interest me, Lord Shin."

"Shin, please."

Yasamura smiled widely. "And you may call me Yasamura."

Konomi snorted. "And now we're all friends. How nice."

Yasamura cut his eyes at her but didn't reply. Instead, he looked at Shin. "But I do not think you came to talk philosophy, however pleasant a diversion it might be."

Shin sighed. "No, in fact, I came to greet Lord Azuma before the performance and to see that he was comfortable."

Azuma inclined his head. "Oh, yes, very comfortable. Not to mention entertained."

"Well, I am glad for that," Shin said. "Now, if you'll excuse me, I believe it is time for me to return to my own box." He made to rise to his feet, but a slight gesture from Yasamura made him pause.

"So soon?"

"The show is about to begin," Shin said. "What might the patrons think if the owner's box is unoccupied?"

"If their attention is where it should be, they will not notice," Yasamura said. "And if yours is where it should be, you will not notice either." He stood and clapped his hands. Konomi and

Azuma stood as well as one of the servants entered the box and rearranged the cushions so that the four of them could watch the stage without turning their heads.

As they resumed their seats, Yasamura said, "It is not the performance I would have chosen, I must say." He glanced slyly at Shin. "*Love Suicides in the City of Green Walls*? A trifle common, don't you think?"

"Perhaps a trifle," Shin admitted. "But that is the point. I could have chosen something more sensational, of course – a political drama or even a romance. Even one of Meko's tragedies, such as *Tears in a Paper Shop*. But in choosing a nontraditional choice, I might have denied myself a full house."

"Is such a thing really so important?"

"It is the most important thing." Shin gestured to the audience below with his fan. "All these people will go home and tell their friends and family what a wonderful experience this was. And then those friends and families will come to the next performance or the next after that."

"Wild horses, cousin," Konomi murmured. Shin glanced at her in puzzlement. Yasamura chuckled and patted Shin's forearm. Shin hesitated but said nothing. The Unicorn, at least in his experience, had a culture of casual affection they often extended to outsiders without warning.

"When you want to capture a wild horse, you don't chase it. You lure it with food or a ready mare. You offer it something familiar, something it knows it wants. By the time it realizes the trick, it's gotten used to enjoying those things. Then you can break it and train it at your leisure."

"Ah, well, having never chased a wild horse, I shall take your word for it." Shin paused. "Can't stand the beasts myself. Untrustworthy brutes."

Konomi made a strangled sound, and Shin allowed himself a small smile. Yasamura laughed out loud as Shin had expected he would. He gave Shin another quick tap with his fan and said, "That they are! Rather like courtiers in a sense. Untrustworthy, unless you know the secret to taming them."

"And do you?" Shin asked without thinking.

Yasamura smiled invitingly. "A good question."

"Both of you shush," Konomi said not unkindly. "It's starting."

It began with the piercing trill of a flute counterpointed by the thump of a drum. The music was brittle and eerie – a magician's ritual, moving the audience from one place and time to another. The curtains slid aside slowly so that the eyes of the audience had time to adjust to the changing light. They revealed a walled garden or rather an expensive facsimile thereof. A shamisen was plucked to signal the scene's opening.

A distraught woman, dressed in noble raiment, her hair artfully arranged, her face as white as snow save for slashes of red and black to mark the contours of her cheeks and mouth, stepped up onto the central dais from behind and motioned as if calling out. As she did so, a singer offstage set the scene in a powerful, warbling tone.

Shin knew the story. Everyone did. It was as old as Rokugan itself, and while Chamizo's version was the most popular, it was also merely the most recent of the tale's permutations. Shin himself preferred it to its earlier iterations largely because Chamizo, like any good playwright, knew his audience and had grafted on a happy ending. The real world had sadness enough to spare. Shin saw no reason for it to infect the stage as well.

The setting was Journey's End City, more popularly known as the City of Lies. Shin, who'd spent several pleasurable years there as a younger man, had fond memories of the city, though he had not been sad to depart. Necessity made the parting a more entertaining affair than it might otherwise have been. His eyes strayed toward the Scorpion box across the way, and he noted the privacy curtain was pulled.

He thought again about his encounter with Bayushi Isamu. The more he thought about it, the more the other man's visit seemed like a veiled warning rather than a courtesy. As if Isamu had been sizing him up for some purpose yet to be revealed. Shin smiled. Maybe Isamu intended to open his own theater with his new bride as the leading light.

He pushed the thought aside and turned his attentions back to the stage. With the setup out of the way, the actress playing Etsuko's mother was free to give vent to her most dramatic cries. She called for her daughter, demanding she appear, and appear she did.

A hushed murmur swept through the audience as Etsuko appeared at the far end of the theater and strode along the flower path accompanied by the actors playing her attendants. No one was looking at the latter, of course. No, all eyes were on Noma Etsuko, and she damn well knew it from the way she carried herself.

She walked slowly as if reluctant to heed her mother's call. The recalcitrant daughter, unruly and untamable. A meaty role for any actress and one which Etsuko feasted upon with gusto. She paused midway to the stage and looked out over the audience, letting them drink her in. A brief, knowing look between diva and devoted. Was it his imagination, or did her gaze fix itself upon the Scorpion box? Did the curtain twitch? He could not say with any certainty, but the thought stayed with him as she made her way to the stage.

"Magnificent," Yasamura breathed.

"Yes," Shin murmured. "She is that, whatever else." He had seen Etsuko perform before. It was why he'd gone out of his way to acquire her contract. Reputation was one thing but better to see it with one's own eyes. Even so, he was struck by her force of presence. Etsuko claimed the stage the way a warlord claimed a battlefield. It was hers from the moment she stepped off the flower path, and none could gainsay her.

"I am grateful to your cousin for suggesting I seek her out," Shin continued. Yasamura laughed softly.

"You should be grateful to me. It is I who suggested it to her in the first place."

Shin felt rather than saw Konomi tense, and he wondered whether she was annoyed with her cousin for claiming credit so blatantly. He glanced at her, but she wasn't looking at him. He smiled at Yasamura. "Then I must thank you both. Even if we are only blessed with her presence for a short while."

Yasamura frowned. "Oh?"

"She is to be wed apparently."

"Ah." Yasamura didn't sound surprised. "How unfortunate for you."

"Yes. Well, perhaps one performance will be enough." Shin turned back to the stage. Etsuko's voice rose and fell like ocean waves. Her gestures were perfectly controlled moment to moment. The flipping aside of her robes as she knelt, the humble – and yet not – bowing of her head as she accepted her mother's stern chiding. She delivered her responses like an archer sending arrow after arrow into a provided target. Every word hit its mark with the audience.

Shin could not help but compare her to Okuni. The shinobi was possessed of an elemental magnetism to be sure, but her acting... well. Rough was the word that came to mind.

Naturalistic. She did not act; she pretended. She inhabited her roles so thoroughly, so skillfully, that it seemed as if she were not acting at all. While impressive, it was not what audiences paid to see. They wanted to see actors act, and Etsuko *acted*. And yet, there was something compelling about Okuni – something…

"You are frowning. Is something wrong?" Yasamura asked softly.

Shin started, momentarily at a loss. Then he remembered to smile and shake his head. "No. Nothing. Thinking of Etsuko's predecessor here and the difference in their styles." As he said it, he could feel Konomi's eyes burning a hole in his back. She knew something of his dealings with Okuni, but he always had the sense she disapproved, though whether of the actress herself or Shin's interest in her, he couldn't say. He straightened himself and flicked at a nonexistent speck of dirt on his sleeve.

"Ah. Was she a good actress, then?"

"Passable," Konomi said before Shin could reply. Yasamura frowned, clearly perplexed. Shin glanced at her, and she made a sharp gesture. Shin shook his head.

"She was a good deal more than that," he said, looking back at Yasamura.

"Was she?" the other man murmured. His expression became speculative, and Shin pretended not to notice the question there. He still wasn't certain what Konomi had told Yasamura or what the other man might be expecting. "And why is she not here now?" Yasamura asked. "A falling out?"

"A family emergency," Shin said blithely.

"Ah, one of those. Well, that would make it difficult to play certain parts, I expect." He paused, then in a grave tone asked, "I assume you're seeing to the child's care?"

Shin looked at him in surprise. "What?" His mind juddered to a halt as he tried to catch up to Yasamura's insinuation. "What?" he asked again.

Yasamura smiled. "My apologies. I just assumed…"

"I assure you," Shin began, fumbling over his words, utterly nonplussed, "that is certainly not the reason…"

"One can never tell," Yasamura interjected. "Especially these days. One hears such stories, especially about men like yourself." He glanced over his shoulder, and Shin turned to glare at Konomi, who was hiding a grin behind her fan.

"And what exactly have you heard about me, my lord?" Shin asked, slipping on a mask of polite distance. Yasamura made a moue of annoyance and shot his own glare at Konomi.

"Less than I was led to believe, I think."

"Gossip is the weed in the garden, obscuring truth among its shoots," Shin said piously. He turned back to the stage. He heard Yasamura hiss something to Konomi and her answering titter. It was a good reminder that as friendly as Konomi was, she still liked to stir up trouble when she thought it might prove amusing. Out of the corner of his eye, he saw Azuma give him a sympathetic nod.

He tried to concentrate on the performance. As with many of Chamizo's works, the important characters were all introduced up front with the appropriate amount of fanfare. Nao would be making his entrance at any moment as the canny lover aided in his assignation by the drunken monk. There, in the garden of her parents, the young lovers – the faithful children of two warring families – would make the pact that drove the plot.

He was looking forward to seeing how Nao comported himself against Etsuko. Nao was a better actor than Okuni. A master of quick changes with impeccable timing. He did not conquer the stage as Etsuko did, rather he stole it, openly and unabashedly.

Onstage, the mother departed, mollified. Etsuko clutched at the heavens, begging the gods for guidance. The monk tottered onstage, whispering drunkenly and eliciting laughter from the audience with his foolish capering. Then, abruptly, he straightened and approached Etsuko hesitantly. Shin watched her face and frowned. Something was wrong. He'd noticed it earlier, he thought, but had put it down to a trick of the light.

He leaned forward, half rising to his feet. He heard Yasamura ask a question but ignored the other man, so intent was he on what was happening on the stage. Nao was making his entrance, every inch the lovelorn nobleman, his voice punching the air with power and verve. But Etsuko was not moving to meet him. She was not moving at all but rather... staring. Staring at Nao or somewhere else? Impossible to say. She clutched at her throat, a convulsive grasping motion like that of a drowning woman.

Then, with a single choked cry, the greatest actress of her generation collapsed.

CHAPTER ELEVEN
Falling Star

Nao watched his rival collapse, and for a single happy moment, he thought she'd fainted. Such embarrassment. However would she live it down? But as he got closer, he realized it was no mere fainting spell.

Etsuko lay in a twitching heap, gasping like a beached fish. She clawed at her throat, and her eyes rolled wildly and blindly. Frozen, Nao turned to Botan, but the other actor was similarly paralyzed. The audience as well. All eyes were fixed upon Etsuko. Any other day, that might have annoyed him.

Finally, after what felt like centuries, he took a faltering step toward her. She was still breathing, but it was clear it was not without some difficulty – and that difficulty was increasing by the moment. He dropped to his knees by her side and gestured frantically to the men on the curtains. He could see Sanemon standing in the wing, eyes wide, face pale. "Pull the curtain," Nao hissed, knowing the first rows of the audience could hear him and not caring. He wasn't sure what was wrong with her, but he quickly realized that if something wasn't done soon, Etsuko would be dead.

He looked at Botan. "Help me, fool!"

Botan jolted forward like a startled horse. Even as the curtain started its slow slide across the stage, he was kneeling beside Nao. "What's wrong with her?"

"Do I look like a doctor?" Nao snapped. "We need to get her offstage. Help me lift her." He took hold of Etsuko's face, trying to catch her fluttering attention. "Etsuko. Etsuko, listen to me. We are going to take you back to the dressing room."

She gasped something – a name? – he couldn't understand. Her hand clutched weakly at his arm. On impulse, Nao bent and scooped her up, his back momentarily protesting the sudden weight. Botan danced about, hands fluttering uselessly. "Can you – I can…" he began. Nao shook his head.

"I've got her. Distract the audience." In truth, Nao was surprised at how light Etsuko was beneath the costume. He rose awkwardly to his feet, fighting to keep his face composed.

"How am I supposed to do that?" Botan hissed out of the corner of his mouth.

"I don't know… trip over something," Nao hissed back. If they were lucky, the audience would think this was nothing more than a new wrinkle in an old scene. If he'd had the wherewithal, he might have tried improvising a line or two, but his thoughts were too scattered for that. It was all he could do not to stumble into the set dressing.

Botan grunted but did as he was bidden. He improvised a few drunken pratfalls while warbling something amusing about the young woman being overcome by his holiness. The audience responded slowly, clearly aware this was not how things were supposed to go but willing to see where it went.

Nao said a silent prayer of thanks for flexible audiences and started with his burden toward the wing of the stage. The curtain closed a moment later, and the audience applauded, though somewhat less enthusiastically than they might have otherwise done. Sanemon, Choki, and a few others came hurrying over when he was at last out of sight of the audience.

"What happened to her?" Sanemon demanded. "Is she ill?"

"I don't know," Nao snapped. "We need to get her to our dressing room." He nudged Choki aside. "Move aside, boy. Everyone, get out of the way!"

Sanemon pursued him. "What about the performance?"

"Go to the next scene!" Nao shook his head. "I can't look after her and do your job for you." Sanemon flinched back at that, his face hardening. Nao felt a moment's regret for his tone, but there was nothing for it. The first rule of theater was that whatever else, the show must go on. Even if one of the actors appeared to be dying.

The thought sent a shiver through him as he contemplated the woman in his arms. Etsuko stared up at his face, but he didn't think she actually saw him. Instead, she was gazing at something visible only to her as her skin mottled beneath its mask of powder and cream. Her breath was coming in short, painful hitches that rattled through her.

"Is she – is she dying?" Choki whispered at his elbow. He looked as pale as death himself, his expression one of horror. Nao had no answer for the young actor. Instead, he bulled his way backstage, scattering crew and actors alike in his awkward haste. Light as she was, Etsuko seemed to double in weight with every step he took.

Eventually, with some assistance from Choki, he managed to get into their dressing room. Ashina looked up guiltily from the slim, bound volume she'd been reading. Her mouth opened, and the book fell from her hands as she rose to her feet. Choki was beside her before she could scream, whispering softly.

At the rear of the dressing room was a small, semidetached alcove that served as a bedroom on occasion. Nao was the only one who used it, as Etsuko found it insultingly small. He didn't think she'd complain this time, however.

He laid her on the sleeping mat and called for Choki. "Get Rin and Uni. I need to remove her costume, and I don't have time to be gentle. Ashina!"

Etsuko's understudy stepped into the room. She was pale and trembling, her hands so tightly interlaced that her knuckles looked like splinters of marble. "M- my lord?" she quavered. Nao snapped his fingers.

"Where is that knife of hers?"

"My lord?"

"The knife she threatened me with earlier! Where is it?"

Ashina's eyes darted to Etsuko's robes, and Nao grunted in disbelief. "She had it onstage with her? The audacity of the woman." He fumbled around until he found the shape of the knife and retrieved it. As he did so, Choki returned with Rin and Uni. Nao didn't waste time. "I'm going to cut the costume off her, Rin."

The costumer nodded briskly. "Find the seam on the side. It'll be easiest from there. Try not to tear anything if you would. A cut I can repair, a tear – not so easy." He circled the mat and began to draw back the edges of the robes. "What is this, Nao? What's happened to her?"

"Sick, I think. But what sort of sickness I can't say. She's having trouble breathing, though. That much is clear. Uni, I would retrieve her wig if you don't want it harmed." The wig dresser blanched and scrabbled at the wig, quickly plucking it from Etsuko's head as Nao began the tedious process of cutting her out of her costume.

"We need a doctor," Rin said, helping where he could.

"I agree. Do you know any?"

Rin grimaced. "No."

"No, nor do I." Nao frowned. He had some know-how when it came to cuts and bruises, but this was beyond his limited wisdom.

"There's a horse leech over near the hostelry two streets over," Uni said, clutching the wig protectively to her chest. Nao looked at her, and she shrugged. "What? Better than nothing. Better than she deserves frankly. Look what she's done to my poor wig!"

"The woman might be dying," Rin protested. This only elicited another shrug.

"She's just an actress," Uni said, with an unsurprising amount of venom. One did not have a long career in the theater without learning how to nurture a grudge. "This wig is almost seventy years old!"

Both Rin and Nao stared at her for a moment before the former shook his head and said, "She's right, whatever else. A horse leech is better than nothing. Shall I send one of my people to collect him?"

"That won't be necessary," Lord Shin said from the doorway. His sudden appearance startled all three of them. He gestured for Rin and Uni to retreat, and as they did so, he stepped into the tiny room. He knelt beside Etsuko, folding himself up with an elegance Nao envied. Whatever else, the Crane was in full control of himself, of his movements, in a way few men, or even women for that matter, were. "I saw her collapse. Did she faint?"

"I thought so at first, but now I'm not sure." He managed to extricate her from the last of her costume and snapped his fingers presumptively. Ashina handed him a bowl filled with water and a rag. "We need a doctor, my lord."

"I have already sent for one. My own personal physician. He will be here directly. Until then, we must do what we can for her." Shin extended his hand. Nao hesitated, then handed him the rag. Gently, Shin began to wipe away the makeup from Etsuko's face. Nao made to help him, using the sleeve of his own robe.

Etsuko was still gasping for air and had begun to shiver as if cold, but her skin was hot to the touch. Carefully, Nao tested her fingers and palms. "Swollen," he murmured. His skin crawled at the realization. Shin looked at him.

"What was that?"

"Nothing, my lord," Nao said instinctively. Lord Shin studied him for a moment and then bent to examine Etsuko's face. He paused.

"Did she have this rash on her neck earlier?"

"Rash?" Nao looked at him with a puzzlement that was only partly feigned. He felt a chill prickle across his scalp and the nape of his neck. He made a show of looking but shook his head. "No. Not that I recall."

"Curious. Ashina?"

"My – my lord?" Ashina asked, looking as if she wanted to be anywhere else in the world. She shrank back as Shin turned his gaze on her.

"Did you notice if Lady Etsuko had a rash when you helped her get ready?"

She shook her head, a look of confusion on her face. "No, my lord."

Shin sat back on his heels. "And more curious still."

Nao continued to cleanse Etsuko's face and neck of makeup. Already her breathing seemed easier but nowhere close to normal. Her eyes had swollen nearly shut, and the rash had spread down her neck and chest to her hands and arms. "Cold compresses," he said, catching Choki's attention. "Rags soaked in cold water directly from the well. Now!" He caught Shin's look and added, "It might help with the swelling."

Shin nodded. "Have you ever seen this before?"

"No, my lord," Nao said. He had to be careful here. His lordship was too clever by half. He could read between the lines as well as any actor. He'd smell a lie, so best not to even try. Shin cocked his head. He'd heard the hesitation in Nao's voice but wasn't sure what it meant. Thankfully, he did not press the issue.

Before Shin could ask any more uncomfortable questions, Sanemon burst in. He was sweating and flushed. "Take a breath before you collapse," Nao said as he stood. Sanemon's retort died on his lips as he spotted Shin. He sketched a wheezy bow.

"My lord!"

Shin gestured airily. "Be at ease, Master Sanemon. How's the audience?"

Sanemon frowned. "Restless, my lord. Wondering what happened." He swallowed and looked down at Etsuko. "What did happen?"

"That is what I hope to determine," Shin said, somewhat melodramatically, Nao thought. While he appreciated a bit of melodrama from time to time, now was not one of them. He glanced at Etsuko and felt a flush of guilt. He wanted to apologize, to tell her all was forgiven. Too late now, though. Too late for anything but regret.

He pushed the thought aside and smoothed his robes. "We have a few scenes before Etsuko is due back onstage. Between the two of you, I hope you can come up with some sort of plan for either getting her back onstage or replacing her before then. Now, if you'll excuse me, I must make ready. I'm due onstage to murder a man – excuse me, duel a man – and I must get changed."

He stepped into the dressing room proper. Rin and Uni had chosen the better part of valor and departed as soon as they were out of Lord Shin's sight. He didn't blame them. This was a disaster in the making. He sighed and signaled to Choki. "Help me get changed. Find my costume while I touch up my makeup." He seated himself before his makeup table and scanned the jars. As he'd thought, one was missing, but he said nothing. It would do Etsuko no good now, after all.

Nao caught a glimpse of himself in the mirror and paused. Then, eyes downcast, he began to fix his face. The show must go on. That was the first rule of the theater.

The show must go on.

CHAPTER TWELVE
Doctor Sanki

Shin stepped into the corridor and slid the doors shut behind him. He took a deep breath. He'd left Konomi and the others in a rush and knew he would eventually have to explain his abrupt departure. It wasn't considered seemly for a theater owner to go rushing backstage at the least little problem. He hoped Konomi at least would understand.

Kasami stood against the opposite wall, her gaze flicking from one end of the corridor to the other. When they'd arrived, a crowd had already been gathering, all of them shouting questions. At his request, Kasami had dispersed them with a few encouraging kicks to recalcitrant backsides. She'd enjoyed it a bit more than was appropriate, but he'd refrained from chiding her. She indulged herself so little that he hadn't had the heart.

Even so, the damage was done. Word would already be spreading throughout the theater. He would have to ask Sanemon to keep a lid on things if possible. It wouldn't do to have the cast and crew panicking. "Well?" Kasami asked.

"She's ill," Shin said in a low voice. "Badly ill by the looks of it. Hopefully Sanki is available. If anyone can pull her through whatever this is, it's him." He'd sent one of the backstage crew to bring the doctor as soon as he'd realized something was wrong.

Kasami frowned. "Are you sure that's wise?" she asked. "People might talk. Calling your personal physician in for an actress… some might wonder about your motivations."

"Let them. Sanki is the best physician in the city."

"Not to mention the most disrespectful."

"That, too."

"He is inappropriate. Rude." She lowered her voice. "He treats common sailors." Kasami had a low opinion of Sanki. Sanki, for his part, seemed to have no opinion of Kasami whatsoever. Shin suspected that was part of the reason for her dislike. Kasami expected respect from others or, failing that, fear. That Sanki did not appear to consider her worthy of either incensed her, not that she would ever admit it.

"He takes his duties seriously."

"Doctor Otaru is a perfectly good physician," she continued. Shin rolled his eyes.

"Otaru is an unctuous little quack," he said. "Worse, he's a gossip. An hour in his tedious company and I knew more than I wished to about the ailments afflicting the great and good of this city. As no doubt he told them about mine."

"And, of course, he refuses to help you with your investigations," Kasami said.

"He faints at the sight of blood! What sort of doctor does that?"

"In fairness, it was quite a bit."

"Yes, well, that's still no excuse," Shin said. At the time, Otaru had been excited – eager, even – to help Shin with one of his cases. But when they'd paid a visit to the scene of the crime, Otaru's exuberance had turned to horror.

It was one thing to read about ghastly murders in pillow books, Shin supposed, and quite another to experience them in person. Needless to say, Otaru had declined further opportunities to assist Shin in his investigations.

Sanki, however, was made of sterner stuff. Shin had sought him out on the recommendation of Captain Lun. The one-eyed former pirate had sought out Sanki's ministrations herself on more than one occasion. From her, he'd found out Sanki had learned his trade on the battlefield in service to the Lion. Sawing off limbs and sewing up spear wounds gave a man a stomach of cast iron.

Since then, he'd retired to the city and taken up a practice tending sailors, something that kept him busy but provided little stimulation. Shin had made the old man's acquaintance, found him to be as irascible and intelligent as Lun proclaimed, and quickly put him on retainer as his private physician. He had yet to regret it.

Kasami stiffened suddenly, breaking him from his thoughts. He followed her gaze and saw a familiar form lingering at the end of the hall. "Is that…"

"Lady Minami's bodyguard," Kasami said. The sour-faced Lion samurai seemed as if he were about to approach, but he hesitated and abruptly turned away, vanishing down the corridor. It was as if he'd thought better of whatever he'd been planning.

"Now what was he doing here?" Shin murmured. The answer came to him even as he voiced the question. Of course Minami would have sent someone. It would have been odd if she hadn't. He sighed. "Never mind. He won't be the last, I'm afraid. There'll likely be a veritable legion of well-wishers and snoops trying to get into this dressing room."

"Try being the operative word," Kasami said with a thin smile.

"Show Sanki in as soon as he arrives," Shin continued. "But no one else, you understand? I want no one in this room without my express permission."

Kasami nodded brusquely. Shin slipped back into the dressing room where Nao was in the process of finishing his costume change with some help from Choki.

"There's going to be an invasion," Nao said as he touched up his eyebrows.

Shin paused. "What?"

"An invasion. Of her admirers. They're all going to want to know what happened. I have it on good authority there are at least half a dozen of them in the audience."

"Kasami is outside."

Nao's lips quirked in a smile. "Then I see my warning was unnecessary."

"But appreciated all the same. As were your efforts onstage. You got her back here with admirable swiftness." Shin watched as Nao finished his touch-ups. "Has anything like that ever happened before?"

"As I said before, not to my knowledge." Nao paused and then stood so Choki could help him on with his costume for the next scene. "Will she recover, do you think?"

"One can but hope so," Shin said.

"For all our sakes, you mean," Nao said with the trace of a bitter smile. "After all, without her, what hope have the rest of us?" He flicked dust from the embroidery on his sleeves and looked at Shin.

"That's taking a somewhat dim view of the matter, I think."

"You would not have contracted her otherwise, my lord," Nao said somewhat pointedly. "We needed her, and she has failed."

Shin studied the actor. Nao was something of an enigma; his face, his posture, all of it was in a constant state of flux – masculine to feminine, young to old, then back again when the mood took him. There was more to him than was evident at first glance. He wore many masks, and one could never be sure one was seeing the true face beneath.

"Has she?" Shin asked finally. "One might say she has ensured this performance will be talked about in days to come."

"Yes, but what exactly will they be saying?" Nao asked, again somewhat pointedly.

Shin made an airy gesture. "What does it matter? That they talk about it is surely enough for our purposes. Money well spent." He clapped his hands together, and Nao bowed his head, acknowledging Shin's argument if not acceding to it. They both turned as the sound of drums came from the direction of the stage.

"Time for me to kill a man," Nao said. "The best part of any performance."

Shin said nothing as the actor departed. He wondered if Nao's parting words had been meant to sound so sinister. Knowing Nao, he probably had meant it that way. Suddenly feeling at a loss, he went back into the bedroom.

He resisted the urge to run his hands through his hair as he looked down at Etsuko. Such a display of nerves would do more harm than good at the moment. Sanemon, seated next to the pallet, looked up after a few moments of silence had passed. "Nao's right, my lord," he said with visible reluctance. "We must figure something out, and quickly, else the whole performance is ruined."

"Etsuko has an understudy, yes?" Shin said absently.

"Ashina? Yes, but…" Sanemon began.

"But nothing. There comes a time when every understudy must take to the stage. Unless you think she is unready?"

Sanemon frowned. "If anyone is ready, she is. But Etsuko won't like it."

"Etsuko is currently in no condition to do anything about it," Shin began. Before he could finish his thought, Kasami called out from the front of the room. Shin stepped out of the bedroom and saw his bodyguard ushering a familiar stooped figure into the dressing room. "Ah, Doctor Sanki. Thank you for coming."

"Didn't think I was given much choice," Sanki grunted. Then, almost as an afterthought added, "My lord." Sanki was a brittle figure, bent by age and a life lived on the sword's edge. Bent as he was, he walked without aid of a cane. He had a wispy beard shot through with silver, and his long hair was knotted atop his head in an untidy bun.

He carried a satchel, much stained and worn shiny in places. His robes were clean but utilitarian in both color and decoration. Sanki was a man who didn't care for attention. He patted the bag with a wrinkled hand. "Where are they?"

Shin slid the bedroom door open and gestured for him to enter. "Back here. We've made her comfortable, but beyond that…"

"Beyond that, you're useless," Sanki said, shuffling past him. "What you know about medicine could fill a thimble with room to spare."

Shin glanced back and saw that Kasami was staring at him in outraged silence. She gestured at Sanki's back, and Shin shrugged. He waved her back outside and followed Sanki in. The doctor had already situated himself beside Etsuko and was peering into her eyes. "She's unconscious. Breathing is ragged. How long ago was the attack?"

"Not long. Half an hour, perhaps a little more."

Sanki picked up one of the damp rags Nao had placed on Etsuko's neck. "I take back what I said earlier. You aren't totally useless. These rags might have kept her alive. Reduced some of the swelling at least." He leaned over and checked the rash on her skin, sucking on his teeth in a familiar, unpleasant fashion. "Haven't seen this in a while."

"What is it?"

Sanki ignored the question. "Is she allergic to anything?" He touched the side of her throat, feeling for her pulse. "What has she eaten?" Sanki stiffened and muttered a curse. Before either Shin or Sanemon could react, he flung the blanket covering her aside and pressed his ear to her chest. Sanemon lunged for him with a strangled cry, but Shin held him back. Sanki looked up. "Her heart's beating too fast."

"What does that mean?"

Before Sanki could reply, Etsuko began to thrash on her pallet, her tortured gasps growing louder and more desperate. Sanki dove for his bag. "Hold her, damn it," he barked. "She's having a spasm!"

They did their best, but Shin could feel the strength of her convulsions. It was as if her body was trying to tear itself apart. Sanki was steadily cursing as he pulled a philter and several long needles from his bag. But by the time he'd dipped a needle into the philter, it was over. Shin felt the life leave her body. Sanemon made a strangled sound.

Sanki sat back on his heels and sighed sourly. "Too late." He looked at Shin. "You have to catch it as soon as the swelling starts, or it's too late. Frankly, I'm surprised she hung on as long as she did. She had a lot of fight for such a small woman."

"She's dead…" Sanemon muttered, staring at the body in shock.

Sanki nodded. "Very much so."

"How?" Shin demanded.

"You saw. Her heart seized. Couldn't take the strain. It just gave out."

"Yes, but why, doctor?"

Sanki grunted. "It looks like an allergic reaction. Something on her skin, judging by the rash. Though that can come with some foods as well. What was she allergic to?"

Shin looked at Sanemon, who shook his head and said, "Nothing that I am aware of."

"Must be something," Sanki insisted. "Once it was in her system, the effect would have been almost immediate. Your messenger said she fainted?"

"Yes," Shin said absently.

Sanki nodded. "There you go. She was dead as soon as she hit the stage. It just took her body a while to figure it out." He paused, weathered features crinkling in speculation. "You say she wasn't allergic to anything?"

"Not to my knowledge. Why?"

Sanki used his sleeve to wipe at a trace of makeup on Etsuko's face. He peered at the smear of white with a frown. "Because from what I can tell, it was her makeup that caused this." He sniffed it, nose wrinkling. "If she wasn't allergic to it before, I'd be inclined to believe someone tampered with it."

Sanemon hissed in disbelief. "You mean…"

"Poison." Shin looked down at Etsuko, her face startlingly composed given the situation. "Lady Etsuko was murdered."

CHAPTER THIRTEEN
Disruption

Ashina was afraid. She was trembling so badly Shin wondered if he ought to ask Sanki to prescribe something. But she took a deep breath and straightened as he cleared his throat. She was attractive but not in the same way as Etsuko. There was an understated quality to her. Not fire but moonlight. In a way, it reminded him of Okuni.

She glanced past him at the bed and Sanki. "Will she recover?" she asked. She did not meet his gaze. Whether due to nervousness or guilt, he could not say at the moment. Hopefully he would find out before Etsuko's replacement was due to retake the stage.

Shin hesitated, then shook his head. "Unfortunately, Lady Etsuko has – that is to say, she is – well…"

"Dead," Sanki said from where he still sat beside the bed. Ashina's eyes widened in startlement. Shin reached over and slid the door shut. He turned back to Ashina.

"Indisposed," he said firmly. If word of Etsuko's death spread, there was no telling how either the audience or the cast would react. Best to keep it quiet for now. "Lady Etsuko has suffered what appears to be an extreme allergic reaction to her makeup. She is not dead. Sanki is exaggerating."

He watched the young woman carefully as he spoke. Though she trembled, her face remained composed throughout. It was only when he mentioned makeup that he saw something in her eyes. "I understand you have been her understudy for several years. Has she suffered such reactions before?"

Ashina hesitated. Shin saw her eyes stray to the makeup benches. Shin stood and went to them. "Which of these is hers?"

Ashina cast her eyes down to the floor. Shin picked up the different pots off the largest of the benches. He knew a little about everything, even stage makeup. The principal colors were red and black, often daubed over a white background. But variations did exist when it came to individual actors, especially actors like Etsuko and Nao.

Shin picked up a brush and sniffed it. Then he put it back down and looked at Ashina. "I ask again, has she ever suffered such a reaction before?"

She did not look at him. "Once," she said in a small voice. "After that, she insisted on mixing her makeup herself. She would craft a new batch for every performance."

He looked back at the table. "And where did she get the supplies?"

"Different shops every time," Ashina said. She glanced at the closed door. "She would send me with a list before a performance, and I would procure what was needed." She took a breath. "She was continually changing the composition of her cosmetics."

Shin nodded. If Ashina was telling the truth, there was little chance of an intentional poisoning – unless Ashina herself was behind it. He paused, then asked, "Is there anything else I should know?"

"I- I heard her accuse Master Nao of stealing something," Ashina said hesitantly. "Before the performance began."

"And did he?"

She paused, then shook her head. "Not that I am aware of, my lord."

"What was it she thought he had stolen?"

Another hesitation. "I- I am not certain, my lord. I was otherwise preoccupied."

Shin studied her. Her first lie and not a good one. He decided to let it lie for the moment. "You are older than many understudies, are you not?"

She blanched and looked down again. "I am not ready. Lady Etsuko says – said – I have not yet learned the proper discipline."

"And in the meantime, she gets an unpaid servant," Shin murmured. Ashina tried to make herself smaller. If it was an act, she was clearly ready for the stage. Shin knocked a knuckle against the makeup table. "Well, proper discipline or not, now is your chance to show what you can do. Lady Etsuko is in no condition to take the stage in her next scene. I trust you've rehearsed her lines?"

Ashina looked up sharply, shock evident on her face. "I – yes, my lord."

"Good. Get into costume. Quickly now. You'll have to use the other dressing room, obviously. We'll make an announcement, so the audience is prepared." Shin gestured airily as she made to stammer her thanks. "Go, go. Hurry!"

As she reached the door, he called out to her. "Ashina, one last thing… I wish to keep Lady Etsuko's condition quiet. At least until after the performance. Can you do that for me?"

Ashina hesitated but after a moment nodded. "Yes, my lord."

"Good. Now why are you still standing there? Go!"

She hurried to get dressed at once, and Shin went to the bedroom. Sanki looked up as Shin slid the internal door open. "I'm sorry," he said. "I wasn't thinking." Sanemon had already departed to do what he could to calm the rest of the cast and let them know Etsuko would be indisposed for the rest of the performance.

"It's not something you usually have to worry about, I expect," Shin said, looking down at the still form on the bed. "You're certain it was an allergic reaction?"

Sanki grunted and pulled a long, thin pipe out of his satchel. He began to fill the bowl as he answered. "As certain as I can be under these conditions. I've seen swelling like this before when a patient of mine was stung by a bee."

"Did they survive?"

"Yes, but only because I cut a hole in their throat before they suffocated." Sanki tamped down the bowl of the pipe and lit it with a bit of flint and steel. "Though that was an extreme case. There are certain tinctures that can reduce the effects of such a reaction, but as I said before, you have to apply them quickly."

"Is there any way of identifying the poison in question?"

"If it was a poison, you mean?"

Shin gestured irritably. "Yes, yes. Is there a way of identifying it?"

"There are tests I can do, of course," Sanki said. "If there is something, I might be able to identify it but no promises," he added sternly.

"I ask only that you do your best."

Sanki snorted. "That's not what you said last time."

Shin saw no reason to dignify that with a response, so he let it be. "If we can identify what ingredient caused her death, we might be able to determine how it wound up in her makeup.

Once we do that, it will be a simple matter of determining who is responsible."

"If anyone at all," Sanki murmured. He puffed on his pipe for a few moments, filling the air with a sweet smell, then explained, "The smoke will cover up any untoward smells, at least until the end of the performance."

"How considerate of you."

"I could leave if you like."

Shin paused. "No. I might require your expertise. If you were willing, that is."

Sanki grunted. "This isn't going to be like the time with the body in the rice barrel, is it? Because I've only just stopped having disturbing dreams."

"I make no promises," Shin said as cheerfully as he could manage. Sanki sighed.

"I am at your service, my lord. But I will expect compensation for my time."

"Of course," Shin said. He looked down at Etsuko again. It had not been a painless death, he thought. Unfortunate, if it was an accident. But if it wasn't an accident...

"You think someone poisoned her, don't you?"

Sanki's words startled him. "Is it that obvious?" Shin asked.

Sanki settled back on his stool, arms crossed, puffing contentedly on his pipe. "You have that look in your eye." He sniffed. "If anyone finds out, you can bid any future ticket sales goodbye."

Shin looked down at him. "Which is why Kasami is on the door, and you're not leaving this room. With luck, no one will even notice until after the performance is over, eh?" He turned as the sound of raised voices came from outside. Sanki laughed but quickly choked it off as he caught sight of Shin's glare.

Shin stepped out of the bedroom, slid the door shut behind him, and headed for the corridor. He felt his headache from earlier returning. He wondered if there was something he'd missed that had allowed this. A ridiculous thought, but it was his responsibility, nonetheless.

The voices were getting louder. He took a breath and a moment to compose himself and stepped into the corridor. "What is going on out here?"

The tableau that greeted him was a tense one. Kasami stood facing a robed Ujik, who had apparently interposed himself between her and a short, heavyset man. Shin vaguely recognized the latter – Gota, a merchant and nobleman of some small standing. The Ujik had one hand on his sword and his free hand extended as if in the act of signaling Kasami to halt. Her own hand was mere inches from the hilt of her sword.

If she drew it, the Ujik would die. Of this Shin was certain. Very few men could endure the attentions of an angry Kasami. A second glance at the Ujik, however, made him reevaluate the speed of his inevitable demise. The Ujik might last a few moments longer than the average. He had the look of a swordsman to him.

Shin decided it would be best to intervene before things reached the point of no return. "Lord Gota, I believe," he said, nonchalantly pushing the Ujik's hand aside as he addressed the man's master. "We have not been introduced. I am Daidoji Shin. Owner of this venue and employer of Noma Etsuko."

Gota hesitated, and Shin took the opportunity to study him. He was a big man, muscular once but now running to fat. But the way he'd set his feet when Kasami had confronted them, and the position of his arms, spoke to martial training or the remnant of such. "You were trained in the art of Sumai, I believe," Shin said.

"Yes, I was a wrestler in my youth," Gota agreed. "How did you know?"

"A guess. It is something the Badger are famous for if I recall correctly," Shin said. As he spoke, he tried to recall what he knew of the Badger, which wasn't much. They were a minor clan, their holdings mainly in the northern mountains. An industrious, if isolated, people with an extensive trade network that spanned the lowlands.

Crane merchants often purchased raw silk from them, though few admitted it openly. Shin himself owned several kimonos made from Badger-produced silk and found them to be among the finest in his wardrobe. Gota was likely a merchant, and one of high status at that, given his surname. Konomi had mentioned a Badger as part of Etsuko's menagerie. This must be him. He waved Kasami back. She retreated reluctantly, her displeasure evident in the force with which she sheathed her sword.

Gota nodded. He patted his paunch ruefully. "I have shrunk some since I was last in the ring, however. Age crumbles even the mightiest mountain."

"Now you are a hill," the Ujik said in heavily accented Rokugani. Gota shot his bodyguard a glare. The Ujik did not seem unduly bothered.

Shin turned his attentions to the nomad. The man had sheathed his blade and stepped back. Dark eyes met Shin's own, and he gave a respectful, if shallow, nod. Shin returned it. Ujik traders were not unheard of, or even particularly rare this close to Unicorn lands, but to see a warrior in service to a Rokugani merchant was curious. "A good joke," Shin replied in the Ujik tongue. The Ujik blinked, startled perhaps to hear his own language coming from the lips of a southerner.

"You speak Ujik?" Gota asked in obvious surprise.

"Not well," Shin said. "I know a few words thanks to a merchant of my acquaintance. You might know him, a fellow by the name of Ito."

Gota frowned. "I know him. An iron dagger in a velvet sheath."

Shin inclined his head. "A good description. He himself learned it from a Moto trader." He studied the Ujik, who was now much less relaxed. "I am sure there is an interesting story here."

"Not especially," Gota said brusquely. "I was owed a debt. Arban's service is the payment. Thus far, I have had little cause for complaint." Arban's lips twitched, and Shin had the distinct impression the Ujik wanted to laugh.

Shin nodded. "Ah. And what are you attempting to achieve by approaching my bodyguard in the corridor?"

"I wish to see Lady Etsuko."

"She is not receiving visitors at the moment, I'm afraid."

"She will see me," Gota said.

Shin rose to his full height and looked down his nose at the smaller man. "She is in no condition to entertain guests, my lord. As you must have seen from your seat, she is ill."

"Then I will call a physician to care for her."

"I have already made arrangements with my own personal physician for her care. He is seeing to her now. I am afraid your presence would only cause undue and unneeded distraction. For the moment, you can do nothing."

"I will be the judge of that," Gota said, puffing out his chest.

"There you are mistaken. As I said, I am the proprietor of this establishment, and I can give you but two choices. The first is that you return to your box, and I will be happy to keep you informed on her condition."

"And the second?"

"I have you ejected from this building." Shin smiled. "It is your choice, of course."

Gota glanced at Kasami, whose eyes were fixed on Arban. Arban, for his part, looked somewhat intrigued by the idea of continuing the fight Shin had interrupted – or perhaps something else entirely. Shin snapped open his fan and gave it a flutter. "It is in no one's best interest to cause any more of a scene, especially Lady Etsuko's. I'm certain she will wish to speak with you once she recovers, but for the moment, she must rest."

Gota glowered at Shin but gave a terse nod. "Very well." He thrust a thick finger into the air beneath Shin's nose. "But I will be kept informed of her condition every step of the way, Daidoji. Else I will remove her ladyship from this place myself."

Shin nodded, politely ignoring both the threat and the finger. "Of course, Lord Gota. And might I add that your gallantry does you credit."

Gota grumbled something under his breath as he turned away. He gestured curtly, and Arban fell in behind him, though not without a backward glance at Kasami. The Ujik had a funny look on his face, rather like a poleaxed ox.

"I think you have an admirer," he said, glancing at Kasami.

Kasami relaxed slightly. "What are you muttering about?"

"Arban. Interesting fellow. Have you ever met an Ujik before?"

"No."

"Nomads, mostly. Fine warriors, though. Their idea of discipline is somewhat sideways to our own as are their notions of propriety. But a tough, hardy folk. Much like your own." Shin snapped his fan shut and popped it against his palm.

"And why are you telling me this?"

"I just thought it might interest you," Shin said innocently.

"It does not."

"You must broaden your horizons, Kasami."

"I must do no such thing," she snapped. She looked at him. "They will try again."

"Is that your professional opinion?"

"It is."

"Then you will stay here and see that no one enters that room without my permission," Shin said in a tone that brooked no argument. "I do not wish Sanki to be disturbed. Is that understood?"

Kasami nodded. "And what will you be doing while I'm sitting here?"

Shin tapped his palm with his fan and frowned.

"Hopefully finding out who poisoned our lead actress."

CHAPTER FOURTEEN
Due Diligence

"He's certain then, this doctor of yours?" Azuma said. "Poison?"

Shin nodded. They sat in Shin's box, the door guarded by two of Azuma's best and the privacy curtain partially drawn. Shin's servants, including Kitano, had been dismissed for the moment so there was no risk of eavesdropping. "As certain as he can be without further investigation. But I trust Sanki. If he says someone tainted Lady Etsuko's makeup with a contact poison, I'm inclined to believe him."

Azuma grunted and rubbed his chin. "I do not like this. We should stop the performance. Question everyone…"

"By everyone, you mean everyone backstage, I take it?"

"Who else would I mean?"

"Etsuko had relationships beyond the stage," Shin said pointedly. Azuma frowned.

"So?"

Shin scratched his chin. "She was engaged to be married. To Bayushi Isamu."

Azuma's eyes narrowed. "You think the culprit might be a jilted lover."

"It's an avenue worth exploring," Shin said. He glanced toward the stage where the performance was continuing. Neither Nao nor Ashina was onstage at the moment. An actor dressed as a monk was performing a slapstick routine for the amusement of the audience as several actresses portraying servants berated him. The audience seemed pleased if the trickle of laughter was anything to go by.

Azuma nodded slowly. "Perhaps. Perhaps we should ask her what she thinks."

"Unfortunately, that is the one avenue of investigation denied us."

"Meaning?"

Shin hesitated. Attempting to hide anything from Azuma was unwise. If he wanted the man's cooperation, he would have to trust him. "She's dead."

Azuma's eyes widened. "What?"

Shin nodded solemnly. "She succumbed to the poison not long after Nao got her backstage. There was nothing anyone could have done, or so Sanki maintains."

"This makes things more complicated," Azuma said softly. "Especially if, as you say, she was to be wed. The Scorpion will demand vengeance."

"I am aware. Just as I am sure you are aware that if things go poorly today, this theater's reputation, and my own, will suffer a blow neither might recover from."

"Sad though that may be, it is not my concern," Azuma began. Shin held up a hand, forestalling the rest of his statement.

"I did not expect you would feel any different, but I would like to make a simple request if I may."

Azuma's eyes narrowed. "You wish to investigate the matter yourself."

"It is my theater, after all. Who better? Call it due diligence if you like."

Azuma snorted. "One day, you will go too far with this business, Crane."

"Is today that day?"

"No," Azuma said after a moment's consideration.

"Then you will let me investigate?"

"Could I stop you?" Azuma asked. He waved aside Shin's reply and shook his head. "A bad business. How will you go about it?"

"As quickly as possible. Once the performance ends, our chances of identifying the murderer go from slim to none. That is why I will need your help."

Azuma rubbed his face. "What do you need?"

"A few of your retainers to guard the entrances and exits." Shin paused. "Leaving before the performance is over is grounds for suspicion, wouldn't you say?"

"What about intermission? The teahouses will howl if you deny them custom."

Shin waved a hand. "Easily solved. I'll send a page to let them know to bring their wares to the theater. People will be served in their seats."

Azuma grunted. "Unorthodox but efficient."

"My stock in trade," Shin said. Azuma laughed. In the time since their first meeting during the affair of the poison rice, he and Azuma had become, if not friends, then close acquaintances. In a certain sense, they both served the same master.

"Even so, I will not order my retainers to keep people here against their will."

Shin shook his head. "Nor am I asking you to do so. I merely want them to watch and, more importantly, to be seen to be watching."

"Ah." Azuma nodded in understanding. "'The promise of the blade is often as dangerous as the blade itself.'"

"Or so Kakita had it," Shin said, acknowledging the quote. "I will do all I can to keep word of Lady Etsuko's… condition quiet, but gossip is the lifeblood of the theater. People will figure out something is wrong the moment Etsuko's understudy steps onto the stage. After that, it will be a matter of time until the truth outs itself."

"Where will you start?"

"Backstage," Shin said. "Etsuko made few friends in her time here but plenty of enemies. So I will talk to them first." He hesitated. "But, eventually, I will need to talk to her friends. Including her fiancé."

Azuma took a deep breath. "You will need to tread carefully there."

"I always tread carefully."

"I mean it, Crane."

"I understand. I've already had an encounter with one of them. Just now, backstage. Lord Gota. Do you know him?"

Azuma nodded. "Trade envoy for the Badger."

"Yes. I don't know much about him. He seems quite… forceful." Shin scratched his cheek. Gota was definitely a jilted lover, but he didn't seem the sort to poison anyone. Even so, his behavior was suspicious. "He's made himself a pest of late. He believes he has a proprietary claim on Etsuko's time. When I start with them, I'll start with him." He turned as Kitano opened the door and bowed respectfully. "Ah. You found him?"

"As you requested, my lord," Kitano said. He gave Azuma a wary glance as he spoke. "Master Sanemon insisted on coming with him, though."

"Did he? Well, that saves me having to send you to find him,

I suppose." Shin retrieved his fan and snapped it open. He'd sent
Kitano to locate Choki, Nao's assistant. Besides Nao, Etsuko,
and Ashina, he was the only one with immediate access to the
dressing room. While he didn't think Choki had anything to
do with Etsuko's death, the youth might have seen or heard
something of importance. He turned to Azuma. "If you'll excuse
me?"

"Of course." Azuma levered himself to his feet. "I will see to
putting people on the doors." He straightened his robes. "And if –
when – your guests come to me to complain, I shall direct them
to you, shall I?"

"If you would be so kind, yes."

Azuma grinned. "Should save you some time at least."

"You are always so thoughtful, Azuma. It's one of the reasons
I like you." Shin paused. "If you could not mention any of this
to Konomi or her cousin, I would be very grateful. It would be a
shame to cast a pall over their entertainment."

Azuma paused at the door. "He asked about you, you know.
After you ran out of my box earlier. Seems a fine man if somewhat
arrogant. Reminds me of you a bit."

"I suppose I must take that as a compliment," Shin said.
Azuma laughed again and departed. A few moments later, Kitano
ushered in Sanemon and Choki. Shin gestured for them to take a
seat. They both did so if somewhat reluctantly.

Shin studied the pair without speaking for a time. They were
both nervous. He decided to put them at ease. "Thank you for
coming, Choki. And you, Sanemon. I am sure you are both busy,
but… well."

Sanemon bowed his head. "We are happy to help, my lord…
Aren't we, lad?" He glanced at Choki and nudged him.

"Y- yes, my lord," Choki said.

Shin smiled. "Excellent. You are a native of the city, Choki, are you not?"

"Yes, my lord."

"You were hired by Mistress Okuni, then?"

"No, my lord. Master Sanemon." Choki glanced at Sanemon, who nodded.

"Ah," Shin said. "Had you acted before?"

"Some, my lord. Bit parts. I have some musical talent and can juggle."

"Useful skills," Shin said. "I am something of an amateur juggler myself. Did you see what happened earlier?" He asked the question suddenly with no warning. Choki froze.

"I- I... Yes. I helped Master Nao take her to the dressing room." He paused. "Is she... is she ill?"

"Resting," Shin said. He felt Sanemon's eyes on him but ignored the other man for the moment. The troupe leader knew better than most what was at stake and what word of Etsuko's death might do to their chances for success today.

Choki swallowed. "Good. I thought – I was afraid that she'd – well. You know."

Shin gestured with his fan. "No. Tell me."

Choki swallowed again. "That she'd died."

"Why?"

"I just – well. She looked so – and she was breathing like ..." He gestured to his throat. "It didn't look good is all." He fell silent. Shin peered at him. Choki, he suspected, was cleverer than Nao gave him credit for. More observant, at least.

"No, well, it wasn't, was it?" Shin tapped his chin with the folded shape of his fan. "Choki, this might seem a curious question, but can you think of anyone who might wish to harm Lady Etsuko?"

Choki glanced again at Sanemon and then said, "I – well, that is, my lord – plenty of people?" He shrugged helplessly. "She isn't the friendliest person if you'll forgive me for saying so."

"Yes, but is she unfriendly to anyone in particular?"

"Master Nao," Choki said without hesitation. "They don't like each other."

Shin sat back. "Does anyone else come to mind?" He didn't like the thought of Nao being involved, though the possibility had crossed his mind earlier. Nao was something of an enigma. As much so as Okuni herself.

Choki shrugged again. "A few of the other actors. Chika, for sure. Botan, once."

"What were her reasons?"

Choki licked his lips. "She – ah – she thought Chika had, well, had stolen something from her." He cut his eyes to Sanemon, who frowned in what Shin took to be annoyance. "Botan, I'm not sure. I think he interrupted one of her – ah – her trysts." He flushed. "Backstage, I mean."

"Really?" Shin said. "Did Botan say who it was he'd seen?"

Choki shook his head. "No, my lord. It was only a few weeks ago, though."

"After she'd become engaged, then," Shin said.

Choki's eyes widened. "She was engaged?"

Sanemon cleared his throat. "I think it is time Choki went backstage, my lord. He needs to get ready. He's playing one of the craftsmen in the marketplace scene."

Shin looked at him and then nodded. "Very well. I would like to speak with you, though, Master Sanemon."

"Of course, my lord," Sanemon said. Choki stood, bowed, and hurriedly departed. Sanemon mopped at his sweating pate with his sleeve. "Thank you, my lord. I did not mean to interrupt, but…"

"Etsuko's intention to wed was not widely known, I take it," Shin said.

"No, my lord. For obvious reasons, I chose not to mention it." Sanemon looked at him. "I suppose I should not be surprised you already knew of it, my lord."

"I was told by her intended. How did you come to find out?"

Sanemon hesitated. "Well… it was Nao, my lord. He told me."

Shin nodded slowly. "Presumably she told him." It was just a guess on Shin's part, but Sanemon nodded.

"They had a confrontation backstage earlier." Sanemon frowned. "I'm sorry to say Lord Kenzō witnessed it."

Shin paused. "Did he?" Unfortunate, but Shin suspected the auditor had witnessed worse in his time. "No matter. This confrontation, was it the usual nonsense or something specific?"

Sanemon grimaced. "The usual. But they went another round afterward in their dressing room. That's where she told him her plans."

"And then he told you."

Sanemon nodded. "He wanted me to tell you. Which I was planning to do, but…" He trailed off and gestured helplessly. He didn't meet Shin's eyes as he spoke. That in itself was not suspicious. Sanemon rarely looked at Shin if he didn't have to.

Music swelled from the stage. Ashina was making her entrance. Shin gestured for Sanemon to wait and turned to watch through the crack in the curtain. They sat in silence as Ashina crossed the flower path and onto the stage, trailed by a gaggle of actresses playing her ladies in waiting. Her voice quavered as she accosted the monk but only at first before gaining in strength.

"She is good," Shin said softly.

"She will get better in time," Sanemon said. He paused and dabbed at his hairless pate again. "Your doctor is certain then? She was poisoned?"

Shin nodded. "Can you think of anyone who might have wished Etsuko harm?"

Sanemon hesitated. "I – that is to say – it might be easier to name those who didn't. Wish her harm, I mean." He grimaced. "As Choki told you, she made few friends here. And actors nurse their grudges like beloved children."

"Like Botan?"

Sanemon shook his head. "The grudge there was all Etsuko's. Botan stumbled onto one of her trysts, or so he said. She tried to browbeat me into getting rid of him, the poor fellow. And for what? Because she wasn't careful enough to dally somewhere more private."

"Did Botan tell you who he saw her with?"

"No. And I didn't ask."

"Probably wise," Shin said, somewhat disappointed. Whoever her dalliance was with, they were a suspect – not that he needed another. He already had a theater full of them. "Who else might have held ill feeling for her? There must be some names that come to mind more quickly than others."

Sanemon stroked his chin, a thoughtful look on his face. "Rin, perhaps, and Uni. Between them, they know everything about everyone in the troupe. Incorrigible gossips, the pair of them. Often as not, they are my eyes and ears among the crew."

"They were present when Nao brought Etsuko in, were they not?"

"They were, my lord."

"They left rather quickly when I arrived."

"They did," Sanemon said with a crooked smile. "You have a reputation, my lord."

Shin frowned. "I thought it was a good one, at least among the troupe."

"It is, my lord," Sanemon said placatingly. "But it is not one that all are comfortable with. You ask awkward questions at times."

Shin accepted this, though not without some chagrin. He forced a smile and said, "Then let me ask another. Choki mentioned that Chika stole something. I don't recall hearing about this before… Would you care to tell me of the matter?"

Sanemon hunched forward and shook his head. "It is nothing, my lord. Etsuko accused Chika of stealing some private correspondence from her dressing room. But there was nothing to it. Actors accuse each other of theft all the time. Sometimes it's true but mostly not. In this case, it was empty air."

"You investigated, then?" Shin asked, somewhat impressed with Sanemon's initiative.

"I didn't need to. Chika had been nowhere near the dressing room at the time." Sanemon coughed awkwardly. "She was – ah – entertaining a friend."

"Oh? Oh." Shin straightened. "And who was this friend?"

"I'd rather not say, my lord."

Shin frowned. "I assure you, I will keep the name in the strictest confidence."

Sanemon sighed. "Master Odoma."

Shin blinked. "Really?"

Sanemon shrugged. "Yes." He looked unhappy as he said it, and Shin considered letting the matter drop then and there, but he was a slave to his curiosity.

"How long has this been going on?"

Sanemon flushed. "Since Lady Etsuko laughed in his face."

Shin paused. "When was this?" he asked carefully. Odoma had made no mention of it earlier. Then again, why would he?

"A few months ago. Just after she first arrived." Sanemon shook his head. "I'm sure you heard of her exploits, my lord. Odoma attempted to ingratiate himself – he sent gifts – but she was having none of it. Chika and some of the other actresses, well, they swooped in to console him."

Shin almost asked why, but the answer was obvious. Odoma was wealthy and unmarried – a good prospect for an actress of humble origins. Even if marriage wasn't on the cards, there was some benefit to enduring his attentions. Perhaps that was why Odoma was so interested in reacquiring the theater. Shin folded the thought away for future consideration. "And what was Etsuko's reaction to this?"

"Well, the accusation, my lord," Sanemon said.

Shin sat back, somewhat startled by Sanemon's reply. "You believe she made the accusation out of, what? Spite?"

Sanemon inclined his head but said nothing. Shin ran a hand through his hair and wondered what else Etsuko had gotten up to… and whether it was the reason she was dead. "I will need to speak to Botan and Chika as well as Rin and Uni."

Sanemon nodded. "I will let them know they need to make themselves available to you." He hesitated. "But surely you can't think one of them is responsible?"

"I won't know until I speak with them," Shin said. "At the moment, I have only a theater full of questions and precious few answers."

CHAPTER FIFTEEN
Hira

Kasami sat on the stool and stared at nothing in particular. Her mind occupied itself with tracing the patterns on the paper of the door and walls, performing a kata of looping lunges and sweeping retreats. Each stroke of paint was the movement of an imaginary blade, and her muscles tensed and relaxed in time to the illusory motion.

She was not bored. Boredom was a weakness of the undisciplined mind. It was a flaw in one's defenses, to be compensated for and corrected. When she reached the end of the pattern, she began again. Again and again, practicing while remaining motionless – serene in her form, yet aware of the world around her. She'd taken note of every face that passed her going to and fro down the corridor.

She was not overly worried about Shin. It was a waste of her abilities to be sat here, watching over a dead woman, but he was her lord, and he had – for once – given her a direct order. Thus, she would fulfill it.

Even so, she could not help but wonder at the point of it all. A part of her thought it would be better if Shin lost all interest in being a patron of the arts. It cost money and time, and his reputation was tarnished enough as it was. But knowing him, this incident had only reinvigorated that flagging desire.

Perhaps it was a good thing. A sign of maturity. Shin rarely stuck with anything longer than a few months. Between his new fascination with puzzles and his responsibilities as a theater owner, he was developing into someone almost respectable. He might even get married. That would please his family to no end.

There were a number of possibilities in that regard – Iuchi Konomi foremost among them. The noblewoman was of good reputation with strong ties to the leaders of her clan. She was intelligent, strong-willed, and capable. Kasami had it on good authority that Konomi had once broken a would-be suitor's ribs with a well-placed kick. More than that, she was sensible. A good match, all in all.

Shin, of course, did not see it that way. Or perhaps he did and simply refused to admit it. That was usually the way of it. She had faith he would see the obvious and do what was expected of him. If not, she would do her best to make him see reason. His family had allowed him to play the fool, but their patience was not infinite. Eventually, they would demand he do his duty, whatever his feelings on the matter. Better for everyone if he jumped before they decided to push him.

Besides, she liked Konomi. It would be no hardship to serve under her in the event of a union. At the very least, it might mean an end to Shin's more dangerous pursuits.

The thought was a pleasing one, but she almost immediately shoved it aside. She felt someone approaching.

It was not the first time someone had come to the dressing room since Etsuko's collapse. Actors and crew alike had come snooping, hunting for gossip. A stern look was usually enough to send them fluttering on their way. Thankfully, the performance was keeping most of them busy. This was someone different, however.

The newcomer cleared her throat diffidently. Kasami's gaze flicked in their direction. Koshei Hira stood some distance away. "My – ah – that is to say, Lady Yua…" she began.

"Sent you to ask after Lady Etsuko," Kasami said. She studied the other woman closely. Hira was a few years younger than Kasami – the same age, in fact, that Kasami had been when she had been assigned to watch over Shin.

Hira swallowed and nodded. "Yes."

"She is resting."

Hira cut her eyes toward the door but made no move toward it, for which Kasami was grateful. The young bodyguard was nervous. Kasami wondered whether it was simply the awkwardness she had detected earlier or something else. "I should like to see her. Lady Yua ordered me to…" Hira began but faltered when she saw the look on Kasami's face.

Kasami gave the slightest twitch of her head. "No one is to enter without Lord Shin's permission." She found it odd that the Dragonfly was the first to come calling on Etsuko – discounting the Lion's earlier, halfhearted attempt. Surely the Scorpion should have been first. But thus far, no sign of them. Then again, perhaps that wasn't surprising. The Scorpion weren't noted for their empathy.

"Oh." Hira shifted her weight uncertainly. She glanced back the way she'd come but made no move to depart.

Kasami watched her for a moment, then said, "Is she so fearsome, then?"

Hira frowned. "Who?"

"Lady Yua. Is she so fearsome a lady?"

Hira blinked. "No. No, not fearsome." She sighed. Kasami felt a flutter of pity and gestured to a spot on the wall beside her.

"Come. The longer it takes you to return, the less upset she will be."

Hira looked at her in surprise but did as Kasami suggested. She sank easily into a crouch and tilted her head to look at the other woman. "Thank you. She was most insistent that I come, otherwise I would not have left her side."

Kasami grunted. "I am not unfamiliar with such frustrations."

Hira ducked her head, but Kasami saw her smile. "So I have heard. Lord Shin is... infamous among the Tonbo. Lady Yua dislikes him intensely, though today was the first time they'd met as far as I know."

"Oh?" Kasami asked. She did not doubt Hira's words, but she was curious as to how Shin had managed to annoy an entire minor clan.

"Yes. I'm not sure why. Something to do with that business with the poisoned rice, I think. Lady Yua does not speak of it. None of them do."

Kasami nodded wordlessly. That made sense. Shin's investigation into a batch of poisoned rice resulted in the death of a Tonbo clerk. That the clerk had ultimately been responsible for the deaths of others, including the attempted murder of Shin himself, did not matter. The Dragonfly, like all clans, greater or lesser, found it easier to blame an outsider than one of their own.

"It must be exciting to work with a man like that," Hira continued.

Kasami looked around. "Yes. Very exciting."

Hira glanced at the dressing room. "Is she ill, then?"

"So I am told."

"I didn't see her collapse. I was outside in the corridor."

"As was I. That is where we should be."

"Lady Yua was frightened. I've never seen her so frightened. Then, maybe that was just because of the Scorpion."

Kasami frowned. Gossip was unseemly, but she did not chide the other woman. Experience told her that Shin might find such information interesting. Instead, she said, "Bayushi Isamu, you mean."

Hira nodded slowly. "He came to speak with her before the performance. The Lion too, if what Yoku said is true."

"Yoku?"

"Lady Minami's bodyguard. Have you met him?"

"Yes," Kasami said, recalling the sour-faced samurai. They'd met before, during the affair of the poisoned rice, and almost come to blows. "He is unpleasant."

"Really? He was very courteous when we spoke," Hira said in evident surprise. Kasami waved this aside.

"The Scorpion visited the Lion as well. When?"

"I'm not certain. He didn't stay long. Apparently, Lady Minami sent him away with a flea in his ear." Hira grinned. "I should have liked to have seen that."

"So would I," Kasami admitted. Hira giggled, and Kasami gave her a stern glance. Warriors did not giggle. But Hira didn't notice. Her eyes were on the door again.

"Lady Yua has never had a bodyguard before," she said after a moment. "I don't really know why she requested one." She glanced at Kasami. "Do you think it might have something to do with the Scorpion?"

Kasami shrugged. "It might. What were they talking about?"

Hira looked alarmed. "I didn't listen! That would have been eavesdropping."

"No, it isn't," Kasami said. "Eavesdropping is a prurient

pastime, fit only for courtiers. We listen so that we might better protect our charges." She fixed the other woman with a stern look. "Now, what did you hear?"

Hira flushed. "Not much," she admitted. "I was too busy trying to outstare those Scorpion bodyguards. The one in the demon mask kept tapping her sword. I thought she was going to challenge me at any moment."

"Yes. She is discourteous." Kasami looked Hira up and down. "Though I suspect you would prove more than capable in any duel she initiated."

Hira flushed an even deeper crimson. Whatever her other skills, she had not yet learned to wear a warrior's mask. Kasami sympathized to some extent. She often found herself losing her temper or surrendering to exasperation, especially around Shin. "Thank you for the compliment," Hira murmured, head bowed.

Kasami hid a smile. "Earlier, you mentioned the Shiba. How did you find their training?" she asked out of genuine curiosity.

"Comprehensive," Hira said. "Exhausting."

Kasami nodded in approval. The warriors of the Shiba were considered among the finest bodyguards in Rokugan. Hira was no doubt as well trained as Kasami herself. "I know something about it myself. Did they make you do the bucket walk?"

Hira laughed. "Yes. Dirt at first, then stones."

Kasami nodded. "Water for me." The bucket walk was an effective method of building up endurance. The aspirant was given a pole to balance across their shoulders with a full bucket hanging from either end. Then they had to walk along a path of overturned buckets or wet stones or, in Kasami's case, reed floats strung out across the marsh. The idea was to move without spilling anything or losing your footing.

Hira's smile faded. "I do not like this."

"Talking?"

"Being sent away by my charge." Hira looked at her. "How do you do it?"

Kasami smiled thinly. "It helps if they can look after themselves." She paused. "Why did she send you and not one of her servants?"

Hira's eyes slid away. "She told me to go in and accept no denial. I was to ask Lady Etsuko a question."

"What question?"

"I do not think I should say."

Kasami nodded. She had expected as much. Hira stood abruptly. "I think I have dawdled long enough. Lady Yua will be wondering where I am." Even as the words left her mouth, however, she stiffened and turned, her hand trailing along the hilt of her blade.

Her sudden turn startled Choki as he made his way down the corridor. The young actor froze and then retreated, hands raised. "Who's he?" Hira demanded.

"No one," Kasami said bluntly, eliciting a wince from Choki. She didn't care for the youth. He seemed unreliable, even for an actor. She couldn't imagine why Nao kept him around. "Is there something you need, Choki?"

"N- no. Well, yes," Choki said hurriedly. "Master Nao will need to touch up his makeup. I came to see that it was ready for him." He edged toward the door to the dressing room. "Is that okay?"

Kasami nodded. "Go. But be quick." Choki darted into the room with unseemly haste and slid the door shut behind him. Kasami looked at Hira, who was frowning. "Is something wrong?"

"One of the Scorpion bodyguards was sent to look for someone named Nao just before Lord Isamu spoke to Lady Yua."

"I thought you weren't eavesdropping," Kasami said in

amusement, but behind her smile she was wondering what the Scorpion could possibly want with Nao. She didn't know the actor well – or at all really. He was utterly conceited with an inflated opinion of his own importance in the scheme of things. A thoroughly unlikeable individual from her perspective, much like Etsuko. She was no judge of acting ability, but she assumed he must have some talent or else why would Sanemon keep him around?

Hira hesitated and then gave a weak smile. "In retrospect, I might have eavesdropped just a bit." She looked back at the dressing room. "Why do you think they wished to speak to this Nao person?"

Kasami frowned and shook her head. "I don't know. But Lord Shin will certainly find it of interest."

CHAPTER SIXTEEN
Investigations

Shin sat in his box, one eye on the stage and one on his manservant. "Kitano, I will need you to conduct a series of discreet interviews with the backstage crew. I cannot do so for obvious reasons."

Kitano bowed low, a slight smile on his face. "You mean because they're scared of you, my lord?" he asked, careful to keep any hint of amusement out of his voice.

Shin turned his full attention on Kitano. "Yes, though for the life of me I do not understand why. I have made every effort to endear myself to Ishi and the rest."

A shadow passed across Kitano's face so quickly that Shin barely noticed it. But notice it he did. He cleared his throat. "Speak your mind, Kitano. Kasami is not here. You do not have to fear for your remaining fingers."

"You are generous, my lord," Kitano said, clearly choosing his words with care. "Often too generous. It… frightens people."

Shin blinked. "I don't understand."

Kitano licked his lips, clearly uncertain as to how his next words would be taken. "They're wondering when the sword will fall, my lord. And where."

"What sword?"

Kitano shrugged. "The sword that is always there, my lord. Just out of sight. Just above our heads. The sword you hold by virtue of who and what you are."

Shin stared at him. It was the most erudite thing he'd ever heard come out of the former gambler's mouth. Kitano mistook his silence for anger and hurriedly added, "Not that I feel that way, my lord. Not me. But them, certainly."

"Yes, well, I should hope not," Shin said, slightly uncomfortable with Kitano's blunt honesty. He gestured to the door. "Go. Find me something useful."

"Very good, my lord," Kitano said as he bowed and backed out of the box. Shin returned his attention to the stage where Nao was addressing a wall of angry samurai. This would be the third swordfight in as many scenes, and somewhere in the wings, a pair of fake heads waited to roll amid a profusion of red silk. Let it never be said that Chamizo did not give the people what they wanted. Blood and romance – the two keys to making any work memorable.

Shin closed his eyes, not really listening to the performance. He sifted through the grains of knowledge he'd acquired over the past hour, looking for something that would point him in the correct direction or at least allow him to ask the right questions. Etsuko had been poisoned, but was it intentional or an accident? There was a question of motive as well. Why poison her in so public a fashion? He wondered if it indicated a desire for publicity – a public execution of sorts. A punishment for some as yet unknown crime. A quiet cough from behind him caused him to crack one eye. "Yes?" he asked, curious.

"You have a visitor, my lord," Niko, one of his other servants, said. She looked nervous, but then, she always did. Something to do with being a spy, he thought. She'd been assigned to his household by the Daidoji Trading Council the day he'd arrived in the city. Kasami had sniffed her out almost immediately, but Shin had decided to say nothing. Better the spy you knew, after all.

"Tell them to go away, Niko. I'm busy."

"You don't look busy to me," Konomi called from the doorway. She stood almost a head taller than Niko and could easily peer over her and into the box. Shin sighed, smiled, and gestured for her to enter. Rin and Uni would have to wait it seemed.

"Lady Konomi. As always, your presence brightens my day." He patted the cushions beside him. "How does this day find you thus far? Well, I trust."

"Better than you, I think. What happened? You never came back to Azuma's box after Etsuko collapsed." She sat down in the spot he'd indicated. "I thought we must have done something to offend you."

"Never." He reached for the tiny bell set on a tray beside his cushion. He gave it a gentle ring, and Niko poked her head back through the door.

"My lord?"

"Tea, please. Thank you."

Konomi watched him, her teasing expression softening into one of concern. "Really, what happened, Shin? Azuma won't say, no matter how much I pry."

"Something unexpected," Shin said.

"Do tell," came a new voice. Niko stepped inside, bowing awkwardly, tray of tea balanced precariously on her palms as the newcomer neatly sidestepped her. Shinjo Yasamura sketched a more graceful bow than Niko had managed and sat down without being invited. "And how is Lady Etsuko?"

"Resting," Shin said smoothly.

"Will she be able to continue the performance?" Konomi asked.

Shin hesitated, wondering if he ought to tell her the truth, if he ought to tell them both. Caution won out, and he nodded slowly. "We shall see. Ashina, her understudy, is capable enough."

"I am sure, but people paid to see the great Noma Etsuko."

Shin heard something in the other man's voice. There was more there than curiosity. "Unfortunately, that is not possible at the moment."

"She is ill, then?"

"You might say that."

"What else might one say?"

Shin paused. "Nothing at the moment."

"A shame. I was so looking forward to the performance."

"The performance will continue," Shin said quickly. Too quickly, perhaps, for Yasamura studied him speculatively. "As I said, Lady Etsuko's understudy is eminently capable of taking on her role as you will see for yourself."

"I am glad to hear it," Yasamura said. "More, I look forward to it. Still, I am curious." Yasamura gave Shin's knee a playful tap. "You are investigating something. What is it? Tell me. I beg you."

Shin tried to laugh it off. "An unrelated matter." Yasamura was charming. Too charming. He had to be careful what he said to the other man. If he allowed himself to be lulled, he might reveal too much.

Yasamura frowned and glanced at Konomi, who shrugged. "I am no fool, Shin. Coincidences are for children. Something is going on. Lady Etsuko collapses in front of the audience and then you absent yourself. I beg you to tell me."

Shin hesitated. As Yasamura had said, he was no fool. To treat him as if he was would be to risk insulting him. He would have to tread carefully. "I would if I could, but in doing so I might endanger my investigation."

Yasamura laughed and clapped his hands. "I knew it!" He looked at Konomi. "Did I not say there was something odd about it?" Konomi nodded, her eyes on Shin. Yasamura leaned back, clearly pleased with himself. "Was she poisoned, then?"

Shin frowned. "Why would you say that?"

"It seems the obvious conclusion," Yasamura said, frowning. "Am I correct?"

"Shame on you, cousin," Konomi interjected. "He has already said he cannot say. Why press the issue, save impolite curiosity?"

Yasamura raised his hands in mock surrender. "You are right, of course. I overstep. I can only apologize for my eagerness." He clapped his hands on his knees and unfolded, rising to his feet with enviable grace. He bowed to Shin. "I shall leave you to your thoughts, my lord. Konomi, shall we return to our box?"

"I shall be along in a moment," Konomi said after a moment's pause. Yasamura bowed wordlessly and departed, an impenetrable look on his face. Shin wondered at it, suspecting something had passed between the cousins.

Shin and Konomi sat in silence for some time. Then Shin said, "Well, I don't care what others say, I like him." It was the truth. Yasamura was effortlessly charming, intelligent... handsome. But he was hiding something. Shin could feel it.

Konomi snorted and almost spilled her tea. "I hoped you might."

"I gathered."

"What do you really think of him? Tell me the truth."

"Very handsome," Shin said.

"And?"

"Clever."

Konomi read something in his face. "But?"

"But what? But nothing. He is a fine man. Respectable. Unlike myself."

"Shin, I hate to break this to you, but you are only considered disreputable by people who take such matters far too seriously. You are a babe in the woods compared to some I could name."

Shin drew back. "I want you to know that is quite possibly the most hurtful thing anyone has ever said to me."

Konomi snorted. "What is the issue, then?"

"I cannot help but feel as if I am of secondary concern to Lord Yasamura." The thought bothered him but not as much as it might have otherwise. Given the current situation, it was almost a relief. One less thing to worry about.

Her eyes narrowed. "What do you mean?"

"Well, he's not here for me, is he?" Shin indicated the stage with a wave of his fan. "He was here for Lady Etsuko." It was a stab in the dark, but sometimes those drew blood.

"Preposterous."

"Really? Then why all the questions?"

"He was trying to show some interest," Konomi said. Shin watched her eyes and saw a flicker of something – disappointment? No, satisfaction. Odd.

"Yes, in Lady Etsuko's mysterious ailment."

"No, you great nitwit. In you." Konomi studied him for long moments. Then she set her hand atop his. "It's the actress, isn't it? That's what's making you hesitate."

"Etsuko?"

"The other one, Shin."

"Ah." Shin sat back on his heels. Konomi knew something

about Okuni but not much. "No. Not as such." It was lie but only a little one. He thought about Okuni often, in fact. More, perhaps, than was good for him.

"Good. Because from what little you've told me of her, she doesn't sound suitable at all." Konomi patted his hand. Her touch was affectionate and familiar.

Shin gave a snort of laughter, and Konomi smiled. "There we are. I prefer it when you smile." She patted his hand again and sat back.

Shin sighed. "If nothing else, Yasamura's presence will ensure that today's performance is talked about in the proper circles." He glanced toward the door. "Still, for a man who thinks the Kitsuki Method is ridiculous, he seems eager to take part in the investigation."

"He comes by his enthusiasm naturally." Konomi paused, then added, "But you are right. He knows her. Etsuko, I mean."

Shin looked at her. "When you say knows her, you mean..."

"A dalliance, or so he assured me. Though you've got me wondering if seeing her again was part of the reason he accepted my invitation to attend this performance." She sighed and tapped her lips with her fan. "It did not end well, I'm told."

"By him?"

She shook her head. "No. Others. He speaks of it only in jest. But I believe she threw him over for another."

Shin frowned. "She threw him over? Him? The son of the Unicorn clan champion?"

"I do not know the details, Shin. It could be even as he said, just a passing dalliance. But I do know he was eager to see her again."

"He said nothing of this." Yasamura's interest in Etsuko was starting to make more sense. Shin wondered why the other courtier was really there. It wasn't for him; he was certain of that now. The thought was mildly disappointing but intriguing.

"Because I told him to be on his best behavior," Konomi said firmly. She peered at him. "Was she? Poisoned, I mean?"

Shin hesitated, then took a chance. "It seems that way, yes." He smiled. "I wonder if Yasamura is conducting an investigation of his own."

"What do you mean?"

"The way he was questioning me." Shin tapped his lips with his fan, considering the matter. Konomi's eyes widened as she realized what he was thinking.

"You can't mean to say you think he had something to do with it?"

Shin hesitated. "No. I do not think he did. But as Yasamura said, coincidences are for children." A thought occurred to him. "What do you know about Lady Etsuko?"

"What makes you think I know anything?"

"Because I know you well enough by now to know you subsist on gossip as much as food and drink. Besides, you were the one who recommended her to me." Shin gestured at her with his fan. "So, tell me."

Konomi frowned. After a moment, she said, "I know she has quite the reputation as a social climber. She began life as the minor daughter of a minor vassal family of a minor clan. A veritable nonentity."

"A harsh assessment," Shin demurred.

"But apt, dear Shin. She was no one at all before she put on face paint and a wig. Now, she is acquainted with many in the gentry." She paused and then pointedly added, "Some to their detriment. I would not want you to get too close to her, in any event."

Shin raised an eyebrow. "That sounds like another warning."

Konomi smiled. "Well, I have come to know you quite well, Shin."

"She is to be married, you know," he said, wanting to see how she reacted.

Konomi looked startled by the idea, but there was something artificial about her expression as if she'd been ready for the revelation. "I can't imagine to whom."

"Bayushi Isamu."

She gave another slow blink, a pretense of surprise. Shin's suspicions crystalized. She already knew or had at least suspected. That clinched it.

Konomi and her cousin were up to something. He was certain of it now. But what did it have to do with Etsuko? He considered just asking Konomi but decided that might be construed as rudeness. So instead, he continued, "Unexpected, I know. I wonder if it was a surprise to anyone else?" His smile faded. "And if so, what they might have chosen to do about it."

CHAPTER SEVENTEEN
Change of Scene

Onstage, the first act was nearing its end. Sanemon watched Nao engage in a duel with a rival suitor for Etsuko's hand. This part never failed to make him nervous.

The fight was more energetic than the norm. Usually, stage combat was a languid affair, full of slow, rote movements. This one, however, was more akin to a dance, full of quick, acrobatic action.

Using the set of writing implements he kept about his person, he scribbled a note and handed it to one of the several pages who sat nearby, crouched on stools or against the walls of the stage wing. "Take this to Ishi. I want to do the body switch in this scene. Make sure he's ready."

The page, a boy of less than fifteen years, nodded eagerly and darted away, heading backstage. Ishi was in charge of everything that happened below the stage. That included getting the actors down safely through the trapdoors.

Onstage, Nao spun, wooden blade clacking loudly as it connected with that of his opponent. The bells set into the hilts of both swords commenced to jingling, lending a festive air. Sanemon winced. Normally, you didn't connect with stage weapons. The bells gave the illusion of ringing steel. But that wasn't enough for Nao. He liked the thump of wood, the sound of true contact. It made the audience flinch.

Watching the actor, Sanemon found himself wondering, not for the first time, whether Nao had some real training with a blade. His movements were not so exaggerated as one might expect from someone trained in stage combat. There was a smoothness to his footwork that sent a familiar chill down Sanemon's spine. He'd only ever seen a man move like that on the battlefield. As always, he forced the thought aside. Those weren't days he wanted to recall or relive in any capacity.

"He is so fast," someone whispered at his elbow. Sanemon started and looked around. Choki crouched nearby in the gloom, his eyes on his master. "He never taught me to move that fast."

"No, I don't expect he has," Sanemon said. "It's not really something one can teach, I fear. Nao is fast because he is fast, not because he learned to be fast."

Choki grimaced. "Then how am I to ever play such a role?" He was dressed as a merchant and had just fled the scene with the other journeymen actors, exiting stage left.

Sanemon, who had heard similar questions before from any number of young actors, smiled. "The same as any actor. In your own fashion." He liked Choki. The lad put in a good day's work when needed. He could memorize lines and deliver them in the proper manner. If you had an empty slot on a cast list, you could do worse than Choki. The only real problem with him was that he wanted to be a lead actor – a role he was not yet suited for.

At least, that was Nao's opinion. He'd been unhappy at first when Sanemon had hired the young man and made him an understudy. But in the months since, he'd come to treat his role

as mentor seriously – when he wasn't making Choki run errands
for him.

As if he were thinking the same thing, Choki shook his head,
his gaze still focused on the stage. "He says I am not ready."

Sanemon caught his attention. "So he says. Tell me this – have
you memorized this play? This scene? Can you tell me what
happens next, without thinking?"

Choki blinked. "He, uh, the suitor dies, and then Master Nao
flees down the flower path and then the, ah, the guards – no – the
cousins arrive. That's right, isn't it?"

"Not quite. Cousins arrive first, forcing our hero to retreat.
Why?"

"Why what?"

"Why does he not flee before they arrive?"

A puzzled look came over Choki's face. "I- I'm not sure."

"A hero does not flee like a common murderer. He stands
defiant until he is forced to retreat by the realization that to remain
means more death. Their deaths, not his." Sanemon indicated
the stage. "Our hero is a warrior without equal. That's what gets
him into trouble, see? He kills his lover's favored cousin, whom
she was promised to. She did not wish to marry him but neither
did she wish him dead. When she learns of what happened, she
naturally assumes her lover slew her cousin out of jealousy, rather
than self-defense, and finds herself caught between loyalty to her
family and loyalty to her lover."

"I know all that," Choki said somewhat irritably. He tugged
at his robes as if their touch irritated him. Maybe they did. They
were cheaply made in comparison to the costumes worn by the
lead actors.

Sanemon didn't take umbrage at his tone. "I should hope so."
He paused. "Ashina will be making her grand entrance soon."

"Ashina?" Choki looked startled. A moment later, he asked, "What about Lady Etsuko? Has she not recovered yet?"

"No," Sanemon said with only a moment's hesitation. He spied Ashina making her way toward the entrance to the flower path and signaled her. She looked nervous beneath her makeup. One of Rin's assistants padded after her, finishing up a few last-minute alterations to her costume for the scene.

Sanemon looked her up and down. "Fix her sleeve, there," he said absently. The embroiderer glared at him but did as he suggested. "How are you holding up?" he asked the actress as she held out her arm for the embroiderer to work.

"Do you think they've noticed?" she asked softly, not meeting his eyes. "That I'm not Lady Etsuko, I mean."

"No," Choki said instantly.

"Yes," Sanemon said, shooting him a hard look. "But that's no bad thing. The audience saw her collapse. Most of them were expecting a cast change." He smoothed out a fold in her robes, despite a wordless complaint from the embroiderer, and took in her anxious expression. "You'll only be onstage for a few moments this time," he murmured. "You're doing fine." She nodded, and he stepped back, nearly colliding with Choki. The young man was staring after her with a besotted expression on his face.

Sanemon sighed and gave him a light slap on the back of the head. "Enough. Stop mooning over her, lad. She has enough to worry about."

Choki flinched and rubbed the back of his head. "I was just – I didn't…"

"I know what you were just," Sanemon said. "Go find something productive to do." A sudden communal intake of breath from the stalls drew his eyes back to the stage. The duel was ended. Nao stood triumphant. The hidden trapdoor had opened, depositing the other actor under the stage and leaving a rag dummy with a paper head in her place. An awkward bit of stagecraft. The audience wasn't fooled, but they appreciated the effort.

Sanemon watched Ashina reach the stage. The audience had fallen largely silent. A few querulous voices called out, but they were swiftly stilled by fellow audience members. Complaints were for afterward – or intermission if you couldn't wait that long.

Ashina's nervousness betrayed itself as soon as she spoke. Her voice quavered slightly, but it was better than it had been. She was getting more confident, but he suspected all it would take was one missed line and she'd be right back where she started. As he'd hoped, she hit her marks, and he sighed with relief as the other actors raced onstage and enveloped her in a warm cocoon of buffoonery. Nao retreated.

Mournful wails rose from the actors clustered about a paper head, red silk spilling from its neck stump. Vengeance was sworn. End scene. The curtain was drawn. Applause rose from the stalls.

As soon as the curtain had been pulled, Sanemon scribbled another note and gestured to a page. "Take this to the musicians. Let them know we have a change in the scene order coming up. Go quickly!" The page took off running.

"Something I should be aware of?" Nao asked, coming up behind him. The actor was already stripping off his costume. As he did so, he handed bits and pieces of it to the waiting Choki. "Are we at last giving up all pretense at serious drama and instead giving in to our natural inclination to farce?"

Sanemon rounded on him, finger raised to a point just under the actor's nose. "I do not have the patience for you at the

moment, Nao, so feel free to keep your witticisms to yourself."
He lowered his hand. "Botan will be going on before you."

Nao frowned. "Why?" He paused. "Oh. You're still worried
about Ashina."

"Aren't you?"

"Now that you mention it, no. She's doing fine, Sanemon."

"You're just saying that to make me feel better."

Nao snorted. "When have you ever known me to do that?
No. I've watched her practice. She's head and shoulders above
many actors I could name." He straightened the hang of his
sleeve. "True, she had a frantic first few minutes onstage, but she's
getting better. I'll be with her for the majority of her next scene. If
she falters, I can carry it, even as I did with Okuni."

Sanemon looked at the actor. Nao oozed confidence, he
always did. He'd only ever seen Nao at a loss once, and then only
because he'd caught Okuni creeping back through a window with
an arrow in her shoulder. He sighed. "I wish she were here now."

Nao frowned and gestured for Choki to leave them. "Go get
my costume ready for the next scene. I'll be along directly." The
young actor went reluctantly. "You're not the only one who
misses her," Nao said when he'd gone. "But there's nothing for it
save to soldier on as best we can in her absence."

"Funny words coming from you. You weren't exactly weeping
when she left."

"I only weep when the script calls for it. You know that." Nao
adjusted his wig. "How is Etsuko, by the way?"

Sanemon took a deep breath. Lord Shin had asked him not to
say anything, but didn't Nao deserve to know? The actor peered
at him. "What is it? What's wrong?"

"She's dead."

Nao paled but didn't seem otherwise surprised. "Dead?"

"Poisoned."

Nao looked away. "You're certain?"

"Lord Shin's physician is. That's good enough for me."

Nao grunted. "Well, that's not going to help our cause any."

"No." Sanemon looked at the actor, hesitated, then softly said, "Was it you?" The question had come unbidden to his lips. He hadn't intended to ask it, but now he wondered whether he ought to have done so sooner.

Nao blinked. "What?"

"Did you poison her?"

Nao's face went still and masklike. "How can you ask me that?"

"You were fighting with her. You had access to her makeup. I am surprised Lord Shin has not asked you himself."

"Maybe he knows me better than you," Nao spat, drawing back.

For once, Sanemon did not retreat in the face of Nao's wrath. If Nao was angry, it meant his question had hit a sore spot. "It is because I know you that I ask. Maybe you did not intend to kill her. Maybe it was an accident. Tell me, and I will do what I can to help you…"

Nao stared at him in shock – possibly feigned – but Sanemon wasn't sure. "You've finally gone mad. That's it, isn't it? The stress has finally broken you. That's the only reason I can think of that you might accuse me of such a thing." He touched his chest as if in pain. "After all we have endured together, you think me capable of such a crime?"

Sanemon hesitated. "Then tell me, who do you think did it?"

Nao gave a bark of laughter. "Maybe it was Ashina, eh? She wouldn't be the first understudy to use such means to get their turn onstage."

"You can't mean that."

"Why not? If Etsuko was poisoned, Ashina is the most likely culprit. You saw how that woman treated her."

"No worse than how you treat Choki," Sanemon said. Nao paused, frowning.

"I beg your pardon?"

"You treat him like a servant rather than a fellow actor."

Nao's frown deepened. "I am teaching him responsibility."

"By making him get your costume ready?" Sanemon waved a hand. "No, don't bother to explain yourself. I have no ear for excuses today." As he spoke, he watched the stage crew change the scenery. A few pieces here and there and suddenly a marketplace was a secluded glade. Almost like magic. He looked back at Nao, decision made.

"The truth is, if you did it, I don't want to know. But if you did, you'd better make sure no one else finds out. For all our sakes."

CHAPTER EIGHTEEN
Backstage

Shin decided to make the costume master, Rin, his first stop upon heading backstage. Of the two, Rin was more gregarious than Uni. At least in Shin's experience. He'd intended to meet with them alone, but that had not happened. He looked over at his companion. "I can't believe you insisted on accompanying me," he murmured as he and Konomi made their way backstage. Her bodyguard, Hachi, followed silently in their wake.

"I can't believe you agreed," she replied, her arm hooked around his elbow. She fluttered her fan at a passing knot of actors, and they bowed in surprise. She tittered politely, and several of them flushed beneath their makeup as they hurried on their way.

"Yasamura will be wondering where you are," Shin said.

"Let him. This is more fun. I've never seen the stage from this side before. I hope you'll give me a tour one of these days."

Shin smiled and shook his head. "I'm sure that can be arranged."

"I'll hold you to it." She glanced at him speculatively. "Do you think it was the Scorpion? They are known for poisoning people."

"That doesn't mean they poisoned Etsuko." Shin had considered that Isamu might be behind it, but as yet he saw no reason for such an act. The Scorpion had a reputation for subtlety to rival that of the Crane, and Etsuko's demise had been anything but subtle.

"It doesn't mean they didn't," she countered.

Shin chuckled. "You're starting to sound like Kasami."

Konomi smiled. "She's a wise woman. You should pay more attention to her." She paused. "Have you spoken to Bayushi Isamu yet?"

"Yes. Do you know him?"

"I know everyone," she said with a sniff. "So should you, by the way. You are the trade representative, after all. It might behoove you to act like it on occasion."

Shin grunted. "Crane merchants require little oversight thankfully."

"It's not the merchants I'm concerned about but their masters." She snapped her fan shut and swatted him on the arm. "Why do you think I invite you to all my parties?"

"I thought you liked my company."

"In modest doses, it's tolerable, I suppose." She grinned, taking some of the sting out of her words. "You are being talked about, Shin. Gossip flows through this city like water. And like water, it spreads. Further and faster than you can imagine."

"What are you trying to say, Konomi?" She wasn't telling him anything he didn't already know. He was used to being a figure of gossip, especially among his fellow courtiers. He had made himself such and intentionally so.

"Simply that you must take more care." She paused again. "Who do you think did it?"

"I don't know."

She tightened her grip on his arm. "Surely you must suspect someone."

"Any number of people."

"Like who?"

Shin gave her a shrewd look. Konomi was feeling him out, albeit more subtly than Yasamura had. "Let me ask you the same question. Who do you think did it?"

Konomi tapped her lips with her fan, head tilted. If she was annoyed by his avoidance of the question, she gave no sign. "Her understudy seems the obvious culprit. I'm surprised you haven't spoken to her yet."

"I have, actually. And yes, I agree, she does seem the obvious answer. Etsuko treated her poorly and kept her from the stage. It only makes sense that she would poison her. But... well. She was as surprised as anyone by Etsuko's collapse."

"Or she's a better actress than you thought," Konomi said primly.

"Or that," Shin agreed. "The problem is that I do not know what questions to ask. Not yet. I need to know more."

"Hence this visit to – what did you say his name was?"

"Rin. He's in charge of the costumes. And yes."

"You think he'll be able to help you with your questions?" Konomi asked doubtfully.

"At the very least, he might be able to provide some context for what happened earlier," Shin said. He gesticulated with his fan. "She was poisoned in such a way that she could not help but collapse onstage. Whoever did it either knew that would happen or didn't care. They could have dropped it in her tea, poisoned her rice, dripped it down a wire into her mouth as she slept. Instead, they did it here and now. Why?"

"What if she wasn't the true target?"

He frowned and looked at her. "What do you mean?"

"You know what I mean, Shin. I'm surprised you haven't come to the conclusion yourself. You're supposed to be the investigator." Her tone was teasing, but he could tell she was serious. "Your reputation, your investment, all of it might well be forfeit if this performance goes badly."

Shin shook his head but didn't immediately reply. He was not so arrogant as to think himself a target. Or maybe it was arrogance that caused him to discount himself – the arrogance of a lord, imagining himself above the squabbles of the common herd. Either way, there was no evidence of it yet.

Konomi nudged him in the ribs, but before he could say anything he spotted the familiar figure of Lord Kenzō hurrying toward them, an inappropriately cheerful look on his face. "Lord Shin! Lord Shin!" He smiled ingratiatingly as he came to a stop before Shin and Konomi. "I came to speak with you in private, but I was told you'd come backstage… and with Lady Konomi as well." He sketched a bow. "Hello again, my lady. A pleasure to see you. I hope to get the chance to meet your cousin before the day is out."

"I'm sure Lord Yasamura would be most pleased to meet you, Lord Kenzō."

Kenzō's smile widened. "How wonderful to hear." His gaze flicked to Shin. "Lord Shin, I do hope everything is all right. With Lady Etsuko, I mean. Did she take ill?"

"I am no doctor, so I really can't say," Shin said. "My apologies, Lord Kenzō, but we are rather busy at the moment…" He gestured for the man to step aside, but Kenzō obstinately remained where he was.

"I was in the audience. When it happened, I mean. Since you did not invite me to share your box with you." The last was said rather pointedly, Shin thought. He wondered if Kenzō was insulted. A small, childish part of him hoped so.

"My apologies for the oversight," Shin began.

Kenzō waved his words aside. "No matter, my lord, no matter. I've never watched a performance from the stalls. Truly an invigorating experience."

"Well, I'm glad you're enjoying it," Shin said.

"Not at all! Terrible play. Can't stand it. But the enthusiasm of the common crowd is something to witness at least once in a lifetime."

Konomi tittered. "I thought it was your recommendation, my lord."

"Oh, it was, it was. But I recommended it on the basis of its popularity, not my own preference." The auditor tapped the air with a finger. "One must often look beyond preference in order to achieve success in one's endeavors."

"Wise words," Shin said somewhat sourly. "My grandfather said something similar once, I believe."

Kenzō nodded. "Your grandfather is a most canny man, my lord. He possesses an acumen second to none." He glanced at Konomi. "Have you had the pleasure of…"

She shook her head. "Sadly, no. Though I would like to meet him someday."

"You simply must. Especially if you two are to – well, that is to say, it would only be expected if you were to…" Kenzō trailed off awkwardly. Konomi laughed and patted Shin's arm, which only seemed to fluster the auditor more.

Shin was tempted to lean into the ruse, if only to see what new shades the other man's face might turn, but decided to err on the side of restraint. "Yes, well, we'll see," he said. "Is there something I can help you with, Lord Kenzō? As I mentioned, we are rather busy."

"Of course, my lord, my apologies." Kenzō leaned close as if to share a secret. "Between you and me, my lord, said crowd is growing a bit unhappy with the performance. That's why I hurried backstage to find you when your servants mentioned where you were. It might behoove you to cancel the rest of the performance, given that our star attraction is ill."

"It's not going to be canceled, Kenzō. Ashina is fully capable of playing Etsuko's part. As you would know if you'd been paying attention."

The auditor waved this aside as well. "I'm not saying the girl isn't capable, but people did not pay to watch her, did they?"

"You are the second person to tell me that today. I will tell you what I told them. The performance can and will continue. There is no need to be concerned, Lord Kenzō. Everything is as it should be."

"But the audience paid to see Lady Etsuko…" Kenzō began. "They'll never stand for a replacement. I shouldn't wonder if half the seats will be empty come intermission. That won't help your reputation."

"Perhaps. It remains to be seen." Shin studied the other man. Kenzō acted as if he was almost disappointed. Maybe he was. For a brief instant, he wondered whether Kenzō himself might be a suspect. But just as quickly, he discarded the idea. Kenzō had easier ways of sabotaging Shin's efforts, and earlier opportunities, and as far as he knew, the auditor had never met Etsuko.

Kenzō frowned. "Yes, well, I'm sure you know best, my lord." He paused. "In that case, might we discuss the expenses for this performance? I was just informed that you decided to allow the teahouses to sell their wares inside the building…"

"Yes."

"And how much did it cost to convince them to do so?"

Shin paused. "Not as much as you might expect." In fact, it had cost nothing. The teahouses had been enthused by the idea of selling to a captive audience. Or so his go-betweens had reported. Shin himself had not spoken to the owners of the teahouses.

"And what about the extra security on the doors?" Kenzō asked quickly. He must have mistaken Shin's hesitation for chagrin, for he continued, "I don't recall authorizing such an expenditure when we discussed the budget last week ... "

Shin held up a hand, forestalling any further complaints. "As much as I am thankful for your help in these matters, Lord Kenzō, I must remind you that you are not in charge. I am. And there is no need to worry about any expenditures. The additional security is being provided free of charge by Lord Azuma."

"I see," Kenzō said stiffly. "Might I ask the reason for such generosity?"

"You may not," Shin said pleasantly. Kenzō flushed slightly but otherwise gave no sign of his annoyance. Shin took pity on him and clapped him lightly on the arm. "Never fear, Lord Kenzō. I've seen to it that your efforts to make this venue profitable will not be in vain. Now, I'm afraid I must leave you. I must talk to Master Rin about a matter of costuming."

With that, Shin bowed and gently but firmly pushed past the other man, leading Konomi and Hachi away. Konomi glanced back. "He looks as if he's bitten into something unpleasant."

"He always looks like that."

"I did tell you to watch out for him, didn't I?"

"You did," Shin murmured.

"Let me reiterate, then. He's trouble."

"Yes, but until I'm certain just what kind, there's little I can do save be polite."

Konomi frowned. "You know, his presence does lead me to wonder at how easy it is to get backstage, even during a performance. Especially for us."

"It is, in fact, very easy and very common. Or so I'm told. The stage crew and the cast are often too busy to take note of anyone who looks out of place. There are dozens of people going in and out of every room at all times. Especially the dressing rooms. And, well, who's going to tell a nobleman – or noblewoman – that they can't go somewhere?"

"I'm beginning to see why you're having so much difficulty identifying the culprit."

Shin nodded. "It's a fool's errand to even try to identify who would have been in the dressing room at the time Etsuko was poisoned. The backstage hierarchy alone makes it all but impossible. The actors barely acknowledge each other, let alone the crew or the pages." He paused. "That is why I need context. I need to clear some brush and expose the path."

"The right path, one hopes," Konomi said.

"Any path will do at this point." Shin stopped in front of the costume room. "Here we are. Would you like to wait out here, or…?"

"Oh, absolutely not. I'm not missing this." Konomi glanced at her bodyguard. "Hachi, watch the door, please." Hachi nodded and took up a position against the far wall. Shin nodded to him in thanks. He felt somewhat naked with Kasami still watching Etsuko's dressing room. Hachi was a comfortingly stolid presence if nothing else.

Shin slid open the door and turned to Konomi.

"After you."

CHAPTER NINETEEN
Arban

Kasami jolted to her feet, startling the well-wisher. He was a dumpy little man, a clerk for one of the independent firms that clung to the docks going by the state of his robes and the ink on his fingers. "Did I not make myself clear?" she growled. "No one is to see Lady Etsuko. No one."

"But I–" he began. Kasami thrust herself toward him in a pugnacious fashion.

"Especially not you," she clarified. The clerk took the hint and fled. Kasami straightened and blew out an annoyed sigh.

"That was mean," someone said. Kasami turned to see Chika leaning against the wall, a clay bottle dangling from her hand. The actress was still in her makeup but had replaced her costume with a loose robe.

"He's the fifth one to try to get in since the scene change," Kasami said. It was infuriating. Anyone could get backstage at any time. They just had to know where to go. She was going to have to do something about the lack of security for the next performance, whether Shin liked it or not.

"Only five? I expected a stampede." Chika extended the bottle. "Drink?"

"What is it?"

"Rice wine."

Kasami shook her head. "Not while I'm on duty."

"Well, I'll drink your share," Chika said, working loose the stopper and taking a delicate swallow. "How is she?"

"Resting," Kasami said, studying the actress. Chika didn't appear inebriated, but she smelled strongly of wine. "Are you celebrating something?"

"What? Oh. The wine. No." Chika shook her head. "Just keeping things lubricated." She took another swallow and sank into an inelegant crouch beside Kasami's stool. Kasami sat down. "So, what happened? Sanemon isn't saying."

"She took ill. That's all I know." Kasami did not enjoy lying to Chika or in general. Shin seemed to get some pleasure out of it, but Kasami had always thought of lies as double-edged swords, prone to cutting their wielder. Chika laughed softly.

"Couldn't happen to a nicer person. She tried to stab me once, you know."

Kasami raised an eyebrow. "What had you done?"

Chika smiled prettily. "Nothing that deserved that sort of response." Her smile faded. "She's getting married. Thought none of us knew." She took another swig from her bottle. "She'll be right at home with the Scorpion. Like calls to like."

Kasami scratched her chin. "How did you find out?"

Chika indicated her eyes. "I am very observant. And they are not very sneaky. They've been scuttling around backstage for weeks. And not just them. Servants of the Tonbo and the Akodo as well, asking impertinent questions and bothering the crew."

Kasami tapped her chin. "What sort of questions?"

Chika shrugged. "Who knows?" She reclined against the wall. "We thought they were just accompanying their masters to Etsuko's bower." She nodded toward the dressing room. "But maybe that was just the Scorpion."

"Lord Isamu, you mean."

Chika shrugged and took another swig from her bottle. "I suppose. I never found out his name. Etsuko did her best to hide her suitors from us. They always met after hours, at night, when most of the cast and crew was gone."

"But not all?"

Chika smiled. "Theaters are never as empty as they seem. There's always someone lingering where they shouldn't be."

Kasami returned her smile. "And you were one of them?" She wondered what Shin would make of Chika's revelation. It didn't seem of much interest to her, but Shin had funny ideas when it came to innocuous bits of information. Clues, he called them. More of that Kitsuki nonsense as far as Kasami was concerned.

Before Chika could answer, someone said, "A good question. It might be said that none of us are where we should be." Kasami frowned as Lord Gota's Ujik bodyguard, Arban, sauntered down the corridor toward them. He stopped in front of them and grinned at Chika. "Celebrating something?"

"She isn't," Kasami said. She glanced at Chika, and the young woman nodded, rose, and retreated without a word. Arban watched her go.

"Pretty woman."

Kasami grunted. The Ujik sat down on the floor beside her. She turned away from him, intent on ignoring him. After a time, she noticed a particular pungency in her vicinity. Unable to stop herself, she glanced at him.

The Ujik was eating something that looked like old leather.

He caught her looking and offered a strip. "Dried meat," he said, chewing. "Want some?"

Kasami grunted again and turned away. The Ujik shrugged and went back to his gnawing. After a time, he finished, wiped his hands on his robes, and said, "I'm supposed to distract you. Are you open to distraction?"

Kasami did not reply. The Ujik scratched his chin and settled back, legs crossed. "Didn't think so. Gota said I was supposed to challenge you or some fool thing. I don't think that would work myself."

"It would go poorly for you," Kasami said without looking at him.

The Ujik grinned. "So you can talk. I wondered about that. I heard the Crane liked to cut out the tongues of their retainers to prevent them from gossiping."

Kasami looked at him, startled by his fluency. Earlier, he'd seemed barely able to comprehend Rokugani. "Ridiculous."

"Obviously. Not even your people are that savage."

"What do you mean 'my people'?"

"Rokugani, of course. It's common knowledge among my folk that there are no crueler people in this world than yours."

Kasami glared at him. "Don't Ujiks use wild horses to tear their captives apart?"

"Only when we're trying to make a point. Your people have made cruelty into an art." He grinned at her. His teeth were surprisingly good for a nomad. "You look angry. Are you angry? If not, I can keep talking."

"Do not trouble yourself on my account."

He laughed. "My name is Arban. What do they call you?"

"None of your concern."

"Well, none of your concern, I think you are getting angry.

That's a shame. I would like to talk more before we move to steel." He leaned close, still showing his teeth. "I think you are very good with your sword."

Kasami was staring at him now. His hands were nowhere near his weapon, but he'd moved very fast before. Quicker than she'd expected. "Where is your master?" she asked softly. "Is he waiting out of sight like a coward?" The last she said loudly. She heard a curse from down the corridor and smiled. "Yes, there he is. You should return to him before he hurts himself."

"Gota can take care of himself," Arban said as loudly as she had.

"Lord Gota," came a bellow in reply.

Arban didn't break eye contact with her, but his smile widened. "Is yours so concerned with proper titles?"

"No. I wish he were. It is better when everyone knows their place."

"I have always thought the opposite myself." He paused, a thoughtful look on his face. "Then I suppose that is why I am here rather than with my people on the great grass sea." His smile returned. "I doubt they miss me all that much."

"I doubt it as well. You seem very troublesome."

"That I am. I was born under a devil star, or so my grandmother insists." He looked past her. "Hello, my lord! I am being very distracting as you commanded."

Kasami snapped around, pinning Gota in place with her glare. He froze, halfway to the door of the dressing room, a scowl on his face. "Damn you, Arban," he snarled. "Can you not do one simple thing I ask of you?"

"I thought I was doing fine," Arban murmured. He glanced at her. "What do you think, eh?"

"I think you should both leave." Kasami stood abruptly.

Startled, Arban fell on his rear, and Gota retreated several steps. "Now. Lord Shin has commanded that no one enter this room without his permission. That includes you, Lord Gota."

"How dare you speak to me in such a manner?" Gota blustered. "I am of noble blood!"

"I do not think she particularly cares," Arban said, rising smoothly to his feet. Kasami placed her back to the door so she could keep an eye on both of them. She let her hand rest on the hilt of her sword. Arban grinned, and his hand fell to his own blade. "See? She doesn't care."

Gota looked back and forth between them, consternation on his face. He obviously hadn't intended it to go this far. Arban, on the other hand, seemed overjoyed. Kasami kept her expression neutral, letting none of her annoyance show.

Arban swaggered to her left, turning so only his right side faced her. His smile had turned sharp and lethal, not the expression of a warrior but that of a killer sizing up his prey. She was not overly concerned. The Ujik was full of himself. He either underestimated her or overestimated himself. Gota was the real danger. If he got involved, she would be faced with a stark choice to either give way before him, for he was of superior rank, or hold fast and risk bringing shame to her family and the Crane.

Thankfully, it proved to be a decision she did not have to make. A trio in robes of red approached, Chika trailing reluctantly in their wake. Their intent to enter was obvious, but they slowed as they realized a confrontation was taking place.

All three were masked; one wore a filigreed eye mask of gold with a veil of red silk covering his mouth and nose; the second wore a plain mask of porcelain painted in stripes of red and black; and the third wore a demon's face to hide her own. All three were armed. They were samurai and bore the insignia of the Bayushi and the Scorpion. The one wearing the veil said, "Move aside. We are here to see Lady Etsuko."

"I have been ordered to see that no one disturbs her," Kasami said as politely as she could manage under the circumstances.

The Scorpion made an impatient noise. "That is no concern of ours. Move aside."

"No."

The Scorpion hesitated. He was clearly not used to being defied. His hand hovered over the hilt of his sword. Finally, he turned his attentions to Arban. "Ujik. Remove her. You will be well rewarded."

Arban frowned. "You are not my master." He glanced at Gota, whose expression was thunderous. "What do you think, Lord Gota? Should I remove her for these men?"

"Don't be an idiot," Gota snapped. He crossed his arms and turned his glare on the newcomers. "Who sent you?"

"We wear our master's colors openly, Badger. You have but to look."

Gota flushed. "And what is your business here?"

"To see Lady Etsuko."

"Why?"

"Why do you think, Badger?" the Scorpion said in a mocking tone. "Or has she not made her intentions clear enough to you?"

Gota's flush deepened, and his big hands flexed. Kasami was suddenly aware of the muscle lurking beneath the flab. Shin had said Gota had been a wrestler. She wondered if she was about to get a demonstration of that prowess. The Scorpion obviously had similar concerns, for they tensed as one as if worried he might rush them in his mounting fury.

But instead of rushing them, he took a deep breath and said, "If I am not allowed in, neither are you. Let your master come himself if he wishes to see her." He gestured and Arban stepped back, taking up a position beside Kasami.

The tall Scorpion sighed and tapped a finger against the hilt of his sword. "I will tell him no such thing. Nor will I allow you to insult him."

"The only one being insulting here is you, my friend," Arban said.

"Quiet, Ujik. Your betters are speaking."

Arban's smile vanished as if he'd been slapped. His hand went to his sword, not playfully now. Deadly serious. He did not draw it, not yet, but he was only seconds from doing so, Kasami thought. Blood would be spilled a moment later, whatever happened.

Kasami heard the door hiss open behind her. Doctor Sanki coughed. "Bad time?" he asked in a gust of pipe smoke. Kasami didn't turn around. The doctor either had incredible timing or was attempting to preempt the violence.

"Yes," she said. "What is it?"

"I need to speak to Lord Shin."

"I'm sure he'll be along directly," she said and slid the door shut in his face. She caught Chika's eye and mouthed Shin's name. The actress nodded and hurried away. The Scorpions either didn't notice or didn't care.

Arban laughed. "You have a remarkable way about you. And you still have not told me your name. I thought your people were supposed to be polite."

"When it is earned," Kasami said. She looked at the Scorpions. "If your master, whoever he might be, wishes to pay a call on Lady Etsuko, he must first ask my lord, Daidoji Shin. Attempting to barge in will earn you nothing save a firm rebuke."

"And who will deliver this rebuke, woman?" asked the one

wearing a demon's face complete with horns and toothy grin. "You? Or maybe you will let the Ujik do it for you. I have heard it said that the Crane prefer to let others do their fighting for them."

Kasami tilted her head. "Funny. I have heard the same about the Scorpion."

"You dare–" the Scorpion snapped. But Kasami heard the satisfaction beneath the outrage. They were looking for an excuse. Which was all just as well, for so was she. She bared her teeth.

"Always."

CHAPTER TWENTY
Rin and Uni

Inside the costume room, it was controlled chaos. A frenzy of productivity greeted their eyes, and Shin barely knew where to look, much less what it was for. He found his eye drawn to several costumes in the midst of alteration, their seams plucked, and myriad folds exposed. He thumbed the material of one, admiring it. He paused as his fingers found a hidden seam – a pocket. "How curious," Konomi said at his elbow.

Shin nodded. "It's for the blood – the silk, I mean. They store it in these pockets until it's needed." He smiled. "Some actors I know even store their lines in here. A quick slip and peek can help in a tight spot." He set the costume aside and turned as he heard Rin call out.

"My lord, it is a pleasure to see you again. And so soon after your last visit." Rin bustled toward Shin and Konomi. Costumers scattered before him, often helped along with a quick swat of his stick. He bowed as much as he was able and smiled at Konomi. "And is this the Lady Konomi about whom I have heard so much?"

"All good things I hope, Master Rin," Konomi replied, smiling. Rin bobbed his head.

"So many that one cannot help but wonder at the truth of

them." He glanced at Shin. "Might I ask the reason for this unanticipated visit?"

"I am in need of guidance, Master Rin."

Rin spread his arms as if in wonder. "Nonsense, my lord. Your sartorial elegance is obvious to even the most jaded costumer!"

Shin laughed at the obvious flattery. "Not about clothing, I'm afraid. On another, less pleasant matter." He paused. "I wish to speak to you about Lady Etsuko?"

Rin's smile faltered just for a moment. "And how is she?"

"Resting," Shin said. "Do you know her well?"

"She and I are barely acquaintances."

"Unfortunate, but still," Shin said. "I understand she has had some difficulty making friends among the troupe."

Rin laughed. "Difficulty is one way of putting it, my lord."

"And how would you put it, Master Rin?"

"Aversion, my lord. Lady Etsuko has a distaste for those she considers her social inferiors. A funny thing coming from – well, no more need be said about that." He glanced at Konomi as he said it.

"No need to soften it on my account, Master Rin," she murmured.

Rin ducked his head and simpered, "I have it on good authority that her father was a common fisherman. And her mother, well, a drudge. A simple drudge. Hardly blessed soil that, if I might be so bold."

"And yet it produced a flower of incalculable beauty," Shin said, wondering what Konomi made of Rin's good authority. To her credit, her expression showed nothing.

"Rough soil often does that, I find," Rin agreed, turning his opinion on the moment. He paused. "She does not like to be reminded of those humble beginnings, my lord. That is what I think. Some actors wish to pretend they are of a kind with the characters they portray."

"And Etsuko is one of them?"

"Lady Etsuko is a complicated woman, my lord. She wears many masks." Rin turned to bark an order at one of his people and swatted the unfortunate man on the rear with his stick. "Forgive me, my lord. We're having to adjust the costumes for Ashina. She is not quite so, ah, voluptuous as Lady Etsuko."

"Forgive me, but I will only keep you for a few moments more," Shin said smoothly. "You said Lady Etsuko has an aversion to making friends... what about enemies?"

"Ah, well, those she collects avidly, my lord," Rin said, turning back to Shin. "Mistress Uni foremost among them, though she will not thank me for saying so."

"Then why say it?"

Rin's eyes twinkled merrily. "Only because I know the old harridan will say the same of me when you speak with her. She is your next port of call, I expect?"

Shin inclined his head. Rin had a quick mind and a talent for patterns. The costume master nodded, pleased to be right. "Of course. Between us, there is not a thing we do not know." He tapped his cheek with his stick. "Lady Etsuko has her share of enemies, it is true. Every actor in this troupe would gut her happily if they knew they could get away with it. Some, even if they knew they couldn't."

"Does that include Nao?"

Rin paused. "Nao more than most. He takes her insults against us personally. With Lady Okuni's departure, Nao has become our... lodestone if you will. Sanemon is master, but Nao is the heart and soul of the troupe. It is to him that we look for leadership."

"That does not speak well of Master Sanemon."

Rin gestured. "That is not what I meant, my lord. Master Sanemon is tireless in his efforts to make something of our humble company. But his is a mind of anxieties and invoices. But Nao... Nao is an actor's actor. There is nothing he would not do for this troupe."

"That is good to hear," Shin said. "Besides Nao, who else might bear Lady Etsuko some grudge?"

"As I said, any number of people, my own assistants among them. She is a violent wind blowing over us all." Rin paused. "But really, our grudges are small compared to some."

"Meaning?"

Rin leaned close. "You know of Lady Etsuko's dalliances then, my lord?"

Shin glanced at Konomi. "It is not the sort of thing I normally concern myself with."

Rin smiled conspiratorially. "Of course not, my lord. Such disreputable gossip is hardly worth listening to. But one cannot very well stuff one's ears with wax, can one? She has made few friends among our company... and fewer still in the city since she came."

"A trail of broken hearts, is it?"

"Something like that, my lord." Rin turned and said something to one of his assistants in a low voice, then looked back at Shin. "You had an encounter with Lord Gota earlier, I heard. He's one who can't take no for an answer. But there are others. They've been sending their servants here at all hours for weeks. All sorts sneaking about backstage, making nuisances of themselves. None of these affairs ended happily, I am told."

Shin frowned. That was quick work. "Were you told why?"

Rin shrugged. "Any number of reasons, my lord. Some of them

might even be true." He hesitated, again glancing at Konomi as if embarrassed by what he was about to say. Shin motioned for him to continue. Rin sighed. "They say that she had many fish on the same lure if you catch my meaning."

"I do," Shin murmured absently. More and more, he suspected he was looking in the wrong place for the killer. Rin peered at him.

"Might I ask a question of my own, my lord?"

"If you like."

"These questions – they imply that Lady Etsuko's sudden illness is not… natural."

Shin looked sharply at the other man. "Whether it is or not is no concern of yours, Master Rin. Today's performance will continue without Lady Etsuko."

"And the next show, my lord?" a woman's voice asked from behind them. Shin turned to see Uni standing near the door, a wig clutched protectively to her bosom. The room had gone silent. Shin was suddenly aware they were being watched by the gathered assistants. He could almost hear what they were thinking. Worry was plain on every face. He cleared his throat.

"Insofar as I am aware, Mistress Uni, all is well in that regard. But it is fortunate that you are here, as I wished to speak with you as well."

She tensed, a frown spreading across her wrinkled features. "I was expecting you earlier, my lord," she said. "Is she dead, then?"

Shin frowned. "Why would you ask that, Uni?"

Her gaze slid toward Rin. "She isn't, is she? That wouldn't be good."

Shin shook his head and clasped his hands behind his back. "No. It wouldn't. Answer my question if you please." He'd hoped to talk to Uni in private, but she seemed willing enough to converse here. Maybe she felt safe, surrounded by Rin and his embroiderers.

"Wishful thinking, my lord," Uni said.

"One might almost think you wished her harm, Uni."

The old woman snorted. "I do not pray for it. But I do not pray against it." She swept past Shin and thrust the wig she held into Rin's hands. "It will need oiling after you take the measurements, so be careful with it."

"I take it that you do not care for Lady Etsuko," Shin pressed.

Uni did not answer immediately. She was a stubborn old woman and as prideful in her way as any lady of the great clans. When she did reply, it was with obvious reluctance. "She is not a lady. Merely an actress."

Shin let that pass. "Master Rin intimated to me that you and she have had some difficulties since she joined the troupe."

Uni glared at Rin, who hurriedly found something else to do. "Did he now?" she muttered, watching as the costume master retreated. "How helpful of him." She paused and flushed. "I am sorry, my lord. My tongue oftentimes has a mind of its own."

Shin gave a forgiving smile. "An affliction we all suffer from, from time to time. But tell me – is there any truth to this?"

Uni looked away. "She does not make it easy, my lord. She treats us – me – as if we are no more than servants. She has no appreciation for what we do." She sighed. "Of the sacrifices we make so she and her kind might look good onstage."

"And what sacrifices might those be?"

"Time, my lord," Uni said. She held up a wrinkled hand. "I have spent my life among false scalps. Tending them as if they were my own children. Some of them I crafted myself. Some are older even than me." She paused. "Sometimes, late at night, I often fancy I hear them murmuring among themselves."

"Perhaps you do," Shin said. "A priest of my acquaintance once told me that upon an object's hundredth birthday, it might acquire a life of its own. Even the most innocuous of household objects might have a spirit inhabiting it if it is old enough."

"I know nothing about such things, my lord."

"Then what do you know about?" Konomi broke in. Shin glanced at her, but let the question stand. Uni, somewhat startled by Konomi's interjection, looked away.

"Unlike Master Rin, I do not lower myself to gossip with pages and embroiderers." She looked about her haughtily, and not a single embroiderer met her gaze.

"What about actors?" Shin asked quickly. Uni flinched slightly.

"Actors, my lord?"

"Do not play coy, Mistress Uni. I have it on good authority that you are privy to much that goes on backstage. If, by your own admission, you do not speak with those of lesser status, then it only stands to reason that you must speak with those of higher." Shin approached her, and she watched him as a hare might watch a circling hawk. "So, what do Nao and Botan and the others say?"

Uni frowned and shrank into herself. Shin was about to repeat his question when Konomi laid a hand on his arm. He paused and glanced at her. Her expression was almost teasing, but there was a warning there as well. He took a deep breath, thought for a moment, and said, "Ah, well. It seems Master Sanemon was wrong."

Uni hesitated. "About what?"

"He assured me you were the one to speak to about this matter. But if you say you know nothing, well ..." Shin raised his hands in a gesture of surrender. Uni's frown deepened. Shin heard a titter from among the clustered embroiderers. Uni glared them into silence, and then turned her gaze on Shin.

"I didn't say I knew nothing. Merely that I do not hold with gossip, my lord."

Shin waited. He spied Rin watching them from the other side of the room. The costume master was frowning but didn't seem inclined to interfere. Finally, Uni said, "She was nothing but a troublemaker, my lord."

"Lady Etsuko, you mean."

"She harried him, my lord. Called us thieves and worse. Said someone had ransacked her belongings and demanded that no one but that poor child she calls an understudy be allowed in her dressing room. Accused poor Chika of stealing from her. And Botan as well, though he's never even spoken to her that I know of. Even tried to get Master Sanemon to send him packing, and he is the only decent clown we've got!"

Shin nodded but didn't interrupt. Choki had said much the same. And while Sanemon had confirmed that there was nothing to it, that didn't mean Chika or one of the other actors might not have taken offense. Or someone acting on their behalf. He recalled that Chika had been entertaining the merchant, Odoma. The same Odoma who'd apparently been enamored with Etsuko... though he hadn't mentioned it when they'd spoken earlier.

Uni continued, "Well, Master Nao had words with her on that score." The old woman forgot herself and clapped her hands in remembered glee. "Such a fight that was! You should have seen it. The two of them went at it like foxes fighting over a fat hen."

"Did they often fight?"

Uni paused. "I would not wish to get Master Nao in trouble, my lord."

"I am not asking you to accuse him of anything, Mistress Uni. I merely wish to know how often he and Etsuko clashed."

"I am not one to spread gossip, my lord, but, well, yes. Quite often as it happens. Not a day went by, really."

"And who provoked such clashes?"

Uni's gaze fell. "Whatever has happened to her onstage, she deserves it," she said finally. Shin sensed that as far as Uni was concerned, that was the end of it. But she'd told him more than enough. More than he'd wanted to hear in fact.

The thought that Nao might have had something to do with Etsuko's death was not a pleasant one. But there was much he didn't know about the actor; much Nao kept hidden. Shin knew he would need to talk to him again, perhaps with Sanemon there this time.

Shin inclined his head and gave both Rin and Uni his best smile. "Thank you for your help, both of you. You have been most informative. I will leave you to your efforts." With that, Shin and Konomi left them to their business.

As they stepped into the corridor, one of the embroiderers followed them. The young man bowed and ducked past. Shin gestured to Hachi, who now crouched opposite the door. "Fetch him for me if you would, Hachi. Gently."

Konomi nodded in agreement, and Hachi rose to his feet and stepped into the embroiderer's path. The embroiderer tensed as Shin's shadow fell across him and turned with wide eyes. "My-my lord? Have- have I offended you in some way?"

"No... Asahi, isn't it?" Shin said, plucking the young man's name from the depths of his capacious memory. "You're the senior costume assistant, aren't you?"

"Yes, my lord," Asahi mumbled, bowing. He clutched a costume to his chest and darted glances at Shin and Konomi.

"Is this for Ashina?" Shin asked, pinching a fold of material between his thumb and forefinger. "For her next scene, I assume."

"Yes, my lord. I must get it to her, my lord." Asahi darted a glance down the hall.

Shin smiled. "Obviously. But if you have a moment, I have a question."

"For me, my lord?" Asahi seemed scandalized by the prospect.

"If you've no objections. No? Good. Master Rin mentioned 'all sorts sneaking backstage'... what sorts might those be? A Scorpion, for instance? Or someone else?" Shin glanced at Konomi. "A Unicorn, perhaps?" Konomi frowned.

"Shin," she began.

Shin stepped back and gestured. "Never mind. Thank you, Asahi." He turned to Konomi. "You have something to tell me?"

"What makes you think that?"

Shin snapped open his fan. "Why did Yasamura recommend Etsuko to you? And why did you recommend her to me?"

Konomi drew herself up. "Are you implying something?"

Shin considered the question. "Yes, I believe I am."

Konomi was about to reply when Sanemon appeared at the other end of the corridor, looking distinctly unhappy. At the sight of them, he hurried over. "My apologies for this interruption, my lord. But, well, I had no choice."

Shin waved his apology aside. "What's wrong?"

"Chika came to me in a panic. It's the Scorpions, my lord," Sanemon mumbled, still face down. "Three of them. They, ah, wanted to deliver a gift to Lady Etsuko, or so they claimed, but your bodyguard... she, well, she, ah..." He trailed off.

"She did as I ordered her to do. Was anyone hurt?"

"Not yet, my lord. At least not according to Chika. It's, ah, ongoing, as it were. Lord Gota is there and his Ujik... well... I don't need to tell you about that, I suppose."

"Oh, this sounds exciting." Konomi clutched Shin's arm, an eager look on her face. "By all means, let's go see what's going on."

Shin sighed. "Lead the way, Master Sanemon. Before Kasami decides to declare war on the Scorpion."

CHAPTER TWENTY-ONE
Kitano

"Scorpions," Ishi snorted as he passed the jug of rice wine to Kitano. "Good wine, by the way. Better than that junk you usually have." He smacked his lips appreciatively.

Kitano smiled. "Borrowed it from Lord Shin's stocks. He doesn't drink the stuff, so I doubt he'd mind." Of course, Kitano also had no intention of telling him, just to be safe. He paused, however, with the jug halfway to his lips. "What about the Scorpions?"

"They were sneaking around backstage last week."

"Anywhere in particular?"

"The dressing rooms mostly," Ishi said.

"Is that odd? Given who she's marrying, I mean."

Ishi snorted. "I'd heard that. Don't believe it." Ishi was a short man, hardly larger than a child, clad in grimy stage whites and with a head shorn clean by a sharp knife. He had dirt caked into the skin of his hands and neck, and his fingernails were black half-moons. Kitano, who'd gotten used to regular bathing, wondered if he'd ever looked half as bad.

Ishi had been with the troupe since Okuni had revitalized

it. They'd hired him away from a puppet theater where he'd purportedly been adept at designing ingenious mechanisms for the display and control of puppets and scenery.

Having seen some of the workarounds Ishi had come up with since they'd begun the repairs to the theater, Kitano could believe the stories. He was a clever man. Smarter than most. Kitano felt something of an affinity for him because of that. He'd once thought himself smarter than most until he'd met Lord Shin. He rubbed his prosthetic finger absently.

Ishi and he sat high up on the catwalk overlooking the stage. No one could see them or hear them from up there, or so Ishi swore. It was a good place for a quiet drink, or maybe a quiet place for a good drink, depending on how you looked at it. Kitano took a pull from the jug and passed it back. "What's to believe? Her fiancé told Lord Shin himself."

Ishi rolled his eyes. "Scorpions," he said again, packing the word with dismissal. "You know what they say about Scorpions."

"They say a lot of things about Scorpions. Narrow it down for me," Kitano said, scratching his cheek with his prosthetic finger. It itched at times. And the stump hurt when it got cold. But he was mostly used to it now. He didn't even resent Kasami that much anymore, despite the fact she kept threatening to cut his other fingers off.

"Their words carry poison," Ishi said.

"You mean he was lying."

Ishi shrugged and took a long drink. Kitano paused. "Everyone is talking about it, though. Seemed like it was common knowledge to me." Kitano had been prowling backstage since leaving Lord Shin's box, but he'd found out precious little in that time, despite generous applications of Lord Shin's stock of rice wine. He'd spent most of the past two hours talking to the journeymen actors – those of too low status to be allowed in the dressing rooms. They had to make do with the corridors. Most of them played background characters – beggars, drunks, and the like. All of them had known. Etsuko had either been singularly bad at hiding her intentions or else hadn't cared that people were gossiping.

"Everyone ain't," Ishi said dismissively.

"The actors are."

"Actors aren't everyone," Ishi said. "You know what I'm talking about."

"I do," Kitano said as Ishi passed the jug back. Hierarchy was a constant in their lives. Nobles ignored peasants, actors ignored crew – as above, so below. Lord Shin was unusual in that he listened. It was also what made him so unnerving to be around. "So you and yours, you don't believe it."

Ishi paused, considering his next words. "Etsuko isn't the marrying sort."

"How do you know that?"

"She told me so."

Kitano nearly choked on his mouthful of wine. "What?" he spluttered. Ishi pounded him on the back. Kitano waved him off. "She… told you?"

Ishi took a swig from the bottle. He looked down at the stage, and Kitano followed his gaze. The actors looked like swirling bursts of color from this angle. It was another fight scene. There were a lot of them from what Kitano could tell. "Actors are like cats in a sack. They're bound to claw one another. For the most part, they ignore us or blame us when something goes wrong."

Kitano nodded. Ishi went on. "Etsuko is different. She doesn't like actors, but she likes us. The stage crew, I mean. We aren't a threat, and I made it clear right off we weren't servants."

"You're safe," Kitano said. He knew something about that just from watching Lord Shin. Status was a double-edged sword. You never felt safe with anyone of lower or higher rank, only with those who held no rank whatsoever.

Ishi grunted. "Don't know about that but maybe so. Either way, she talks to me." He took a long drink. Kitano stared at him in fascination.

"What'd you talk about?"

Ishi paused. "Don't know that I should tell you, Kitano. You're a good sort, but Etsuko wouldn't like it much if I went about spilling her secrets."

Kitano eyed him. Lord Shin always made this bit look so easy, but it was harder than it seemed. He decided to go for the direct approach. "You know she was poisoned, right?"

Ishi blinked. "What?"

"Keep it quiet. Lord Shin doesn't want it getting around. You know how actors are." Kitano leaned toward him. "But yeah… poison."

Ishi frowned and looked away. "Wondered about that. Thought it might have been the case, but I wasn't sure."

"Why'd you think that?"

"She was worried about something happening."

"Did she say why?"

Ishi shook his head. "Not as such. But it ain't hard to figure out the reason." He hesitated. Kitano offered him the jug. Ishi took it and had a long swig. "She isn't getting married. She's entering a business arrangement."

Kitano frowned. "What does that mean, exactly?"

"You tell me. All I know is that's how she described it. A business arrangement."

"With the Scorpion," Kitano pressed. Ishi grimaced.

"Must be if what you say is true." He paused and offered Kitano the jug. "She didn't go into detail, you understand, but I put it together after a while. She wasn't happy about it, but she was... satisfied, I guess. Between that and the stuff she had me hide, didn't take a genius to see something was going on."

Kitano tensed. "What stuff did she have you hide, exactly?"

Ishi shrugged again. "Don't know, really. Papers or some such."

"Are they still there?" Kitano asked, trying to hide his sudden eagerness. Lord Shin was definitely going to be pleased with this, whatever it proved to be. Ishi hesitated.

"Poisoned," he said again.

Kitano nodded.

Ishi sighed and slapped the jug into Kitano's chest. "Follow me," he said as he rose smoothly and started toward the opposite end of the catwalk. Kitano climbed to his feet and carefully followed Ishi. They hurried down to the backstage area and then deeper still, through a trapdoor behind the curtain that led below the stage.

"Watch your head," Ishi called up as they clambered down the wooden ladder. "Being tall isn't much of an advantage down here."

Kitano followed him warily down into the musty dark. "Where exactly are we going?" he asked, ducking beneath a wooden support frame. He wasn't a tall man, exactly, but Ishi wasn't exaggerating. The space was cramped – claustrophobic.

"We're underneath the stage proper," Ishi murmured. They pitched their voices low, so as not to be heard by either the audience or those onstage. Ishi was used to the tight confines and moved swiftly and confidently through the labyrinth of wood and paper that made up the world beneath the stage. Kitano followed more slowly, stepping over coils of replacement rope and navigating between pallets of wood and rolls of paper.

He saw at least a dozen members of the stage crew, seeing to their duties in the shadowed recesses beneath the stage. Several noticed him and nodded in greeting. Kitano knew most of them by face if not name. A few of them even owed him money.

Ishi stopped suddenly, and Kitano nearly crashed into him. "There it is. You see?" Ishi pointed into the darkness ahead. It took Kitano's eyes a few moments to adjust to the gloom, but when it did, he saw a rectangle of light above. He realized they were standing under one of several trapdoors scattered about the length of the stage.

Each trapdoor opened onto a small bamboo platform that was connected to a counterweight pulley system of Ishi's design. The idea was that the trapdoor would open, depositing an actor onto the platform, which would then descend due to their weight.

Ishi was pointing at the pulley system. Kitano squinted into the gloom but saw nothing out of the ordinary. "Yes?" he said. Ishi snorted.

"I thought gamblers were supposed to be observant."

Kitano grunted. "Fine. I observe a pulley system."

Ishi laughed softly and made his way over to the pulley, careful to skirt the space where the platform would descend. "Here. Look at this." Kitano followed him and saw an extra layer of wood attached to the frame of the pulley. Ishi tapped the wood and then swiftly rotated it aside, revealing a hollow compartment. "Made these to store tools, extra rope, that sort of thing. Nothing worse than when a pulley breaks and you don't have the proper materials to hand to fix it."

Kitano peered into the compartment and saw not tools, but

papers wrapped in silk ribbon. Kitano could read and write some, and he recognized the beeswax seals that marked some of the folded papers as he flipped through them in the compartment. He saw the insignia of the Iuchi, the Akodo, even the Tonbo – and one set that bore the fanciful seal of the merchant, Odoma: a stylized soybean.

"You recognize these sigils?" Kitano asked.

Ishi shrugged. "Some of them. Not my business, though."

"Mine either," Kitano murmured.

"You're still looking at them, I notice."

"Yes, I am." Carefully, gently, he scooped the papers out and looked at Ishi. "I'll be taking these to Lord Shin. I trust you have no objections."

Ishi didn't look happy, but he shook his head. "No. No objections."

"Good. When did she have you hide these?"

"A few months ago," Ishi said. "Etsuko said they were valuable, and she was worried about thieves."

"Lot of thieves around here?"

"Lot of unfamiliar faces, I know that." Ishi ran a hand over his shorn pate. "Servants like you. All of them sneaking about like they were looking for something."

"Did you tell anyone?"

"Everyone knew," Ishi said bluntly. "Most thought they were spying on Etsuko for their masters."

Kitano peered at him. "What about you? What did you think?"

"I think she was more worried about her new in-laws."

"Before, when you said the Scorpions were creeping about, you think they were looking for this stuff?" Kitano asked, eyeing the papers. Letters, most of them. Professions of devotion, love poetry, some of it fairly erotic, at least insofar as he defined the term. He shook his head. In his experience, the nobility overcomplicated such things.

Ishi shook his head. "I don't think anything. But you tell me, why they were going into her dressing room with her not there."

"You didn't say it was her dressing room."

"It was implied," Ishi said.

Kitano decided not to argue the point. "So, who was there?" he asked, turning his attentions back to the letters. He wasn't expecting an answer, but the look on Ishi's face caught his attention. It was an expression of consternation. Kitano peered at him. "You know who it was, don't you?" he said.

Ishi stepped back, shaking his head. "No. Not for certain."

"Tell me," Kitano insisted. "Or tell Lord Shin. Your choice."

Ishi glared at him. "You're a hard man, Kitano."

Kitano bared his teeth in a grin. "So I've been told."

CHAPTER TWENTY-TWO
Scorpions

Things weren't quite as bad as Sanemon had made out, but they were close. Shin could feel the violence in the air as he rounded the corner and saw the standoff taking place in front of the dressing room. Kasami stood side-by-side with Arban and Gota, facing off against a trio of Scorpion retainers. The latter were between him and the door, and they whirled when he gave a polite cough to alert them to his presence.

Shin snapped open his fan and fluttered it before his face as he observed them. Konomi stood behind him, her own bodyguard watching the Scorpions warily. As if realizing they were outnumbered, the Scorpions moved their hands well away from their weapons. Shin gestured with his fan. "Well? Would you care to explain this?"

One of the Scorpions stepped forward. "My master bids me deliver a gift to Lady Etsuko to aid in her speedy recovery," he said. His mask was made of gold and silk. He wore robes of red and black, as did the others.

Shin clasped his hands behind his back and eyed them warily. These weren't simple servants; they were samurai. That was interesting. Why send samurai to deliver such a gift? "Lady

Etsuko is resting at present. The attending physician has asked that she not be disturbed under any circumstances."

"Our lord also requests that his own physician be allowed to see to her."

Gota stepped forward. "If they send for their physician, I will send for mine as well." He glared at the Scorpions as if they were responsible for Etsuko's condition. In contrast, Arban seemed at ease, his fingers tapping against the horsehide-wrapped hilt of his sword. The Ujik smiled slightly as he caught Shin's eye. Amusement gave way to something more speculative as his gaze strayed to Kasami.

Shin had no time to wonder what that might be about. He could feel the tension in the corridor like a storm brewing. The Scorpions were angry but also – nervous? Impatient? As if they had something they needed to attend to. Not just delivering a gift, he thought. "That will not be necessary. Doctor Sanki is the most capable physician in the city, and he is by her side even as we speak. She needs rest. This… disruption is anything but helpful in that regard." He looked down his nose at the offending parties.

Gota, at least, had the good grace to look embarrassed. It was hard to tell what the Scorpions were feeling given that their faces were hidden. From their body language, they'd relaxed somewhat. Maybe bloodshed could be avoided after all.

The spokesman for the Scorpion bowed. "We will inform our lord thus." He gestured, and the others turned as if to depart. Shin raised a hand, and they paused.

"A moment."

"My lord?" the spokesman said.

"The gift."

All three hesitated, looking at one another. "I do not understand, my lord," the spokesman said carefully.

"You said you brought a gift. Where is it? Might I see it?"

The spokesman's eyes narrowed behind his mask. He'd realized his error, but he recovered quickly. "My apologies, but it is for Lady Etsuko alone, my lord."

"Of course. But I am happy to deliver it to her if you like. On behalf of your lord." Shin did not take his gaze off the Scorpion as he spoke. He watched the eyes. You could tell a lot about what a man was thinking if you watched his eyes. The eyes gave away more than the face much of the time. They revealed the turmoil behind the mask.

But there was no turmoil in the Scorpion's eyes – just a cold flicker of evaluation. A warrior's judgment of whether the battle could be won or only lost. He knew which it was the moment the Scorpion made the decision.

"That will not be necessary, my lord. Thank you."

Shin inclined his head. "It is my pleasure. Please inform Lord Isamu that I wish to speak with him again – at intermission, say. If he could make himself available, I would be most obliged."

Again, a deep bow, and at Shin's gesture, they departed. Shin waited until they were out of earshot and turned to Lord Gota.

"Lord Gota, I thank you for your intervention. No doubt your timely arrival prevented Lady Etsuko from being unduly disturbed."

Gota flushed slightly. "I would like to pass along my apologies to her personally if I might." He glanced at the door to the dressing room, an almost plaintive look on his face. Shin felt a moment's pity for him but quickly quashed it.

"I would ask that you return to your box, Lord Gota. Your presence here is disruptive. It does neither the cast nor Lady Etsuko any good."

"Not until I know she is all right," Gota said.

"Fine. I will check on Lady Etsuko and let you know how she is. Then you will leave." At first, Gota made as if to argue but subsided with a brusque nod instead, much to Shin's relief. Shin turned to Kasami. "Wait here."

She bowed her head and turned to give Arban a hard look. The Ujik slouched against the wall, posture relaxed. He grinned lazily at Kasami, and she snorted and turned back to Shin. "Hurry back. Otherwise I might spill his guts on the floor."

"Try to restrain yourself." Shin stepped into the dressing room and called out for Sanki. The doctor was waiting for him beside Etsuko's body.

"I see we had another incident," Sanki said, looking up.

"Yes."

"Gota again?"

"Scorpions, actually."

"Well, that makes for a change."

"Kasami said you wanted to see me."

"Yes." Sanki peered at him. "I just wanted to tell you that I might have some answers for you in regard to how she died."

"You said she was poisoned."

"And so she was." Sanki leaned over the body, his head wreathed in pipe smoke. "The swelling is – was – localized to her throat and face where the makeup was applied thickest. The reaction would have taken a few minutes to set in. Likely she was already feeling the effects when she got onstage. It is… quite impressive that she lasted as long as she did."

"Ashina mentioned she'd suffered allergic reactions before."

"She might have thought she could endure it, my lord. Some people have an exaggerated opinion of their own capabilities."

Shin blinked, wondering if that last comment had been directed at him. He decided to ignore it as he usually did when

Sanki acted disrespectfully. A certain leniency was useful when it came to men like him. Even if the old man did not admit it, he appreciated it and understood how rare such a gift was.

"From what Ashina said, the previous reactions were embarrassing but not debilitating. Why was this one so different?"

"Look at this." Sanki picked up a wooden palette smeared with something white. "This is a sample I took from the jar. Note the discoloration."

Shin took the palette gingerly and studied it. The white paste was going yellow, and beads of something oily rested on the surface. "Is this because of the poison?"

"Yes. It wasn't well mixed. It's begun to separate."

"Then it must have happened sometime today." Shin sniffed the concoction. There was a faint, bitter odor to it. Noticeable, especially if you were slathering it on your face. Etsuko would have almost certainly noticed had it been left to sit. "What is it?"

"A derivation of wasp venom. I can't identify what type exactly, but I'm certain it's a derivative compound. They added it to the makeup sometime after it was mixed, so it was likely done recently."

"Then it happened after Ashina brought the ingredients back here," Shin said, putting the pieces together in his mind. Ashina had said she bought the ingredients and then Etsuko mixed them herself. That meant the poison had been added afterward.

"Most likely," Sanki said. "I hope that's of some help."

"It means I was right. Whoever did it is likely still here in the building." Whoever was responsible wanted to see Etsuko collapse. The method of delivery was too public. This wasn't simply a murder. It was an execution.

"You can't know that for sure."

"No, but it's a better hypothesis than the alternative." Shin handed the palette back. "If whoever did it has already escaped, then all this is for nothing."

"Cheery thought," Sanki said. "There are a few more tests I can run, of course. But I think I've squeezed every droplet of information I can without – well, you know." He gestured lazily to the body, and Shin grimaced.

"No. That won't be necessary, I think. Not at this time."

Sanki settled onto his heels with a relieved sigh. "Good. This isn't the ideal spot for investigating the contents of a human body." He looked at Etsuko. "What will we do with her... afterward?"

"I will pay for her funeral myself," Shin said softly. "It seems the least I can do."

Sanki gave a perplexed grunt. "It's hardly your fault, my lord. You didn't poison the poor woman, after all."

"Yes, but if I hadn't brought her here, she would not have died." Shin sank to his knees beside the body and bowed his head. It was the first time since her death that he'd allowed himself to think such thoughts. The sudden rush of guilt was almost too much to bear. "If I had not convinced myself it was the only way to save this troupe, she would not be here. She would still be alive, married perhaps. Happier, at least."

Sanki was silent for a moment, then he gave a bitter laugh. "It's not for us to say whether she'd have been happy or not. Someone might just as easily have killed her there as here." He fixed Shin with a steady look. "At least here, there's you."

Shin couldn't bring himself to meet the doctor's gaze. "Yes. Here is me." In death, Etsuko was smaller than he remembered. It was as if all that had made her who she was had fled at the moment of dying. What was left was nothing at all like the woman she had been. Just a shrunken shell. He tore his eyes away and stood.

"Are you willing to stay for a while longer?" he asked.

"Of course. The dead are convivial companions." Sanki paused. "Are you all right, my lord? You look peaked."

"Tired. I am just tired. But I do not think I will get the opportunity to rest until after all this has been taken care of." Shin went to the door. He paused and cast a final look at the body. A part of him felt he ought to apologize despite the ridiculousness of the impulse. Instead, he merely nodded to Sanki and left.

Konomi was waiting for him in the corridor. "You should probably be getting back to Yasamura," Shin said before she could ask him anything. "I'd hate for him to think I'd kidnapped you or some such nonsense."

Konomi patted his arm. "More like he'll be wondering where you are."

Shin smiled. "Yes, well, he wouldn't be the first in that regard."

"Is he the one who…" She trailed off with a surreptitious gesture in the direction of Gota, who stood some distance away. From his body language, the Badger clearly wished to speak to Shin but seemed uncertain as to how best approach him. Shin raised his fan in acknowledgment but kept his attentions on Konomi.

Shin shook his head. "No," he murmured. "I am fairly certain Gota does not possess that sort of cold cunning. He's a man of passion. Of sudden fury and quick abatement." He looked at her. "The Scorpion, on the other hand, are infamous for their use of such substances."

"I believe I mentioned that earlier," she said.

"She speaks wisely," Kasami said.

"Yes, thank you." Shin looked down at Kasami. "Did Gota say anything that struck you as unusual?" he asked. "Before the Scorpions showed up, I mean."

Kasami shook her head. "Nothing but the usual bluster." She paused. "I'd say he genuinely wants to see her. But the Scorpions... they might be a different matter."

"Yes, sending three samurai to deliver a gift is a bit much." Shin fell silent, pondering the matter. "Unless they were here for something else."

Konomi frowned. "Like what?"

Shin paused. "That is something I need to find out. I need to talk to Isamu again." He caught Kasami's eye and noted the expression on her face. She had something she wanted to tell him. Quickly, he took Konomi's hand in his own. "I fear I've taken up too much of your time, Konomi. I'd hate for you to miss the rest of the performance on my behalf. Would it be rude of me to ask you to find your own way back to your box?"

Konomi gave him a knowing look. He suspected she knew full well what he was up to. "A bit. But I think Hachi and I will manage. Still, I expect a full accounting at intermission, Shin. Don't make me come look for you." She gave him a friendly swat with her fan and motioned to Hachi. "Come Hachi. Let us return to our proper place in the heavens."

Shin watched them go, then turned to Kasami. "Well?" he asked softly.

Kasami leaned close. "The Scorpion have been hanging around a lot more than we knew about. They paid a call on Lady Yua and on Nao."

"Nao?" Shin said, raising an eyebrow. "What would they want with him?"

"Not just him. Chika said they've been hanging around backstage for weeks."

"Chika?" Shin turned. "Where is she, by the way? I need to speak with her." He spied the actress loitering near the opposite end of the corridor, speaking quietly with Sanemon. He gestured to her, but she turned and hurried away. He frowned and motioned to Sanemon, who came over, albeit somewhat reluctantly.

"My lord?" he asked.

"I must speak with Chika – and Botan as well – at their earliest convenience. By which I mean my earliest convenience. Where are they?"

Sanemon bowed his head. "Getting ready for the last scene before intermission, my lord. If you hurry, you might be able to catch them before they go onstage."

Shin nodded. "Excellent. But first, I must speak to Lord Gota."

Gota was waiting impatiently for Shin when he at last turned to face the Badger. The big man looked anxious. Not nervous, but worried. Shin smiled in a friendly fashion and gestured. "Come, Lord Gota. Let us walk a bit and talk." He caught Kasami's eye. "I'm sure you and Arban can occupy yourselves for a few more minutes."

Kasami glanced at the Ujik, and her jaw tightened. But she didn't protest. "Is she well?" Gota asked softly as he and Shin ambled down the corridor. The performance was still going on, and the noise of it could be heard through the paper walls. Gota didn't seem to mind that he was missing it.

"As well as can be expected," Shin said with only a slight hesitation. Gota did not appear to notice. Instead, he knotted his thick fingers and looked at the wall.

"That is good. She has been through much. The life of an actress is a hard one."

"Yes. So I am told. I will come to speak with you at intermission if I might. There we can discuss the events of today in a more convivial environment."

Gota frowned. "I don't see what there is to discuss."

"And that is the difference between us, my lord." Shin tapped him gently on the chest. "The way I see it, you and I have much to discuss. But later." Shin turned away, folding his hands behind his back. "For now, please enjoy the show."

CHAPTER TWENTY-THREE
Stagecraft

Shin made his way to the communal dressing room, trying to organize his thoughts as he went. The Kitsuki Method of investigation placed an emphasis on physical evidence – too much emphasis in his opinion. He preferred to determine motive and work backward from there. Once you knew the why, you quickly found the who and the how.

Etsuko had been poisoned. Sanki had proven that beyond a shadow of a doubt. Someone had gotten access to her makeup and tampered with it, but why? What purpose did her death serve? What was the killer's motive? Revenge seemed the most obvious answer, but whose revenge? A wronged assistant, an ex-lover – the possibilities seemed endless. He paused. According to the music coming from the stage, it was almost the end of the scene. One to go, and then intermission would follow. He was running out of time, and so far, all he really knew for certain was that a woman was dead, and it was no accident.

The communal dressing room was crowded between scenes. Screens had been set up to provide a modicum of privacy, but mostly they were left folded so the actors could talk among themselves as they got ready for their next appearance onstage.

Pages scurried underfoot as Shin entered the room, bringing new wigs and costume changes to the actors who needed them. Assistants helped actors get dressed or apply makeup, and others passed around food and drink.

A hush fell over the assemblage as Shin navigated the room, searching for either Botan or Chika. Conversation resumed in his wake, but it was of a more subdued variety. He gave a halfhearted wave and a smile to those watching but was rewarded with hurried departures. He was an intruder here despite his best efforts. Not unwelcome; never that. But his presence was making them uneasy. He resolved to be quick.

Botan was easy enough to find. He was seated near the wall, working on a cup of tea and a bowl of rice. The actor smiled nervously around a mouthful of rice as Shin came to a halt before him. He made to stand, but Shin waved his fan. "No, no, please sit. My apologies for this interruption, Master Botan. Did Master Sanemon tell you I wished to speak to you?"

Botan swallowed. "He- he did, my lord," he gulped. "Though I don't know how much help I can be. Does- does this have something to do with Etsuko – I mean, *Lady* Etsuko?"

"Indeed, it does," Shin said. He opened his fan and attempted to stir the muggy air. "I am told she held something of a grudge against you. That, in fact, she tried to have Sanemon expel you from the troupe."

Botan nearly choked on a swallow of tea. He dabbed hurriedly at his lips, taking pains not to smudge his makeup. Shin could not help but admire the man's dexterity. Botan put his meal aside and nodded. "She did, my lord, yes. Tried to have me expelled, I mean."

"Might I ask why?"

Botan glanced around. Shin noted that the actors closest to them were doing their best to appear as if they weren't eavesdropping. Botan didn't seem to mind. In fact, it seemed to please him. Perhaps he liked being the center of attention. "I lingered where I should not have, my lord. That is all there was to it."

"If that is all there was to it, I would not have asked you to elaborate." Shin smiled as if making a jest, and Botan chuckled dutifully.

"Yes, my lord, of course. I, well, I was backstage, practicing my tumbling, when I noted the presence of someone who was not part of the cast."

"And who was this person?"

"I don't know," Botan said plainly. "Never seen them before in my life."

"Man? Woman?"

"Could have been either. Wearing a mask." Botan tapped the side of his nose gently so as not to smudge his makeup. He leaned toward Shin conspiratorially. "I've heard that she's engaged to be wed, to a Scorpion no less."

Shin inclined his head slightly, neither confirming nor denying this. Instead, he said, "Could this person you saw have been a Scorpion?"

Botan sat back. "No clue, my lord. Anyone can wear a mask, after all. I wear them myself for certain roles." He smiled and shook his head. "I followed them, of course. Sometimes thieves try to slip in and steal a bit of rope or something. Thought I might dissuade them, you know…"

"How very commendable of you," Shin said, not believing it for a moment. Botan didn't strike him as a man given to flights of courage. More than likely, he'd simply been nosy, looking for something to gossip about. "And this stranger, they went into Lady Etsuko's dressing room?"

"The very place, my lord. I must have stepped on a board wrong or something, for I gave myself away just as Etsuko greeted them. She spotted me right off and gave me such a glare I feared for my life."

"And then?"

"Well, the next day, she tried to have Master Sanemon expel me. Said I was skulking about. Called me a thief." Botan assumed an air of wounded dignity. "I've never stolen anything in my life, except maybe the spotlight on occasion."

Shin snapped his fan closed. "Did she have reason to believe you might have stolen something? I understand she also accused your fellow cast member Chika of theft as well."

Botan frowned. "You'd have to ask Chika about that, my lord."

"I intend to. You said a moment ago that you'd heard she was to be wed. Was that an open secret? What I mean to say is, was it a topic of backstage gossip?"

"It was, my lord," Chika called out from across the room. The constant murmur of voices fell silent. Shin turned. Chika was crouched on a stool set near the far wall, hunched over a small mirror and an even smaller makeup bench. She paused, brush in hand, and said, "We all knew it was only a matter of time. The way she prowled about, she was going to pounce sooner or later."

Shin paused, then thanked Botan for his help and strode across the room. Chika looked up as he approached. "Is there something I can do for you, my lord?" Her arch tone set off an eruption of giggles from her nearest neighbors.

Shin paused. The question was a loaded one, and Chika knew it. It was as much a tease as an invitation. Shin knew his reputation, and though he had never propositioned any member of the troupe, some of them likely thought it was only a matter of time and were impatient to get on with it. "I'd like to talk if you have a moment," he said, emphasizing the word *talk*. It didn't help.

Chika smiled, and one of the other actresses nearby gave a sharp whistle. The others attempted to smother their laughter as Chika rose gracefully to her feet. "Of course, my lord. It would be my pleasure."

Shin gestured toward a screen at the back of the room. "In private, please."

More laughter and more eyes on them now. Shin felt a sudden flush of annoyance, which he quickly stifled. He swiftly unfolded the screen to its fullest, blocking sight of them from the rest of the actors. When he turned to her, Chika was looking at him expectantly. Shin hesitated, wondering if he'd made an error in judgment. He pushed the thought aside and tried to concentrate on the matter at hand. "Tell me about Lady Etsuko," he said.

Chika peered at him, a calculating expression on her face. "Okuni was well-liked, my lord. When she departed, she left a hole that anyone would have a hard time filling. We were – are – a family of sorts. The best troupes always are."

"And Lady Etsuko has not endeared herself to the family."

"Rather the opposite, my lord. It was all Master Sanemon could do to keep some of us from murdering her…" She paused. "Is that why you're here, my lord? Did she collapse because someone did something to her?"

Shin gave a wry smile. "That is what I am trying to determine."

Chika laughed and clapped her hands. "I knew it! One of Rin's assistants was by here earlier, mentioning you'd been talking to his master. I said it to the others then. Lord Shin is investigating a case!"

Shin's smile became somewhat strained. It hadn't occurred to him at the time how quickly gossip might travel backstage. Despite his admonishments to Rin and the others, it was clear everyone likely knew what he was doing if not the real reason why. Still, it couldn't be helped. "Yes, well, that is why I am here now. Uni mentioned you'd had an unfortunate encounter with Lady Etsuko some weeks ago. She accused you of stealing something of hers, did she not?"

Chika flushed beneath her makeup. "I didn't, my lord, I swear to you."

"What was it you were supposed to have stolen?"

"Papers of some kind, my lord. Letters, I think. Though why anyone would want her letters I don't know. She said someone had been rooting around in her things and demanded that Master Sanemon declare her dressing room off-limits to everyone save herself and that wilting flower she calls an understudy."

"Ashina," Shin supplied. Chika nodded. "There's a sad sight if you don't mind me saying so, my lord. Etsuko has that poor girl on a tight leash. She refuses to stand up for herself." She paused. "If we're being honest, Master Nao is the only one who can stand up to Etsuko without flinching."

"Has he had cause to do so often?"

Another nod. "After the incident with the letters, Master Nao started interceding every time she so much as raised her voice. The moment she starts in on someone, he's there." She looked at him. "He's the only reason most of us have stayed, my lord."

Though he knew it wasn't intended as such, Shin couldn't help but feel he was being chastised. Despite his best intentions, his decision to employ Etsuko had nearly torn his troupe apart. He wondered if perhaps he should have asked the troupe before hiring her. He wouldn't make that mistake next time. "Master Nao has my compliments in that case." He paused. "Why did she accuse you?"

Chika tensed. "I don't know."

Shin read the lie in her eyes. He paused, wondering whether to let it rest, then said, "Would it have anything to do with Odoma?"

Chika looked away. "Of course you know about that, my lord," she said after a moment. "I should have realized." She sighed and gave him a sad grin. "Yes, I think so. She squeezed him for all he was worth and then moved on. But I'm not so greedy. There was a bit left in him. Plenty for me."

"Do you intend to…" Shin began.

Chika laughed, and her fingers traced the embroidery on his sleeve, fingering the material. "No, my lord! Not with him at least. I value myself more highly than that. No, Odoma is a rich man with bad habits and little common sense."

"Entertaining, in other words," Shin said. He absently took a half-step back, and she made a moue of disappointment. "Have you spoken to him lately? Today, say?"

She gave him a cagey look. "Briefly, my lord."

Shin paused, wondering if Odoma's earlier reluctance to attend today's performance had been a sham. "Might I ask about what?"

"A lady never tells, my lord," Chika said, eyes downcast.

"Did it have to do with Lady Etsuko?"

Chika hesitated. "We might have discussed her but only a bit. She's a sore subject for him as you might imagine."

"I'm told she has a reputation for being spiteful."

"So do I," Chika said with a savage smile. "Why do you think I snapped up Odoma?"

Shin nodded. He'd suspected as much, but it was good to have it confirmed. That still left one question unanswered, however. "These letters you were supposed to have stolen – did she say who they were from?"

Chika frowned. "Not that I heard, my lord. They must have been important, though. I can't imagine her getting so angry otherwise."

"Could it have had to do with her engagement?" he asked, watching her expression carefully. The bewilderment he saw there was real.

"I suppose, my lord."

Shin closed his fan and tapped it against his lips, thinking. He recalled something Konomi had said about Etsuko and blackmail. Could that be the answer? Possibly. He thought perhaps he needed to find those letters. They might hold the key to everything. He looked at Chika. "Thank you, Chika. You have been most helpful."

"You are most welcome, my lord," Chika said. She paused, a speculative look on her face. "Is it true Shinjo Yasamura is in the audience today, my lord?"

Shin peered at her. "It is, yes. Why?"

Chika tossed her head. "No reason, my lord." She tapped her lip. "Though, if I might be so bold, he is a handsome man."

Shin frowned. "I hadn't noticed."

"You could do worse, my lord."

"Thank you. I think you can return to your preparations now," Shin said, sliding the privacy screen aside. He stopped, struck by the sight of half a dozen actors pretending not to have been eavesdropping. He wondered what it said for the future of the troupe that none of them were very good at it.

"My lord…" Chika asked from behind him. He turned. Her

expression was serious. "Regardless of what you might think, none of us would ever harm Lady Etsuko. Embarrass her? Certainly. But harm her? We'd only be harming ourselves."

Shin looked at her. "What do you mean?"

Chika looked around. "We know you brought her here to change our fortunes, my lord. We need her. You would not have inflicted her upon us if that was not the case. Master Sanemon made that very clear." She folded her hands before her and bowed her head. "We were all willing to endure her tantrums if it meant our success as a troupe."

A murmur of agreement went around the room. Shin turned, studying the assembled actors. All had the same look on their face as Chika – a sort of grim determination utterly at odds with their previous behavior.

"That is to your credit," he said softly. "But it is not something you should have had to endure. In the future, I will endeavor to be more attentive to the needs of the troupe. What else is a patron for, after all?"

Chika smiled brightly. "In that case, we could all use an increase in wages." Laughter followed her comment, and Shin smiled.

"Let's see how the performance goes first. If we can make it through without any further problems, we'll discuss it." With that, Shin made his departure.

He found Kitano was waiting for him in the corridor. "My lord, I found something," he said without preamble. He pulled a folded piece of paper from his robes and offered it to Shin. Shin took it, saw the Iuchi insignia stamped on the broken seal, and flicked his eyes to his servant, wondering at the serendipity of it all. Kitano grinned. "There's more where that came from. Lots more."

"And what is this, exactly?" Shin asked as he unfolded the paper. He scanned it, frowning. "Ah. Oh. Oh my," he murmured. Kitano nodded.

"They're all like that."

Shin glanced at him. "You read them?"

Kitano shrugged. "Thought I ought to see what they were, my lord." He grinned somewhat sheepishly. "Before I bothered you with them, I mean."

"Obviously," Shin said. "Do you know what these are?"

Kitano, who clearly did know, said, "No, my lord."

Shin laughed. "That's what I thought. It's what we've been looking for, Kitano." He smacked his palm with the missive. "I do believe you've found our killer's motive."

CHAPTER TWENTY-FOUR
Intermission

Nao stamped his foot and made a wide, wild slash – a desperate blow, thrown by an injured man. Streamers of red silk spilled from a concealed pocket on the side of his robes, representing his wound. A lucky slash by an enraged cousin. Paper blossoms drifted down from the catwalks above, lending a surreal air to the scene.

Cousins, wearing ornate masks, bounded and spun about him, wooden weapons spinning in their hands. A frenzied duel between a lone swordsman and half a dozen determined foes. Ashina watched from the dais, her face composed and solemn. The look of a woman forced to lead her lover into a trap certain to claim his life.

It was a brazen scene meant to test a critic's composure. Every line, every gesture, dripped with the sort of melodrama that made the better class of audience wince. But it played well in the benches. The few times he caught a glimpse of the stalls, he saw rapt faces. That encouraged him to draw things out a bit.

Normally, the scene was over swiftly. A few spinning slashes, some shouts, and the betrayed lover flees to an unknown fate. At least until after intermission. But Nao thought the audience deserved a bit more entertainment than that, especially given Etsuko's collapse. He'd made his intentions clear to the others early in the scene. It was a poor actor who improvised without warning.

The flower petals were also an improvisation, though this time on Sanemon's part. He'd thought such a pivotal scene needed a bit of extra oomph. Sometimes, Nao wondered whether there was a poet hiding inside Sanemon. Not a good poet, perhaps, but a poet nonetheless.

He mimed blocking a blow that might have decapitated him had it actually connected and had the sword been real. He stamped again, uttering a wordless cry that could be heard in the farthest stalls. His opponents retreated like startled birds before swooping in again. As he turned, he found his gaze drifting up toward the boxes. The curtains were open on all of them, save one – the box belonging to the Scorpion.

Nao wondered if they were even watching, then he wondered why they'd even come at all. Perhaps to check on Etsuko. It did not surprise him that she had chosen a Scorpion for her husband. Like called to like. He was curious as to whether Lord Shin had yet told her fiancé that the engagement was off.

A shout from one of his opponents drew his mind back to the scene. It was time to retreat. He parried a tentative strike and took a step back. The flower path beckoned – his flight would take him through the audience. He cast a last, lingering look toward Ashina and saw she was weeping real tears. He could tell by the tracks they left in her makeup. He paused. For a moment, everything was off-kilter, but he recovered swiftly. With a dramatic flourish, he spun and stumbled away from the stage. The suitors pursued to the edge of the flower path where Ashina's cry stopped them. Her voice quavered eerily, and Nao resolved to compliment her on her skill at the first opportunity. If he didn't know better, he would have sworn she was actually distraught.

The audience stirred as he ran past. Behind him, a swell of music signaled the scene's end as the curtain began its inexorable slide. Overhead, the drum sounded, letting the audience know intermission was about to begin.

He vanished through the black curtains of the concealed walkway and found Choki waiting for him, still clad in the costume of a courtier from the previous scene. "That was wonderful, master," Choki enthused as they headed backstage. "The audience was eating it up with both hands. I've never seen them so enraptured."

"Yes," Nao said. "A good day's work if I do say so myself." He pulled the rest of the red silk out of its hidden pocket and thrust it into Choki's hands.

"And Ashina, she was amazing," Choki continued.

Nao glanced at him, slightly irked. "Yes, though I think the tears were a bit much. Real emotion has no place onstage." He handed Choki his sword as well. "I shall have to have a talk with her later once the theater empties out for intermission."

"Haven't you heard, master? Lord Shin has decided to keep the doors closed."

"He what?" Nao frowned. "Is he mad? The audience will riot."

Choki shrugged. "I can't say whether he's mad or not, but I heard he's bringing the tea sellers inside and letting them sell directly to the stalls. They're crowded at the doors now, waiting to be let in."

Nao shook his head, bemused by the thought. It was scandalous. Against years of tradition. It would probably catch on quite quickly. Nothing shopkeepers liked more than a captive customer. "Hopefully he'll remember to send someone backstage for us." He paused. "Speaking of which, I heard there was some ruckus earlier. What was that about?"

"The Scorpions, master. Three of them."

Nao froze but only for a moment. "What about them?" They stepped through the curtains separating the passage from backstage. Things were bustling – scenery was being moved, and pages were scurrying on various errands. The actors playing the cousins wandered past, laughing, already stripping out of their costumes.

"They wanted to see Lady Etsuko. They were very insistent."

"I expect they were. What happened?"

"Lord Shin saw them off." Choki hesitated, and Nao thought there might have been something else he wanted to say, but the moment passed swiftly. "They were not happy, master. Neither was Lord Gota."

Nao sniffed. "How like Etsuko, leaving a mess for everyone else to clean up." He shook his head. "Ah, well. Let Lord Shin deal with it. That's his job anyway."

"Yes, master." Choki frowned. "Master Sanemon has said that I'm to play one of the monks in the next scene after intermission."

Nao grimaced. "Yes."

"Was that your suggestion, master?"

"Yes, Choki. It was."

"They don't have any lines," Choki protested. "They just wander across the stage."

"They don't wander, Choki. They kneel in prayer before the shrine our hero flees to in order to recuperate. They are, in fact, very important to the scene."

"When are you going to let me do something – anything – other than just stand in the background?" Choki asked heatedly. "Ashina is out there right now. I should be as well!"

Nao rounded on him. "Why? What does one have to do with the other?"

"I'm ready," Choki said. "Tell Master Sanemon I'm ready. *Please*." His hands had balled into fists, and his face was set in a determined expression. "You know I'm ready."

Nao hesitated. He was saved from having to answer by a voice from behind him.

"Nao."

Nao frowned. The voice was familiar as was the derision in it. He gestured. "Go get my costume ready, Choki, if you would. We'll discuss your request later."

"Master, are you–" Choki began hesitantly. His eyes darted to the newcomers. Nao snapped his fingers imperiously, drawing the young man's eyes back to him.

"Costume, Choki. And have Uni ready a selection of wigs, please." He waved a hand in dismissal. "Go. I will be along shortly." Only when Choki was safely out of sight did he turn to face the newcomers. There were three of them. Scorpions. Probably the same ones Choki had just mentioned. He recognized their masks. Among the Scorpion, a mask was as good as a face when it came to familiarity.

"Arata, how lovely to see you again." Nao held out his hands to the one in the lead. "Come, let me embrace you, cousin."

Arata did not move to embrace him. But he'd always been the icy sort. His eyes glittered with malice above the red of his veil. "We are not cousins any longer, Nao. Or had you forgotten?"

Nao gave his best winsome smile. "You're not still upset with me about that, are you? It was so long ago. We were barely past our naming ceremonies." He plucked a flower from a nearby basket. It was fake, of course. The blossom was made of carefully folded paper and the stem was wood.

"Some things one does not forget," one of the other Scorpions – a woman in a demon mask – said.

"Is that you, Nagisa, hiding behind the demon's smile?" Nao asked, pretending to smell the flower. The woman tensed. Nao smiled. "Ah. Last I saw you, you were but a child, chasing chickens with a paring knife."

Nagisa glared at him from behind her mask. "I am no longer a child."

"And I am no longer beholden to the traditions of the Scorpion." Nao tossed her the flower, but she did not catch it. Instead, it tumbled down her chest and settled on the floor. He clucked his tongue chidingly and turned to the third of the Scorpions. "And where Arata and Nagisa go, can stoic Ozuru be far behind?"

Ozuru grunted. It might have been a greeting. Then again, knowing Ozuru, it probably wasn't. He'd never been the talkative sort. Nao smiled and looked at the three of them. "You three – always tagging along with Isamu, hoping the older boy would let you play his little games. The more things change, the more they stay the same."

"You slimy–" Nagisa began, reaching for her blade. Arata gestured sharply.

"He's trying to provoke you."

"And you always fall for it," Nao said.

"You are lucky, Nao. Isamu told us you were not to be harmed. Otherwise, we might be inclined to give you the beating you have so long deserved."

Nao tittered, not because he found Arata's words particularly amusing but because he knew it annoyed them to be laughed at. If there was a sense of humor between them, he couldn't recall seeing it. "Promises, promises," he said in a soft falsetto.

"I suppose you three were the ones who tried to break into my dressing room?"

"It is Lady Etsuko's dressing room," Nagisa said.

"Our dressing room," Nao corrected, letting a bit of steel creep into his voice. "We shared quarters as well as top billing."

"She must be delighted with that," Nagisa shot back.

Nao ignored her and looked at Arata. "What is it you want, then? Be quick. Some of us have to change clothes." He gestured to his costume.

"Lord Isamu wishes to see you."

"Does he? How flattering." Despite his words, Nao had no intention of going with them. "But I am simply too busy at the moment to greet a fan, I fear. After the performance, perhaps." He turned as if to go, and Ozuru grabbed him. Nao froze. "Let go of me," he said, his voice deepening. "Now."

Ozuru hesitated, then released him. Nao turned. "Such disrespect does you no credit, cousins. Nor does it do credit to Isamu."

"Do not speak his name with such familiarity," Nagisa said. "You no longer have that privilege. Speak so of him again, and I will take out your tongue."

"And what will you do with it, I wonder? I dread to think," Nao shot back. Nagisa hesitated, clearly confused. Then, she'd never been the sharpest. But before she could reply, Arata intervened.

"Did you receive our message, Nao?"

"Message?" Nao hesitated. He remembered the puzzle message that had been delivered to Sanemon during the first act but let no sign of the realization show on his face. "What message?"

Arata's eyes narrowed. "You know what I'm talking about. Don't play the fool."

Nao shook his head. "I genuinely have no idea what you are ranting about," he lied. "Just as I genuinely have no intention of speaking to your master… unless he comes to see me himself. I am not some lackey to be chivvied by bodyguards."

"You disrespectful little fool," Arata murmured after a moment's shocked silence. "He is trying to help you."

"Not that you deserve it," Nagisa muttered. Arata glanced at her, and she fell silent.

"Do not be so quick to cast our master's offer back in his face," he said. "The past is a closed book, and the future is as yet unwritten."

"How pithy," Nao said. "Did he write that for you?"

Arata's gaze sharpened, and Nao felt a chill. It was hard to get under Arata's skin, but when you managed it, the results were never pretty. He stepped back, putting some distance between himself and the three of them.

"Tell Isamu I am happy to meet with him but only on my terms. My days of serving at the pleasure of the Bayushi are done. I am a free man."

Nagisa laughed at this, but Arata silenced her with a gesture. "I will tell him. He will not be pleased."

"When has he ever been pleased with me?" Nao said without thinking.

Arata surprised him by nodding. "True enough." The cold look had faded from his eyes. He gestured, and the others turned to depart. Arata hesitated. "You are many things, Nao, but not a fool," he said softly. "Never that. Do not let your pride lead you into making a foolish mistake."

Startled by this advice, Nao said nothing. Only when they'd left and he was alone did he find his voice. "It wouldn't be the first time," he murmured.

CHAPTER TWENTY-FIVE
Letters

Shin made his way back to the dressing room, reading one of the letters Kitano had brought him. The letter was a brief thing – poetry, mostly, and poor poetry at that. Declarations of love and demands for the same with a few veiled threats mixed in. The writing was neat and tidy. Too neat. The scrawl of a clerk, perhaps, or a scribe. He sniffed the letter and detected the faintest remnant of a curious odor – perfume, perhaps?

Kitano trotted in his wake. "What now, my lord?" Shin glanced at him, reflecting on his good fortune in stumbling across a man like Kitano. The former gambler had proven himself a useful sort of fellow more than once of late. He aided Shin's investigations immeasurably and had proven himself worthy of trust – at least to a certain extent. He was fairly sure Kitano regularly raided his stores of wine, but he could overlook such indulgences so long as it yielded results.

Shin tapped his chin with the letter. "Now I need you to take a message to Lord Isamu for me. I would like to speak with him in my box if he finds it convenient."

"And if he doesn't?"

Shin paused. He sniffed the letter again. Ordinarily, he had a good nose for perfume. He found it annoying not to be able to identify the scent. He took a deep whiff, trying to provoke his thought processes. When the answer came, he blinked in surprise. "Ah," he murmured. Then, "Oh."

The odor he'd detected wasn't perfume at all. It was tea. Spring's Smile to be exact.

"My lord?" Kitano pressed. Shin blinked, startled.

"What?"

"What should I do if Lord Isamu doesn't find it convenient?"

"I think he will," Shin said, but before he could elaborate, he heard Kasami shout from the direction of the dressing room. He brushed past Kitano and rounded the corner to find his bodyguard in a standoff with a familiar, if sour, face. Shin recognized the Lion samurai from earlier – Minami's bodyguard.

"Out of my way," he barked, glaring at Kasami.

"I think not," she said with what Shin thought was commendable mildness.

The Lion grimaced. "If you do not move, I will–"

"You will what?" Shin interrupted. The Lion whirled, his eyes widening as he realized who Shin was.

"My lord, I–" he began, but Shin raised a hand to silence him. He looked past the Lion at Kasami. Her hand hovered over her sword, and the look on her face said the Lion was lucky Shin had intervened.

"What happened?" Shin asked her.

"He demanded to see Lady Etsuko. Said Lady Minami wished to check on her." Kasami lowered her hand but continued to stare daggers at the Lion. "I told him she was not to be disturbed, and he tried to push past me."

"I'm surprised you didn't kill him," Shin said.

"You told me to be tactful."

The Lion turned as if to argue with her, but something in her expression made him fall into a curt silence. Shin looked at him. "We keep meeting like this, and you have yet to introduce yourself," he said. He paused and snapped his fingers. "That's where I know you from. You came to my house during that business with the poisoned rice last year. You were rude then as well."

The Lion stepped back, his broad features flushing in what might have been anger or embarrassment. His big hands clenched and then relaxed. He stepped back, a surly expression on his face. "My apologies," he growled.

"Apologize to my bodyguard as well, please. It is she whom you offended."

Again, he looked as if he wished to argue. But again, wisdom won out. He sighed and bowed his head to Kasami. "I... apologize." Kasami stared at him for a moment longer, then nodded briskly and slid aside.

Shin replaced her in front of the door of the dressing room, just to make his feeling on any chance of entry plain. "Good. Well done. Now, what's your name?"

"Yoku," the Lion growled.

"A pleasure to make your acquaintance, Yoku. Tell Lady Minami that Lady Etsuko is resting comfortably and that I shall come see her during intermission at the first opportunity." Shin spread his arms, his hands gripping either side of the doorway. "You may go now."

Yoku stared at him for a moment, then turned on his heel and departed without a word, nearly colliding with Kitano in the process. Shin looked at Kasami. "Interesting, don't you think?"

"Annoying, is what I think."

"That too. Has anyone else come sniffing around other than Yoku there and our Scorpion friends earlier?" Shin paused. "Other than Gota and Arban, of course."

"Not that I've noticed." Kasami hesitated. "I saw one of the Tonbo servants scurrying around, but Lord Azuma's men caught him and sent him on his way with a thump on the ear." She sounded as if she approved of it as well. "They're all very concerned about her."

"I don't think it's her they're worried about."

"What do you mean?" Kasami asked, looking at him in puzzlement.

"Let's just say Kitano has proven his worth," Shin said, holding up the letter he'd been looking at earlier. "Etsuko was engaged in something illicit, something that may well taint by association. Whoever poisoned her was making a statement, possibly in regard to whatever she was up to."

"You think it was one of her... paramours," Kasami said with a frown of disapproval. Whether she disapproved of the implications or the idea of paramours in general, Shin couldn't say, and he didn't feel it polite to ask.

"I think that is more likely than any of her fellow cast members. Poison is not the tool of the angry. It is a tool of the calculating. One can be both, obviously, but it takes a certain sort of mind to conceive of such a tactic."

"What about Nao?" she asked.

"Yes, what about me?" Nao said as he swept down the corridor toward them. He stopped in front of Shin. "Can I be of some service? Only I really would like to change and have a cup of tea before the end of intermission."

Shin hesitated. "You have an hour at least. Perhaps you could spare me a moment or two of your time."

Nao studied him for a few seconds, then nodded. "Of course, my lord. Anything for our illustrious patron. If I might..." He gestured to the door, and Shin stepped aside, sliding it open as he did so. Shin motioned for Kasami and Kitano to wait outside and followed the actor into the dressing room.

Nao turned away as Shin closed the door behind him. "You've made quite the stir, my lord. Rin and Uni are beside themselves, I'm told."

Shin bowed his head. "My apologies. It was not my intent to upset anyone."

"What is intended and what actually occurs are often two different things, my lord," Nao said as he began to undress in the center of the room. His fingers moved briskly, and he'd disrobed almost before Shin was aware of the act. His lean frame was pale but marked by several vivid scars that stood out like crimson bands against his flesh. Shin stared at them, bewildered, wondering how and where the actor had acquired them until Nao said, "You wish to speak with me about Etsuko, I suppose."

"Yes."

Nao glanced toward the bedroom. "Is she still in there?"

Shin nodded. "Yes."

"Sick, is she?"

"Poisoned."

Nao stopped, mouth open, clearly shocked. So clearly, in fact, that Shin knew it was an act. "Poisoned? How dreadful," Nao said.

"You knew."

Nao paused. "I suspected."

"But you did not share these suspicions."

"I would have, had you asked," Nao said with an air of injured dignity.

"I didn't have time. You fled as quickly as Rin and Uni."

"I had to be onstage."

Shin let this go. "You are here now. Tell me."

Nao was silent for a moment. Then, "Etsuko had few friends. None, in fact. At least that I knew of. But she made enemies easily."

"So I have heard."

"Knowing this, I merely jumped to the obvious conclusion. She wouldn't be the first actor to wind up swallowing something she shouldn't have."

"She didn't swallow it. It was in her makeup."

Nao flinched. It was so sudden, so quick, that Shin almost missed it. He filed it away. "When did it happen?" the actor asked.

Shin paused, considering whether to answer. Something told him Nao already knew and was asking only for appearance's sake. "It would have had to have been sometime before she went onstage."

Nao pressed a hand to his chest, the picture of horrified distress. "I just spoke to her, it seems. We traded barbs in the wings. When she collapsed, I thought…" He trailed off. Shin seized on the words.

"You thought what?"

Nao selected a new kimono from one of the mannequins in the corner. "That she was faking, honestly. She had a reputation, you know."

"So I have been told. But I have never heard of her leaving a stage in such a manner."

Nao paused. "No. Whatever else, my lord, she was a professional. At least when it came to the performance itself."

"What about afterwards?"

"Afterwards, my lord?"

Shin nodded. "After you had gotten her backstage, and seen the swelling – the rash… what did you think then?"

Nao hesitated before answering. "That she'd somehow suffered an allergic reaction. Though I could not fathom how it might have occurred." He looked at Shin. "Have you found the poisoner yet?"

"No. I hoped you might help me with that. Who might have had access to Etsuko's makeup? Besides yourself, I mean."

Nao frowned again. "Ashina is the only one I can think of. But you can't suspect her, surely? I can't imagine that girl so much as treading on an ant."

"No. That brings us back to you."

"Of course!" Nao laughed and turned to look at the rack of costumes in one corner of the room. It did not surprise Shin to see that Nao had his own collection. "I would suspect me if I were you. We clashed often enough, Etsuko and I."

"I've also been told she accused you of stealing something."

Nao turned. "And who told you that?"

Shin ignored the question. "What did she think you'd stolen?"

Nao stared at him for a moment, then selected a costume. "What does it matter?" he asked as he made a show of examining the robes he'd chosen. "I stole nothing."

Shin paused. Nao was clearly hiding something, but what? He decided on a gamble. It might yield something or nothing. "Was it a letter, by chance?" Shin pulled one of the letters he'd gotten from Kitano out of his robes and held it up. "Like this one?"

Nao looked at the letter, but his face gave nothing away. "It might have been. She accuses me of so many things that I've just stopped listening. Is it from one of her suitors?"

"It appears to be."

"That would explain it, then." Nao hesitated. "It was probably one of them. Her suitors, I mean. That is where I would look for your poisoner if I were you." He smiled. "Then, you've probably already thought of that."

Shin tapped his lips with the letter, thinking. "Not as deeply as I might like."

"She was blackmailing them, you know."

Shin blinked, noting the use of the past tense. A slip of the tongue, or an indication that Nao knew Etsuko was dead? He couldn't say for certain, not yet. "What?"

Nao indicated the letter in Shin's hand. "Her suitors. She was blackmailing them."

"You know this for certain?"

"I suspect it." Nao shrugged. "Ask Ashina if you want confirmation. She was privy to Etsuko's secrets, after all."

"I will when she arrives." Shin paused. More past tense. Nao either knew she was dead, or suspected. He decided to leave it for the moment. He didn't feel comfortable accusing Nao of anything until he had something more substantial to go on. "Did you know she was to be wed?"

Nao tapped his nose. "Ah. Sanemon told you then, did he?" He sighed. "Yes, I did. She was gloating about it before the performance. She was quite pleased with herself." He hesitated. "Before you ask, his name is Bayushi Isamu."

"Yes. He came to see me."

"Did he?" Something in the way Nao replied caught Shin's attention. It was as if the actor had realized something. But what that something was, he never got the chance to ask, for Ashina chose that moment to arrive, Choki in tow.

The two young actors were talking quietly as they opened the door. Both of them froze as they caught sight of Shin, then bowed hurriedly. "My- my lord," Choki blurted. "Forgive us. We did not know you were speaking to Master Nao…"

"Up, both of you. No need to bow." Shin gestured, and they rose hurriedly to their feet. "It is fortunate you are here. I wished to speak with you."

"Me?" Choki squeaked.

"Of course not," Nao barked. "He wants to speak to Ashina."

"Me? But- but why?" the young woman asked. She looked almost… afraid. Shin felt a moment's pity but forced it aside.

"It has come to my attention that Lady Etsuko had in her possession certain correspondence. I wish to know about them. I believe you can help me with this."

Ashina hesitated, clearly unprepared for this line of questioning. "My lord?"

He waved the letter for emphasis. "The letters, Ashina. What do you know of them?"

He thought her face paled somewhat beneath her makeup. "My lord, I do not know what you mean. I know of no letters." She darted a glance at Choki, who made to speak until Nao silenced him with a hard look.

Shin drew her attention back to him. "Come now. Chika told me Lady Etsuko accused her of stealing some private correspondence. Surely you must recall that at least?"

Ashina flushed and looked down at her feet. Shin frowned. "Ashina, look at me, please." She did with visible reluctance. Shin held her gaze. "This is important," he said softly. "I believe Lady Etsuko's illness is no accident. You said earlier that she'd suffered from an allergic reaction. It seems someone tampered with her makeup."

Ashina flinched. "No, that's not possible."

"Unfortunately, it is. I have had it tested, and I am assured that it is so."

Ashina's eyes widened as the implications struck home. "I

didn't – my lord, you must believe me!" She fell onto her face, shivering. With an inarticulate cry, Choki made to go to her side but froze at a look from Shin.

"Nao, I would ask that you take Choki and finish your preparations later," Shin said softly. "I will send someone to let you know when I am done."

Nao hesitated but only for a moment. He rose gracefully and pushed Choki toward the door. "Be gentle with her, my lord," he murmured as he stepped past Shin. Shin didn't reply. He waited for Ashina to compose herself.

"Lady Etsuko has treated you poorly," he said after a moment. "Everyone agrees on this. I would not find it strange if you wished some measure of revenge. Even just to embarrass her. You knew of her allergies, and you collected the ingredients... It would have been simple for you to add a bit of extra spice to the mix."

She looked up at him then, and he saw nothing but horror in her eyes. No guilt. No anger. Just raw, naked fear. Ashina was a good actress, but no one was that good. Wordlessly, she reached for the hem of his robe, and he retreated a few steps.

"I do believe you, Ashina," he continued gently. "Else we would not be speaking in private. But nevertheless, I think you know something that will help me in finding out who poisoned your mistress. My question is, will you?"

CHAPTER TWENTY-SIX
Blackmail

Ashina was quiet for several moments, her head bowed and eyes closed. If he had not known better, Shin might have almost thought her asleep. Finally, she looked up. "You found them, then?"

"Yes. Under the stage. A clever hiding place."

"Not clever enough," Ashina murmured without rancor. Shin studied her. She lifted her chin and swallowed convulsively. "She's dead, isn't she?"

Shin nodded. "Yes." He wasn't surprised by her realization. He wondered if perhaps she had suspected it all along.

"This whole time she has been dead?"

"Yes."

She swallowed again and looked away. "Someone killed her."

"I believe so."

She bent her head and took a long, shuddering breath. "She thought the letters would protect her. That is what she always said."

"And how were they supposed to have done that?"

Ashina hesitated but only for an instant. "They were from

her suitors. She made sure they would send her letters. As proof of their affections. If the letters found their way into the wrong hands, they might prove embarrassing."

Shin nodded. It was a hoary old scheme as such things went – but effective. By the time her suitors realized what they'd done, Etsuko would likely have safely stashed the incriminating missives where no one could find them. Over time, the stash had become a hoard, a cache of blackmail material spanning cities and clans.

It was impressive in its way. Etsuko had clearly been more cunning than her attitude implied. Perhaps she'd simply learned to hide that cleverness beneath a mask of audacity and arrogance. An audacious woman was a desirable woman. But a clever woman? Possibly not. Possibly only to a discerning suitor. Someone like Bayushi Isamu, maybe.

"I am guessing the content of these letters was somewhat scandalous?" he asked carefully, wondering how much Ashina knew. The young woman nodded. "Blackmail, then," he said.

"No!" Ashina looked up. "No, it wasn't like that."

"Then tell me what it was like," Shin pressed.

Ashina flushed. "It was just for protection. She never used the letters for anything other than making sure none of them had claim on her." She looked at him, her eyes wide and dark with sadness. "You do not understand what it is like for us, my lord. We are scorned and desired in equal measure. Sometimes the one bleeds into the other, and we are punished for the vagaries of others."

Shin did not deny this. Could not. Instead, all he said was, "And do you think that is what happened to Lady Etsuko?"

Again, her eyes slid to the floor. They were red rimmed now, but she was not yet weeping. He wondered if she would. "I do not know, my lord." She glanced toward the bedroom. "May I – may I see her? Please?"

Shin stepped back and extended his arm. Ashina stepped past him after a second's hesitation. As if he'd been listening to their conversation, Sanki slid open the door and motioned for her to enter. The doctor looked at Shin quizzically, but Shin merely shook his head in reply. Sanki grunted.

Ashina froze in the doorway, staring down at the body of her mistress. She seemed unable to speak and thrust her knuckle into her mouth as if to keep from screaming. Seeing Shin's hesitation, Sanki took her arm. "There, there, girl. It was quick enough, as these things go, and she fought it longer than any man might have. Take some consolation in that if you can." He guided her to his stool and helped her to sit.

Ashina nodded her thanks and held tight to the old man's hand. After a time, she said, "I don't understand how it could have happened. I picked up the ingredients myself, just as she ordered. I watched her mix them. How did it happen?" She looked at Shin pleadingly. "How did it come to this, my lord?"

"That is what I am trying to determine," Shin said gently. "The answer to who did this might lay in those letters."

Ashina continued to stare at the body. "What do you need from me?" she asked in a soft voice. "You have them already."

"Why did she choose to hide them in such an out of the way place?" Shin asked.

"What do you mean?"

"It was hardly convenient, especially for quick retrieval. It was also done rather recently, according to my sources. Did she fear they would be found in their previous hiding place? And if so, who did she think was looking for them?"

Ashina bent her head. "It is not for me to say, my lord."

"She is dead, girl," Sanki muttered. "No sense protecting her now." Ashina jolted slightly at his words and looked up first at him, then at Shin. She took a deep breath and rose unsteadily to her feet, releasing her grip on Sanki. Without a word, she retreated to the dressing room. Shin exchanged a glance with Sanki and followed her.

Slowly, she went to the makeup bench Etsuko shared with Nao. She bent as if to wipe something off the front. There was a click. "Of course," Shin murmured as he went to join her. "A hidden drawer. How clever." He paused. "Does Nao know about this?"

"No." Ashina smiled slightly. "When we first arrived, they had an argument about his old bench taking up too much space and she had it thrown out without his knowledge. Master Sanemon insisted she allow Master Nao to share hers until such time as they could procure a new one."

Shin laughed. "I bet neither of them were pleased with that particular compromise."

Ashina shook her head. "No. Forgive me for saying so, my lord, but neither of them was the sort to compromise." She gave a guilty glance toward the bedroom. Sanki stood in the doorway, smoking his pipe and not inconsequentially hiding her view of the body. Ashina indicated the makeup bench. "But mostly she was upset because she was worried that Nao, or someone, might discover its secret."

Shin frowned. "It seems impossible that anyone might stumble across such an ingenious hiding spot."

"She had it specially designed," Ashina said. "I only know of it by chance. I was cleaning the mirror and accidentally found it. She was quite upset about it. She swore me to secrecy, though I did not know what I'd found at the time."

"Did she tell you later?"

Ashina's smile was a brief thing, there and gone again even as he registered it. "No. I saw them for myself. When she was elsewhere."

Shin laughed. "Very good." He gestured. "May I?" She stepped aside, and he sat down in front of the bench. He peered inside the drawer. "Empty, of course. Did she decide to move them because of Nao?"

"It was after the theft. Some of them went missing." She'd stepped back to give him room and had turned her attention to Etsuko's costumes, hanging on a rack opposite Nao's own. Out of the corner of his eye, he watched her trail her hand through them as if searching for something. The gesture was seemingly an idle one, but at one point, she paused and made a sound that drew his full attention. He turned.

"Is something the matter?"

"No," she said hurriedly. "No. Nothing."

Shin sat back. "These letters that went missing, were these the ones Chika was supposed to have stolen?"

"Yes. She moved them then. But when it turned out Chika couldn't have done it…" Ashina trailed off. Shin nodded in understanding, though privately he suspected she was hiding something.

"She decided Nao was the culprit."

"Yes."

Shin paused. "Why did she blame Chika in the first place?"

Ashina looked uncomfortable. "I- I'm not certain, my lord. She- she was in our dressing room, but many of the actors came and went early on."

Shin frowned. Chika hadn't seen fit to mention that when he'd questioned her earlier. He was starting to understand why. "Would it have anything to do with a merchant named Odoma?"

Ashina blinked. "Oh. You know about him?"

"More than I like but less than I ought. Was he involved?"

"I don't think so. The letters that went missing weren't his."

Shin paused. "Did Chika know about the letters? Did anyone in the cast, other than yourself? Or how to access them?" And Nao, he thought. Nao obviously knew, but how had he learned of it? A question he intended to ask the actor at the very next opportunity. "What I mean to say is, was it an open secret in the same way as her engagement to Bayushi Isamu?"

"No, my lord." Ashina shook her head for emphasis.

Shin digested this for a moment. "Which letters went missing?"

Ashina hesitated. Then, softly, "Those belonging to Bayushi Sana."

"Not Bayushi Isamu?" Shin asked.

"Lord Isamu sent her no letters," Ashina said, clearly choosing her words with care. Shin sat back, considering this revelation. He vaguely knew the name Bayushi Sana – an influential courtier in the imperial capital. Beyond that, he knew nothing about the man, save perhaps an interest in audacious women.

"She was to marry Lord Isamu," he said finally.

Ashina bowed her head, saying nothing. Still protecting her mistress's reputation, despite everything. Such loyalty was admirable, even if displayed toward one so obviously unworthy of it. Shin recalled what Kitano had said about Etsuko regarding her nuptials as a business arrangement, and all at once, things began to click into place. He took a deep breath and said, "I think I have it now. Or at least the shape of the thing. These missing letters, they were the reason she was marrying Lord Isamu. Am I correct in that assumption?"

"I do not know for certain, my lord," Ashina said diffidently.

But her tone convinced him he was on the right track. He scratched his chin and looked again at the empty drawer, mulling it over. It was clear there was more going on here than he'd first thought. He looked at Ashina.

"Do you have any idea where they might have gone?"

"No, my lord. If I did, I would have returned them to her."

"Would you have?" Shin asked. Ashina frowned.

"Of course, my lord. Why wouldn't I?"

"For the same reason Lady Etsuko kept them. Protection. After all, what was to become of you when she departed?"

Ashina hesitated, and Shin saw something in her eyes. A flicker, there and gone so quickly he almost missed it. She knew something she wasn't saying. Maybe she'd stolen them. He waved his words aside and changed the subject. "I'm told the Scorpion visited this dressing room many times over the last few weeks. Presumably, they were visiting Etsuko. Were you present for any of these visits?"

Ashina's expression was momentarily one of puzzlement. "One, at least, my lord. Etsuko wished a witness and had me hide in the bedroom. But I know of no others."

"Tell me about the one, then," Shin said.

"Nothing to tell, my lord. Not really. They discussed the marriage and the proper, ah, dispensation of the dowry…"

"The letters, you mean."

She nodded. "Yes."

"All of them or just the ones written by Lord Sana?" Shin asked quickly.

Ashina licked her lips. "All of them, my lord."

"She was trading her leverage for a marriage," Shin said. That added an unpleasant wrinkle to things. If one of her suitors had found out about Etsuko's plans, about her dowry, they might have been inclined to try to either recover the letters or silence the only one who knew their location.

Ashina looked away. "She was tired, my lord. Tired of the stage, tired of this life… tired of being Noma Etsuko. She wanted to change. To be someone different."

"And she thought the Scorpion provided her with the best chance of it?"

Ashina frowned. "They were the ones who agreed."

Shin paused. "She tried this before? When? On whom?"

"Only once." Ashina clutched her hands together. "In the capital. A Unicorn nobleman. The son of the Clan Champion. She thought she had him, but he… well…" She smiled weakly. "He was uninterested in making any arrangements."

Shin stared at her for a moment. "Shinjo Yasamura," he said flatly. Annoyance warred with anger in him, and he ruthlessly stifled the surge of feeling. Now was not the time. Later. Later, he would ask Konomi several pointed questions and then possibly ask Yasamura several more. "He is here today. Was she aware of that?"

Ashina gave him a startled look. "No. I – we – had no idea. Why is he here?"

"A better question might be why he recommended Etsuko's name to me." Shin turned away, thinking furiously. Had they used him to set a trap for Etsuko? The thought was not a pleasant one. He didn't like being made a fool of – *especially if it had cost a woman under his protection her life.* Shin stood paralyzed for a moment, his anger threatening to boil over.

"My lord?" Ashina asked softly. Her voice snapped him back to his senses. He turned and forced a smile.

"Thank you, Ashina. You have been most helpful."

"Then I- I am free to continue the performance?" she asked.

Shin looked at her. "Of course. Unless you do not wish to?"

Her eyes were downcast. "I thought if you learned of the letters, you might wish to be rid of me." She paused, still looking at the floor. "With Lady Etsuko dead, I have no reason to stay. If you wish me to leave, I understand…"

Shin smiled gently. "I wish nothing of the sort. But that discussion is for later. For the moment, rest assured that you will have a place here for as long as you wish."

"Oh, thank you, my lord. Thank you!" Ashina bowed low, her voice trembling with relief. Suddenly uncomfortable, Shin gestured for her to rise.

"Up, please," he said. He turned to Sanki. "Doctor, I will be back, likely after intermission."

"I'll hold the fort, as the Lion say," Sanki said, turning and closing the bedroom door behind himself. Shin turned back to Ashina.

"I ask that you keep what we've spoken of to yourself for the time being," he said. He fixed her with his gaze. "Tell no one." Ashina nodded jerkily and, satisfied, Shin left the dressing room. He found Kasami and Kitano waiting for him. He spoke to Kitano first. "I believe I sent you on an errand, Kitano. Go now and inform Lord Isamu I wish to speak to him. And make haste."

Kitano made as if to speak, but a hard look from Kasami sent him on his way. She turned to him expectantly. "And me?"

"I know it's tedious, but I ask that you remain here for the moment. At least until we're certain none of her admirers killed her."

She frowned but didn't argue. "And where will you be?"

Shin sighed and ran his hand through his hair. "Talking to the bereaved fiancé, among others."

CHAPTER TWENTY-SEVEN
Stinger

Back in his box, Shin sighed and waved the messenger away. Another note from a tea shop owner complaining he wasn't allowed to sell exclusively to the audience. The protests were rote; there was no real bad feeling there. Just a need to prove that they weren't being taken advantage of by an arrogant aristocrat.

Thankfully, there were no complaints from the stalls. The audience appeared bemused by the idea of not having to leave to get their tea or rice. There was laughter from them, and he'd sent out a few of the troupe's musicians to play for the crowd and keep them sedate.

Shin sat back and tapped the pot of tea before him impatiently. It didn't help with the steeping, but it made him feel better.

Azuma, sitting opposite him, said, "Explain it to me again if you would." The Kaeru shifted on his cushions, leaning toward his host. "As if I'm a child. Also, stop tapping the tea. You'll mar the flavor."

Shin checked the tea and gave it another tap. "That's an old wives' tale. And it really is quite simple. Lady Etsuko was involved in a complicated blackmail scheme involving various notable personages, including Bayushi Isamu. She was trading her blackmail material for a marriage."

"Her dowry," Azuma said with chill amusement. Shin inclined his head.

"That's how I thought of it, yes. It also seems Isamu is taking the arrow on behalf of another Bayushi."

"And what about Lord Yasamura? How is he involved?"

"I'm not certain yet. All I know is that it is likely he's caught up in it. Nor is he the only audience member to be such. Both Akodo Minami and Tonbo Yua are former suitors of our fallen actress as are Lord Gota and Master Odoma."

"And you believe one of them killed her," Azuma said. "I think I'm caught up now."

"Glad to be of help. Any further complaints on your end?"

Azuma grunted and sat back. "Several. Mostly from Lady Yua and Odoma. Both of them want to leave, but neither have so far pressed the issue, thankfully."

"What about Lord Isamu?"

"No. He seems to be content to crouch in his box. Small favors, I suppose." Azuma cocked an eye at Shin. "You think he'll come to see what you have to say?"

"Whether he does or not, I will learn something," Shin said. The tea was finally ready, and he filled two cups. "Hopefully it will be enough to point me in the right direction."

"What if it doesn't?"

Shin passed Azuma his cup. "Then I will simply have to think of something else."

"Intermission will be over in little less than an hour. After the performance ends, I will not be able to keep anyone from leaving. Not without a very good reason."

"Murder isn't a good reason?" Shin asked, only half in jest.

Azuma frowned. "Sadly, no." He took a sip of tea. "It would have simplified matters if the culprit were one of the cast. An easy solution and all concerns assuaged."

"The simplest explanation is not always the correct one," Shin said pointedly.

Azuma gestured dismissively. "I am aware. I was merely commenting." He set his tea down. "On that note, what about this other actor, Nao?"

"I admit, he is still a suspect. But blackmail is a better motive for murder than professional jealousy, don't you think?"

"If it was murder."

"Sanki says that whatever it was, it was added after the makeup had been mixed. That speaks to the mixer's intention, I think."

"Has he discovered what it was?" Azuma asked, sipping at his tea.

"Not yet. He believes it to be a derivation of wasp venom, but his tests have been inconclusive. Whatever it is, it relies on the victim having a specific allergy to be fatal. Otherwise, she would have only suffered a temporary, if embarrassing, rash."

"So someone learned of her allergy, concocted a poison, and ensured she would apply it herself." Azuma paused. "The girl, Ashina, what about her?"

"Another possibility, but one I've dismissed. She was badly shaken by Etsuko's death. And she admitted her part in Etsuko's schemes."

"Perhaps to divert suspicion."

Shin inclined his head, acknowledging the possibility, but saying nothing. Azuma sighed. "Fine. Who will you be speaking to first?"

"Odoma," Shin said decisively. "Then Lady Yua. They are the most eager to leave. Better to talk to them now. After that, Lady Minami and Lord Gota."

"Saving the Unicorn for last, then?"

"Yes, well, I think that will be a most unpleasant conversation." Shin clutched his cup in both hands and stared down into the depths of the tea. Some soothsayers claimed they could read the future in tea leaves, but all Shin saw was steam. He knocked back the scalding liquid and set the cup aside. "More and more, it appears I have been a pawn in someone else's game. I do not care for the feeling."

"You get used to it," Azuma said simply. Shin stared at him for a moment, then laughed somewhat ruefully. He was about to reply when there was a quiet knock at the door. He called for them to enter, and Kitano stepped inside, bowing immediately upon noticing Azuma's presence.

"My lord, your guest is on his way," Kitano said.

"Lord Isamu, you mean?"

"Yes, my lord."

"Excellent." Shin glanced at Azuma.

Azuma grunted. "I believe I will return to my box now." He pushed himself to his feet, and Shin rose with him. Azuma paused. "I hope when next we speak, you have some answers. For so far, it seems we have nothing but questions."

"That is my hope as well, Lord Azuma." Shin retrieved a fresh cup from the selection arrayed on the tea tray and set it aside for Isamu. Then he settled back to wait as Kitano showed Azuma out. Though he kept his expression studiously bland, he was in fact ecstatic. Isamu was as good as admitting he was up to something.

Kitano showed Isamu in a moment later. The Scorpion stood in the doorway for a moment as if studying the interior of Shin's box for hidden traps or assassins. Shin indicated the cushions Azuma had just removed himself from. "Thank you for coming, Lord Isamu. Please, sit."

Isamu arranged himself on the cushions. "What do you want?" he asked bluntly. It was a calculated provocation, the sting of the Scorpion courtier. Poke, poke, poke… that was how the Bayushi got things done. In a way, it was not dissimilar to the Daidoji Method. If courtesy was a shield, discourtesy was a blade. When in doubt, strike the right spot, or simply strike often enough, and your opponent might reveal something.

"To talk," Shin said, parrying the thrust.

"About what?"

Shin bent and refilled his own cup. "Are you in need of refreshment?" he asked.

"Well?" Isamu asked.

"Tea?" Shin inquired, indicating the pot.

"No. Well?"

"Something else? Rice wine, perhaps?"

"No." Isamu fell silent.

Shin paused for effect and then said, "I feel like we got off to a bad start, you and I. My fault as much as yours, obviously."

"Debatable."

"Compromise is preferable to debate, I find," Shin said.

Isamu snorted. "Spoken like a true Crane."

"Have some tea," Shin said, pouring his guest a cup. He set it in front of Isamu. The Scorpion looked down at it, then grudgingly picked it up.

"Fine. Now will you get to the point?"

"I wished to speak about your coming marriage to Lady Etsuko." Shin made a show of blowing on his tea. "I note that you have not asked me how she's feeling."

Isamu ran a finger around the rim of his cup as if testing it to see whether it had been laced with poison. "I sent my servants to inquire as to her health. You sent them away."

"I cannot help but notice you still haven't asked."

Isamu fixed him with a level stare. "How is she?"

"Ill."

"Something she ate?"

"An allergic reaction to her makeup," Shin said, watching the other man's eyes for any sign of a reaction. He was rewarded by an ever so slight tightening of the skin between Isamu's eyes – a crease of puzzlement.

"That is unfortunate. Perhaps I should take her home."

"She is resting under the care of my personal physician."

"How kind," Isamu said. "'Kindness is a circular gift and singular in its purpose.'"

"Utayu," Shin said, identifying the snatch of poetry. "*The Kiss of Winter.*"

"No. *The Lover's Sojourn.*"

Shin bristled but did not let it show on his face. "From which, of course, the verses which make up *The Kiss of Winter* were derived. I find it stands best as a separate work."

"Your opinion is noted and disregarded," Isamu said. "You cannot judge a work of art by a single brush stroke, after all."

"The discerning mind can judge a work based on nothing more than the medium," Shin said. He did not hold such a view himself, but he felt such a statement would suitably annoy his guest. He was pleased to see he was correct.

"And do you judge yourself a discerning mind, then?" Isamu asked.

"I have been judged such on occasion."

"Not by me."

"No, but the day is young," Shin said lightly. "Tell me about your relationship with Lady Etsuko. How did you come to meet?"

Isamu was silent for a moment. "'The village bell has rung,

time for all to sleep, yet thinking of my love, how can I succumb to slumber?'" he quoted.

"*Lady Kasua*," Shin said. "A classic of the genre." He cleared his throat. "'The breakers of the sea roar down upon the shore like thunder, as fierce and proud as they, is she who pounds in my heart.'" He looked at Isamu. "Poetry aside, I do not think your feelings for Etsuko were as strong as all that. In fact, I think you regarded your impending nuptials as something onerous at best."

"And why would you think that?"

"I am very observant."

"So I have been told. I have yet to see any evidence of it myself."

Shin's smile didn't waver. "I have learned that Etsuko was in the habit of collecting correspondence. That she intended to trade said correspondence to you in return for a suitable marriage. However, certain elements of her dowry have gone missing."

"Thus, you believe, what? That we poisoned her?"

"I do not believe I mentioned poison."

Isamu flipped a hand in dismissal. "I am a Scorpion. To hear others tell it, poison is our only weapon. Allow me a question if you will…"

"Of course," Shin said.

"What does it matter?"

Shin paused. "To what do you refer?"

"Etsuko is dead, no? Why bother with any of this?"

"Why do you believe she is dead?"

"If she weren't, you could merely ask her who the likely culprit is. There would be no need for one of these tedious investigations of yours." Isamu sat back on his heels. "And if she is dead, then I am no longer required to attend this function."

"Save that leaving early might imply guilt," Shin said quickly.

"Of course, you are a Scorpion and therefore adjudged guilty by default."

Isamu's eyes narrowed. "I didn't kill her."

"I didn't say she was dead."

"It was implied."

"Implications are subjective. What you choose to read into my words is not my responsibility. More tea?"

"No, thank you. Trust a Crane to deny responsibility."

"Trust a Scorpion to insist others are engaged in wrongdoing." Shin sipped his tea, never breaking eye contact with Isamu. "Tell me about the letters."

"I do not know what you are talking about."

"If you didn't, you wouldn't be here."

"I came because I wished to know what was going on with my fiancé seeing as you prevented my servants from checking on her." Isamu rose to his feet. "Now I know."

Shin set his cup aside. "And how do you feel about that?"

Isamu paused. "Again, what does it matter?"

"Humor me."

"'This is not the sun, nor is it the winter; I alone am still unchanged,'" Isamu quoted.

Shin rose and followed him to the door. "'May I live on until I long for this moment, in which I am so troubled and recall it with bliss,'" he quoted in reply. Isamu spun, eyes glinting with anger.

"Are you threatening me, Crane?"

"Me?" Shin clutched himself in faux shock. "Fortunes, no. Never. Besides, what have you to fear from me?"

"Nothing, and you would do well to remember that," Isamu hissed. Abruptly, he straightened and smoothed his robes. "I will not be speaking with you again, Crane. Not today or any other day. For Etsuko's sake, I will endure the remainder of this performance, but once it is done, I will leave. You will not try to stop me."

"Of course not," Shin said. "I wouldn't dream of even attempting such discourtesy."

Isamu stared at him a moment longer, then nodded sharply and showed himself out. Shin sighed and turned toward the stage. He'd learned less than he'd hoped, though he was still certain Isamu was hiding something. The question was, how could Shin provoke him into revealing what he knew?

Shin paused as a thought occurred to him. A smile spread slowly across his face. "When in doubt, strike the right spot," he murmured. Decision made, he turned back to the door and called for Kitano.

It was time to pay a visit to the Badger.

CHAPTER TWENTY-EIGHT
Badger

Intent and result often differed. Shin knew this, for he'd experienced it himself on a number of occasions. He'd intended to visit Gota, but he never made it. He'd taken only a few steps out of his box when he was accosted by one of Azuma's men. "My lord, my lord," the warrior panted as he hurried down the corridor. "Lord Azuma said we were to alert you if someone tried to leave!"

Shin nodded. "Yes, well, who was it?"

"Lady Yua, my lord," the Kaeru retainer said. "She's not alone either. They're in the foyer. They've demanded to speak to Lord Azuma, and he told me that if anyone asked to see him, I was to bring you instead."

Shin bit back a laugh. "Of course he did. Very well. Let's be about it." Shin followed Azuma's retainer back the way he'd come, annoyed by the interruption but not wholly unprepared. Someone was going to have made the attempt sooner or later. That it was Lady Yua was something of a surprise. He'd expected it to be Isamu. Then, the Scorpion had good reason to remain where they were.

The scene in the foyer was a tense one. Shin saw Lady Yua's bodyguard facing off against Azuma's retainers. And behind her, he spied the two disheveled samurai who were acting as bodyguards for the merchant, Odoma. Odoma himself stood next to Lady Yua, though not so close as to imply any association.

The merchant was the first to spot Shin and the first to speak. "And here comes our captor now, Lady Yua. Full of himself, I don't doubt."

"Ah, Master Odoma. How nice to see you again," Shin lied. He nodded politely to Lady Yua. "And Lady Yua. You wish to leave, I'm told."

"I have matters that require my attention," Yua said stiffly as she waved Hira back. She looked uneasy. Shin wondered whether it was due to the situation or something else.

Odoma nodded. "As do I." He gestured, and his bodyguards relaxed. Azuma's retainers, however, did not. The Kaeru were not ones for games of bravado. If there was to be bloodshed, they were ready for it.

Shin glanced at the merchant. "But you'll miss the rest of the performance." Unlike Yua, Odoma didn't look particularly nervous. Perhaps he had more practice at hiding his feelings. Shin wondered whether the merchant had spoken to Chika lately. Had the actress told him she'd been questioned by Shin?

"Unavoidable, I fear," Yua said.

Shin nodded. "How disappointing. Not to mention somewhat insulting."

"That is not my intention," she began.

"And yet, I fear that is how I will take it," Shin said. "I went to great efforts to ensure you were both made comfortable, and now you will leave early, ensuring my efforts are for naught. What will people say about that?"

"I never thought you one to care about that sort of thing, my lord," Odoma said. He smirked unpleasantly. "I'm glad to see I was wrong."

Shin fixed him with a steady look. "Are you now?" Odoma flushed and looked away, clearly unsettled by Shin's gaze.

"Where is Lord Azuma?" Yua demanded, stepping in front of Shin. "I wish to protest this treatment. It is not proper that we should be prevented from leaving."

"Nor do I intend to do so," Shin said smoothly. "As to Lord Azuma's whereabouts, I assume he is in his box, enjoying some refreshments before the show continues. Something we could all do with, I think. Don't you agree?"

"I told you, I must leave," Yua said sharply.

Shin spread his hands in studied helplessness. "My permission is not necessary, though it is flattering you think otherwise."

Yua stared at him as if perplexed by his stubborn passivity. Finally, she said, "I perceive that you have something you wish to say to me. Say it and leave me in peace."

Shin decided it was time to be direct. "Spring's Smile," he said.

She looked at him in confusion. So did Odoma. "What?" she asked.

"It's the type of tea you prefer. It has a distinctive odor. One which lingers. On paper, especially. Even after several months." He gave her a gentle smile. As he'd hoped, she caught his meaning immediately. She shrank back from him as if he were a viper, and Shin felt momentary pity for her.

"What nonsense is this?" Odoma demanded, looking back and forth between them. "Have you taken leave of your senses?"

"A good question," Shin said. "One I might ask both of you, though perhaps we should do so somewhere private."

Yua bowed her head. "Yes," she said in a small voice.

Odoma snorted. "No. I'm leaving."

"If you must," Shin said. "Chika will be disappointed, of course."

Odoma glared at him. "What's that supposed to mean?"

Shin snapped open his fan and said, "Tell me, did she offer to look for the letter, or was it your idea?" It was a stab in the dark, a theory based on nothing more than circumstantial evidence. But it was apparently the correct one, for Odoma paled and clutched at his chest as if in shock.

"You- you…"

"Yes," Shin said simply. He looked at them both. "I think we three have much to discuss. I ask that you both wait for me in your boxes. I will be along before the end of intermission to discuss the matter in more detail."

Odoma swallowed. "You- you can't just…"

Shin peered at him. "I can. I have. You will. But first, why leave now? What provoked this sudden urge to depart?"

Odoma looked away. "I was told it might be in my best interests," he muttered. Shin glanced at Yua, who nodded silently but did not meet his gaze.

"And who told you this?"

Neither spoke. It was Hira who answered him if only in oblique fashion. She caught his eye and made a slight gesture – a twitch of a finger – alerting him to an eavesdropper behind them. Out of the corner of his eye, he spied a familiar demon mask, watching from the steps that led to the second level of the theater. By the time he'd turned, however, Isamu's bodyguard was gone. Shin frowned. "I am beginning to regret inviting that man," he murmured. He turned back to Odoma and Yua. "We will speak later. Rest assured your secrets, such as they are, are in safe hands. Now go."

Kitano was waiting for him at the top of the stairs. "Lord Gota is getting impatient, my lord," he said, casting a curious glance at Odoma and the others as they followed Shin up the steps. Shin flicked his fan and kept walking. Kitano hurried to keep up.

"He's not the only one. Did you see her?"

"Who, my lord?"

"The Scorpion, Kitano. The one in the demon mask."

"Nagisa, my lord," Kitano supplied. Shin glanced at him. Kitano smiled. "I, ah, made the acquaintance of several of Lord Isamu's servants, my lord. Friendly bunch when you get past the masks. They filled me in on the names of his retainers. Nagisa, Arata and the big one whose name I've forgotten."

"I'll take your word for it. Did you see her?"

"Only briefly, my lord," Kitano said. "She passed me in the corridor."

"Probably scurrying back to her master." Shin glanced over his shoulder. Yua was heading toward her box, and Odoma was shuffling in the direction of his own. "I need you to keep an eye on them. Make sure they don't try to slip out without me knowing."

"You think they'll try, my lord?"

"It would be inconvenient if they did so," Shin said. "That is why I would rather it not happen." He gestured with his fan. "Go. Watch. But try not to be seen. I must speak with Lord Gota, but I will pay a visit to Lady Yua next."

Kitano bowed low and drifted unobtrusively away. Shin continued on to Gota's box. Arban was seated outside, leaning back against the wall beside the door. He lazily extended one foot as Shin approached the door, blocking the latter's path. "He's waiting for you," the Ujik said, peering up at Shin.

"Then perhaps you should move your foot."

Arban ignored him. "I like Gota. He's a good man. Just…

hotheaded. Try not to upset him. He might do something rash, and then Kasami would be upset with me."

"Well, we wouldn't want that, would we?" Shin said in amusement. Arban shifted his leg aside, and Shin entered the box. Gota was inside pacing, his thick hands clasped behind his back. He glowered at Shin as the latter announced himself.

"You took your sweet time."

"I was momentarily distracted. My apologies."

Gota snorted and turned, arms crossed over his barrel chest. "I have heard about you, you know. You have a reputation."

"A good one?"

"No. They say you're a meddler. A busybody."

"My vices are many, I fear," Shin sighed. "It is the sorrow of my family."

Gota grunted and ran a palm over his head. "Whatever you think of me, I am no fool. What is going on here, Crane? Why can't I see Etsuko?"

Shin tapped his fan on his palm. "Lady Etsuko is ill." He paused. Honesty might better serve his purpose here than prevarication. Especially if he could use Gota's anger to his advantage. "The illness is not natural."

Gota paled. "Poison?"

"It appears that way," Shin said, watching his reaction. Gota looked dumbfounded, incredulous. If he was an actor, he was better than any of those currently onstage.

"Who did it?" he asked finally. His voice cracked.

"I do not know."

"Why not? Another actor. It must be! They were always jealous of her." Gota turned as if seeking someone to attack. "She always said they hated her. One of them must have – have ... How? How did they..." He reeled around and made as if to grab the front of

Shin's robes. Shin deflected the grasping hands gently with a swat of his fan. Gota shrank back, startled. The tines of the fan were steel and sharp.

"When was the last time you spoke to her, Lord Gota?"

Gota shook his head. "I don't – what does that matter?" His eyes widened in realization. "You think I poisoned her."

"No. I do not think you would poison anyone. If her neck had been broken or she had been throttled, you would have been my primary suspect. But poison is not where your mind goes when something displeases you, is it?"

Gota hesitated and then looked down at his hands as if seeing them for the first time. "No," he said hoarsely. He lowered his hands. "No," he repeated. "Who did it?"

"That is what I am trying to determine." Shin decided to be as straightforward as possible. Time was of the essence, and Gota might be more forthcoming. "How long have you known Lady Etsuko?"

Gota blinked. "Years. Many years."

"How many?"

"Since we were children." Gota's expression softened. "She is – was – one of my clan, you know." Shin, who had not known this, let no sign of surprise cross his face. "A long time ago. I ... knew her then," Gota continued. He looked at his hands. "She left to find a new way. I did not see her again for many years."

"That must have been hard for you," Shin said carefully. He was starting to understand why Gota had made himself such a nuisance.

The Badger gave him a sharp look. "No. I – we – there was nothing between us." He looked away. "Not until later. Until we saw each other again. Many years later. I was a wealthy man then. Still am."

"So I have heard. You made quite a stir among certain circles when you chose to move your business here from the capital." Shin paused. "At around the same time Lady Etsuko came here, I believe."

"The same time you stole her away," Gota growled. He hunched forward, his hands balling into fists, a human mountain. He glared at Shin. "You came and took her away."

"From you?"

Gota blinked. The mountain crumbled. He looked away again, hands flexing uselessly. "No. Not from me."

"If it helps at all, I regret doing so."

"It does not."

Shin accepted this with a nod. "You followed her. Why?"

Gota was silent for several moments. "I thought she would grow tired of it all."

"Of what? Acting?"

"Maybe. No." Gota shook his head. "She wanted more than I could give her. Than anyone could give her really. It was like a ladder she had to climb. She couldn't come down. She could only go up." He paused. "I hoped she would see there was nothing waiting for her at the top."

Shin hesitated, then asked, "Did you know she was engaged to be married?" If he'd ever truly suspected Gota, those suspicions would have been wiped clear by the agony he heard in the other man's voice. Gota was a man at sea, lovelorn and helpless.

Gota tensed. "I did."

"Did you know to whom?" Shin asked, watching Gota's face for any hint of deception. He didn't expect to see it, however. If he had known, Shin suspected that Isamu would already be in pieces.

"No."

"Bayushi Isamu. Is that name familiar to you?"

"No. Why are you asking me this?" Gota looked at him. "This Isamu... is he the one who she was to marry?" His hands flexed and Shin wondered what sort of damage Gota could do with just his fists.

Shin unfolded his fan and looked away. "I've said too much." In point of fact, he thought he'd said just enough. If Gota was a mountain, he was an unstable one... prone to avalanches. But an avalanche could be a useful thing if it was aimed in the right direction. Even so, Shin felt a flicker of guilt. This was not a kind thing, though it was a necessary one all the same.

"Wait. Just now, you said she was poisoned. That Bayushi you mentioned, do you think he did it?"

"I am not certain."

Gota looked at him, and Shin felt a momentary unease at the expression on the other man's face. He wondered if he had made an error in telling Gota anything. He pushed the thought aside. Too late now. "Perhaps I should ask him," Gota said softly.

"I think that would be unwise," Shin said, prodding the rocks down the cliff. "The Scorpion are not to be taken lightly."

"Are you scared of them, then?" Gota growled. "Because I am not."

"I am not scared, Lord Gota, merely practical. If they are responsible, I will find out. But it would be foolish to confront them without being certain." Shin met Gota's glare with a bland gaze he knew others found infuriating.

Gota grimaced, his face flushing red, but rather than explode, he said only, "When you find out, let me know. I would regard it as a personal favor."

Shin bowed. "Of course. You will be the first to know." He

turned but stopped at the door. "Remember what I said. Do not challenge them."

Gota gestured sharply and turned away. Shin studied him for a moment, noting the tension in his shoulders and the set of his head. Then, satisfied the avalanche was in motion, he showed himself out. He had more grieving lovers to speak with, and intermission would soon be over.

CHAPTER TWENTY-NINE
Intervention

Shin quickly made his way to the box set aside for the Dragonfly, only to find he wasn't the only one paying a last-minute visit. As he turned the corner, he was startled to see several samurai crowding the narrow space at the far end of the corridor. Kitano, who'd been leaning unobtrusively against the wall nearby, fell into step with Shin.

"What is going on here?" Shin asked. A warrior bearing the crest of the Shinjo stood near the door, resolutely ignoring his Tonbo counterpart, who was doing her best to look similarly unconcerned. Nearby, Hachi, Konomi's bodyguard, and Yoku, the Lion samurai, stood at attention, glaring daggers at Odoma's pair of rapscallions.

Kitano shrugged. "Lady Konomi was waiting for Lady Yua. Lord Shinjo arrived not long ago with Lady Minami and Odoma in tow. I decided to keep my distance, just in case one of them decided to take offense at my presence."

"Wise thinking." Shin paused and looked at his servant. "Take yourself over to Lord Isamu's box. I have a feeling something is going to happen there very soon, and I want to know about it when it does."

Kitano's brow furrowed. "What's going to happen?"

"You'll know it when you see it. Hurry." Shin turned back toward the Dragonfly box, frowning. He was annoyed with himself. He'd known Yasamura was up to something, but he hadn't expected this. What was the man thinking? He snapped open his fan in frustration and started toward the crowd of samurai.

All of them turned as Shin arrived, and he thought he detected a look of relief on the Tonbo's face. He smiled expectantly behind his fan, but no one spoke. Finally, he gestured to the Tonbo bodyguard. "Hira, isn't it? I believe you're supposed to announce me."

Hira started, an embarrassed look on her face. "Of course, my lord. My apologies." She made to reach for the door, but the Shinjo samurai grunted in displeasure and extended an arm protectively.

"My master is currently visiting the Lady Yua," he said, not looking at Shin.

The Lion, Yoku, turned to glare at the Shinjo. "Lady Minami wishes to speak with Lord Shin. You will let him in."

"Thank you, Yoku," Shin said appreciatively.

The Shinjo frowned and matched Yoku's glare with his own. "Lord Yasamura asked not to be disturbed."

"How sensible of him." Shin used his fan to force the samurai aside gently. The man went but grudgingly. "I assure you I have no intention of disturbing anyone. Now step aside if you would. Thank you."

Shin paused in the entrance to the box proper. Shinjo Yasamura knelt across from Lady Yua, a pot of tea between them. Konomi sat beside her cousin, and Minami and Odoma sat nearby. From Yua's expression, she did not seem happy about her visitors. Shin cleared his throat, and Yasamura turned, beaming. "Ah, Shin! A pleasure to see you again – and so soon after our last chat."

"Lord Yasamura. I did not expect to see you here," Shin said politely. He looked around the box. "I did not expect to see any of you, come to that."

"We were just enjoying some of this marvelous tea you've provided, Shin." Yasamura held up the cup in salute. "Truly, you've spared no expense." He glanced at Yua, who did not appear to have touched her own tea. "Though perhaps it was a wasted effort in the case of some."

"I prefer wine," Odoma said. Yasamura bestowed a lazy glance on the merchant, who flushed and looked away.

"I think we would all prefer to keep a clear head in this instance," Yasamura said. His smile was sharp enough to cut wood. He set his cup down and gestured to Shin. "I suppose you'd like to join us?"

"How kind of you," Shin murmured, but he didn't move. Instead, he looked at Konomi, who was fanning herself with an air of serenity. "I cannot help but feel somewhat foolish about this whole matter."

Konomi lowered her fan. "What are you implying?"

"I think you know exactly what I'm implying."

"I don't," Minami spoke up. She looked around, clearly annoyed. "In fact, I'm still not sure why I'm here, save that Yasamura insisted."

"For the same reason we all are," Yasamura said, not looking at her. "All of us save Shin, of course. And my dear cousin." He picked up his tea and took another sip. "We all share the same problem. Even our humble merchant friend here. Isn't that right, Odoma?" Odoma glared at the cup of tea in his hand and said nothing.

"Etsuko," Shin said bluntly. Yasamura cut his eyes in Shin's direction.

"Took you longer than I expected," he said. "Frankly, I was starting to wonder if you'd ever figure it out. Really, it's a good thing you're handsome."

"Well, I was at a disadvantage, given that I had no idea any of this was going on," Shin said, trying to ignore the little flutter of pleasure he felt at being called handsome. "I think I've just about caught up, though."

"Do tell," Yasamura said, lifting his chin. He smiled invitingly. "This should be entertaining if nothing else."

Shin gave his fan a mocking flutter. "You're here because Noma Etsuko was getting married. And that meant all the blackmail material she'd collected was soon to become the property of someone far more dangerous than an ambitious actress."

Yasamura frowned. "Was. Past tense. You said she was recovering."

Shin saw looks of puzzlement and consternation on the faces of the others. "A necessary lie. I did not wish to provoke a panic."

Yasamura sniffed. "More like you did not wish to lose money. I know how you Cranes think."

"Do you?" Shin asked, peering at him. "Then what am I thinking now, pray tell?"

Yasamura hesitated. He composed himself and said, "You found the letters, then?"

"I did." A definite stirring among the others now. Minami glanced at Odoma, and Yua hunched forward with a strangled moan.

Yasamura smiled thinly. "One of mine?"

"Among others." Shin glanced at Yua and the others, trying to judge their reactions. As he'd expected, only Minami met his gaze. He looked back at Yasamura, who was still smiling. The man seemed to think this was a game.

"Out of curiosity, did you read mine?"

Shin nodded. "One of them, yes."

Yasamura's smile widened. "Did you find it enjoyable?"

"Not to my taste," Shin said.

"Pity."

"How?" Yua asked abruptly in a voice raw with emotion. "How did you find them? She told me she'd hidden them where no one could find them."

"Luck," Shin replied, turning his attentions to her. "The exact circumstances do not matter. You were in love with her, weren't you?"

Yua flushed deeply, then said softly, "No. It was… a dalliance. Nothing more."

"You ended it?"

"No. She did." Yua paused. "Etsuko never left the stage, save of her own volition. She told me that I- I was not interesting enough." She smiled sadly. "I cannot fault her for that, for I am many things, but interesting is not one of them."

"Why did you come here today?" Shin asked again.

"Because she told us we had to come," Minami broke in.

Shin looked at her. "Why would she do that?"

"To show her power," Minami said after a moment. "Etsuko was like that. Even when it came to little things. Life was a war, and she was determined to win."

"Not just that, I think," Shin said, his mind working even as he pushed past the disappointment of realizing his honored guests had almost certainly been blackmailed into attending the performance. "She wanted you here to show her power, true, but not as a simple exercise in egotism. Rather, she was doing it to prove a point. To illustrate her hold over you to someone else." He shook his head. "Yet surely the letters you wrote her would be no more than an embarrassment."

Minami snorted. "You know better than most that embarrassment is a keen blade in the right hands. Especially in this city. If the commander of the Lion garrison were revealed to have wasted her time mooning over an actress, some might come to question her decisions in other matters. Even, perhaps, her fitness for command."

"It is the same with me," Yua said softly. "I have many responsibilities. If my superiors believed me unfit, I would be removed from my position."

Odoma grunted. "I would have lost the respect of my fellow merchants. I am looked upon with much esteem in this city. Word of my dalliance would surely have shattered my reputation."

"Unlike your gambling," Shin said. Odoma grimaced.

"A merchant can be forgiven for losing money, not his wits." Odoma shifted on his cushion, a sour look on his face. "I thought – well, it does not matter now."

"You thought Chika would get them back for you," Shin said bluntly.

Odoma looked away, gnawing his bottom lip. Shin sniffed derisively and turned to Minami. "You sent that great lump you call a bodyguard to try to get into Etsuko's dressing room." He pointed his fan at Yua. "And you sent poor Hira."

Yua's eyes widened, and she made to protest, but Shin waved it aside. "No, no. She said nothing. I deduced the reason for her presence backstage. There was only one individual concerned enough to seek out Etsuko in person. Coincidentally, he's the one person she has no hold over, at least not one of ink and paper."

"Gota," Konomi murmured. Shin nodded.

"Even so."

"Wonderful. True love yet exists in this fallen world," Yasamura sighed. "I suppose it's too much to hope that you intend to give the letters back?"

Shin nodded. "Afterward, certainly."

"After what?" Odoma blurted. "The performance?"

"No. After I determine which of you killed her."

There were gasps from Yua and Minami. Odoma grunted. Yasamura was too experienced a courtier to react as the others did. Instead, he merely raised an eyebrow. "That is a grave accusation. Do you have proof?"

Shin snapped open his fan. "If I did not, would I be here?"

"Almost certainly." Yasamura paused. "How can you be sure she was murdered?"

Shin paused. "She was poisoned."

Yasamura clapped his hands and looked at Konomi. "Ha! As I said."

"Yes, cousin. Very clever." Konomi looked at Shin. "Why do you think one of them poisoned her? Why not the Scorpion?"

"For that matter, why not one of her fellow actors?" Yasamura interjected. "Does it matter whether the actual perpetrator is apprehended? Arrest one of the actors or, better, one of the stagehands. I doubt she had any friends among them and probably not a few enemies."

Shin frowned. "That is not my way."

Yasamura stroked his chin. "It would be easier if it was."

Shin glanced at Konomi. She had the good grace to look embarrassed. "I have often been told that before. Yet I do not see myself changing anytime soon."

Yasamura smiled. "You would not be the man whom I have heard so much about if you did." He clutched his knees and leaned forward. "Fine. You have the letters. You have the poison. What more do you need?"

Shin leaned forward as well. "The truth, for preference. Why are you really here, Shinjo Yasamura? Not because you were eager to flirt with me, I think – painful as that is to admit." He was rewarded by a slight tightening of Yasamura's lips. Was it a moue of regret or annoyance? He wasn't sure. Maybe Yasamura wasn't sure either. "Is it true Etsuko once tried to marry you?"

Yasamura was silent for a moment. Shin felt the eyes of the others on them. Finally, Yasamura said, "She is – was – a vivacious woman. Spirited. Argumentative. I have a preference for that sort." He looked at Shin as he said it. "I allowed myself to be overcome by her wiles, and I wrote her a few affectionate letters. She was quite insistent on that. Of course, I knew very well what she was up to. I have been blackmailed before and likely will be again. Her attempt was clumsy and, ultimately, forgivable."

"Why?"

Yasamura shrugged. "I have no doubt she was seeking a prospect for a noble marriage. If she could not get it by dint of her wiles, she intended to get it another way. Unfortunately for her, she went about it in a clumsy fashion. Her only saving grace as a conspirator lay in her method of defense."

"The letters," Shin said.

"Yes, quite. Innocuous enough, at least mine were, but as Lady Minami said, embarrassment is a keen blade when wielded correctly. Other people have killed to keep their peccadillos quiet."

"At least one has in this case."

Yasamura frowned. "Yes. I do not approve of such methods. Etsuko was harmless."

"Harmless or not, she seems to have succeeded in her goal," Shin said. "She was engaged to Bayushi Isamu." He looked around, but none of the others seemed surprised. Evidently, he was the last to find out.

Yasamura laughed softly. "I know. She had a Scorpion's heart, that one. Of course, there may be another reason they chose to yield to her blandishments."

"The letters themselves."

Yasamura nodded. "Yes. Years of them. Ever since she began her career. What a dowry they would make, don't you think?" He smiled sadly. "I have no doubt the first few were nothing more than memories, sweet remembrances from lovers past. Then she saw a use in them. A form of protection and eventually of advancement." He trailed off and shook his head. "I have often wondered what set her on that path, whether somewhere there is a letter explaining it all."

Shin thought of Gota and said, "Perhaps. It is immaterial now. Etsuko is dead."

"But her secrets – our secrets – live on," Yua said.

Shin looked at Yasamura. "And that's why you truly came today, isn't it?"

Yasamura grimaced. "Yes, though not on my own behalf, I assure you. I was satisfied with our interaction, but I was not the only member of our clan to commit an indiscretion when it came to Lady Etsuko."

Shin, who'd noted more than one Iuchi sigil among the

letters, nodded slowly. "How many?" Konomi blurted in evident surprise.

"More than you'd think but less than you might suspect," Yasamura sighed. "As I said, she was a vivacious woman and argumentative. To a certain sort of person, that is an irresistible combination."

Shin sat back on his heels to consider this. "Which is why you recommended her to Konomi, knowing she would pass along the recommendation to me. You must have been looking for an opportunity to remove her from the capital and thus away from those she might influence."

"That was my initial thought, yes. A simple enough task, and one I was happy to do. But then word came that she was to be married and to a Bayushi no less. You see the problem, of course." Yasamura emptied his cup and set it down.

"Of course. The Bayushi – and the Scorpion – have a reputation for making use of embarrassing information." Shin shook his head. "Though I have reason to believe Isamu is a victim himself, thrown to Etsuko in order to protect another."

"That wouldn't surprise me," Yasamura said. "It is a very Scorpion way of thinking. But do you have proof?"

"Not as such. But what I have is enough." Shin studied the other man across the top of his fan. "Why involve Yua and the others? In fact, how did you even know... Of course. How silly of me." He looked at Konomi, but she did not flinch from his gaze. "Earlier, we spoke of the gossip surrounding Etsuko. You knew more than you were letting on."

Konomi nodded. "I did warn you, Shin."

"Obliquely." Shin snapped his fan shut and tapped his lips. "It is most irksome to find myself as a thread in another's tapestry."

"Irksome or not, it is done. As to involving these fine worthies, well, that was my darling cousin's advice." Yasamura sat back. "Isamu refuses to speak with me, though he has spoken with the others."

"So Lady Yua said," Shin murmured, glancing at her. She flushed and looked away.

"Isamu paid a call on all of us, all who Etsuko insisted attend," Minami said. "Oblique courtesies, wrapped around vague intimations that he had some advantage, followed later by a suggestion that we leave at the earliest opportunity." She bared her teeth, and her eyes blazed with heat. "Couldn't deliver that one himself, of course. Sent his servants to tell us. As if we were his subordinates."

"Yes. Likely he hoped to prevent a gathering such as this," Yasamura said. "Konomi thought presenting a unified front might serve to back down our Bayushi rival. I'm inclined to agree. I doubt Isamu wants a fight."

There was a sudden commotion outside. Yua's servant peered nervously into the box. "M- my lady, Lord Shin's servant is here. He- he says he must speak with his master."

Yua looked at Shin. "What is this? Some ploy of yours?"

"Yes, and right on schedule." Shin rose to his feet. Yasamura stretched out a hand.

"What about the letters? What do you intend to do with them?"

"For the moment, nothing." Shin looked around. "Understand, I am not interested in the letters save that they might well point me to the identity of the killer. But that is for later. For now, I intend to pay another visit to Lord Isamu."

"From what I've heard, he doesn't want to speak with you either," Yasamura said.

Shin smiled brightly and slapped his fan into his open palm.

"Oh, I think he'll change his mind when I keep Lord Gota from throttling him."

CHAPTER THIRTY
Badger and Scorpion

Shin made his way toward the Scorpion box but not alone. Yasamura had insisted on coming along as had Konomi. They were trailed by Hachi and Yasamura's bodyguard. Shin had decided there was no point in arguing with his guests. Better to have Yasamura as an ally than an opponent. Besides, as Konomi had pointed out, there was something to be said for presenting a unified front.

Konomi leaned toward Shin with her fan held up to hide her mouth. "Are you actually angry with me?" she murmured, doing her best to look innocent.

Shin avoided the question. "I think you were distracting me earlier. Giving Yasamura time to go about his business. That's why you weren't worried about him wondering where you were. Am I correct?"

"Perhaps somewhat. Mostly, I was just having some fun."

Shin grinned mirthlessly. "And Yasamura?"

Konomi paused, then sighed. "I suppose I was trying to fit two horses with one bridle, as my father says. Yasamura was sent here on family business. I was asked to help him. I thought I could help you at the same time." She fluttered her fan. "For what it's worth, he really does find you fascinating, though I can't say why."

"For the same reasons you do, I expect." He'd meant the comment as a joke, but she fixed him with a sidelong look that unsettled him.

"You know, perhaps I erred in keeping all this from you," Yasamura interrupted, moving up between them. Konomi, obviously used to such rudeness from her cousin, sidled aside gracefully. "After all, you have as much to lose as we do." He chuckled. "Your reputation hinges on today's success, doesn't it? A murder onstage can't be good for the reviews."

"That depends," Shin demurred. "If I were to bring the culprit to justice, I would imagine it might do wonders for my reputation."

Yasamura chuckled. "Perhaps we can arrange for you to do that onstage as well. I wager the audience would eat it up."

"Do you think Isamu did it?" Konomi asked. She peered at Shin over the top of Yasamura's head. "You said you believed Bayushi Isamu was a sacrifice, someone offered up by the Scorpion to placate Etsuko. If I were him in that situation, I might well poison my betrothed."

"You did stab that fellow one time," Yasamura said.

"And broke the ribs of another," Shin added.

Konomi glared at them. "We're not talking about me. We're talking about the Scorpion. How difficult would it have been to hire someone to add poison to her makeup? Even someone from the troupe itself, especially if they didn't tell them what it was."

Shin paused. Something about what Konomi had just said struck him, but he couldn't be sure. It fluttered there, at the edges of his mind, and then was gone. Before he could ask her to repeat herself, in the hopes it might spark the lost thought anew, Kitano came hurrying toward them down the corridor. Shin had sent his servant ahead to keep an eye on things, and Kitano had obviously seen enough. "My lord, you'd best hurry. Things are becoming unpleasant!"

Shin and the others picked up the pace. As the box came into sight, he recognized the two guards outside the box from his earlier encounter with them – the woman in the demon mask and the other in a mask of ceramic with red and black stripes. But they were not paying attention to Shin or the others. Instead, their attentions were focused firmly on the Ujik, Arban, and his master, Gota, who squared off with them in an aggressive fashion.

"Move aside," Gota snarled, his big fists twitching by his sides.

"Our lord does not wish to be disturbed," Nagisa, the one in the demon mask, said. Her hand was on her sword, but Gota did not appear to notice. "You would do well to return to your own box, my lord." Her voice was dripping with condescension, and Gota, predictably, bristled.

"Arban," he said.

"Yes, Gota," the Ujik replied lazily.

"Kill them."

Arban raised an eyebrow but reached for his sword nonetheless. "You're the boss."

Shin coughed loudly. Everyone stopped. Slowly, the Scorpions turned. "I feel I should point out that technically, as this is my theater, I am the boss," he said.

"Isn't that only on ships?" Konomi asked unhelpfully.

"Goes for theater as well," Shin said, not looking at her. He snapped open his fan and waved it about. "This is my fiefdom, and I am master here. No blood can be shed, save by my explicit permission. Since none of you have said permission, I insist you cease glaring at one another." He met Gota's angry stare. "Lord Gota, I feel like we have had this conversation before."

"I want to speak to the Scorpion," Gota said stubbornly.

"So I see. And if they refuse?"

"They won't if they know what's good for them." Gota turned his baleful gaze on Nagisa and her companion. Neither seemed that impressed, though the masks made it hard to tell. "I want to know what he did to Etsuko," Gota continued.

Shin studied him for a moment. "I don't propose to stop you, my lord. I propose to join you. A united front might achieve more than a lone voice, don't you think?" He looked back at Konomi and Yasamura. "Any objections?"

"Not a one," Yasamura said, smiling thinly. Shin inclined his head. He turned to Nagisa and her companion and gestured to the door.

"Well? What are you waiting for? Announce us."

"My lord has requested that he not be–" Nagisa began.

"So you said. But the odds have shifted ever so slightly, I think." Shin looked around. "Perhaps a strategic withdrawal is in order, don't you think?"

The two samurai looked at one another. Something silent passed between them, then the one in the porcelain mask turned and entered the box. He returned a moment later and slid the door open in invitation. Shin led the way inside. Kitano, Arban, Hachi, and Yasamura's retainer remained outside with Nagisa and her companion.

Unlike the first time Shin had visited, Isamu was alone in the box. Briefly, he wondered where the other Scorpion courtiers had gotten to but realized Isamu had no doubt sent them away once he figured out Etsuko was dead. He was standing when they entered and made no move to sit. Nor did he invite them to do so.

"I did not expect such discourtesy from a Crane, even one that has fallen so far from the nest as yourself," he said in the same tone he might have used to comment on the weather. He peered past Shin at the others, and his eyes narrowed. "Given the company you choose to keep, perhaps I should not be surprised."

"Well, that's just hurtful," Yasamura murmured.

Gota bristled and jabbed a thick finger at Isamu. "Watch your tone, Bayushi, or I'll show you just how discourteous I can be."

"Do not rise to the bait, Lord Gota," Shin said. He gave his fan a flutter. "Like all Scorpions, he's merely trying to find the best place to sting you."

"'Thus cries the crane, that now stalks forgotten in reedy marshes, far from the joyous cloudland,'" Isamu quoted. Shin laughed.

"Tajiwara," he said, identifying the line. "A bit utilitarian but a classic for all that." He peered at Isamu over the top of his fan. "I prefer his ode to economic stability." He cleared his throat and recited, "'Like the steadfast trees that stand on northern sands, in Father's Home, the cherries yet bloom full.'"

"How dull," Isamu said. "Then, I expected no better from a soul as pedestrian as yours." Shin heard an intake of breath from Konomi and hid his frown. Rudeness was a weapon like any other, and the Scorpion were more adept at its use than most. Isamu was baiting him. But two could play that game.

"That you consider the state of my soul is a great compliment," Shin purred.

"I have not wasted a single thought on your soul or anything else about you," Isamu said. "In fact, I would be most obliged if you would remove yourself from my presence at once. All of you."

Yasamura whistled softly as if impressed by Isamu's cheek. Gota took a step toward Isamu but paused when Shin extended an arm to block his path. Konomi chuckled softly. "Scorpion courtesy is truly a thing to behold," she said. Isamu glared at her.

"And the Unicorn would know what about courtesy, exactly?"

"Enough to know that vinegar requires more preparation than honey," she said in a slightly singsong tone, tapping at the air with her fan. Isamu grunted dismissively and turned his attentions to Shin.

"What do you want?" he asked.

"To talk," Shin replied.

Isamu hesitated, but only for a moment. "About what?"

"Etsuko."

"Of course," Isamu said in resignation. "I should have realized." He sighed. "I have told you I know nothing about these letters you spoke of." He glanced at Yasamura. "Perhaps Lord Yasamura might know something of them. Have you asked him?"

"Oh, yes," Shin said. "He knows quite a bit. I wager you know more."

"And I have said I do not. It appears we are at an impasse."

Shin waved his fan. "I do not think so."

"I do not see how it could be otherwise."

"Well, you are not a trained investigator," Shin said.

Isamu fixed him with a glare. "Neither are you."

Here, Gota laughed, a bellicose chortle that filled the box. "He's got you there, Crane," the Badger said. Both Shin and Isamu looked at him, and Gota glowered back. "Enough of this back and forth. I want to know what he did to Etsuko."

Shin raised a hand, and Gota fell silent, though grudgingly. "Earlier you spoke to Lady Yua," Shin said. "Might I ask what the topic of conversation was?"

Isamu paused. "You may not."

"You spoke with the merchant, Odoma, as well. Was it on the same topic?"

"It is none of your concern."

"What about Lady Minami? She was most vocal about your threats." Shin heard a stifled laugh from behind him. Yasamura, he thought.

"I threatened no one," Isamu said. "I do not know what you are talking about. I do not know why you think I am involved in whatever nonexistent scheme you have concocted out of whole cloth, but I am growing decidedly weary of it."

"'There is no bower where I might rest my horse or brush my laden sleeves,'" Shin quoted. "Tajiwara again. His verses are plain, but they get his meaning across."

Isamu stared at him. "Whatever you think is going on, it has nothing to do with me. Anyone can see that the culprit – if there is one – is lurking backstage. Everyone knows actors are untrustworthy at best."

"And yet, you're planning to marry one," Shin said.

"Who I intend to marry is my business and mine alone." Isamu gestured. "Some might say your interest in my marriage borders on obsession."

"Some might," Shin said cheerfully. "No one with any intelligence, obviously." He looked around. "Speaking of your servants, where's the third one?"

Isamu gave him a sharp look. Shin smiled. "I wonder... is he trying to get into the dressing room again? Is he hoping to ascertain Lady Etsuko's condition or looking for the letters?"

"Letters?" Gota said querulously. "What are you nattering about?"

Isamu ignored him and kept his eyes on Shin. "What business is it of yours where my bodyguard is?" he challenged.

"What letters?" Gota snarled. "What are you two talking about? What does this have to do with Etsuko?"

Isamu looked at the Badger, then at Shin. "You haven't told him, have you?"

"Told me what?" Gota asked, looking back and forth between them.

Shin hesitated. Isamu's brow wrinkled. He was smiling. "That Etsuko is dead."

"Dead?" Gota said in a hollow voice. He'd gone pale, and for a moment, Shin thought he might faint. "Dead. No. No. She cannot be." He looked at Shin wildly. "You told me she was ill. You said she would be fine!"

Shin took a step back. "A necessary lie. I am sorry, Lord Gota, but yes, she is dead."

"She has been dead since she took the stage," Isamu said. There was something in his voice. Regret? But Shin couldn't be sure.

Gota whirled on him. "You did this," he snarled accusingly. Isamu took a step back. "You did it," Gota roared again. "It was you!"

And with that, he lunged for Isamu's throat.

CHAPTER THIRTY-ONE
Restitution

Nao sat at his makeup bench and wondered what the future held. A persistent murmur from the direction of the stalls spoke to the impatience of the audience. Intermission would be over soon and then he would be needed onstage. But he could not muster the energy to finish getting dressed. Instead, he surveyed the jars of makeup that sat before him.

They'd been forced to share a makeup bench after she'd gotten rid of his for reasons that escaped him. His long fingers flicked across them, moving them in slow circles as if performing sleight of hand. Not all of them were his.

To the uneducated, there was no difference between the jars. But Nao could easily tell them apart. His were made from the clay of a certain river to the north and had a somewhat reddish hue. They'd been made by a peasant potter and showed a certain crudity he found aesthetically pleasing.

Etsuko's on the other hand had been made by a professional potter. They were smooth where his were rough and had cost more than a week's wage for a journeyman actor. No doubt they had been a gift by some besotted courtier or merchant.

He lifted one of the jars and studied it. "Idiot woman," he murmured. "You can't tease the scorpion's tail and not get stung." He set the jar down and rose. It was almost time for the end. The end of what? The performance, certainly. But maybe everything. Bad luck, that was all it was. Bad luck or maybe fate catching up with him.

Maybe it was all just a coincidence. Maybe Isamu wanted nothing more than to talk over old times. But somehow, he doubted it. Isamu had never been one for small talk. Whatever he wanted, it was bound to be troublesome. Especially if it involved Etsuko. Such annoyances were one of the reasons he'd left the City of Lies for greener pastures.

He'd had plenty of reasons for leaving. Too many to name, really. More than he cared to think about. While he hadn't exactly found happiness, he'd at least found satisfaction. To think that it was all so close to being taken away was maddening. All because of Etsuko.

"Damnable idiot woman," he breathed. He'd outlasted her, but she'd had the last laugh after all. He sighed and without thinking turned toward the bedroom. He hesitated and spun as the door to the dressing room clattered open. "Choki," he said. "What do you think you are doing, startling me like that?"

The young man froze. "I- I brought you your wig for the next scene as you asked," he said, proffering the wig as if it were a shield.

"The right one this time, I hope." Nao paused and cursed himself silently for snapping at the youth. "Never mind. Of course. Yes. Thank you." He took the wig from Choki and set it aside. "How are things backstage?"

Choki wrapped his arms around his chest. "Everyone is nervous. You heard about what Ishi found under the stage, didn't you?"

"Yes." Nao had to admit Etsuko had been clever. She'd hidden the letters in a place no one would ever think to look. "Put it from your mind, Choki. It has nothing to do with us."

Choki went to the costume rack and began looking through them. "Master Rin says Lord Shin is unhappy with how things are going." He paused, half-pulled one out and then chose another. "Here. This one, I think."

Nao took the costume and studied it. It went well with the wig at least. Maybe the boy was learning after all. "And why shouldn't he be?"

"Because we're doing our best," Choki snapped. "I shouldn't have told him anything earlier. Now Ashina is in trouble and… and…" He hung his head and trailed off. "It just… It feels as if the troupe is coming apart."

Nao paused and said, "You did nothing wrong. Ashina is not in trouble." He felt a flicker of guilt as he considered what the younger man must be feeling.

Choki glanced at the bedroom. "And what about Lady Etsuko?"

"Are you trying to say that's your fault as well?" Nao asked, smiling.

The look on Choki's face would have been funny had Nao seen it onstage. But here, now, it startled him. It was a look of fear and something else – anger? But it vanished so quickly Nao couldn't say. The youth turned away. His hands curled into fists. "I just… I just want to be an actor. I am an actor. But without a troupe…"

"You don't need to worry about that," Nao said firmly.

"Because you won't let me onstage as anything other than background." Choki turned back. "And now I might not get the chance. Because of you."

Nao drew himself up to his full height. "Watch your tone, Choki. I am still a lead actor, and you are still my apprentice."

"I am your understudy," Choki said. "Not your apprentice."

"You are what I say you are," Nao insisted. He felt heat rise to his cheeks and a pounding in his chest. He forced himself to relax. "But you are right," he said after a moment's consideration.

Choki looked at him, startled. "I- I am?"

"Yes. Yes, you are. I will talk to Master Sanemon."

"You... you will let me onstage? With Ashina?"

Nao nodded. "Yes. After today's performance is over." He paused. "I... might have to leave. The troupe will need someone to take my place. That could be you."

Choki's eyes widened. "Leave? Why?"

"It doesn't matter," Nao said, waving the question aside. He handed the wig back to Choki and gestured. "I've changed my mind. Tell Uni I want something special. She'll know what to give you. Go. Be quick."

Choki nodded and hurried out, fairly dancing in his haste. Nao sighed and turned to the costume rack. He replaced the costume Choki had chosen with the first one the young actor had examined. Folding it over his arm, he went to the bedroom. He slid the door open quietly and looked down at the dead woman on the mat. The doctor, Sanki, turned slightly where he sat. "You shouldn't be in here," he said softly.

"Neither should she," Nao said.

"You don't seem surprised. By her condition, I mean."

"I'm not." He stood over Etsuko and studied her. "What was it?"

"I'm not sure I should tell you."

"Was it a type of venom mixed into the makeup?"

Sanki frowned and took his pipe from his mouth. "How do you know that?"

"I am familiar with the effects. Though I've never known it to kill anyone." Nao sighed. "But then, she was allergic, wasn't she?"

"I believe so, yes."

Nao closed his eyes. He was not one for prayer, but he tried to muster some feeling for the dead woman. Something other than frustration and relief. "Did you know her well?" Sanki asked, startling him. Nao looked at the old man.

"Better than I wished."

He turned to go but stopped as the familiar figure of Arata stepped into the dressing room. He'd entered so silently that Nao hadn't heard him. The samurai closed the door behind himself. "How did you get in here?" Nao demanded.

"A bit of misdirection," Arata said.

"How unlike you. What did you do, poison her tea?"

"I paid two of the pages to start a brawl. She went to break it up. Or to watch. I'm not sure. Either way, I am here." He studied Nao coolly. "Intermission is almost over," he said.

"Where are the others?" Nao asked. He made to close the door to the bedroom, but a slight gesture from Arata stopped him.

"I left them to watch over Isamu," the samurai said as he approached. "I thought one might succeed where three failed. Is she in there?"

"She's resting."

"I do not think she is." Arata made as if to shove him aside, but Nao moved too quickly for him. He retreated and Arata peered in. He ignored Sanki, took in Etsuko's body at a glance, and turned to Nao. "You fool."

"Me?"

"You are many things, but I never thought you capable of this."

Nao stared at him. Arata seemed surprised. That was unexpected. "I did not do this."

"I do not believe you." Arata took a step toward him, and Nao retreated. "Lord Isamu will not believe you. Your only option is to throw yourself on his mercy. Perhaps he can protect you from justice."

"Justice?"

"Lord Shin. He searches for the killer."

"As I said, that is not me."

"But it could be," Arata said softly. "It would be so easy. You've left yourself open, Nao. You've made yourself weak. Your garden of forking paths has narrowed to but one." He paused. "Or rather, one that ends well."

"Is that a threat, Arata?"

"A promise, Nao. The same promise I made to you all those years ago. Come back. Make restitution. Let Isamu protect you. It is the only way you will survive… cousin."

Nao laughed softly. "And how would I go about doing that, *cousin*?"

"The letters. Where are they?"

Nao snorted. "Of course. Well, you're too late. Lord Shin has them." He indicated Etsuko's makeup desk. "She hid them there."

"Not all of them."

Nao looked at him. "There are more?"

"Yes. The ones from Lord Sana. You stole them."

Nao suddenly recalled his last conversation with Etsuko. So that was what this was about. "I stole nothing."

"Of course you did. How could you not when you realized what they were worth?" Arata peered at him. "Lord Isamu entertained a hope that you might have done so out of some familial loyalty, but I know better. You've never cared for anything but yourself."

"What you or Lord Isamu believe is of no concern to me, Arata."

Arata was silent for a moment. Then, "A month. That is how long he mourned your departure. A month. He barely ate, did not sleep. For a month, he did nothing save scribble poetry, which he then burned."

Nao sighed. "Yes, well, he was always a bit melodramatic, wasn't he?"

"You broke him. And now here you are again, taunting him."

"I am doing no such thing. I did not even know he was in the city until Etsuko mentioned him." Nao paused. "I wonder, how did she react when he told her who I was?"

Arata grunted. "Not well. She asked me to kill you. Perhaps I should have. Perhaps I should remove your head from your shoulders and save us all some embarrassment." His hand fell to his sword, and Nao tensed. Arata didn't make idle threats. Not like Nagisa.

"Go ahead. It will be the last thing you ever do," a voice said from the door. Arata turned and, looking past him, Nao saw Lord Shin's bodyguard, Kasami.

"I thought you were supposed to be guarding the door," Nao said.

"I was. I saw him come in. I wanted to hear what you two had to say to one another." Kasami slid the door shut behind her. "Now I have, and it's time you left, Scorpion."

"This is not your concern," Arata began.

"Everything that happens here is my concern," she said, giving Arata a look that brooked no argument. "Step back from the actor."

Arata turned so he could face her. "He is not worth your protection."

"That is for me to decide, I think." She stepped away from the door. Arata mirrored her movement, circling around the opposite way. She did not look at Nao as she said, "Is Sanki still in the bedroom?"

"I'm here," Sanki called. He stepped into the doorway, still puffing on his pipe. "He barely even looked at me."

"I have no quarrel with either of you," Arata said. His eyes flicked to the door.

"Just with me," Nao said. He smiled at Arata. "Then, we've never really gotten along, have we, Arata? Whatever Isamu insisted."

Arata hesitated. Then he straightened and lowered his hands. "No. We never have." He pointed at Nao. "The letters, Nao. He will forgive you in return for the letters."

"I have done nothing that requires forgiveness," Nao said. Arata studied him for a moment longer, then he was gone as quietly as he'd come. Nao glanced at Kasami. "Thank you," he began.

"What letters?" she asked.

Nao frowned. "I have no idea. The only letters I'm aware of are the ones Lord Shin found. And as far as I know, he took those with him." He paused. "Even so, I think I need to speak to Lord Shin."

CHAPTER THIRTY-TWO
Revelation

Instinctively, Shin snapped open his fan and brushed it across Gota's face – hard enough to sting but not to cut – even as he sidestepped the other man's lunge. Gota howled out an obscenity and staggered, clutching at his face.

The door was flung aside as Nagisa and the other Scorpion warrior burst in, followed by Hachi, Arban, and Yasamura's retainer. Isamu flung up a hand. "Hold," he barked. The two samurai froze. Hachi looked around in confusion. Arban helped Gota to his feet. Yasamura waved his retainer back.

"He blinded me," Gota sobbed, pawing at his face.

Arban forced Gota's hands away from his face and examined the already fading marks left by the fan. "No, he didn't. Looks like he just gave you a warning." The Ujik glanced at Shin with something that might have been admiration. Shin snapped his fan closed and sighed. Things weren't going well. He looked at Isamu.

"That was foolish. He might have killed you."

"I doubt that," Isamu said loftily. But even so, he rubbed his throat as if imagining what Gota might have done to him.

Shin pointed his fan at the other courtier. "You said she'd been dead since she walked onstage. That's true enough. But how did you know that?"

"It was poison, wasn't it?" Isamu asked.

"You know damn well what it was," Gota snarled. He glared blearily at Isamu. "You tricked her into marriage and then killed her!"

"I tricked no one," Isamu snapped. "If you think this marriage was my idea–" He cut himself off and shook his head. "Just… tell me. It was poison, wasn't it?"

"Yes. My physician has determined that she died of an allergic reaction to the venom of a certain species of wasp likely mixed into her makeup." Shin watched Isamu's eyes as he spoke and thought he saw a flicker of what? Recognition? "Does that sound familiar to you?" Shin asked.

Isamu shook his head. "No," he said. "Should it?"

"Possibly. Poison is considered an art form among the Scorpion, or so I am told."

"I prefer poetry," Isamu said flatly.

"I know. Did you write any to Etsuko?"

Isamu laughed softly. "No."

"Did Lord Sana?" Shin asked.

Isamu stared at him without speaking. Shin nodded. "Yes, I know everything."

Isamu chuckled sourly. "I doubt that."

"Then by all means, illuminate me."

"Lord Sana is a fool. At least when it comes to actresses." Isamu spoke offhandedly as if he were talking about the weather rather than a scandal. He examined his fingernails as he spoke, inspecting them for dirt. "He wrote her many letters." His eyes flicked up. "Though I doubt they were of the quality of Lord Yasamura's."

Yasamura laughed gaily. "Obviously."

Shin swept his fan out. "And yet you were the one marrying her, not Lord Sana."

"Yes."

"Why?"

"Because Lord Sana is already married," Konomi said suddenly. "Or at least engaged. To the daughter of a prominent member of the Miya family." Shin glanced at her, and she shrugged. "I was sent an invitation to the wedding."

"I wasn't," Shin said.

"Neither was I," Yasamura added. He looked at Shin. "An oversight, perhaps."

"It wasn't," Isamu said. He nodded to Konomi. "But you are correct. He is to be married. Etsuko, however, insisted on a noble marriage. So a willing groom was found."

"I'm surprised you didn't simply kill her," Shin said.

Isamu glared at him. "That was rude."

"Yes, well, I'm a bit annoyed with you. Why didn't you simply make her… go away?" Shin paused. "It was the letters, wasn't it? Not just Lord Sana's but all of them."

Isamu said nothing, but Shin knew his silence was as good as confirmation. Shin glanced at Yasamura. "Which is why you came here. To keep the Scorpion from getting their hands on Etsuko's dowry of blackmail material."

"Only you have it now," Yasamura said pointedly.

"Yes, I do. And Isamu knows it." Shin rounded on Isamu. "So why are you still here? Were you hoping to wring something out of this disaster?"

"Perhaps I felt I owed it to her to wait. To see if you caught the killer."

"Or perhaps you were trying to avoid suspicion." Shin

went to the privacy curtain and peeked out at the auditorium. Downstairs, the crowd was getting restless. Intermission was almost over. Any moment now, the drum would begin to sound, signaling the start of the second half of the day's performance. Time was running out. He turned back to Isamu. "I believe the letters are connected to Etsuko's death. But I do not know how. I was hoping you could shed some light on that."

"I did not poison her," Isamu said. "Nor did I order it. There was no benefit to me in doing so. As I said, I was marrying her."

Shin wondered at Isamu's choice of words. It was very careful, very particular. A courtier's phrasing. "But were you happy about it?"

Isamu fell silent. After a moment, he said, "What does it matter? I was willing, and she was pleased." Gota made a strangled sound. Isamu ignored the Badger and went on, "I had no reason to poison her. And even if I had, I would not have done it with wasp venom."

Shin heard the derision in his voice. "What do you mean?"

"Wasp venom is a child's toy," Isamu said. "It causes nothing more than a rash."

"Unless you are allergic to it," Shin said. Isamu hesitated and then nodded.

"Unless that is the case, yes."

"Did you know she was allergic to such things?"

"Obviously not," Isamu said.

"How could you not know?" Shin asked. Isamu was hiding something; he was sure of it. He could feel the others watching and felt something like nervousness. It was as if he were onstage and they the audience. What was he missing?

"She hid her secrets well, did Etsuko," Isamu said. "Her rough manner hid a cunning far outstripping that of most."

Shin was still thinking of a reply when he heard a polite cough from the doorway. The third of Isamu's bodyguards stood there, looking distinctly ill-at-ease with the goings-on. "Enter, Arata," Isamu said. "As you can see, you missed some excitement."

Arata looked around, clearly bemused. "My lord, I–" he began hesitantly.

"Well?" Isamu pressed.

Arata shook his head. Isamu bit back a curse. "Something the matter?" Shin asked. Isamu turned, and for a moment, his gaze was like fire. Then it cooled and he was composed once more. Shin was immediately alert. Something was about to happen. He could feel it.

"It occurs to me that perhaps you already know who the killer is," Isamu purred.

Shin hesitated. "What do you mean?"

"All this running about, asking impertinent questions. Are you perhaps covering for one of your own, Crane?" Isamu gestured languidly. "I mean, it seems to me the killer could only be someone with access to Etsuko's person at a very specific period of time. If it was wasp venom, I mean."

Shin frowned. He was losing the advantage. Isamu was retaking control. "It was. My physician confirmed it."

"Wasp venom must be mixed quickly, for it soon separates from whatever solution it is added to. That means it could only have been added immediately prior to application." Isamu clasped his hands behind his back. "Obviously, then, the culprit was someone backstage. Another actor with a grudge, perhaps."

Shin looked around and saw Gota nodding slowly. Yasamura met his eyes and gave an apologetic smile. "It would solve the matter nicely, don't you think?" he said. "And you even suspected it yourself at the beginning. Or so Konomi said."

"The lead actor – Nao," Isamu said almost gently. "He is the one with the most to gain, isn't he? Before Etsuko arrived, his name was at the top of the signboards."

"I have spoken to Nao," Shin said. He saw it now. A neat trap – or diversion at least.

"Yes, but did you ask him the right questions?"

Shin hesitated. "What do you mean?"

"What do you know about him?" Isamu asked. "Really, I mean. That he is an actor is obvious. But there are actors, and then there are actors."

Shin frowned. "I'm afraid I don't follow."

Isamu laughed. "I thought you were supposed to be clever."

Stung, Shin snapped open his fan and gave it a flutter. "Speak plainly if you please."

"Do you know where he learned his skills?"

"I have never asked." Shin knew actors of Nao's caliber often attended special academies rather than learning their trade from a single master.

"No, I expect not," Isamu said. "Why would you care, after all?"

Shin's fan stopped in mid-flutter. "If you have something interesting to say, I suggest you say it, Lord Isamu. Otherwise, I might get bored and wander off."

"The Butei Academy," Isamu said.

Shin paused. "What?"

"Impossible," Yasamura said. "He's a Shosuro? Why is he working with such an inconsequential troupe?" He paused and looked at Shin. "No offense."

"None taken," Shin said absently. The Butei Academy was a highly prestigious school. But the actors it turned out weren't the sort who joined the Three Flower Troupe. Not unless something had gone very wrong in their life. He looked at Isamu. "How did you come by this information?"

Isamu paused, and Shin had a moment of clarity. Isamu had given something away, but what? He let his gaze slide away, opening himself up. "It is of no importance, I suppose. What does it matter where he went or what his name is?"

Another pause. Another hesitation. Isamu's eyes narrowed. He'd overplayed his hand, offering up something Shin knew was supposed to be bait but that Shin was artfully ignoring. Isamu glanced at Arata. The samurai gave a slight shake of his head, but Isamu gave an impatient flick of his fingers. Shin had the sense that an entire conversation had taken place in those two gestures.

Isamu looked at him in silent appeal. Shin fluttered his fan and said, "Would you all mind giving myself and Lord Isamu some privacy, please?"

"Are you certain?" Yasamura said.

"Yes, please," Shin said, not looking at him. Yasamura grunted and made as if to protest, but Konomi took his arm in hers.

"You heard him," she said. "Out. That goes for you as well, Lord Gota."

"No," Gota said pugnaciously. Konomi inveigled her arm around his elbow, and he looked at her, startled. Konomi turned the full force of her smile upon him. It was the sort of smile that could calm wild horses or send them fleeing. Shin had endured it before, and he did not fault Gota for his stammering acquiescence.

Konomi caught his eye as she guided the two men out. She winked, and Shin sighed. "Helpful woman," Isamu murmured as his samurai retreated with the rest and closed the door, giving the two of them the box.

"She has her reasons."

"There's a rumor going around that you two are betrothed," Isamu said.

Shin turned. "Is there? I hadn't heard. You wanted to tell me something, I think." He motioned to the empty box. "Well, you have the floor."

Isamu was silent for a moment. "What do you know about the Butei Academy?"

"It is the personal school of the Shosuro family. Many fine actors have emerged from its doors, including Nao, apparently."

"Shosuro Nao was one of the finest actors the school has ever produced," Isamu said, and again, Shin detected something unsaid. "But he was more than that," Isamu went on. "As the academy is more than it seems."

"Ah." Shin closed his fan and nodded. "You are referring to the rumors of its dual purpose. The training of not just actors but spies and assassins." Shin had heard the stories as a young man, but he'd never given them much credence at the time.

Isamu chuckled. "Not just rumors." He locked eyes with Shin. "I tell you in full confidence that you are smart enough to forget everything I am about to tell you once this affair is ended. Any attempt to use this information for personal gain will result in immediate retribution. You are one Crane, far from the shelter of your nest."

"But when you see one Scorpion, rest assured there are a hundred you don't," Shin said. "Yes, yes, I am quaking with fear. Are you implying that Nao is – what? – an assassin? That he poisoned Etsuko over some grudge?"

"It is possible," Isamu said stiffly. "It is also possible that he is in the employ of someone else." He hesitated. "He left us – I mean, rather the Shosuro – some years ago. A falling out. He struck out on his own."

"And I suppose it was purely by chance that you stumbled across him here?"

"Yes," Isamu said softly, and something in his eyes convinced Shin it was the truth. "I had no idea he was here until Etsuko mentioned him."

"In what context?"

"She believed he'd stolen something from her. A theft she'd initially blamed on another actress. But she'd come to believe Nao was the true culprit."

"The letters?" Shin asked.

"Perhaps. She never said." Isamu looked away. "I warned her about him, of course. Told her not to be alone with him. I don't think she believed me." He sighed. "I wish she had. A shame."

"Yes, a shame. Would Nao know of the uses of wasp venom?"

"Of course. Students at the Butei Academy often use it to prank one another."

"Then it's possible whoever used it didn't realize Etsuko would have such a reaction. It might have been an accident." Shin tapped his fan into his palm. But by his own words, Nao had known of her allergy. If it was him, could that be anything other than cold-blooded murder?

"No. Nao would have known."

"You are certain it was him. Why?"

Isamu snorted. "Who else could it have been?" He took a breath. "And as the wronged party, his life is mine."

Shin blinked. "You may need to take that up with Lord Azuma."

Isamu laughed. "Do you think he will care about the life of one actor? Even one of yours? No. He'll hand him over to keep the Scorpion happy if nothing else."

"What makes you happy makes the Scorpion happy. Is that

it?" Shin waved his reply aside. He didn't believe it for a second, but even so, he needed to talk to Nao – and quickly. "I don't know what sort of grudge you have against Nao, but I won't hand him over on your say-so. I'm going to need proof."

"Then by all means, go find it. Ask him the right questions this time. See what answers you get." Isamu paused as the sudden thud of a drum rolled through the theater. Intermission was over.

Shin turned to leave, but a word from Isamu stopped him. "I'd hurry," he called out. "I intend to present my case to Lord Azuma as soon as this performance is concluded. One way or another, Shosuro Nao is mine."

CHAPTER THIRTY-THREE
Shosuro Method

Shin made his way backstage to the beating of the signal drum, Isamu's words chasing one another around inside his head. Intermission had ended, and the performance was set to begin again. Ashina would be going onstage at any moment to mourn the loss of her lover – presumed dead – and her cousin, who was definitely dead. He had another hour, maybe two, to find the killer, depending on whether they could drag out the final scenes.

He'd left Kitano to watch over the Scorpion with orders to come and find him if Isamu or his retainers made any move. He'd made his apologies to Yasamura and Konomi and extricated himself from their company with as much dignity as possible. Konomi had attempted to make some excuse to accompany him, but he'd refused the offer. Too many people now would only confuse the issue.

That and he did not entirely trust them. Not at the moment. Not with this. Yasamura was far too willing to accept Isamu's theory. Shin could see why. It was a tidy solution. One that allowed everyone to go their separate ways with no lingering doubts. The letters were lost, the blackmailer dead, and her killer in custody. Problem solved.

Except that Shin was almost certain Nao hadn't done it. He could not say why or how he knew this, only that he did. But he had to be certain, and that meant talking to Nao one more time before he went back onstage. In doing so, he hoped to spark some leap of intuition that might direct him to the real killer.

"Crane. *Crane!*"

Shin stopped and spun, his fan extended like a sword. Gota slid to an awkward halt. He and Arban had been following Shin since he'd come backstage. Shin had allowed it because he had no time to argue otherwise. But now he was annoyed. "What?" he said. "What do you want now, Lord Gota? To yell some more? To bluster and roar like an overwrought child? If so, do it elsewhere, I beg you."

Gota's face flushed red, but the hue faded, and he sagged. "You used me," he said after a moment. "You knew what I would do. That it would give you an excuse to confront Isamu. I knew it as soon as you showed up."

Shin lowered his fan. "I did. I make no apologies for it."

"I don't want an apology. I want to see her, Crane." Then, more softly, "Please."

Shin was tempted to send him away, but he didn't have the heart. Instead, he turned away and gestured over his shoulder. "Very well. But do not interfere, or I will be forced to give you another swat on the nose."

Gota grumbled slightly at this but did not argue. Instead, he said, "Do you think this Nao person did it?"

"No. Isamu is trying to distract me."

"Why?"

"I do not know."

"Then how do you know that he is?" Gota asked.

Shin didn't reply. They made their way backstage in silence after that. Gota was subdued. Arban whistled tunelessly, seemingly at ease. The sound of the drum accompanied them the entire way. Pages and stage crew hurried to their places, and a group of actors flocked toward the flower path. Chika was among them, and Shin waved his fan in greeting.

Kasami was at her usual spot when they arrived. "He's waiting for you in there," she said, not batting an eye at the sight of Gota and Arban. "Says he wants to talk."

"Who?"

"Nao."

Shin frowned and looked at the closed door to the dressing room. "About what?"

"Presumably it has to do with the Scorpion that came to visit." She looked up at him. "Remember what I said before, about them looking for Nao? I think there's more to this than you imagined."

"So I understand." Shin tapped his lips with his folded fan. "What else?"

"I don't know what he was looking for, but I don't think he found it."

"Good." Shin slid the door open and gestured for Gota to enter ahead of him as Arban sat down untidily on the floor. As Kasami had said, Nao was waiting for him.

He seemed puzzled by the appearance of Gota, but said only, "Well, took you long enough." Shin waved him to silence. Gota strode past the actor toward the bedroom. He yanked the door aside and paused. Shin joined him. "Sanki, if you would…" he said. Inside the room, Sanki rose and stepped out into the dressing room, leaving it to Gota and Shin.

"She is beautiful," Gota said softly, looking down at Etsuko's form. "Even now, she is beautiful."

"Yes," Shin said. He could almost hear the pounding of Gota's heart like a drum echoing deep in a mountain fastness. The big man sat down heavily beside the body. He leaned over the dead woman, closer perhaps than propriety allowed. "I loved her, you know," he said hoarsely. "Always have. Ever since we were children."

Shin said nothing. Gota didn't look at him. Shin thought his gaze had turned inward. "I offered her everything I had, but it wasn't enough," he went on. "She wanted excitement, or so she said." A shudder ran through his massive frame. "May I – may I just sit here with her, my lord?"

"Take all the time you need," Shin said and stepped out of the room. He slid the door shut and turned to look at Nao. The actor read something in his gaze and straightened his previously languid posture. "We need to have a chat, you and I."

"We do indeed," Nao said.

"I spoke to Bayushi Isamu."

"And who is that?" Nao asked. An obvious lie. "A suspect, perhaps?"

"Perhaps. This might simply have been an accident." Shin sat down in front of the makeup table, studying it. He picked up a pot and took out the stopper. An acrid smell stung his nose. "This is the one she used."

"How can you tell?" Nao asked.

"Sanki told me that the poison eventually separates from the mixture. These beads of condensation, the smell – it was this one." Shin glanced at him. "Lucky you didn't accidentally use it, eh?"

"I doubt I would have noticed, save for the smell. I'm not allergic to such things."

"How fortunate." Shin turned the pot this way and that, peering at it from every angle. It was not of the same quality as the others. He hadn't noticed that the first time around. "I have answers for every question – wrong ones, possibly, but answers nonetheless. The only question I have remaining is the least important."

"And that is?"

"How did she not know? She mixed her own ingredients and yet she did not notice something had been added. It only occurred to me recently. She applied it herself. Why didn't she notice that something was off about the mix?"

"Well, for starters, that's not one of hers," Nao said.

Shin froze. "What?"

"Those pots there, they're not hers."

Shin turned to the actor, still holding the pot. "If this isn't hers, whose is it?"

"Mine, obviously." Nao took the pot from Shin and balanced it on his palm. "She stole it. A common occurrence, as I mentioned earlier. If half the stories about her are true, she liked to show her rivals she could take whatever they had with ease. Men, makeup, it didn't matter."

Shin rose to his feet, and he looked at Nao with new suspicion. It seemed inconceivable that Isamu was right. "Did you know?" he asked softly.

Nao blinked. "What do you mean?" The actor frowned. "You can't think I poisoned my own makeup in order to – what – kill her?"

"At this moment, I do not know what to think. Why did you not tell me you were a member of the Shosuro family?"

"Frankly, it was none of your business, my lord." Nao hesitated. "Forgive me."

Shin twitched his fingers in curt dismissal. "You are certain that this is yours?"

"I- I am."

"And you are certain she stole it?"

"As I said, it was a habit of hers. She was angry with me."

"Why?" Shin asked.

"Because she was who she was, and I am who I am."

"And who are you, Shosuro Nao?"

"I have no right to that name," Nao said sharply. "Those privileges and responsibilities are no longer mine." He faced Shin, face bare of its usual haughty expression. Bare of the mask of the actor. Instead, he was simply one man facing another. "I gave them up when I left. When I chose to follow my own path rather than the one laid out for me."

Taken aback, Shin said nothing. Nao squeezed the pot so tightly Shin thought it might break. Instead, he set it back down on the table. Shin saw that his hand was shaking. "Etsuko was a hardened veteran of the stage. She knew better than anyone how to get under the skin of her fellow actors – and she did, often. Some actors attempt to ingratiate themselves when they join a new troupe. Others, like Etsuko, attempt to conquer through whatever means they see fit."

"When you learned she had taken ill, did you suspect the cause?"

Now it was Nao's turn to be taken aback. "No! Why would I?"

Shin paused. Another lie, but an instinctive one, he thought. "Is it true that you were a student of the Butei Academy?"

Nao froze. "Did Isamu tell you that?"

"Is that a yes?"

Nao looked away. "In another life, yes."

"It is said by some that the students there learn arts in addition to stagecraft and singing."

"Spying, you mean?" Nao asked bitterly.

"Among other things."

"I wouldn't know." He peered at Shin. "Was it Isamu?" he asked again.

Shin tilted his head. "You two know one another, don't you? There's something personal between you, isn't there?"

"In another life," Nao said. He looked at himself in the mirror, his expression rueful. "We were younger then. I think you know what that is like, my lord."

"'Youth is another country, and the sea between us is vast'," Shin quoted.

"Chamizo," Nao said, nodding. "The old priest, counseling the parents on their wayward child." He smiled. "A good scene... though my character is not in it."

"Lord Isamu believes you are the one who poisoned Etsuko."

Nao grimaced. "He would say that. And I suppose he wishes me turned over to him for punishment?"

"That was mentioned. You do not seem surprised."

"I am not. As I said, I knew him when we were young." Nao shook his head. "You cannot trust that one, my lord. Even for a Scorpion, he is duplicitous. Always has been."

"When you knew him in your youth, you mean."

Nao bowed his head. "Even so." He looked down at his hands, visibly marshaling his thoughts. Shin did not interrupt. When Nao looked up, the mask was back in place. "While it is true that I trained at the Butei Academy, I was anything but a star pupil. That is why I left. There were things I needed to learn that I could not learn there."

"But in your time there, did you learn anything about poisons?"

Nao hesitated. It was as good as an answer. Shin pressed forward. "Who else might have known that Etsuko intended to...

borrow your makeup?" Nao looked at him as if he were a fool.

"Everyone. She made no secret of such things. She was proud of it."

"When you found yours missing, what did you do?"

Nao snorted. "The same thing I always do. I stole one of hers." He smiled. "The show must go on, after all."

Shin looked around the room, searching for answers. There were none to be found, at least not at a glance. Nao had ceased his preparations. He stood still and silent, looking at nothing. Finally, he said, "Choki is not ready to take over for me, but he may well play better against Ashina than I can. The performance can continue, even without myself and Etsuko." He began to disrobe.

Shin stopped him with a gesture. "That will not be necessary."

Nao paused. "Then you believe me innocent, my lord."

"I don't know. I know only that our audience is upset enough. To lose both leading actors would do irreparable damage to the reputation of this troupe."

"Not to mention yourself," Nao said with some of his former archness.

Shin nodded. "Yes. Selfish of me, I admit. But it would not be the first time I have bowed to enlightened self-interest." It was Shin's turn to pause. "I am trusting you, Nao. Do not disappoint me."

Nao bowed his head. "I will do my best, my lord."

"My- my lord?" Choki quavered from the doorway. Nao gestured, and the young man stepped fully into the room, carrying a wig.

"Ah, Choki, good. I've decided on a new costume to go with the new wig." Nao indicated a costume lying across a nearby bench. Choki glanced at it and blanched.

"That one? Are – are you certain?"

Nao looked at him. "Yes. Why?"

"Oh, no – no reason. I just thought… Never mind. A good choice."

Nao snorted. "All my choices are good choices." He gestured to himself. "Now help me get the dratted thing on."

Shin watched as Choki began to help Nao dress. Suspicion still lingered in his mind. There was something left unsaid here, something important he wasn't seeing. He considered his next words carefully.

"Isamu mentioned that Etsuko said something about missing letters."

Choki flinched. Nao frowned. "I was under the impression you'd found them."

"Not all of them. Some were missing. Ashina confirmed it. Can you think of why that might be?"

Nao checked the set of his wig in the mirror. "It should be obvious, I think. She hid them elsewhere as a precaution."

"Any idea where?"

"None, I'm afraid."

Shin nodded, accepting the statement at face value. He bowed his head. "Unfortunate, but possibly for the best."

Nao looked at him. "And what about Isamu?"

"Leave him to me. He has given me until the end of the performance to produce a culprit, and I intend to do so." He paused, listening to the music echoing from the stage.

He still had no answers. At least not the right ones. None of his suspects seemed to fit the bill. Not as well as he would like. There was something he wasn't seeing. But what was it? What was the missing piece?

He stared into the distance, pondering the matter. Someone

had poisoned Etsuko. But why? For revenge? Or to get at the letters? And how had they known to poison Nao's makeup rather than Etsuko's own?

He stopped. "What if they didn't?" he murmured. It was so simple. Simple enough that he'd overlooked the possibility entirely. He'd been so focused on Etsuko as the victim that he hadn't even considered that she might not have been the true target.

"I'm an idiot," he said aloud.

"My lord?"

Startled, he turned to find Choki behind him. "Yes? What is it, Choki?"

Choki swallowed and glanced at Nao. His expression was wary. Shin, seeing what he was after, took him by the arm and pulled him a short distance away. "Yes?" he said in a low voice. "What is it?"

"I- I think I might know where the letters are, my lord."

Startled, Shin looked at him. "Where?"

"The drum tower, my lord. They're in the drum tower."

CHAPTER THIRTY-FOUR
Drum Tower

Shin followed Choki through the narrow corridors that led to the rear of the theater. The heavy wooden steps that led up to the drum tower were located near the rear entrance, among the stacks of props, coils of rope, folded curtains, and the other detritus produced by a functioning theater. "Tell me again," Shin said, hurrying to keep up with the younger man. "How did you find out about the letters?"

"Ashina told me, my lord," Choki said, not looking at Shin.

"And how did she know where they were?" Shin asked, though he suspected he already knew. That was what Ashina had been hiding. The actress clearly knew more about what was going on than she'd first admitted.

Choki hunched his shoulders. "She- she gave them to me. And I- I hid them in the drum tower." He glanced at Shin. "No one ever goes there except the drummer, Chizu. And she only stays up there long enough to do her job. There's no way anyone would find them."

"Clever," Shin said. He wondered whether Choki had been

hoping to help Nao in his struggles with Etsuko. Or maybe the young actor was cleverer than he let on; blackmail was endemic among actors of all stripes and persuasions. Extortion was a common means of acquiring better parts, at least in some troupes. "And are you certain these are the same letters Etsuko blamed Chika for stealing? And then later Nao?"

Choki bobbed his head. "I am, my lord. I recognized the sigil of the Bayushi."

Shin nodded to himself. Yes, very clever indeed. So clever, he had to ask the obvious question. "Why have you chosen to tell me this now, Choki?"

Choki stopped and turned. His expression was almost comically downcast. "I heard what you said to Master Nao. About where he came from. And what Lord Isamu thinks. I know I shouldn't have been eavesdropping, but I- I was worried."

"About Nao?"

Choki hesitated. Shin nodded in understanding. "Ah. About Ashina. You were worried the Scorpion would go after her next when they realized Nao didn't know anything about the letters."

Choki sagged slightly. "I am sorry, my lord, but, well, yes."

Shin smiled. "How long?"

Choki blinked. "My lord?"

"How long have you and Ashina been… well." Shin waved his fan in dismissal as Choki's face fell. "Never mind. Rude of me to ask."

Choki bowed his head. "A few weeks, my lord." Then, more softly, "Only a few weeks." He turned and started back toward the drum tower. Shin fell into step with him.

"Is that why she gave the letters to you to hide?"

"Yes."

"Did you mean to use them?"

Choki glanced at him. "No! Never. I wouldn't even know how to go about such a thing, my lord."

"Of course, Choki. I merely had to ask." Shin could tell Choki was nervous about something – perhaps he feared punishment. Shin decided to reassure him.

"You have done me a great service, Choki. I will see to it that you are well rewarded."

Choki darted a look at him but didn't reply. Shin felt suddenly awkward as he recalled what Kitano had told him earlier about how his largesse was viewed. Was it any wonder then that Choki looked so nervous? Casting about desperately for a safer topic, Shin settled on the obvious. "Can you think of anyone who might have wanted to hurt Nao? Or even just embarrass him?"

Choki started as if surprised by the question. He frowned. "No, my lord. Everyone here loves him." He didn't sound particularly pleased by the prospect, but Shin chose to let it lie. "Why do you ask, my lord?"

"I fear I have made a mistake," Shin said. "I suspect Etsuko was not the intended victim, as I – and everyone – assumed. It seemed only natural that she would be. But what if she wasn't? What if she was merely in the wrong place at the wrong time?"

"What do you mean, my lord?"

Shin tapped his palm with his fan as he talked. It was the first time he'd articulated his theory. "What if all of this is one grand accident, a comedy of errors. Someone added poison to the makeup jar, but it was not Etsuko's jar. Rather, it was Nao's. I didn't even think to ask, you see… I made an assumption – an incorrect one as it turned out. I assumed Etsuko was the target, and my investigation reinforced that assumption."

"I don't understand, my lord," Choki said, clearly bewildered.

"Intent and result, Choki. Often two very different things. I intended to find Etsuko's killer, but the result is that the killer wasn't after Etsuko at all. This situation is not as I imagined. None of this is as I thought."

"Then why are you looking for the letters, my lord?"

"Because they are a loose end, and loose ends are untidy." Shin clasped his hands behind his back, twirling his fan idly. "More, because I think it's the only way to clear out our Scorpion infestation. They'll keep looking for those letters until they know someone has found them. I'd prefer that someone to be me."

"What are you going to do with them?"

"Nothing. Why, do you have a suggestion?" It was a joke, but Choki seemed to take it as a serious inquiry.

"I'd burn them, my lord. Only way to be safe."

"A good suggestion. I shall take it under advisement."

"What- what about the poison, then?" Choki asked. "Who do you think did it?"

Shin paused. "I'd rather not say."

Choki turned and looked at him. "You think it was Ashina, don't you?"

Shin frowned. "As I said, I'd rather not speculate at this point."

"She didn't do it."

"I don't care to think of it either," Shin said. "But at the moment, she is the prime suspect. After all, why else lie to me about the location of the lost letters? The question now is, why would she attempt to poison Nao? What does she have to gain?" He spotted the steps leading up to the drum tower at the opposite end of the corridor. "Either way, we'll find out soon enough. Come along."

As they drew closer to the steps, Shin realized the guards

Azuma had posted on the door were not at their posts. Choki noticed his hesitation and said, "I think Lord Azuma summoned them, my lord. I'm not sure why."

"Curious. Still, I'm sure it's important, whatever the reason." Shin started up. The steps were encircled by paper walls decorated with scenes from theatrical history. Climbing the steps was a claustrophobic experience – intentionally so, as the steps had been designed to take up as little space as possible.

The drum tower was a simple edifice of wood with a curved, flared roof of blue tile. It had four walls with circular windowlike apertures on each side, allowing the sound of the drums to echo outward across the nearby streets.

Shin climbed up through the trapdoor and paused. The drummer – Chizu – would have already left, her duties completed for the day. He heard the fluttering of wings as a startled bird took flight. He peered down at Choki. "Where are they?"

Choki popped up through the hatch and pointed toward the drums. "I hid them underneath the drums. There's a hollow space beneath the floor."

Shin circled the drums slowly, studying them from all angles. He was suddenly uneasy. This was all a bit too convenient. "Are you certain? I oversaw the installation of these drums myself. I don't recall any–"

A wooden clatter jolted him. It took him a moment to realize it had come from the trapdoor. It had fallen shut. Shin hurried over and found it had been latched from the other side. He was trapped in the tower.

"Choki?" he called out. "Choki?"

No answer.

He sat back on his heels. "Wonderful." A trap. And like a fool, he'd blundered obligingly into it. Kasami would never let him hear the end of it. He'd half-suspected it – the sudden discovery of the letters was far too convenient. Though he wondered whether it was planned or simply an impulse.

Even now, Choki and Ashina might be fleeing the building, especially if Azuma's people were elsewhere. That too, seemed suspiciously timed. "Planned, then," he murmured. Choki must have realized Shin would turn his attentions back to Ashina and made ready. Now he was trapped, at least until the end of the performance, and there was an open path to freedom. Shin ran a hand through his hair. "Clever, clever young man. Nao seriously underestimated you. Come to that, so did I."

Still, he couldn't help but wonder at the why of it all. Why had Ashina attempted to poison Nao? Had she done it on behalf of Etsuko? Or maybe someone else? Isamu? It seemed preposterous on the face of it, but why not? What if they'd promised her something – a starring role, maybe.

He paused and sniffed the air. He could smell something. And whatever it was, it was getting stronger. He squinted at the trapdoor. There was something…

He leapt to his feet with a curse. Smoke. It was smoke. Someone had set the drum tower on fire. With him in it. "Fire," he shouted, stamping on the floor. "Fire!" No response was immediately forthcoming. They'd notice soon enough when the smoke boiled out of the windows, but by then it would be too late for him. If the smoke didn't get him, the fire would.

He looked around, searching for some means of escape. The windows weren't that large, but he might be able to squeeze through. For a moment, he considered attempting to climb down the outside of the tower. Then his eyes lit on the drum.

He paused but only for an instant. He scooped up the drum mallets, gave them a twirl, and made a tentative thump. The sound was loud but not loud enough. He coughed. Smoke was seeping up through the cracks in the floor, and he felt the first brush of heat from below.

No time to be dignified about it. He racked his brain for a moment, then laughed. A moment later, he began to beat on the drum. The rhythm wasn't the sort that usually echoed from the tower – rather, it was a very special tempo; one any sailor would recognize: the signal for *fire*. He just hoped the right person would hear it.

He kept pounding as a wave of heat swelled up from the floor, wrapping itself around him. The heat squeezed at him, and he blinked sweat from his eyes as he kept at it, striking the drum as fiercely as he could. Smoke stung his eyes and scoured his throat. He heard the crackle of the fire right beneath him.

The only thing that distracted him from the panic that threatened to overwhelm him was the realization that he'd solved the mystery. Not through any clever deduction on his part but rather through a simple offhand comment made by his chief suspect.

As the heat pounded at him and he pounded at the drum, the pieces slotted into place in his mind. Etsuko had not been the target – her death was an accident. A mistake. That much was obvious. The wasp venom hadn't been meant to kill but to embarrass. To inconvenience. To send a message that only a graduate of the Butei Academy would recognize. But Ashina hadn't been the one to send the message. Why would she?

He thought about pockets in costumes, and Ashina's strange cry in the dressing room. What had she been looking for among Etsuko's costumes? Whatever it was, its absence had startled her. If it were the letters, who would have known where she'd hidden them? Only someone familiar with the tricks of costumery – just as only one person had access, and the motivation, to attempt to embarrass Nao. But why? What was the point? He needed answers.

And all he had to do to get them was avoid being burned to death.

CHAPTER THIRTY-FIVE
Rescue

Kasami stared at the door to the dressing room. The leaping fish painted on the door stared back. She had never noticed the fish before, but now that she had, she couldn't stop staring at it. Chika, sitting beside her, said, "Why a fish?"

"What?" Kasami said without breaking eye contact with the fish.

"Why a fish? Why not a bird or a frog?"

Kasami blinked. "A frog?"

"Given the city's name, I mean," Chika clarified.

"Shouldn't you be onstage?"

"No," Chika said. "Besides, I'd think you'd be glad of the company."

"She has company," Arban said from the other side of the corridor. He was crouched opposite Kasami and Chika. Kasami ignored him and glanced at Chika.

"I am, but you are somewhat distracting."

"That's what they all say," Chika said teasingly. Arban laughed. Kasami glared at him until he fell silent.

"Why are you here?" she demanded. "Your presence is not required."

"Gota is still in there," Arban said, hiking a thumb over his shoulder. "I'm just making sure he doesn't hurt himself." He looked at the door. "That is a very ugly fish, though. Is that what fish here look like?"

"Fish don't look like that anywhere," Chika said. She leaned forward and rested her chin on her hands as she gazed at Arban. "So, you're an Ujik."

Arban grinned at her. "Am I? That is good to know."

Chika laughed appreciatively. "You're funny as well."

Kasami rolled her eyes. "He's not. Do not encourage him." She settled back. She was annoyed. Shin had gone somewhere with Choki but hadn't given her so much as a warning or even told her where he was going – something she was going to have to discuss with him later. Running about as he had been all day, he might well need reminding that her primary purpose was not sitting in front of dressing rooms but making sure he didn't wind up dead.

"I think Arban is very funny. Handsome too." Chika fluttered her eyelashes at Arban, and he responded with an almost comical leer. She laughed. "Too handsome for me, though. I like an ugly man. Ugly men try harder and only rarely take you for granted."

"I'm glad you feel that way," Arban replied sincerely. "For you are far too skinny for me. Have you ever even ridden a horse?"

"I've ridden on a wagon pulled by a horse. Or maybe it was an ox." Chika tapped her lip with a finger as if trying to recall which it was. She waved a hand. "One of them anyway."

"What about you?" Arban asked, giving Kasami a lazy glance.

"What about me?"

"Have you ever ridden a horse?"

Kasami snorted. "Of course. Every Hiramori knows how to ride."

Arban nodded approvingly. "Good. A woman ought to know how to ride."

"I agree," Kasami said. "She should also know how to use a sword."

"I don't know either of those things," Chika said mock mournfully. She looked at Kasami. "Can you teach me?"

Kasami blinked in surprise, and her reply was instinctive. "It is not proper."

"I'll teach you," Arban said.

"I didn't say I wouldn't," Kasami said quickly. "I simply noted that it isn't proper. But I could – I could teach you something, I suppose. The fundamentals at least."

"And I'll cover whatever she leaves out," Arban said with a laugh. He paused and looked up. "Do you smell something?"

"If you're asking whether you need to take a bath, the answer is yes," Kasami said. Chika laughed appreciatively.

Arban shook his head. "Not that. Something else." He glanced at the door. "Maybe it's nothing. My imagination."

The drums started up a moment later. Kasami frowned and looked at Chika. "I thought the drums were done for the day."

Chika frowned. "They should be." She cocked her head, listening to the rhythm. "That doesn't sound like any signal I've ever heard."

Kasami nodded. The rhythm was almost martial but not one she was familiar with. She looked at Arban, who shrugged. "I don't know anything about drums," he said apologetically. "Doesn't sound like it's a particularly happy beat, does it?"

"No," Kasami murmured. As she rose to her feet, she heard voices from within the dressing room. Angry ones. She moved to the door, but before she could open it, someone else did so for her.

"Why are you standing around?" Sanki bellowed more loudly than she'd thought possible for such an old man. He'd wrenched the door open, Gota standing behind him, looking startled. "Can't you idiots hear the drum?"

"What about it?" Kasami asked, taken aback by the anger in his voice.

"It's the signal for fire," Sanki snarled, shoving past her.

She was about to reply when she smelled it. Smoke. She looked at Arban. "I told you I smelled something," he said.

Thinking quickly, Kasami rounded on Chika. "Alert the crew. Let them know there's a fire near the drum tower." She turned back to Arban. "Get your master to safety."

"What about you?" he asked.

"I have to find Shin." She paused. "Naval signal – of course. He's in the drum tower, the fool." She started down the corridor but turned as Sanki hurried after her, bag in hand. "Where do you think you're going?"

"With you, of course. Lord Shin might need help."

There was no time to argue. Kasami nodded tersely and continued. She didn't slow her pace, and Sanki soon fell behind. She trusted he would catch up. As she was running, she almost collided with someone coming the opposite way. Choki. The actor spun away from her, a look of panic on his face. "Choki, what–" she began.

"Fire," he panted, clutching at her. "Fire, my lady! The drum tower is burning! I have to go tell the others. We have to put it out quickly or else the whole theater might go up!" He pushed past her and darted down the corridor, shouting at the top of his lungs. Kasami immediately pressed on, though a part of her wondered why Choki wasn't with Shin. Had Shin sent him to get help? That sounded like the sort of foolish thing he'd do.

She reached the drum tower a moment later. The fire was crawling up the walls and the beams, though it was finding little purchase on the timbers as yet. But the paper walls would more than feed its hunger. Thinking quickly, she snatched her sword from its sheath and slashed through the closest of them, tearing them down and hurling them aside. That would delay the fire somewhat.

She sheathed her blade and drew her knife. It had been a gift from Shin, and she kept the blade sharp. With a few quick slashes, she had ripped off a section of the bottom of her robes and fashioned a mask for herself to help with the smoke as well as rags to protect her hands and hair from errant flames. A moment later she was starting up the steps, knife in hand.

As she went, she cut and cast aside more of the paper walls, but it was a vain effort. The fire had spread. Whoever had set it had known what they were doing – or maybe they had just gotten lucky.

Smoke filled the stairway, and soon enough her eyes were watering and her sinuses stinging. Heat washed over her and around her, squeezing her tight. Coughing, she reached the top and saw that someone had jammed the latch with a prop knife. "Lord Shin," she called out. "Lord Shin, can you hear me?"

Despite the crackle of the flames, she thought she heard a muffled shout from above. The drumbeat, which had continued all this time, at last faltered. "Stand back," she shouted, coughing as she did so. One blow of her knife was sufficient to shatter the prop into fragments, and a crash of her shoulder was enough to knock the trapdoor upward. A figure loomed out of the smoke above, coughing and wheezing.

A moment later, Shin all but collapsed into her arms. "Kasami," he coughed. "What took you so long?" The smoke swirled about them, making it hard to see and even harder to breathe. She thrust her knife through her belt and glared at him.

"Quiet," she said. "We have to get out of here." She caught him as he slumped against her, racked by a coughing fit. Through her blurred gaze, she could see his robes were stained with smoke and his flesh red.

"Wonderful idea," he wheezed. "Lead the way." A moment later, they were making their way down the blackened stairs. She saw that the fire was crawling across the ceiling, despite her best efforts.

But as they reached the bottom step, a sluice of water struck the timbers next to her. She cried out, covering Shin, and heard a shouted apology. A small bucket chain was forming, organized by Chika. A moment later, one of Azuma's men hurried up the stairs past Shin and Kasami, hauling a bucket of water. Several theater pages followed him, each of them similarly burdened. Shouts sounded from elsewhere, and she could hear the thud of running feet.

Kasami got Shin away from the steps and set him down a safe distance from the fire. She pulled down the rag that covered her face. "What were you doing up there?" she demanded. "Why didn't you tell me where you were going?"

Coughing, Shin tried to reply. "A trick. Someone tried to kill me."

"Of course they did," she said in resignation. She'd hoped that for once they might get through one of Shin's investigations without someone trying to kill him. But if he went around giving people reasons, it couldn't be helped. She glanced back at the steps. The fire was mostly out. "The fire was spotted before it did more than scorch the timbers."

"Thanks to me, you mean," Shin said.

"Thanks to Sanki," she corrected. "We heard the drums, but he's the one who understood the message you were sending."

"Still think I shouldn't have retained him?" Shin asked with a wheeze. He tried to rise, and she put a hand on his chest.

"Don't move. Sanki is on the way." She turned and spied Sanki hustling down the corridor, dodging pages and crew. He had his bag in his hands, and he shoved it into Kasami's arms as he crouched beside Shin, puffing from his exertion. "Still alive, then?" he asked, peering at Shin's face. He grabbed Shin's head and turned it this way and that.

"Thanks to you," Shin coughed.

"You're lucky I heard the drums." He indicated Kasami with a flap of his hand. "I don't think this one believed me until one of those pages came running by, shouting about fire. The nervous one. Always helping that actor of yours. What's his name?"

"Choki," Shin said softly. Kasami nodded.

"He must have seen whoever started the fire," she said. "We should find him. Question him."

Sanki poked and prodded at Shin's limbs and pinched the skin of his neck and cheek. Kasami wasn't entirely certain any of it was necessary. Perhaps Sanki was as annoyed as she was. He stepped back and nodded to Kasami. "He's fine."

"But of course," Shin said as Kasami helped him to his feet. He looked mournfully at the state of his robes. "Though I don't think we'll be able to clean these."

Kasami snorted. "You have more."

"But these were my lucky robes," he said somewhat plaintively.

"Yes," Sanki said pointedly. "They were."

Kasami looked at him. "What possessed you to go up there?" she demanded. "What were you thinking?"

"I was thinking – well, it doesn't matter what I was thinking since it was a trick. By our poisoner," Shin said, wiping ineffectually at a soot stain on his sleeve.

Kasami glanced at Sanki. "The poisoner? But I saw you leave with …" She trailed off, her annoyance with Shin evaporating as she realized what he meant. "Oh. Choki."

Shin pushed himself tiredly to his feet. "We need to find him." He looked at Sanki. "Doctor, stay here if you would. Someone might need your help before that fire is put out." Sanki nodded and turned toward the bucket chain.

"He must be gone by now," Kasami protested.

"He won't leave until he gets what he's after. The letters."

"You have the letters," she said.

"Not all of them." Shin started down the corridor, still coughing. "It was Isamu who gave the game away, though he didn't realize it."

She hurried after him. "Isamu? What does he have to do with anything?"

Shin tossed her a wry glance. "Who do you think gave our understudy the wasp venom in the first place? It's hardly the sort of thing Choki could have procured on his own. No, someone gave it to him."

"But why?"

"To send a message."

"By killing Etsuko?" Kasami asked, incredulous. She shook her head. "Ridiculous."

Shin nodded. "Yes, if the message had been intended for Etsuko, but it wasn't. It was intended for Nao."

"Nao?" Kasami said. "Why Nao?"

"It's too complicated to go into now. Suffice to say, we have to get to the stage. Hurry!" Shin broke into a run. Kasami cursed and ran after him. Even a fire wasn't enough to make him slow down.

There was a crowd of actors and crew in the wings when they arrived. Sanemon was trying to keep people calm, but it wasn't going well. He caught sight of them and said, "It's Choki, my lord. He's lost his mind!" Cries of agreement followed this exclamation. Actors huddled, talking excitedly at the top of their lungs.

Shin glanced at Kasami, and she raised her voice. "Quiet!"

Everyone fell silent. The crowd parted for Shin and Kasami. Onstage, the scene had come to an abrupt halt. Ashina and the other actors stood frozen, staring in shock at her co-star, Nao – and at Choki, who held a knife to Nao's throat.

"No one come any closer," Choki shouted. His voice carried easily across the silent stage. The audience had gone quiet as well, all eyes on the drama occurring before them.

"Choki, this isn't the way," Nao said. Kasami couldn't help but admire his equilibrium. She'd known trained warriors who wouldn't be so calm with a knife to their throats. "I don't know what you were trying to do, sneaking onstage, but all you've managed to do is embarrass both of us…"

"Quiet!" Choki twisted the knife, and Nao fell silent. His eyes were wild, desperate. They widened as he caught sight of Shin and Kasami in the wings. "No! Stay back!"

Kasami growled under her breath and took a threatening step toward Choki, one hand on her sword. Shin stayed her with a gesture. She looked at him quizzically, but he shook his head slowly. "No bloodshed," he murmured.

"He may not give us a choice," she said.

"We shall see," Shin said. He took a deep breath and stepped onto the stage. She followed and was immediately aware of the eyes of the audience on them. Shin took a step toward Choki.

"Stop right there," Choki said.

Shin stopped but only for a moment. "Choki, why?" he asked softly. He kept his hands in full view and moved slowly so as not to startle the youth. Kasami did the same, sidling in the opposite direction. "Why were you trying to poison Nao?"

"I wasn't. *I wasn't!*" Choki said in a choked voice. He tensed, and Nao grunted in pain as the knife bit lightly into his neck. Blood beaded and ran down into the hollow of his throat. There was an audible intake of breath from the audience. If Choki noticed, he gave no sign. "It was only supposed to make him sick so I could take over for him. Just for tonight. Just so everyone could *see...*"

Nao gave a harsh laugh. "See you make a fool of yourself onstage, you mean?" Choki's face scrunched up into a scowl and he tensed. Shin raised a hand.

"Wait, wait," he said, still speaking softly. Kasami frowned in understanding. Shin was trying not to startle him. If Choki twitched at the wrong time or in the wrong way, Nao would be dead. "We both know who gave you the idea, don't we?" Shin glanced meaningfully toward the Scorpion box.

Choki followed his gaze and nodded, swallowing. "He- he told me Nao would be so embarrassed he'd leave the troupe and I could take his place."

Shin licked his lips. "Did he mention Etsuko to you at all?"

Choki shook his head furiously. "That wasn't my fault!"

"No – no, you couldn't have known she would borrow the makeup or suffer an allergic reaction to it. But afterward... afterward, when you realized what had happened, you panicked, didn't you?"

Choki squeezed his eyes shut. "I didn't murder her," he whispered. "I didn't murder anyone. It wasn't my fault."

"Not for lack of trying, I think."

Choki's eyes sprang open. "I couldn't take the chance. If you figured it out..."

"And then what, Choki?" Shin asked in a gentle tone. "Burn the theater?" The young man shook his head, his eyes empty of everything save desperation. Like an animal in a trap, Kasami thought. "Why not simply flee?"

Choki tensed again. His eyes strayed to Ashina, and her expression was impossible to read. Was it fear? Regret? Frustration? Kasami could not tell. Shin continued. "You came back for the letters, didn't you? You hid them in Nao's costume earlier, in one of the concealed pockets, I suspect."

"He was supposed to wear the other one," Choki said in a hollow tone. "Nobody would have known. Nobody would have noticed me leaving. But now it's too late. Too late for anything but this." He twisted the knife, and Nao hissed in pain.

"You don't want to do this, Choki," Shin said. Kasami spied Nao's prop sword laying on the stage nearby and surreptitiously placed herself within reach of the weapon. Choki didn't seem to notice. "Why throw your life away on a useless gesture like this?" Shin continued. "Put the knife down, and let us talk."

Choki shook his head, not answering. The knife trembled and swung away from Nao's throat. Kasami tensed and edged her foot under the sword. Then Choki's expression tightened into a panicked snarl. "There's been enough talking!"

He turned on Nao and raised the knife. Kasami hooked the sword with her foot and kicked it up, snatching it out of the air and then hurling it awkwardly toward Choki. The youth yelped and ducked aside, allowing Nao to scramble to safety.

Before Choki could recover, Shin swooped in. He caught the youth's wrist and gave it a vicious twist, forcing him to drop the knife. As Choki cried out in pain, Shin yanked the youth's arm up behind his back and forced him to his knees. He looked up as Kasami joined him, one hand on her sword. "Well done," she said.

"No bloodshed," Shin said.

In the stalls, the audience began to applaud. Soon, they were standing in the aisles. The musicians struck up a tune, and the curtain began to fall. But the applause continued for some time after.

CHAPTER THIRTY-SIX
Final Curtain

"Is that it, then? A mistake?" Yasamura took a sip of his tea and shook his head. "All this trouble for a simple mistake."

"Not exactly how I would characterize it, but yes," Shin said, sipping his own tea. He sat in his box with Yasamura and Konomi. The theater was largely empty now, and the sets were being broken down. The audience had seemed pleased with the ending if nothing else, and they had chattered excitedly as they left the building. "And to think, none of it would have happened had you not inveigled me to bring Etsuko here."

Yasamura looked at him. "Are you implying something?"

"I think he's doing more than suggesting it, cousin," Konomi said. "And he is correct to do so. We set this thing in motion, however good our intentions, and we must bear some responsibility for that."

Yasamura looked as if he wanted to argue but instead shrugged and took another sip of tea. "Fine. Yes. I accept my part in things. But I could not foresee all this. Indeed, I'm still not certain as to what actually transpired."

Konomi looked at Shin. "That's your cue, I think."

Shin assumed an innocent expression. "Whatever do you mean?"

"Oh, stop it. You've been bursting at the seams to show off how clever you are since the performance ended. So tell us. How did you figure it all out?"

"The same way I always do. Through inquiry and observation." Shin tapped the side of his nose. "The missing letters were the key, though not, I admit, in precisely the way I predicted. I knew Ashina was the only one with the opportunity to steal them and the only one who knew how to access them." Shin gestured lazily. "I noted her interest in Etsuko's costumes when I questioned her for the second time. It occurred to me that those costumes would make an excellent hiding place, given all the concealed pockets."

"Pockets?" Konomi asked.

"For the blood," Shin said, pulling a length of red silk – one he'd hidden earlier, hoping someone would give him cause to use it – from within his robes to illustrate his point. "Unfortunately, Ashina trusted the wrong person. She told Choki where she'd hidden them, no doubt for what seemed like a good reason at the time, and, well…"

Yasamura frowned. "He took them. Why?"

"Leverage," Shin said, wrapping the silk around his hands. "Ashina hoped to use them to procure a future for herself once Etsuko had departed. But Choki needed them for a more urgent reason – to protect himself from the Scorpion."

"Why?" Konomi asked.

"Because he'd failed the task they'd set for him," Shin said. He paused. "Much of this is speculation, of course. Isamu will never confirm any of it nor would I expect him to. The poison they gave to Choki would have caused Nao some embarrassment but nothing worse."

"But Etsuko was allergic to it," Yasamura said in sudden realization. "But how did she get the poisoned makeup?"

"Poor judgment," Shin said. "Etsuko stole Nao's makeup in order to get back at him for an earlier spat. She'd done it before, so she knew his blend of makeup wouldn't aggravate her allergies – except this time, it did. When Choki realized what had happened, he stole the letters, possibly hoping to use them to buy his way out of trouble with the Scorpion and hid them in one of Nao's costumes until he could retrieve them. Unfortunately for him, Nao chose that particular costume to wear for the final act."

He paused and pulled the length of red silk taut between his fists. "If I am right, Isamu knew instantly what had gone wrong. He would've also known he would be suspected once the cause of Etsuko's death was discovered."

"The Scorpion are known poisoners," Yasamura murmured.

Shin nodded. "Even so. But in this case, it was an accident. Isamu, ever-practical, decided to salvage what he could from the situation. It is almost certain that Etsuko gave him a few names from her menagerie – Lady Yua, the merchant Odoma, and Lady Minami – and ensured that those individuals would attend today's performance in order to prove the worth of her dowry. Isamu approached each of them, hoping to find some hook to reel them in before they learned Etsuko was dead and her trove of blackmail was lost."

"He's been a busy little insect," Yasamura said with grudging admiration.

"No less than yourself," Shin said pointedly. Yasamura had the good grace to look away, though Shin was certain he felt no guilt for his machinations, even if they had resulted in Etsuko's death. Shin understood – the games played by courtiers could not be won by the gentle of heart – but could not bring himself to condone it. Yasamura and Isamu were two sides of the same tarnished coin; men playing with lives the way gamblers threw dice.

Shin took a breath and continued, "Of course, once I became involved, the matter became untenable from Isamu's point of view – and Choki's. Choki set the fire backstage to distract everyone, hoping to retrieve the letters and escape in the resulting confusion. Unfortunately for him, as I said, Nao had chosen to wear the very costume he'd hidden the letters in, forcing him to try to retrieve them onstage. Unfortunately, Nao spotted him, and the situation became… fraught."

"But you caught him," Konomi said with some approval.

"For which he should be thankful," Yasamura added. "If I know the Bayushi, they'd have set their hounds on him the moment he reappeared, letters or no letters."

"What will happen to him?" Konomi asked. "Choki, I mean."

"That is for Azuma to decide. He is a magistrate – or as good as," Shin said. He paused, thinking about the look of utter desolation on Choki's face as Azuma's men took him into custody. He shook his head. "I've argued for some degree of clemency, given that Choki didn't intend to kill anyone."

"Except you," Konomi said pointedly.

Shin waved this aside. "I doubt that. It was a convenient way to clear himself a path, that's all. He's no murderer, just desperate and foolish. Regardless, what will be will be."

"Then you intend to just… forgive and forget?" Yasamura asked.

"I never forget," Shin said. "But if I held a grudge against everyone who attempted to kill me, I'd be unable to hold anything else." He said it lightly, but the truth was, he had no doubt Choki would be dead within a week. Azuma took his duties seriously, and Choki had killed a woman with friends in high places. Including Lord Gota and the Bayushi.

Gota had made it plain that he intended to see the youth suffer for what he'd done. Shin thought it more likely that the Bayushi would quietly slip something into Choki's next meal and save everyone the trouble of a trial. Especially themselves.

Yasamura grunted, whether in approval or amusement Shin couldn't say. "And what about the girl, Ashina? What will you do with her?"

Shin shrugged. "That's up to her. She's a fine actress and well-liked by the rest of the cast. There's a place for her here if she wants it. She may not, given the events of today."

"She's a blackmailer," Yasamura said in disbelief.

Shin held up a finger. "She worked for a blackmailer. There's a difference."

"Is there?" Konomi asked in obvious amusement.

"I like to think so," Shin said. "Besides, it's not for me to judge her."

"What about the letters?" Yasamura asked. Shin put his cup down.

"I will destroy them at the first opportunity. I think that is the best course of action for all concerned." Shin tapped the rim of his cup. "You have my word they will never see the light of day."

"I wish it were so simple," Yasamura began.

"It is enough," Konomi interjected. "Shin's word is as good as your own, cousin." Yasamura frowned at this and shook his head but didn't argue. Konomi looked at Shin. "People will be talking about this performance for months, Shin, dear. They'll be lining up around the block for the next one. Have you given any thought to what it'll be?"

Shin picked up his cup and sipped at his tea. "A farce, possibly. Something without any death in it, for preference." He paused and looked at Yasamura. The other man had caused him no end of trouble, but that could be forgiven – under the right circumstances.

Kitano appeared at the door. He cleared his throat. "He's here, my lord," he said. Shin sighed, somewhere between relief and disappointment.

"Good. I was afraid he might decline my invitation."

Yasamura and Konomi looked at him. "He who?" Konomi asked.

"Bayushi Isamu," Shin said. He rose, and they followed suit. "I'm afraid I must ask you both to leave now."

"Kicking us out?" Konomi said as they rose to their feet. "How rude."

"Only temporary, I assure you." He looked at Yasamura. "Though, I suppose you will be leaving soon. A pity. I was… looking forward to further conversations."

"Were you now?" Yasamura raised an eyebrow. "Well, I suppose I could delay my departure by a few days if you like."

Shin smiled. "I do not wish you to inconvenience yourself."

"The first thing you must learn about me is that I never inconvenience myself," Yasamura said, tapping his fingers against Shin's chest.

"And what is the second thing?" Shin asked, trying his best to maintain a poise of mild interest. It was difficult, given how his heart was racing.

Yasamura leaned close and kissed him on the cheek. "That, you will have to discover for yourself." He turned and looked at Konomi, who had an odd expression on her face. "Coming, cousin?"

"Yes, I suppose." Konomi hesitated, then kissed Shin roughly on his other cheek. Shin blinked, shocked. She was always affectionate, but there was something different about this kiss – almost possessive.

To her credit, Konomi looked somewhat shocked herself. "Oh," she murmured.

"Oh," Shin said. He touched his cheek. "What was–"

Konomi turned. "Yasamura is calling me. Coming, cousin!" With a final parting glance, she hurried after her cousin. Bemused, Shin slid the door shut and retreated to await his other guest.

Kitano showed the Scorpion in a moment later. From what little he could see of the other man's face, he did not think Isamu was happy. "Thank you for coming," Shin said.

"I do not believe I had much choice in the matter," Isamu said stiffly. He looked around the box. "Then, the Crane are known for assuming authority where none is granted."

Shin let the insult pass. Isamu was nervous. "You know why I asked you here." It wasn't a question, and Isamu didn't take it as such.

"It has nothing to do with me."

"You and I both know that is a lie and an obvious one at that. Do me the courtesy of telling the truth or at least trying harder when you come up with a falsehood."

Isamu jerked away as if Shin had slapped him. He turned and leaned heavily against the edge of the box. All the fight seemed to have gone out of him. He turned. "I did not give the boy the means to poison her."

"A courtier's phrasing," Shin said. "You didn't, but one of your retainers certainly did. Arata, perhaps. They claimed to be meeting with Nao, but in reality, they were eliciting Choki's aid. I wonder, how did you know he would be open to the idea of betraying Nao?" Shin waved away Isamu's reply. "Etsuko's doing, I suspect. Ashina might well have told her Choki was unhappy. From there, it would have been a simple matter of sounding him out and making the proposal."

"If you know all this, why am I here?" Isamu asked.

Shin frowned. "Because what I don't know is why."

"You expect me to tell you?"

"No. But if you'll indulge me – Nao was a student of the Butei Academy. He was a member of your clan, of your family. The two of you knew one another during that time. You were friends or perhaps more. Am I on the right path?"

Isamu didn't answer. Shin nodded and went on. "Nao has never spoken to me of how he came to join the Three Flower Troupe. I have never asked."

"Why would you? He is just an actor." Isamu's voice was laced with bitterness. Shin wondered whether it was on Nao's behalf or something else.

"Is he?"

Isamu turned back to the stage. "He is now. He made certain of it."

"Why did you want Choki to poison him?"

"It wouldn't have poisoned him," Isamu said softly. "It was merely an irritant."

"Unless one happened to be allergic to it," Shin said harshly.

Isamu hung his head. "Yes. Unless one happened to be allergic." There was real regret in his voice, Shin thought. He might not have cared for Etsuko, but he was not callous about her death. Maybe he'd liked her after all.

"He would have noticed the tampering. Was it a warning?" He didn't give Isamu a chance to answer. "Or an invitation?"

"A game," Isamu said after a moment.

Shin blinked. "A ... game?"

Isamu laughed bitterly. "What other sort of game would a young Scorpion play?" He straightened and knocked his knuckles against the edge of the box. "I did not come to this city for him. I did not know he was here. When Etsuko told me, I was surprised. When she learned that we had ... known one another, she became angry. She was certain we were plotting against her."

"Why?"

Isamu shrugged slowly like someone bearing an uncomfortable weight. "I do not know. I tried to explain, but she wouldn't hear of it. She threatened to call off the engagement and embarrass Lord Sana or worse, sell her secrets to the highest bidder."

Shin considered this. All at once, things began to fall into place. "That's why you sent that message to Nao. You were hoping to pressure him into retrieving Etsuko's dowry for you, weren't you? Perhaps even find the letters Lord Sana wrote and remove the necessity of marrying her at all. After all, she'd already told you he'd stolen them."

Isamu didn't reply, but someone else did. "Obviously, that's what he was hoping," Nao said from behind them. Shin and Isamu turned. The actor stood in the entrance to the box wearing plain robes, his face bare of makeup and his hair unbound. He fiddled with a makeup jar – the fatal one – in his hands as he spoke. "Why else would he bother to contact me unless he needed something, especially if that something inconvenienced me?"

Isamu stared at Nao. For the first time, the Scorpion seemed to be at a loss for words. The actor tossed the jar to Isamu. The Scorpion caught it without looking at it. "You almost got me killed, Isamu. I think you owe me an apology at least."

Isamu looked at the jar, then at Nao. "That was not my intent."

Nao laughed sourly. "Oh, you never intend to hurt anyone. But somehow, you always manage it. It's a talent." He shook his head. "I left because I was tired of such foolishness. Tired of being a spy who played at acting when all I really wanted was to be onstage."

Isamu relaxed. "I did wonder," he said in a soft voice.

Nao's smile turned gentle. "Do not flatter yourself, Isamu. You had nothing to do with my decision."

"Nothing?"

Nao shrugged. "Maybe something." He looked at Shin. "Given what happened here today, I suggest our next performance be a farce, my lord."

"I was thinking much the same." Shin looked at Isamu. "I have the letters. All of them, including those belonging to Lord Sana. I intend to destroy them."

Isamu's eyes narrowed. "Intention is not the same as result."

"It is for me," Shin said firmly. "I understand why you did what you did, Isamu, but I do not condone it. A woman is dead because you decided to play silly games. That it was an accident does not erase the stain on your character. I have said I will destroy the letters. If my word is good enough for the Unicorn, it should be good enough for the Scorpion as well. I trust that will settle the matter to the satisfaction of all concerned?"

Isamu nodded somewhat reluctantly. "I suppose it must." His eyes were fixed on Nao's face as he nodded slowly in either acknowledgment or perhaps gratitude. He made to speak, but fell silent, his eyes turning once more to Nao. Then, "Nao, I–"

"There is nothing more to say, I think," Nao said. Isamu stiffened, then nodded. He left without further word, leaving Shin and Nao alone in the box. They stood in silence for a time, then Nao sighed and said, "Thank you, my lord."

"Think nothing of it," Shin said. "Are you ever going to tell me what all that was about?" He paused. "What it was really about, I mean."

Nao smiled. "Probably not, my lord. It is a sad, sordid story, not fit for the ears of one such as yourself." He preened slightly. "Suffice it to say, I am the better for it ending as it did." He deflated slightly, and his smile became sad. "Isamu as well, though I doubt he'd admit it. He was always too stubborn to admit when I was right."

Shin nodded in understanding and sighed. Love was a funny thing. It made poets of warriors and warriors of poets and turned them all into fools for good measure. "Now that he knows you are here, he might well try again."

Nao gave an elegant shrug. "Let him try. I could stand some amusement. It gets so tiring being me."

Shin laughed. "Does that mean you're staying?"

Nao looked away as if embarrassed. "For the moment, my lord. Someone must show Ashina the ropes, after all." He glanced at Shin. "But I reserve the right to depart in unseemly haste if you ever again suspect me of murder."

"Of course," Shin said, pleased. He clasped his hands behind his back and turned to look at the stage. "All things considered, our first performance could have gone much worse."

"Much, much worse," Nao said. "Next time will be better."

"Yes," Shin said. He smiled. "It most certainly will."

CAST LIST

CRANE

Daidoji Shin – *nobleman & amateur detective*
Hiramori Kasami – *yojimbo in service to Shin*
Kitano Daichi – *gambler & manservant to Shin*
Nagata Sanki – *Shin's personal physician*
Junichi Kenzō – *nobleman & auditor for the
Daidoji Trading Council*

THREE FLOWER TROUPE

Wada Sanemon – *master of the troupe*
Nao – *lead actor*
Choki – *actor & understudy for Nao*
Noma Etsuko – *lead actress*
Ashina – *actress & Etsuko's understudy*
Various actors, stagehands and crew

OTHER

Odama – *soy merchant & former owner of the Foxfire Theatre*
Iuchi Konomi – *Unicorn noblewoman & patron of the arts*
Shinjo Yasamura – *Unicorn nobleman & cousin of Konomi*
Ichiro Gota – *Badger nobleman & patron of the arts*
Arban-Ujik – *nomad & bodyguard in service to Gota*
Bayushi Isamu – *Scorpion nobleman & trade representative*
Akodo Minami – *Lion noblewoman & garrison commander*
Kaeru Azuma – *ronin & advisor to the Governor*

ABOUT THE AUTHOR

JOSH REYNOLDS is a writer, editor and semi-professional monster movie enthusiast. He has been a professional author since 2007, writing over thirty novels and numerous short stories, including *Arkham Horror, Warhammer: Age of Sigmar, Warhammer 40,000,* and the occasional audio script. He grew up in South Carolina and now lives in Sheffield, UK.

joshuamreynolds.co.uk
twitter.com/jmreynolds

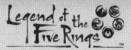

Brave warriors defend the empire from demonic threats, while
battle and political intrigue divide the Great Clans.

Follow dilettante detective, Daidoji Shin as he solves murders
and mysteries amid the machinations of the Clans.

The Great Clan
novellas of Rokugan
return, collected in
omnibus editions
for the first time,
with brand new
tales of the Lion
and Crane Clans.

DESCENT
LEGENDS OF THE DARK

Epic fantasy of heroes and monsters in the perilous realms of Terrinoth.

DESCENT
THE RAIDERS OF BLOODWOOD
The forces of Terrinoth will burn
DAVIDE MANA

DESCENT
THE GATES OF THELGRIM
A realm of darkness has awoken beneath Terrinoth
ROBBIE MACNIVEN

DESCENT
Zathareth
Power corrupts even the mightiest of heroes
ROBBIE MACNIVEN

DESCENT
THE SHIELD OF DAQAN
The invasion of the realms of Terrinoth has begun
DAVID GUYMER

DESCENT
THE DOOM OF FALLOWHEARTH
A new darkness threatens the realms of Terrinoth
ROBBIE MACNIVEN

Legends unite to uncover treachery and dark sorcery, defeat the darkness, and save the realm, yet adventure comes at a high price in this astonishing world.

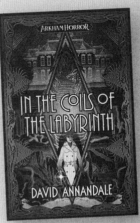

ARKHAM HORROR™

Riveting pulp adventure as unknowable horrors threaten to tear our reality apart.

Something monstrous has risen from the depths beneath Arkham, Miskatonic University is plagued with missing students and maddening litanies, and a charismatic surrealist's art opens doorways to unspeakable places.

A web of terror lurks in the jungle, a director captures unnameable horrors while making his masterpiece, and a thief stumbles onto a necrophagic conspiracy.

WORLD EXPANDING FICTION

Do you have them all?

ARKHAM HORROR
- ☐ *Wrath of N'kai* by Josh Reynolds
- ☐ *The Last Ritual* by S A Sidor
- ☐ *Mask of Silver* by Rosemary Jones
- ☐ *Litany of Dreams* by Ari Marmell
- ☐ *The Devourer Below* ed Charlotte Llewelyn-Wells
- ☐ *Dark Origins, The Collected Novellas Vol 1*
- ☐ *Cult of the Spider Queen* by S A Sidor
- ☐ *The Deadly Grimoire* by Rosemary Jones
- ☐ *Grim Investigations, The Collected Novellas Vol 2*
- ☐ *In the Coils of the Labyrinth* by David Annandale
  (coming soon)

DESCENT
- ☐ *The Doom of Fallowhearth* by Robbie MacNiven
- ☐ *The Shield of Daqan* by David Guymer
- ☐ *The Gates of Thelgrim* by Robbie MacNiven
- ☐ *Zachareth* by Robbie MacNiven
- ☐ *The Raiders of Bloodwood* by Davide Mana *(coming soon)*

KEYFORGE
- ☐ *Tales from the Crucible* ed Charlotte Llewelyn-Wells
- ☐ *The Qubit Zirconium* by M Darusha Wehm

LEGEND OF THE FIVE RINGS
- ☐ *Curse of Honor* by David Annandale
- ☐ *Poison River* by Josh Reynolds
- ☐ *The Night Parade of 100 Demons* by Marie Brennan
- ☐ *Death's Kiss* by Josh Reynolds
- ☐ *The Great Clans of Rokugan, The Collected Novellas Vol 1*
- ☐ *To Chart the Clouds* by Evan Dicken
- ☐ *The Great Clans of Rokugan, The Collected Novellas Vol 2*
- ☑ *The Flower Path* by Josh Reynolds

PANDEMIC
- ☐ *Patient Zero* by Amanda Bridgeman

TERRAFORMING MARS
- ☐ *In the Shadow of Deimos* by Jane Killick
- ☐ *Edge of Catastrophe* by Jane Killick *(coming soon)*

TWILIGHT IMPERIUM
- ☐ *The Fractured Void* by Tim Pratt
- ☐ *The Necropolis Empire* by Tim Pratt
- ☐ *The Veiled Masters* by Tim Pratt
- ☐ *The Stars Beyond* by Tim Pratt *(coming soon)*

ZOMBICIDE
- ☐ *Last Resort* by Josh Reynolds
- ☐ *Planet Havoc* by Tim Waggoner
- ☐ *Age of the Undead* by C L Werner